RUTHLESS MONSTERS

THE DAMNED CREW #1

TATUM RAYNE

Ruthless Monsters
The Damned Crew #1
Copyright © 2022 Tatum Rayne
Published by Hudson Indie Ink
www.hudsonindieink.com

Cover Designer: Tatum Rayne Designs
Proof Readers: Jenn Pepper-Smith

Ruthless Monsters/Tatum Rayne - 1st ed. 2022

To my family and friends. I can't thank you all enough for the support and encouragement you have shown me. Even though it was a secret dream of mine to write, I never had the courage to do it. But your excitement and support mean everything. My girls are my rocks. To my eldest, who has repeatedly said that this is so cool, I just want to say. It doesn't matter how old you are and what life throws at you, always follow your dreams. To my youngest, keep being you, Tiny, little hurricane you have always been and remember you can be whoever you want to be, the world is yours.

To everyone else. My Editor Elizabeth. My Cover Designer Pretty In Ink Creations. Thank you to you both and I apologize for all the questions. You both are amazing.

To my Beta readers. Thank you for diving into my crazy mind and telling me what you think. I couldn't ask for a better group of people. You guys are the best.

WARNING

This book is intended for 18+ readers. Some situations in this book might be disturbing to some people. If you're wanting a powerful female who swears like a sailor and doesn't give a shit, you're in the right place. If you don't like too much swearing or other things people find offensive, this isn't the book for you.

1

REIKA

"C'mon reaper! You got this, knock his fucking head off!"
"Kick his ass, knock him out!"

The crowd is on a whole other level here tonight. I've not heard anything like it, they're amped up and demanding blood.

"Fuck," my brain rattles as the beast in front of me lands a blow to my side. The bastard has broken some of my ribs and pain roars through my veins, my breathing becoming heavier and I've got black spots doing the conga in front of my eyes. *Fuck, that's going to be a bitch tomorrow!*

Rocco's eyes are darting all over the place, anxiety rolls off him in waves, his fingers twitching. I can feel it from my position inside the cage. I know what that means. It's getting close to the time I'm supposed to drop like a sack of shit and act like I can't continue. Big man's orders, "the little girl must lose!" It's like a podcast on repeat in my head; a constant reminder if I don't do what I'm told to I won't get paid. I hate this. I don't lose. I'm undefeated and having to throw a fight because the boss man is worried about his grandson's ego really pisses me off. Apparently, the guy is already annoyed at having to fight a little girl because it's beneath him to do such things.

1

I wouldn't normally fight more than once in a week, but a woman's got to eat and pay bills. That's why on a Sunday night I'm here at a rundown warehouse in the middle of nowhere, in a piece of shit cage that smells of piss, and old blood. A shadow flashes across my vision. *Shit!*

I really need to learn to concentrate, barely jumping back out of the way of a roundhouse to the stomach. The guy seems to hold back and wait, he keeps looking to Rocco who is currently throwing daggers my way. Rocco, the fight coordinator, doesn't usually pair male and female fighters together. The one rule of the house is that women fight women and men fight men, but when the female fighters kept refusing to fight me, it was a case of fight men or don't fight at all.It's a taboo thing, apparently, for the guy who runs this place. I don't know why though; he had no bother putting me in here and breaking his own rule.Hence the reason why I took the order to get my ass beat so my pockets are filled with bills at the end of this.

We continue through blow after blow, round after round, to keep the crowd buzzed. If they knew the fight was fixed, well, shit would hit the fan for boss man. Labored breathing filters into my ears between the crowd's screams. I'm shocked to see big man is slowing down. He is meant to be one of the best fighters on the male's side. It's obvious he has never had to go so long in a fight. He must be one of them that uses brute force and has never really had to work for a win. Jesus, he needs to work on his cardio if I'm messing him up like this. Ha-ha, yeah as if *"I'm just a woman,"* was his shitty comment when he saw me out back earlier. The stupid twat hasn't realized yet I'm just messing with him. This is my usual trick. I toy with them when I'm fighting, running rings around my opponent so when boredom sets in, I pull out my finishing move. A nice combo of a fake kick to the stomach and followed up with a superman punch to the head. That baby makes them drop to the floor, lights out, no matter how big they are.

My eyes connect with Rocco's from my position in the cage. He's begging me with his eyes to do it, drop to the floor and finish this. I know the fight's been going on longer than it was supposed to, but I've been having way too much fun ramping the crowd up, their screams for the impending bloodbath fueling the bloodlust inside me. Big man takes advantage of my lack of concentration by body slamming me to the mat, swiftly following up with a knee to the chest, pinning me under his weight and holding me in place. It feels like I have a concrete block where his knee pins my chest, and he starts throwing blows to my face that feel like bombs as they connect.

I really wish I could get my guard up fully to protect my face, because the blows that do get through hurt like hell. Thank God my partial guard is staying solid so only the odd few make it past. He hooks his left arm around my neck and spins us, my back is now to his front in a chokehold grip. My hand is tucked over his arm under my chin which stops him from getting any leverage to put me to sleep. Yeah, yeah, I know I really should give up, but pride is a bitch and all that, I can't seem to bring myself to do it.

"Do it!" Rocco screams from outside the ring.

"What's the matter, baby?" he purrs in my ear.

"Do it!" Rocco screams again.

"You're holding out on me baby, is it just so I keep my hands on you?" he breathes into my ear.

"Hmmmm bet you would love it, don't you think?" *Who the fuck does this dude think he is?*

"C'mon, sweet cheeks, move ya hand and let me put you to sleep and I'll make you feel so damn good after."

"Like fuck you will." I snarl. "You aren't my type, fuckface.

3

It would be less painful if I poured battery acid into my eyes." Good thing Casanova here can't see my face. It would be pretty obvious I want to make him swallow his Adam's Apple right about now. The thought of watching him turn blue brings a sadistic grin to my face.

"You cheeky bitch!" he screeches, his spit flying everywhere, some even lands on my cheek.

"I'm gonna teach you a lesson after this, doll face. I will fuck you one way or another, even if I have to make you bleed." He licks the side of my face from jaw to ear then sticks his tongue into it. My stomach turns and a violent shiver works its way down my spine. God, this guy is disgusting.

"For fuck's sake, Reaper! Stop fucking around and get it done," Rocco screams from the side.

I turn my head slightly to the right, keeping my hand in place to look at Rocco, I'm not surprised to find his eyes wide and him frantically pulling at his hair. This is making him nervous; he feels like he's losing control. I'm unpredictable at the best of times, but Rocco doesn't know what this fucker behind me, currently grinding his cock into my ass, said. He just threatened me. And no one, I mean fucking no one, threatens me and gets away with it. *Time to teach this bastard a lesson.*

I slip my hips from the center of his body to the right, so my ass hits the mat. I laugh. I can't help it. My adrenaline runs through my body full force, but the best part is my mind has gone quiet. Anyone who knows me knows, if I go calm, you're fucked. I am about to go ninja on his ass.

I dig my elbow into ribs, pulling a grunt from him followed by a savage snarl. I guess he's worked it out now. I am done playing. I switch my hips again and dick punch him. He screams like a girl.

"Damn," I say, jumping up to my feet, "music to my ears."

He's red faced, rolling around on the floor. I dive on top of him and start raining punches anywhere on his body I can reach; jabs to the face, stomach and a right hook to the temple. If he was a car ornament, his head would be wobbling. Oh sweet! That one definitely dazed him. I jump back and stand in my corner, beckoning him with a finger. I want to finish him while he is on his feet, that's the only way I feel the threat should be repaid. I tried to do what Rocco wanted but the boy pushed me too far. I can't allow him to get away with it. The way he tossed the threat out so casually, he's obviously done it before.

"Bitch!" he screams at me as he slowly stands up.

"What's up, baby? Did I damage your crown jewels?" My laugh could send a shiver down the devil's spine. It's cold and heartless.

The crowd is going wild. They can feel the change in the atmosphere surrounding us. They're out for blood. They know this is the end for him or me, and only one of us is walking out of here the champion of the night.

He roars as he rushes at me, all caution gone. Losing you temper is a rookie mistake. You learn growing up and brawling to survive like I have, you never, and I mean never, fight angry.

I sidestep and sweep his legs from underneath him, spinning out of the way to the other side of the cage. My attitude is cocky and I love the way the crowd screams because of the show I'm giving them. He jumps to his feet and charges again; I spin and land a jab to the side of his head, which must have hurt because my bones shook from the force of it. He grabs my right arm and tries to twist it, but I drop to my knee and kick him square in his kneecap. I hear a crunch; the sound is satisfying. With a grin on my face, I move to the other side of the cage and wait.

Any normal fighter with a knee injury like that would bow

out, but not big man; he's got a God complex. He pulls his ass up from the mat and stands the best he can. It's a waste really. He can barely put any weight on it, but I know he won't go out easily. His ego won't allow it. He grins at me like he stands a chance at beating me, running his eyes up and down my body. Our eyes connect and he licks his lips, then grins at me. I've had enough. I charge him and lean out of the way of his outstretched arms and jump, my right foot above his right hip and I use my momentum to get my left leg over his shoulder, I throw a right hook to the side of his face and bring my right leg up and over, so I'm wrapped around his neck. I hook my left foot under my right knee so I'm in a triangle chokehold, throwing my upper body back to dangle. The movement happens so fast that big man is pulled forward into a roll. I hold on and push my hips just enough that he avoids crushing me, but I keep the hold I have on him strong. I increase my pressure on his neck. He tries to pull my legs away, but it's no use; not enough oxygen is reaching his lungs and he's gasping for air.

His movements are becoming sluggish, his strength fading. I could easily snap his neck in this position, but not the best idea considering Rocco is screaming at me like a man possessed. He knows as well as everyone else here this is over. Not one person makes a noise while waiting to see what I'm going to do next, it's an eerie sort of silence as they wait. I apply more pressure, his choked gasps become harsher as I crush his airway. I kind of feel sorry for him, flapping around like a fish. It's not long before he realizes it's a lost cause, he can't get out of the hold. I add a touch more pressure and strike, left fist to his nose and right to his temple. That is poetry right there. I land it perfectly. Instantly he's out cold. Unhooking my legs, I roll him to the side and stand up, his unconscious body at my feet. The crowd is silent for a moment, and Rocco looks like he wants to kill me.

He better get in line. Boss man isn't going to be happy about this. The crowd erupts, at the end turning the noise level from enjoyment into chaos. They love the bloodshed. If they didn't, they wouldn't come back. A cold shiver runs down my spine, you know the kind. The type when you know someone is watching. I try to look around, but all see is the crowd jumping and screaming. I investigate the corners, but the light doesn't reach that far. I can't make out anything. It must have been my imagination.

2

KANE

W e're stood at the top of the makeshift bleachers surrounding the cage to give us a better vantage point of the warehouse floor. We are here to keep an eye on our target, Alexander, a small-time degenerate who likes to think he is better than everybody else. Unfortunately for him, he has a serious addiction to money and gambling it away. It doesn't matter how he gets it or who he asks for it. That's why he runs an underground fight ring. The creep is a con-artist.

It's common knowledge to anyone higher up the food chain that he fixes some of his fights to pay the debts he owes. That's where me and my brothers come in. I'm the leader of the Damned Crew, my brother Liam is my second and his twin Marcus is my third.

Marcus may seem like a lady's man with a happy go lucky attitude making him look like a good little citizen, but what people don't see is the most ruthless enforcer I have ever seen. My brothers and I are here because Alexander borrowed fifteen thousand dollars from me to place a bet on the main fight tonight. The match was meant to give us a massive turnover and he was going to pay us back with the customary interest.

We came to see how this fight went down and make sure the little shit couldn't back out of our deal. From the way he is hiding in the corner like he wants the ground to open and swallow him whole, he must get the sense that he's being watched.

We were surprised by who Mason was fighting tonight. We've all heard the rumors. With his size, you would have expected his opponent to be a man, but I'm frozen to my spot when a tiny, absolutely stunning woman strolls into the cage as if this is nothing new to her. We all stand at attention.

"Fuck me, who the hell is that?" my brother Marcus mumbles, to himself.

"Bro, we need to stop this, she's going to get seriously hurt." Liam frantically waves a hand in front of my face trying to engage me in conversation.

All I can do is stare at her. She's gotta be pulled out of my favorite wet dream. She is a perfect replica of my ideal woman. She stands around five and a half feet tall with long flowing black hair that reaches to the band on her shorts, even in a ponytail. She has a tight little body with more than enough tits and ass. I adjust my stance slightly, trying to take pressure off my rock-hard cock. I wonder if she's a screamer. I can't wait to wrap her ponytail around my hand and pull to the point of pain while I push my cock into her pussy and fuck her until we are both seeing stars. I want to see her eyes; they are the doorway to the soul, you see. You can learn a lot about someone from their eyes. I *need* to see into her soul. I want to find the way I can own and command her to my will. She doesn't know it yet, but she is mine. I own her now and she will do as I say. If she fights me on it, I will enjoy breaking her spirit.

"For fuck's sake, Kane! We need to get her out of there!" Liam roars his anger, pulling me out of my daydream.

"You don't know who she is?" A piss-head below states,

with a surprised look on his face. He stumbles back, the look of surprise now turning into confusion.

"No shit, Sherlock." I deadpan, folding my arms across my chest.

"So, you don't know she's a regular here?" he asks, there's a curious lilt to his voice.

"Why the hell would we? That's why we're so confused about a woman being in the cage with a dude," Marcus snarls starting to lose his patience with the guy he has a hold on, I wonder when he yanked the guy close to him.

"She's the goddamn Reaper!" he screeches, his gaze flicking between our faces as it dawns on him that we still haven't got a clue what he's on about.

"Seriously, you haven't heard of the Reaper? She's the baddest bitch on this side of the tracks. She's the undefeated women's champion in these fights."

"Undefeated?" Marcus says as if he can't quite believe what he's hearing.

"That tiny woman is an undefeated champion?" Liam asks, with a snort. My brother is a brawler by nature, and he has never been undefeated.

"Damn right. She's bloodthirsty and ruthless - never holds back." The wino snorts a laugh as he looks at us, "It's like there's a F5 tornado packed into that little body."

"There were rumors after her fight last week that the female fighters have refused to fight her anymore." I try to imagine everything this bum is saying but it doesn't seem right, he's obviously full of crap.

"Yeah, you see after her last fight, they had to take her opponent out of the ring on a stretcher and dump her outside the ER! It looked like a massacre in there," he says, jumping around like an excited Labrador. My brain is still trying to filter through everything this guy just told us, when we hear the fight coordinator, Rocco.

We all look up to the center of the cage where Rocco is standing. On one side is Mason standing so cocky and on the other she jumps around warming herself up, completely at ease in the ring.

"You ready for a beatdown?" echoes through the air.

I can't keep my eyes off her. This has to be a mistake; the piss head has to be wrong.

"You're all in for a treat tonight." The crowd screams its approval.

"We have two titans about to battle it out. You all know my man, Mason, who is dominating the male side of these fights." Some of the crowd starts screaming louder while others become silent.

"Well, tonight ladies and gentlemen he's taking on The One... The Only... Reaper!" He bellows into the microphone and the crowd goes wild for the woman.

Liam, Marcus and I are all stunned. I'm not really hearing the crowd now, it's like there is cotton wool in my ears. We watch as the two fighters move to the center of the ring, and touch gloves before moving back to their respective corners.

Ding, Ding! The bell goes, both fighters are out of the corner before the last bell stops.

My brain can't keep up with what's going on. All I can see is her fluid movements as she throws blow after blow. She never once loses her footing or slips. It's as if she's done this thousands of times before. I stand in stunned silence, awed at the beauty of her fighting capability.

"Holy shit, did you see that move?"

The first thing my brain registers when the fog starts to lift is the noise of the crowd, and my brother Marcus screaming like a young girl who has just had her favorite barbie bought for her. I look to see what's happening in the cage. Mason is laid on his side with the Reaper's legs wrapped around his neck. From a distance I think it's some kind of chokehold, but I can't be sure. One jab to the nose and a right punch to the temple. Mason is out cold! She rolls him over onto the floor and stands to look around at the crowd which is chanting, "Reaper, Reaper, Reaper!"

My eyes are drilling holes into the back of her head. As if she can feel me, her eyes scan the darkness with a puzzled look on her face. I can't take my eyes off her. My brothers are saying something to me, but I can't hear them.

"Mine!" roars through my head.

"Mine, Mine, Mine!" The chant becomes all-consuming as it grows in volume.

The Reaper doesn't know, but there is something more deadly in this warehouse than she is. That something is me. I will own her - gorgeous body and soul. If you try to run, Baby, it will make it all the sweeter. I love a good chase. I always get what I want. You belong to me.

I turn to my brothers to see shock, awe and lust across their faces. We all look to the cage as the padlock is taken off the door and The Reaper steps out onto the stairs. Slowly making her way down into the crowd and past Alexander, who looks like he's about to have a heart attack at any moment.

He makes a grab for her right arm, catching her above her elbow and drags her through the crowd toward his office shouting at her as he goes. He doesn't know this yet, but he just touched what belongs to me and I plan to collect my money, my woman and remove his hand as a lesson.

"Don't worry, Baby. I'm on my way," I mumble to myself as my brothers and I make our way across the warehouse, following them to his office.

Reika

Once the padlock is removed from the outer door, I brush off the feeling of being watched and step out of the cage. I make my way down in an exhausted state, my ribs hurting like a bitch. I am definitely gonna be a mess by tomorrow. As I take a step to walk through the crowd, still celebrating my win, I come face to face with a bright red Alexander. Whoops! Looks like the boss man wants to shout at me himself instead of having his grunt, Rocco, do it. I am so tired I didn't even register his movement until I felt him grip my arm.

"You little bitch!" he seethes, through gritted teeth. "Who, me?" I question. "Yes, you. Don't play stupid." He starts dragging me through the crowd toward the office. Awe shit, no talking myself out of this one. Once inside the office, Alexander slams the door and stands with his back to it, blocking my exit.

"You stupid, snot-nosed little tart! Do you know what you've done?" he bellows.

"Huh?" My brain is really struggling to keep up with what is going

on, consumed with thoughts of sleep and food.

"Go a few rounds to appease the crowd then drop like a sack of shit. The plan was for you to lose the fucking fight! You were meant to lose!" he screams.

I'm still looking at him as if I don't have a care in the world I really should care though, because it's not likely I will be taking any winnings home.

"Why didn't you drop like you were meant to?" he asks, making me snigger.

"Answer me!" he roars, spit flying everywhere.

I'm still chuckling to myself which turns into full blown belly laughs as my brain registers what he shouted. I can't believe he just tried to command me. The longer I take to answer him, the more agitated he's getting. I can see it in the way his shoulders are set and the grinding of his teeth.

"Dude! Take a breath, your face is so red. Any more pressure and you're going to blow," I say trying to stop laughing, which is making the situation worse.

"Take a breath, take a fucking breath!" he screeches.

"You fucked me over, Reaper. You were supposed to throw the fight. You're gonna pay for this, you stupid bitch. You owe me a lot of money."

"What do you mean I owe you a lot of money? You and your boy Rocco told me you wanted me to eat the mat so your grandson didn't take a hit to the ego!" I seethe, my throat stills and rumbles with a growl. I'm so fucking done with this bullshit. Yeah, I didn't do what was asked, but this is next level. My brain starts running faster and faster, even in its exhausted state, as it puts the pieces together. Alexander wouldn't be so pissed off if it was a case of bruised ego. No, this is more than that.

"What the fuck did you do, Alexander?"

"I told you to lose the fight, Reika." His tone is lower this time.

Oh, shit. Alexander never calls me by my real name in the warehouse. I use the name Reaper to keep my real name out of the mouths of the people who come to the fight circles. You never know how these delinquents will use that information.

"Who do you owe money to?" The color drains from his face at my words as my brain flashes the answer in my head. He owes money to someone who puts the fear of God into him. It is clear from his pale complexion and wide eyes.

"Alexander, who do you owe money to? It's obvious that you owe money to someone."

"You are gonna have to pay the money back, Reika. I borrowed money from some people I had no business dealing with." He starts to pace up and down the length of the office. My brain has worked out what it needs to. I am not to blame for this, it's Mason's problem. If he hadn't threatened to rape me, I would have thrown the fight like I was supposed to.

"Work the club, that's how she can repay the money, yeah she can work at the strip club and dance if she has too." He rushes through his

words, as he paces.

"Like fuck! I'm not dancing in your disgusting STD riddled strip club." That's it, my exhaustion has transformed into full-on rage. *Who the fuck does he think he is to suggest that I strip to pay off a debt that is not mine?*

"You will dance to pay this debt off, Reika!"

"Like fuck I will, Alexander! If anyone fucked you over it was Mason!" I shout, my voice getting louder to the point of no return. I'm shaking and fidgeting. I need to get out of here soon or else I'm gonna get stabby.

"What do you mean it was Mason?" He spins on me so fast I'm surprised his head didn't roll off.

"Mason threatened to rape me in the cage." No shock, nothing registers on his face. This must be a regular occurrence, from

the way Mason threw the threat out to Alexander's lack of surprise.

"What do you mean?" His voice is back to a normal octave.

"He told me I must like his hands all over me. That's why I was dragging the fight out. He said if I didn't give up, then he was going to fuck me one way or another on the outside of the cage."

Reika Martins trying to diffuse a situation. I am more of a punch or stab first, ask questions later kind of girl. Who'd of thought it, huh? If only Dr. Ivanka Ivan could see me now. I snort, the crazy bitch would have a field day with this. I had six months of weekly sessions with the good doctor until she considered me a lost cause; too broken to be able to work through my problems. That story is my own, not a soul outside of her and I know what I've been through in my life. All they know is I was the eleven-year-old girl they found outside a burning building screaming for her family inside. That's why they call me Reaper. My mother, father, little brother and sister died that night. As far as the emergency services were concerned, there was a faulty gas supply, and they wrote it off as a freak accident. Kids started calling me Reaper from that day on, saying I brought death to the people I care about. Guess the name stuck.

"You will repay your debt by dancing in the club, Reika." He spits, with venom.

"Like hell I will, old man. This is your debt, your fucking problem... I will not be used as a scapegoat because you fucked up!"

"You will do as I say girl," he bellows, his frustration clear.

"Just because you got yourself into shit, with people that scare the shit out of you," I seethe. "If you're that desperate, you strip to pay them!"

A throat clears. I spin so quick my eyes rattle in my head, a growl builds in my throat at the interruption, when my eyes land on the guys standing in the office doorway. There's three of them and they're gorgeous, standing all casual like they're used to seeing screaming matches happen. Scanning my eyes up and down their bodies, I know I'm wrong. Calling them men is an understatement, gods would be more fitting. They look like the type of men that good parents warn their daughters about. The type of men who are made to fuck and make a good girl sin. Turning to my side so I can keep an eye on the new additions, I look over to Alexander who has suddenly gone very quiet.

My brain is quick to catch up, as I take in his complexion and body language. These are obviously the people he owes money to, the look of absolute terror in his face is all the confirmation I need. How could three guys like this cause so much fear in the piece of scum? I turn my body again to gauge them better while waiting for one of them to open their mouth. All three of them are wearing jeans and wife beaters with leather jackets. The two standing behind the mountain are without a doubt twins. They are identical in how they look, but it's rather obvious their personalities are polar opposite. The one on the right, closest to the door, is grinning like the Cheshire Cat. Don't get me wrong, he's very easy on the eyes, standing around six-foot five, black hair that's tousled on top and closely shaved on the sides. His bright blue eyes are as clear as some of the oceans you see on holiday and muscles in all the right places, from what I can tell. He's the leanest of the bunch. Even though he comes across as the friendliest, he's got a look of pure mischief. Something is hidden in his depths; a sadistic twinkle like he could flip a switch, slit someone's throat and smile while doing it. A shiver runs down my spine at the mental image that puts in my head. The worst part is he's staring openly at me, like I'm a puzzle that needs to be pulled to pieces just so he can try to put it back together again.

Stooge two is openly staring at me with a frown on his face. He has the same six-foot five frame, black hair in a messy style that looks like he runs his hands through it when thinking. The same blue eyes stare back at me, but instead of the friendly appearance his twin has, his is guarded. It's obvious he would rather be anywhere but here.

Then there's the front man, the mountain himself. Fuck me, he's a lethal injection straight to women's ovaries. Shit, there honestly needs to be a law against looking that good. Yep, you guessed it, my blood is currently rushing south to my vagina. The thirsty bitch that she is definitely likes the look of him. Standing an inch or so taller than the other two, his hair looks to be the darkest black I have ever seen, closely shaved to his head on either side. A well-kept beard graces his face. The guy is fucking huge, there's no way that can be natural muscle. He must walk through a door sideways because of the breadth of his shoulders. Slowly raising my eyes from his feet back up his thick thighs to his torso, chest and shoulders my eyes land back on his face. The eyes staring back at me look black, like the soulless demons you see in films. Just the aura itself coming from him would make anyone want to run into moving traffic. 100% alpha douchebag that knows he's God's gift to women.

He's like the jocks with the God complex you see in school, only a thousand times stronger and his top coating is dipped in sin. Don't get me wrong, I'm a red-blooded female and goddamn this dude is fine, but he would definitely be a detriment to someone's mental health, and mine is already questionable at best.

I've only just realized not one person has said a word in the time it's taken for me to look over the newcomers. A pungent smell fills
the office. Has Alexander pissed himself?

"Who the fuck are these three stooges, Alex?" annoyance clear in my voice, as I demand an answer from the boss man.

"Reaper, for fuck's sake, shut up!" he hisses. I turn my eyes back to the three stooges.

"Who the fuck are you since you've obviously stood here listening to a conversation that doesn't concern you!" Anger coats my tongue at these fuckers listening to our private conversation.

"Reaper, shut it!" Alexander barks at me. "I'm sorry, gentlemen. She's had a bit of a sheltered life and doesn't know when to shut her mouth." This comment makes Stooge Two, fuck it I'm calling him Frosty, snigger. The bastard narrows his gaze at me, while looking down his nose like a king.

"You think that's funny, fuck face?" I question, my anger turning to rage beneath my skin. Alexander looks half a second away from having a coronary. I chuckle at the stupidity of him. Throwing daggers at me to try and get me to shut up.

"You're full of shit, Alexander. I haven't had a sheltered life; you and I both know it. I will call you on your bullshit though, the stench of fear pumping out of your pores is so thick I could cut it with a knife. Plus, I'm pretty sure you've just pissed your pants at the sight of these three!"

"She's pretty observant," says the Cheshire Cat.

"A woman should learn to keep her pretty nose out of things that don't concern her," replies Frosty. *Oh no, this motherfucker did not just go there!*

"Keep my pretty nose out of shit that doesn't concern me?" I ask, dripping in sarcasm. "This situation concerns me and sir piss-a-lot over there. So why don't you and the other two stooges walk your asses back outside and wait your goddamn fucking turn!" I snap.

Frosty goes to take a step forward, but the mountain holds his arm out to stop him. "Brother. Stop letting a little girl wind you up. She is nothing. A nobody!" Ouch, that stings! If I was your typical girl, I would probably cry at a comment like that.

"Yeah, that's it, Frosty. Go back to the corner of your cage and stop rattling the bars because your master says so!" I've got a sickly-sweet grin splashed across my face. *God, smiling like this makes me want to vomit.*

"The thing is, Frosty, don't ever step toward me threateningly again or I'll remove your balls and add them to my collection of keepsakes." The one I've named Cheshire barks out a laugh with a surprised look on his face, like he can't believe I have the guts to say shit like that to Frosty. I have a bigger pair of balls than the majority of the men I've ever met in my life, and no jumped-up prick like him is going to try intimidating me.

"Alexander, is our conversation over? I'm going to go chase down Rocco and get my cut for tonight since it looks like you have more pressing matters that you need to sort out."

"Ummm..." Clearly, he's still trying to process everything. I turn on my heel and aim for the door.

Unfortunately, I have three assholes standing in my way. Well, fuck, that's never stopped me before, so my ass keeps walking until I side check one, two, then three.

"It was nice to meet you Reaper," the leader grins, I can't figure out if he's trying for charming or possessed. "I have a feeling we will see

each other again soon."

I make it through the door and practically sag under the relief of not being in that office any longer. Since my adrenaline is gone, I am beyond exhausted. Time to get the hell out of here and take my ass to bed. I look across the arena and not three feet in front of me is Rocco finishing whatever it is he's doing.

"Hey, Rocco."

"What's up, Reaper? Did boss man rip you a new one for going off script?"

"Yeah, yeah. He was trying to when he received three big-ass visitors in the office."

"Who?" He blurts the question.

"How the fuck should I know? Boss man says to give me

some of my cut from tonight and we are gonna sort it out about me going off script next week."

"Uh, yeah, okay. But if I get fucked for this..."

"You won't, trust me." We head over to the counters' table. They are dealing with the money that was made tonight on bets and Rocco grabs three stacks of bills, handing them over.

"I'll give you three stacks now and then you sort the rest out with boss man, yeah?"

"Sweet. Cheers."

I stuff the bills into my bag, spin toward the door, then stroll across the warehouse floor. I can hear raised voices, it's not clear enough to understand what is being said. Not my drama not my problem, I think to myself as I push open the old, rickety door. It groans as I open it wide and make it out into the fresh air. Walking down the street that leads straight from the warehouse, I take a right at the end of the block and keep walking until I cross the old train tracks that split the industrial part of the town with the actual town itself.

Fifteen minutes later I can see the sign for the garage. My friend, Tom, owns it and lets me live above it for nothing. He says he won't take rent from me because it's like he has his own security guard. Climbing the old metal staircase at the back of the garage, I eventually get my key into the door. with a click, I step into my sanctuary. Making my way through my tiny apartment I decide I'm too tired for food or a shower. Flopping my ass on top of my bed I feel my eyelids close, taking me into dreamland. Hopefully tonight is a nightmare free night.

3

KANE

I watch intently as the dark-haired beauty strolls out of the office with no shits given, the girl has balls I'll give her that one. I've never met anyone with the balls to talk to Liam like that, telling us to walk our asses back out the door and wait our turn, like the Queen of England. My brain can't figure it out. She's either stupid or has a death wish.

"Tut, tut Alexander, you owe me money." I say, watching his reaction.

"I-I-I can get you the money! I just need some time." the vile little cockroach says, as he shudders.

"You promised us when you borrowed the money the return would be more than we bargained for." I start to make my way further into his office. He knows he screwed up, it's written all over his face. Walking past I get a strong smell of something disgusting. I take another small inhale. My pretty bird was right, he has pissed his pants. I sit down behind his desk, lean back in the chair and place my feet on the desk, studying his body language. Marcus slowly makes his way back to the door to block the exit so this fucker can't run. Believe me, he's going to try.

"Don't try to run, Alexander! You and I both know you won't get very far." I twirl my coin between my fingers, waiting to see how he

plans to get out of this.

"Kane, please. I just need some time! I'll get you your money. The stupid bitch didn't do as she was told." His voice, has a little more life in it this time. It's always the same with assholes like him. They try to pass the blame to someone else to get themselves out of shit. Now I am getting pissed off. It's bad enough doing it normally, but throwing a woman under the bus? Nah, we don't roll like that.

"What do you mean she didn't do as she was told?" Liam asks. I know he is intrigued by her, the way she defended herself against him has definitely put her on his radar.

"Reaper! The bitch was meant to lose the fight."

"Why?" I'm curious why someone who would put opposite sexes into a match up and have the weaker of the two go through a beating just to win money, doesn't sit right with me.

"Why?" He looks at me with confusion written on his face. He doesn't know where I'm going with this.

"Yeah, I asked you why?" *For fuck's sake, how hard is the question to understand?*

"Reaper has always been the crowd favorite." I sit up at the mention of her name, wanting as much info on the black-haired beauty as I can get.

"Has been since the day she started here. She's never lost. The crowd loves her. She's a warrior and they love the bloodshed she causes. The thing that makes her valuable is the crowd bets major money when she fights." The room is thick with a strange charge of energy and my brothers and I glance at each other. We all have the same thought.

"Now, imagine how much I would take home if I had my champion female fighter and best male fighter go head-to-head!

24

"It worked in my favor. You see the women refuse to fight her, that's a win-win. So, I told her she had to fight Mason and lose if she ever wanted to fight again. She agreed." he pleads.

Lust roars to life in my veins; I want her, I must have her. Fuck! Why does my brain keep wandering to her? I can't concentrate on this conversation because every time she's mentioned my brain and dick do their own thing.

"Mason said something which set her off, so she decided she

wanted to kick his ass instead of losing." Alexander explains.

"She fucked me over!" he screams out into the open, like this would save his ass. "When you walked in, we were having a disagreement about the fight. I told her she had to dance to pay the money back!"

He wants her to dance at his strip club. He wants her to get naked to pay her debt. My blood runs cold and my right hand starts to twitch. Like fuck! No one is seeing my pretty bird naked! Over my dead body.

I jump up from my seat, scaring the shit out of the little retch who wants to put my girl on display for fuck knows how may creeps to leer at.

"She is not dancing in your God-awful club. That isn't fucking happening." My voice is filled with deadly intent, both a warning and a promise. Liam and Marcus look at me like I've lost my damn mind. Women don't appeal to me in that way, and none have ever intrigued me like this. They are a means to an end. I love to fuck; women relieve the itch then I send them on their way. All women are a weakness, they'll turn you into a lovesick fool. Not me; I fuck them, they fuck off.

"I'll contact Andre then. He wanted her. I'll see if he still wants to buy her." Alexander rushes out.

"Buy her?" My bellow, nearly shakes the foundations of the

building. I must have misheard that. Surely, he wouldn't sell her.

"Are you fucking serious right now?" I roar as I stride towards him. He needs to be very careful what he says next, because depending on his answer, I'm likely to kill his ass.

"Yeah, he runs a fight scene too. He heard about her and wanted to buy her a few months ago. My turnover has been mental for the last six years since she's been a regular." He rushes through his words, holding his hands up.

"You want to sell your money maker like that? You've just said she's the one who they pay to see and bet on, so why would you sell her?" Liam asks.

"Shit, yeah. I didn't think of that, fuck!" Alexander paces, grinding the heels of his palms into his eyes.

"Why don't you loan her out to Andre every other weekend? He has a chance to increase the money coming in on his side and you don't lose your money maker." I look at Marcus who is causally leaning against the office door, with a grin on his face.

"Andre wouldn't go for that. He'd want to either buy her or not at all. He would fuck me over just to get her there."

The room is quiet while everyone thinks. I know the bad guys being amenable is funny. I may be an asshole, but my pretty bird isn't going anywhere unless it's into my bed or bent over my desk. I've already claimed her as mine and I'm not having anyone think they have control over what's mine. Alexander hasn't realized it yet, but Reaper isn't his property.

I want to own, consume and break her. That isn't a possibility while someone else owns her. A sadistic grin grows on my face slowly, as the plan comes to mind.

"I know that grin, brother. What have you decided?" Liam asks with a raised eyebrow.

"Alexander, how about we make a new deal that will

benefit us both greatly?" My tone is calm, like I'm a suit at a business meeting.

"How so?" He looks scared.

"You want your debt cleared with me and my brother's, don't you?" I ask, before he can answer, "Why don't you sell The Reaper to us?"

"What?" He gapes at me like he hasn't understood what I've just said. God this guy is slow.

"You sell her to me, and I'll clear your debt. You don't owe me anything and I own her." Yeah, I like this idea. He will sell her to me one way or another.

"But, but how? You want my best fighter. I'll lose my cash flow."

"Simple, really. I'll own her, she fights for me and my brothers here. You keep your money but we get a percentage of the house. Everybody is happy."

"But..."

"Alexander, you will do this because if you don't, I will take your money maker, your fight scene and everything you hold dear, and destroy it piece by piece as you watch. Then, I'll chop you up and feed you to the pigs."

"You're saying if I sell Reaper to you, she is still able to fight here?" he asks, deep in thought.

"Yes." What's taking the dipshit so long to decide?

"How big of a percentage of the fights are we talking about or is it a nightly percentage?" he asks eagerly.

"What percentage does a fighter take home from their fight?" I ask.

"Five percent from the fight, the rest goes to the house." he says.

I don't care about the money, but it will help me to secure this deal. There's just something about her. She's strong willed with an iron shell wrapped up in gorgeous packaging but there has to be more and I want it all. I want her broken and laid at my feet like a sacrifice ready to be possessed and consumed by the evil in front of her.

"The house keeps sixty percent and we take thirty-five percent and the fighters keep their five. Do we have a deal?"

"Kane, what the fuck bro?" Liam looks pissed at my suggestion. He likes money more than he likes sex. That percentage, to him, is an insult.

"Liam, we will talk about this later."

"Damn fucking right, we will." He glares at me.

"Do we have a deal?" My blood is buzzing waiting for him to answer.

"I get sixty percent and you aren't going to go back on the deal once you have her? My debt is clear? My family is safe?" the idiot questions.

"Yes. Do we have a deal or not!" I shout, losing my patience.

"Yes!" he shouts, as relief shows on his face. "She's yours! I accept she belongs to you, but I would like her to fight on Saturday's like she always has." I knew he would take the deal. He knows I would have followed through on my threat. We are called The Damned for a reason. None of the others have much of their souls left, but mine is nonexistent.

"Deal! You have until Friday to tell her and deliver her to me." With a handshake the deal is done. This is perfect. I can have what I want and slowly clip her beautiful feathers so she can never leave me. I have just found myself a very interesting toy to play with. The thought makes my dick hard. I'll allow her time to get used to the idea of belonging to me; I can wait a little while longer.

4

REIKA

Someone needs to hit daylight with a brightness tax. Jesus, why is it so bright this goddamn early? I feel worse than I did last night. I roll over to grab my phone. Fuck! I forgot about my broken ribs. I didn't shower or ice them before I fell asleep last night. Grabbing my phone, I find a text from Tom asking me to meet him downstairs. I stand up and make my way to the shower to get all the blood, grime and stink off me from last night. Flicking the light switch, I get a good look at myself in the mirror.

My reflection confirms that I look like hell. I have a slight bruise on the underside of my jaw. I carefully pull up my top to get a better look at my ribs. My eyes nearly pop out of my head as my gaze lands on the bright purple and blue splotches on both sides. Coffee and painkillers are going to be needed to function. I switch on the shower and turn the temperature up. Hopefully the heat and steam will help my battered muscles and bring some of the swelling down on my face. I head back to the kitchen to make a drink, giving the shower time to warm up. As I flick the kettle on, my phone starts to ring. Whoever is calling better be dead, dying or about to tell me we are having a zombie apocalypse. Great, it's Mel. I do not have enough brain function for this. I click to answer and wait to see how cheery her mood is.

"Ry! You there?" Not too cheery. I might make it through a whole conversation.

"Someone best be dying, Mel. I've just woken up." I growl, morning isn't my friendliest time of day.

"Really, dude? It's two-thirty."

I turn to grab a cup, adding in two sugars to coffee. Finishing with a splash of milk, just the way I like it. I would drink black coffee if I could, but I don't think that would be a good idea.

"Is there a point to you calling, Mel? I'm just about to grab a shower." I huff down the phone. She always rings as I'm about to get in shower or doing something.

"Such a grinch when you wake up, Ry. Will you come to the den with me tonight? That guy I'm dating wants to meet up, but some of his friends are going to be there. Please, you'll be doing me a solid." Her voice is pleading down the phone, and I just know if she was here she would be giving me huge puppy dogs eyes.

"What time? Honestly, I could use a drink after last night." This isn't an argument I can win.

"Is eight good for you? I can swing by and pick you up if you want?" she squeals.

"Sweet. See you tonight." I mumble, trying to rush her off the phone.

"Ry!" she barks, just as I'm about to hit the end call button.

"What?" I growl.

"Can you please be on your best behavior tonight? I really like him. I don't want you to run him off like you did James!" I snort a laugh, which causes coffee to shoot out of my nose everywhere.

"I didn't run James off. I just explained to him the consequences of hurting my friend. Not my problem if he lost his balls somewhere." I grin at the memory, that dude was terrified.

"Ry, you told him if he hurt me, you would tie his ass up, remove his balls and feed them to him. Then remove his fingers and toes. Plus, when you got bored you would give him to the gators as a present." Her voice is a mix of anger and laughter. I know she was pissed at me for saying that to him, but she understood why. The girl is a part of my family, and I'm fiercely protective of my family.

"Yeah, and I was only telling him the truth. Not my problem he was a scared little bitch." I blurt, continuing before she can give me the third degree, "Mel, anyone would do the same thing for their sister from another mister and honestly, if they run because of that, they aren't worth your time. Period!"

"Yeah, yeah. Just please behave. Got to go. I'll see you at eight. Love ya."

The line goes dead, before I can say anything in reply. Best get ready for tonight.

I have the quickest shower ever, jump out and pull on my grey joggers with a white t-shirt. Throwing my hair up into a bun, I slip my shoes on and head to Tom's office with a new coffee in hand.

"Damn. Ry, when are you gonna let me take your fine ass out?" Mark shouts across to me.

"Not in this lifetime, Mark. You need to find yourself a good girl. I'll suck your soul from your body and dance in the rain with it." I smile, which has him turning more googly eyed.

"I'm not afraid to lose my soul, Ry." He shouts with his arms spread wide.

"You should be. Not having a soul isn't all it's cracked up to be! Catch you later, Mark." Walking through Tom's office door I'm met with a Starbucks coffee instead of the cheap shit I normally drink.

"Have I ever told you how much I love you, dude?"

"Bahahaha. All the time, especially when I give you decent coffee." Tom laughs. Sitting down, my ribs twinge in pain bringing a growl to my lips. "Before you ask, I was fighting last night. The big bastard broke some ribs." After wiggling a bit, I get myself in the perfect position to ease the pain and get a better view of Tom, who is sitting across from me in the chair.

"Bastard? Ry, that sounds to me like you were fighting a guy? Please tell me that's bullshit?" I stare, open mouthed at how quick he spat those questions without giving me a chance to answer any of them.

"Yep, yep and nope." His eyes darken, his jaw ticks. Here we go again, Tom hates it when I fight. He says I shouldn't have too. He knows the reasons why I do, but doesn't like it.

"Fuck's sake, Ry! Why the hell are you fighting guys? You could get seriously hurt." I can't look him in the eyes. I know he's begging me to stop. It's both an obsession and addiction to feel my flesh split when someone lands a punch, but the best thing of all is the numbness that comes with it. I feel like I belong, and I'm in control.

"If you need money, I'll give you it. Please, I'm begging. Don't fight anymore."

"Tom, I love you like a brother. Thank you for the offer but you know it's not about money for me. It never has been.

"I fight, because the demons get too loud in my head. Giving in to them, feeding the bloodlust to them is the only peace I can get." My words sound hollow, even to my ears.

"You still blame yourself for what happened, Reika? You were a child!" He's pissed. All I ever asked of him and Mel was to never talk about what happened when I was younger.

"Don't!" I warn, my skin starts to prickle as he carries on picking the scab of the wound I forever carry.

"Fuck you, Ry. You're not a robot. You can feel pain, heartache, loss. It's not healthy to close yourself off from the world and keep yourself on a destructive path. I can't stand by and watch you destroy yourself." He's really starting to piss me off. I don't need a lecture. I'm happy with how my life is. Why can't people just leave me be?

"My past is my past, and it will stay that way. You wanted to talk, here I am. If you're going to drag up other shit, I'm out!" Standing up, I turn to the office door to get out of here before we both say things we'll regret. My fingers barely touch the handle when I hear, "Running again? I thought *the great Reaper* never ran from anything! You're still that scared little girl who can't face her problems!" My anger is building, my chest heaving. I try to reign it in, why won't he shut up? He knows what I'm capable of when I lose my shit. 10...9...8...7...6. "You're lost, Reika. You never gave yourself closure and never allowed yourself to realize you're not the monster you think you are!"

White hot rage flashes through my head. I spin fast and stalk across his office towards him. Looking at me with wide eyes, he knows he went too far. Throwing my arm forward, I grab around his throat and sweep my leg to knock his legs out from under him. I have murder clearly written across my face. I'm unhinged.

"R...R...Ry, I'm sorry!" I scoff, "Sorry! You're fucking sorry!"

"Closure," I seethe. "How the fuck would I get closure from seeing my family brutally murdered!" I roar. "I couldn't save them. That makes me just as much of a monster as the people who did it." The edges of my vision begin dimming. I know I'm being dragged back to that horrific day, but there is nothing I can do to stop it. I fight to pull breath into my lungs, as Tom's office fades. Slowly, it's replaced with the walls of the past.

I'm sitting on my bedroom floor reading; Mommy will be in soon to tuck me into bed. The door flies open. "Mommy, what's the matter?"

"Baby, I need you to come with me and stay as quiet as a mouse. Can you do that for me?"

Dragging me across the hallway toward the dining room, my mom spins to face me.

"What do you need me to do?" I ask.

"Stay as quiet as a mouse!"

"Mommy, you're scaring me." She's taken the hatch off the air vent and motions for me to get in. A crash comes from the front of the house.

"Climb in, baby. Remember to stay quiet, Reika. Promise me. No matter what you hear, do not come out." I am just about to say I promise when she clicks the hatch back into place and runs out of the room. Silent tears trace their way down my cheeks. I can't make a sound, I promised mommy I wouldn't. I must be as quiet as a mouse. Screaming starts. I hear my mommy asking someone to leave them alone. A man comes into the room I'm hiding in. I stay super still. I don't want him to find me. Another man walks in, dragging my daddy with him. Daddy has blood all over his face and he can't stand. Another man comes in, takes a chair from the table and puts it in the middle of the room. The man holding my daddy sits him in the chair and puts something around his arms.

"No, no. Please leave them alone. They have nothing to do with this. It's me you want." cries Daddy. I'm shaking. I put my hand over my mouth to stop them from hearing my breathing. I

hear screaming getting closer to the dining room. Another man comes in, dragging my mommy by her hair.

"I found her trying to call for help." Daddy starts moving around to get to Mommy. One of the men hit him on the back of his head. Someone whispers something in my daddy's ear, and he starts thrashing more and more. I'm trying hard to stay quiet, but I'm so scared. The man holding Mommy throws her to the floor. She starts to crawl away, but the man grabs her leg and pulls her back. He starts pulling at her clothes. The man climbs on top of her and I hear something clinking. My eyes are blurry from tears, but I can see what is happening. Mommy is screaming; the man is making strange noises. I remember I found Mommy and Daddy once and they made strange noises. Mommy told me it was ok. Her and Daddy were playing a game. The noises are getting louder and Daddy is screaming. Mommy is so quiet; she's as quiet as a mouse, but not moving. Another man comes, I cover my ears. I don't know how long I've been in the vent, but my body hurts. The men are laughing. The man stands up and pulls her up into his arms and puts something shiny to her neck. Daddy screams and the man holding Mommy laughs again.

Blood, all I can see is blood covering my mommy's face and clothes. The man lets her go and she falls. Daddy screams and tries to get to her. She hits the floor and doesn't move. There is blood all over her. One of the men laughs and pulls something out of his pants and points it at Daddy. There's a loud bang and then Daddy doesn't move. The men all laugh and go somewhere. I stay where I am. What if the men come back? I made a promise. I look out of the vent as much as I can and see Mommy's eyes. She's looking at me but the brightness that used to be there is gone.

I don't know how long I stay in the vent; my chest and legs hurt. I open the vent, then crawl out.

"Mommy, I'm sorry. I stayed quiet, but I hurt in there. Are you okay?" Nothing. *"Mommy!"* I touch her cheek and she's ice cold. I can't hear her breathe and she doesn't move. *"Mommy, Mommy wake up please, the bad men have gone! Mommy please, Mommy please, wake up...Mommy?"* Nothing. She doesn't wake up. I lie down and hug her. I know something is wrong. *"Mommy. Mommy, please don't leave me."* I hug her until my body is so cold, then someone grabs me and carries me away.

"No! Mommy, I can't leave Mommy, no!"

Endless darkness. I can still hear the screams of the little girl begging to stay with her parents. I hate when a flashback comes on as quickly as that one just did. My breathing techniques normally work. I haven't had an episode like that in years. The fog slowly starts to lift, my senses coming back. I can hear movement somewhere in the room, but it sounds slightly muffled.

The brightness from the room is clearing the fog behind my eyes. "Ry... Reika, can you hear me?" Tom's voice echoes in my head.

The darkness lifts and everything comes rushing back like a movie on rewind. Adjusting my eyes so I can see in the room after being in my memories, I realize Tom is beside me, gently trying to shake me out of it. I feel ice cold, like there isn't any warmth in my body at all. I'm so heavy, I slowly move to my knees and get my feet underneath me to stand. Closing my eyes to make sure everything stays where it's meant to be, open them and look into a set of tortured blue eyes that beg me to forgive them.

"Are you ok? Do you want some water? Food?" He fusses over me, his voice trembling with unease. My stomach rolls at

36

the idea of trying to eat or drink anything now. I look around wondering how long I have been lost to the memories this time. "How long was I under?" I ask quietly, still trying to get my brain to function properly.

"About twenty minutes. Ry, will you sit before you fall down?" he snaps as I try to pull myself to my feet.

Years of work, building me into the person I am are just shattered, like the walls I built were never there at all. I've been in control of my life since the day I started taking self-defense classes, learning everything I could to keep control of my world. The little girl from my memories is fading into nothing. The little girl who had dreams about sunshine and rainbows, about growing up, finding love and marriage, happiness, about a perfect life, learned a hard lesson. It's not always sunshine and rainbows. I made a promise to myself then that I would never be that broken again. I've built myself up over the years to be stronger, better, and more deadly than anything I've ever faced. Stronger than the nightmares which still haunt me. To be in control of my life. To be prepared for the unexpected.

Shaking off the cold feeling and putting my emotions back into the box where they have long been hidden, I start to feel more like myself.

"Ry?"

"I'm fine. Nothing to worry about!" I snap.

"Ry, you just hit the deck. I tried to talk to you, but nothing. The fear on your face… it was pure terror. I have never seen you go into a trance like that before." His eyes are on the floor as I stare at one of the people I adore; family isn't always blood.

"Tom, I'm fine. It was an overreaction to being caught off guard. Honestly, there's nothing to worry about." I try to lighten the situation.

"R…"

"Enough! You asked me to come down because you wanted to ask me something. What was it?" I ask trying to change the topic.

"I….um!" Tom said as I picked my phone up from where it fell out of my pocket.

"Fuck, it's five. I've got to be ready for tonight by eight. Shit." My anxiety grows as I think about whatever Mel has planned for tonight.

Not even bothering to find out what he wanted, I bolt out the door and up the steps toward home. Once inside, I start to relax. I throw a frozen pizza in the microwave and make another coffee. Making my way over to the sofa, I tuck into my food. I do not get why Mel and I are friends, sometimes. We are complete opposites. She loves clothes, makeup, shoes, and bags. I love my boots, my leather jacket and my bike. Twenty minutes later, I have just sat down to dry my hair when I hear the door open.

"Where are you at, biatch?" I knew it. Hmm, how long till she bitches about my outfit choice? She strolls into my bedroom, done up to the nines in a little black dress, killer heels, make up on point and not a hair out of place. I turn a little green. Mel is gorgeous, always attracting the attention of men wherever we go, as if she's a homing beacon for the male species. Me, I blend. I've never been one for makeup, honestly, I don't even know what to do with the stuff. I tried once to put it on and I ended up looking like a Pennywise look alike with a taste for heroin. I finish the last section of my hair and turn to Mel.

"You look gorgeous. From your outfit, I guess you're planning on getting laid tonight?" I chuckle, as she wiggles her hips.

"Damn right I am. Antonio is fine! What are you wearing?" she asks, her tone suspicious.

"My usual." I throw the comment out, trying not to draw too much attention to the fact that I don't plan on looking like one of the Olsen twins with her.

"Like hell you are! The den isn't the run-down shack it used to be. You aren't wearing jeans and boots. C'mon, Ry!" It's a lost cause, so I wave my hand to the closet. I know that's what she wanted anyway. She disappears instantly into my tiny excuse for storage space. Within seconds, my stuff is being launched over her shoulder, and a pile is starting to grow on the floor. I need a beer; this is going to be torture. I grab a Bud from the fridge and head back to the room. After a lot of banging and swearing, Mel finally comes out with a grin on her face. I'm fucked! That look means she wants to cause trouble.

"What about this?" She holds up a black dress which would barely cover my ass.

"Where did you pull that from? I don't own any shit like that." I accuse. She just grins savagely at me.

"I hid it here a while ago, hoping you might get over your no dresses rule." Her grin spreads wider at my horrified expression.

"You sneaky bitch." I chastise her like a child, but I did wonder why she kept disappearing into my room every time she came to visit. *How much more shit has she hidden in there without me knowing?*

"Nope, not happening. I'm not wearing that. My pussy and ass would be hanging out!" Rolling her eyes, she heads back in to hunt down something else. I hope her ass gets lost in Narnia, if she's going to keep suggesting stuff like that. Snorting to myself, I sit down on my bed and wait. Ten minutes, that is all it took for her to screech she's found it.

"I've got it. You don't do dresses, so I'll make you a deal." she shouts out.

"Hmmmm..."

"Wear this and the only thing I'll do is put makeup on you," She squeals again. Someone please kill me now. She's jumping around like an excited puppy. "Fine," I groan.

She hands me the clothes. Huh, never thought to put these together. Pulling my leather pants up and over my ass, I grab the ACDC top she's pulled out with it. I love this top. I haven't worn it in years; just seeing it brings back loads of memories. It's ripped in a lot of places looking like it barely stays together. Putting it on, it shows my stomach and falls off one shoulder. Before I get to check if my bruising is showing, Mel grabs me, pushing me into a chair so she can do my makeup.

God knows what has been put on my eyes, eyebrows, lips and cheeks. After a couple of touches to my hair, so it falls in waves down my back, she finally allows me to look in the mirror. Looking at my reflection I am surprised at what I see. My makeup looks fierce, with dark eyeshadow to really make my grey eyes pop and red lips. I have the whole look of a sexy as fuck woman. With my no shit attitude, it all works. I like where this is going. Fuck it, I have been ghosting my fuck buddy lately because he wants more than I am willing to give. But seeing myself like this, I think it's time to find a new one.

Mel applies more lipstick when we pull up outside the club on the outskirts of town. There is only one road with one building, on its own. The car doors slam behind us as we make our way to the line. I start walking to the back when she grabs my arm. "We don't have to wait, Ry."

"Mel, have you seen the amount of people here?" I ask puzzled, a lot of the people in the line glare at us.

"Trust me, we don't have to wait in line." She grins at me, leading me to the door. I spot the bouncer, checking people's IDs then ushering them through the door. The guy is fucking huge, like a minotaur and Godzilla had kids. Tattoos run up the full length of his arms. To complete his look, he has a bald head and a don't fuck with me expression. He spots Mel as we make our way over. "Hey, Cam. What's it like in there?"

"Busier than usual. Who's your friend, Mel?" He grins at her, with his eyes glued to me.

"Ry, this is Cam. Cam, this is Ry." Could he be any more predictable? It's written across his face that he likes what he sees and is about to spew some shit.

"You fancy a drink when I get off work, gorgeous?" he grins at me, with an air of eagerness that causes my skin to crawl.

I can't be assed with any more drama today. I want to get pissed and dance my ass off. Giving a wink, we walk past him into the club. According to the groans and shouts, the people in the line are pissed. I can't really blame them. Halestorm's "I Miss the Misery" is blaring from the speakers. I grin as I hum away to the song, as its one of my favorites. It's definitely changed in here; nothing like I remember. There's a dance floor in the middle now, tables around it giving a perfect view over the floor. Booths line the back wall behind the DJ box, probably for VIP's. The bar is lit up in blue lights to my right, giving it a freaky ice look to it.

"What do you think?" Mel leans into me, shouting in my ear so that I can hear her.

"Definitely different. I'm going to get a drink. Do you want one?"

"Nah, I'm gonna look for my date, if that's ok with you?" Her feet shuffle as she waits for an answer. I can't help myself; I um and ah about it for a few seconds. Her anxiety grows as I continue to hold out on my answer.

"Go, I can look after myself. Find me later on or I can make my own way home later." She eyes me suspiciously "Don't worry, I'll be on my best behavior," I say dripping in sarcasm.

She will find her date and I won't see her for a while, if at all, for the rest of the night. Instantly she melts into the crowd, and she's gone.

"What can I get you, gorgeous?" I was in my own little world thinking it would be a while to get a drink with the amount of people here. Turning to face the owner of the voice, my eyes widen slightly as they land on a blond-haired, blue-eyed guy with a couple of tattoos and a cheeky grin. He's nice to look at, in the boy next door kind of way, and definitely not my type of trouble. Way too friendly with a happy vibe, which is not who I am or what I look for. I need someone a lot darker to match what I have within.

"You finished checking me out, gorgeous?" he smiles wide, as his gaze rakes over my body.

"Yeah, you're cute, darling, but I'm not your type. Can I have a bottle of Bud?"

"Not my type? What do you think my type is?" He narrows his gaze at me a little in mock anger.

"The bubbly cheerleader type." I grin, as I watch his face for the reaction to my assumption.

"Wrong. That's not my type at all." He passes me my drink, looking slightly offended by my comment. I laugh.

"Don't ask a question if you're easily offended." I grin as I grab my drink. The feeling of the ice-cold beer rolling down my throat is a godsend with how warm it is in here. He's staring at me as I finish the drink in record time, just as a pretty blonde-haired girl strolls up to the bar and asks him if they are meeting up after he finishes work. Lifting my eyebrow, I smirk at him. Spotting a table free, I squeeze through the crowd. Some bastard managed to cop a feel as I tried to get to the table as quick as I could. Thank God I'm not wearing heels, or I would have been face first on the floor by now. Mel is nowhere to be seen, but I'm not bothered, honestly. I enjoy my own company.

Still, I scan around the room as far as I can see to try to spot her. I always do it no matter where we are; I always keep an eye out for her. If my girl is getting shit, then you know my ass will be there. On my return scan back to where I started, I see a tall blond-haired guy looking straight at me. Huh, weird. I feel like I've seen him somewhere before. I squint through the smoke to try and get a clearer picture of his face, but people block my view. When they move, I look again and the spot is now empty. Why would he be staring at me, of all people?

"Mi Gente" by J Balvin comes on. Finishing my beer, I make my way to the dance floor. The beat is building, my hips are moving, I throw my head back and just feel. Everything is bliss. The best feeling ever.

5

KANE

Sitting behind my desk in the office at the club, I look through the stock orders and profits taken in the last two weeks. I pay someone to do this, but from time to time I have a look through, just to be certain. With a huff, I drop the pile in my hands back onto the desk. It's no use, I can't concentrate on them. All my mind is showing me is stormy grey eyes belonging to a mouthy-ass female. I didn't sleep at all last night. Every time I started to drift my brain would conjure up an image of her eyes. A growl builds in my throat at the stupidity of it. Why am I reacting like this? She's a piece of property, that's all. Granted, I want to fuck her brains out, but that's it. I know she's a damn good fighter, but that's not enough for me to continue with this obsession. Property, that's all she is! One that will bring a nice sum into the crew's businesses, and something for me to toy with and fuck when I'm bored. But she's a feisty female, that's why this thing doesn't make sense. I don't like them with an attitude. I like submissive women, who do what I want, when I want and are happy with what attention I give them. Everyone has a weakness. I'll find hers and break her so she becomes submissive, compliant and willing to please. I snort a laugh, there's more of a chance of me seeing a unicorn than that happening. But if I can break her enough and she does submit, then maybe I might keep her. The office door swings open and my brother Liam strolls in, chewing on his bottom lip and running his hand through his hair in jerky movements.

"Kane, you sure about this deal with Alexander?" he asks with a frown.

"Why wouldn't I be? It's a win-win for us." I shrug like it's no big deal, "You were the one who wanted to bring a good fighter on board. Now we have one. What's the issue?" Unease rolls off him in waves as he stares everywhere but at me. I can't figure out if it's because I cleared Alexander's debt to purchase her or if it's something else entirely. I lean back in my chair; it squeaks as I get comfortable. My fingers lock together as I wait for whatever internal battle he's having to be over with.

"Yeah, I wanted a fighter, but she's unpredictable. A wild card." He yanks at his hair as he runs his hands through it again "She's cocky, look at what happened in the office. She doesn't even know who we are." I knew it, his problem is because she showed us zero respect. That has always been a major thing with Liam. It all boils down to the respect he assumes we are due.

"What's done is done. Either she fights and earns us money, or we remove the issue." My stomach clenches at my flippant words, but they do exactly what I had hoped they would. Liam's face smooths out as he grins at me. I chuckle and pick up my glass of whiskey.

"You sure? I saw the way you were looking at her in the cage. I don't want pussy getting in the way of all this. I know you're the boss man, but I watch your back and that girl is trouble with a capital T!"

"She is a transaction, a means to an end. That is all. You

don't need to worry about that." My stomach tightens even more, I stamp the feeling down and lock down everything warring inside me. They don't call me Soulless for nothing.

"If you say so." With an eye roll, he stands to leave.

Once the office door closes, I lean back with my eyes closed and try to relax. I don't know how much time passes before I hear the click of the door opening. Looking up, I notice one of the girls I see regularly, entering the office. She has a huge grin on her face, as she strolls in. I think her name's Dahlia? She's looking at me with lust filled eyes, and my skin tingles as I realize she was obviously seeking me out because she's horny.

Perfect, I need a distraction from my thoughts. Without speaking a word to her, I nod at my cock in a command that she knows all too well. Her hips sway as she walks over, dropping to her knees in between my legs without a word. She reaches for the button and slowly pulls the zipper down, my cock springs free instantly from the confined space. Her eyes widen, her tongue runs across her bottom lip, as she eyes my rock-solid length. I grab the back of her hair and pull her toward my dick. Prizing her mouth open, "Don't do anything." I snarl the words as I slam her head down on my cock, pushing it as far into her throat as possible. She gags, as I groan. I pump in and out of her mouth brutally. It's not enough. I need more.

I launch myself to my feet, one of my hands fisted in her hair. My length is so far down her throat her breathing is shallow as she tries her best to breathe through her nose. Moving in and out of her throat as fast as I can, her hands land on my stomach as she tries to push me away. With a savage snarl, I tighten the hold I have on her, causing her to squeak at the pain as I pick up the pace.

I drop my hold on her, pulling my still hard shaft out of her mouth as tears stream down her face. As she sucks in air frantically, I grab her again, and like the good girl she is she opens up without question. As I continue to use her mouth for my pleasure, I feel the resistance of her tonsils. "Swallow," I grit out. I am so deep her nose is buried into my flesh as I press forward again. "Good girl. That's it, keep it open," I order, my hips picking up the pace. I'm grunting and groaning. I feel the tingle start from my balls and radiate throughout my body. I fuck her mouth faster, harder, deeper. She gags and struggles to breathe once again, but I really don't give a shit. I need to come. "That's it! Good Girl. Fuck." The feeling is spreading faster, sweat pours between my shoulder blades. Any minute now I'll blow my load down her throat.

Crackling comes over the radio. "Erm, boss? Thought you should know your girl just walked into the club." *The fuck!*

I pull whatever her name is off my cock and make a grab for the radio on the other side of the desk. I find her wide eyed in a heap on the floor, staring at me as she cleans all the spit off her face, her eyes are clouded with anger. "Get out!" She scrambles to her feet, rushing out the door with tear-stained cheeks.

"What do you mean my girl just walked in?" My words come out quickly as I speak into the radio. The static is instant as Cam's voice comes through. "You know that picture you showed the crew this morning of the gorgeous, black-haired woman?"

"Reaper?" I stupidly ask.

"Yeah, that's it. She's just walked into the club with Mel, and damn boss, the picture doesn't do her justice. She's drop-dead gorgeous."

"Shut your mouth!" I roar down the radio, "She's mine. If anyone even looks at her, I will have their intestines as garlands at the next meeting." My anger dissipates slightly as he gulps on the other end.

48

Cam starts muttering about something, but I don't hear it. She's here, in my club. What the fuck is she doing here? Cam just said she's drop dead gorgeous. How many of the others have eyed what is mine? She was in the cage when I first saw her; I don't need that fucker telling me how gorgeous she is, I know. My emotions swirl at the thought of someone down there, having their paws all over her. The door slams behind me as I get to the bottom of the stairs leading onto the main floor, in search of my property.

Alexander has until Friday to deliver her to me, per the rules of the deal. I own her ass, even though she doesn't know it yet, and she is in my club. Excitement thrums through me knowing I am going to see her in her normal element. I need to know what she's like when she's not surrounded by assholes. Does she have a carefree attitude? Or is the whole bad girl fighter vibe constantly in place?

Need drives me forward. I don't see or hear anything as I make my way through the crowds. Fingers brush across my arms and back, but I don't stop to see who is trying to catch my attention. I check near the toilets and outer tables first, nothing. She isn't standing anywhere near here. As I scan the room again, I spot Mel in the corner sitting with one of my guys. But her attention isn't on him, it's somewhere else.

Following her line of sight, I realize what her smile is for. There she is, in the center of the dance floor without a care in the world. Her hips swaying to the music, arms raised, head thrown back, as if she is the only person out there. I step closer to get a better look. My cock instantly goes harder than it was in the office. Fuck me! The sight of her has me gritting my teeth. Her leather pants hug her ass perfectly. The ripped shirt shows off her bronzed skin. The outfit as a whole shows off how gorgeous she is. Men in the vicinity are all staring, transfixed by her. I don't mind them looking as long as they

don't try to touch or I will make their innards into garlands. She caught my attention in the cage in a nanosecond, but now all put together, she's a lethal dose straight to my dick. Lust roars through my body. I can't take my eyes off her.

She's still dancing in her own little world. She hasn't noticed the guy dancing behind her. I watch as he moves closer to her, then backs off again. If she ignores him to continue dancing on her own, I will reward her; if she doesn't, well, I will make her punishment worth my while. C'mon, Pretty Bird. What the fuck! She steps back into him and grinds into his junk, his hands running all over her. Rage ignites in my body. I grab the radio, "Cam, get ya ass in here and remove someone for me before I slaughter the bastard in the club." I grind my teeth as I try to keep my anger in check, darkness roaring to life in my chest. "On my way, boss." Cam shouts into the radio, closely followed by panting.

I watch this fucker and my girl grind on each other like they're fucking on the dance floor. I'm frozen in place, as my limbs turn to stone. What the fuck? She just kissed him! His hand runs down her legs and lifts her. Everything goes dark. My fist connects with the fucker's nose and I start smashing his face in. My vision is tinged in red, as I pound his face. I'm going to kill this bastard for touching what's mine. All I hear are screams filling the air. Someone is trying to pull me off this fucker. I snarl savagely as I continue my assault. He's a dead man. She's mine. I get to touch her and feel her body under my hands, not him. Not anybody as long as I walk this fucking earth.

"What the fuck is wrong with you?" A voice booms out at my side, as I'm hauled backwards off the guy, as he wails like an animal on the floor. Liam's face comes into view as his words register, his face is pinched in anger as he glowers at me. I can see he's pissed.

"Me? Did you see how he was touching her? No one gets to touch her but me!" My voice booms, Liam's eyes widen, surprised by my outburst.

"Are you shitting me? You beat the guy within an inch of his life because he was touching someone." He huffs in disbelief as he shakes his head.

"Not someone. He was touching her! She belongs to me, Liam, and no-one else." My body vibrates with uncontrollable rage.

"Shit!" Liam starts pacing up and down the office. Now he knows who the fucker downstairs had his hands all over. Processing the whole situation, I don't even remember moving. One-minute I'm watching from the side, then the guy is on the floor, blood pouring from his nose and anywhere else I did damage.

"You're telling me you nearly killed someone because he danced with The Reaper?" He demands as his lip curls.

"I knew she'd be nothing but trouble. For fuck's sake they were dancing. You fucking idiot!" he screams in my face.

"Dancing? They were practically fucking on the dance floor." I bellow back in his face. He takes a step away from me. What the hell is happening? Women are nothing but toys to me. Why am I so affected by seeing her make out with someone else? I don't give a shit if the other women see other men. I get my cock wet and leave. I don't care about them, but seeing him touch her like that set me off.

"Kane, seriously. That girl is trouble. Don't keep this deal with Alexander," Liam begs. "You're already fucked up over her and she's not even been handed over yet."

"Not going to happen. I'm not breaking this deal." I'm not fucked up over this girl. He's wrong. I'm pissed off I didn't get to finish earlier, and then seeing that just pissed me off. That's all. The office door opens and Marcus strolls in.

"What happened? I overheard some customers saying you went Blade on someone's ass?" he snorts. The packet of crisps in his hand crinkles as he pulls one out and throws it into his mouth.

"That's a fucking understatement," Liam snaps out. "He lost his shit because a guy was dancing with The Reaper." Marcus' eyes widen in surprise.

"The fighter? Really you fucked him up for dancing with her?" Marcus grins as he looks between the pair of us, neither one looking to the other. He's enjoying this. The little shit loves drama. He thrives off it.

"They were practically fucking each other." My voice is calmer now, but the venom is there.

"Kane. Get a fucking grip on yourself." Liam booms, throwing his arms up. "I'm telling you, break this fucking deal. I'm not dealing with you losing your shit all the time over some pussy." Liam slams the door. Him being pissed over me beating someone doesn't make sense. Marcus is studying me with his eerie, calculating gaze. My breathing is still heavy as all my emotions war within my body. A grin appears on his face as he starts to chuckle.

"Fuck me. I never thought I'd see the day!" He mumbles, then shakes his head. He moves over to the door when I blurt, "The fuck you on about, Marcus?"

"Shit's about to get interesting, that's for sure!" He leaves the room still chuckling to himself.

Reika

What the fuck is going on? This big man is kicking the shit out of my dance partner. I just stare as blood splatters everywhere and the poor guy screams. What the fuck is he doing here?

Some of the crowd scream while others just stand far away from the pissed off man that looks like he wants to end this guy's life. Fuck this, I wanted a fun relaxed night to just chill from all the crap earlier. I need a fucking beer. I head to the women's toilets first. Hopefully it will be quieter in there so I can process what I've just witnessed. He was brutally savage with a psychotic aura rolling off of him. Honestly, it was hot as fuck.

The ladies' stalls are empty, thank fuck. Standing in front of the mirror, I stare at myself wondering how the hell my life has had more drama in the last two days than I've had in the last three years. Something moves in the mirror, I zero in on the reflection finding a blonde-haired girl staring at me. She's looking me up and down like I'm a piece of shit. What the hell? I don't even know this chick. Seriously, is it one asshole after another today?

"You want a picture sweetie?" I growl out. Seriously, what's her problem?

"I don't need a picture, sweetie," she spits. "He'll be coming back to me when he's done with you tonight." I cock my head as I take in her appearance. Her clothes are disheveled and her make up is smudged, but the bitch looks like she wants to throw down. Now who am I to back away from a challenge? She better be prepared; she doesn't know who the fuck I am.

"What're you on about?" I ask, her accusation has me stumped.

"You heard me. Kane will come back to me." What the fuck has this bitch been snorting, and who the hell is Kane?

"I haven't got a clue what the hell you're going on about, but drop your attitude before someone gets hurt!" I'm getting pissed.

"Don't play stupid with me, bitch!" she screeches. "I bet you're wet from seeing him beat the shit out of that guy you were dancing with?"The penny drops Kane is the big man. Nice to know, but I still can't figure out what the fuck she is doing in here, screeching like a goddamn banshee. Her words rattle in my head as I play catch up, trying to piece it all together. Then it slaps me in the face like a brick. This bitch is here to mark her property. That's cute, and hilarious.

"Let me guess. You're here to make sure I don't step on your toes?" I fight to hold back the chuckle at the stupidity of the situation.

"Like you could. I'm his favorite. He comes to me the most," she says.

"Back the fuck up? Did I just hear you right?" She doesn't reply, just glares at me. Snorting to myself, I can't believe what I'm hearing. His favorite? What the fuck? Has the guy got a house full of bitches he keeps in rotation? To each their own, I guess, but fucking hell.

Don't get me wrong, I like to fuck a lot and don't give a crap who is fucking who when they leave my place or I leave theirs, but like hell would I be in a day-to-day competition with other women, wondering who he's going to go see.

"I don't want your man." I say slowly so she understands what I'm saying, "The fact you're here pissing all over your property. Like a dog does to its territory. All because he beat the shit out of someone, and you think I'm the reason behind it." I snort as I try to explain to this bimbo that I don't give a shit about her or her man. They can skip off into the sunset holding hands or die in a twelve-body orgy. I won't lose sleep over it.

Getting in my face she spits, "He wants me!" Oh no, she fucking didn't. Stepping closer so our noses are practically touching I smile, "Baby, if you're happy to be a nob gobbler when he's probably had his dick in something else five minutes before, that's your choice. Don't get in my face because you feel threatened!" Wide eyed she starts spluttering.

"I. Don't. Want. Him. If I wanted to fuck him I would, but I haven't. If you really want to try to intimidate someone, make sure you pick the right person next time, because I won't hesitate to fuck you up." My grin is malicious as I press the point.

Fuck this chick. I spin and leave. I'm no saint, but fuck me. I should have dropped her, the stupid bitch. It's chaotic out in the hallway, bodies are squished together like sardines in a tin can. The chatter is loud as everyone laughs and jokes, clearly still high from the shit show that went on earlier. Just as I'm about to exit the darkened hallway, I hear my name from two guys who are leaned against the wall talking. I have never seen these guys before in my life, but they used my fight name. Now my interest is piqued.

"Yeah, bro, didn't you see boss man lose his shit because of who the guy was dancing with?"

"It doesn't make sense. You've seen how Kane goes through pussy." The guy huffs out a breath. "What's so special about this chick?" I step back further into the shadows of the hallway, so they carry on their conversation. What a set of fucking idiots. You never know who's listening.

"I hear she's The Reaper from the fight ring!" The words burst out of him loudly as he hops from foot to foot.

"You're shitting me?" The other one gasps as he looks at his friend and I can see the profile of his face. "Nah man you got it wrong. The Reaper is one bad-ass bitch. Didn't you hear what she did to Mason last night?" Keep talking boys. I step closer, the noise in the hallway covers the sound of my movements perfectly, they don't even notice when I chuckle.

"Yep, she fucked him up! They were there to make sure Alexander didn't take off on the loan. You know boss man, though. He always looks for ways to make money." Tweedle Dee and Tweedle Dumb are as thick as pig shit. Seriously, they haven't checked their surroundings? It's obvious this isn't a conversation they should be having out in the open like this.

"What are you getting at, Bone?"

"Ice man was looking for a fighter to put into the rings to earn money! Alexander was here a few days ago, if you remember, then Boss man fucks that guy up for dancing with her!"

"You saying Kane bought her off him to have her fight in the ring?"

"Yep, it makes sense. He owns her ass. That will be why he did what he did." He chuckles as he takes another swig of his drink.

"You've heard about The Reaper. You know the stories; you really think she's going to just accept that?" The other questions, the excited one's eyes drop into a frown. Thankfully I am still in the shadows and I watch as his friend's questions roll around in his mind.

Just like they rattle around in my head tormenting me. He fucking bought me. That motherfucking bastard sold me like a piece of fucking cattle. I don't know why I'm surprised about Kane buying me, the aura of the guy was on another level, but that motherfucker sold me. Kane thinks he owns me? Like fuck! I don't belong to anyone; I will not be owned. I'm not a circus animal that will dance to my master's tune. Livid, I'm fucking livid. Who the fuck do they think they are? My rage builds as the words continue to repeat through my head. My teeth crunch so loud under the pressure of my jaw, I think I'm half a second away from cracking teeth. You've just fucked yourself in the ass with a prickly dildo, Kane. I bow to no one and after meeting your bitch earlier, I will not be a toy to use. I haven't even noticed Tweedle Dee and Tweedle Dumb have left the spot they were in.

Shooting a message to Mel telling her I'm heading home, I

make my way to the front door. The ice-cold air blasts me as I step out onto the sidewalk with a nod to Cam. I set off to get away from the club as quickly as I can because I am half a second away from boiling the bastard alive. I make it to the end of the block, my rage a living, breathing thing, beneath my skin. Two women pass by giving me a once over, cackling to themselves at something when one of them mentions his name. I'm rooted to the spot; they're talking about what they would give just so he fucks them once and how they've heard he's a beast in bed. Desperate bitches. Seriously, why do most women turn to a blubbering mess when a guy is hot? It's as if they lose all brain function.

My ears perk up even more as the conversation turns to how much money he has with owning a club like this. Hmm, that's why he was there. That makes sense now I know he owns the place. But still, why the fuck would he think it's to put a beating on the dude when he watched me in the cage. It's not like I'm a damsel who can't look after myself. Mel was adamant we come here as this is her go to place; she doesn't even know what went down at the warehouse. I can't get pissed at the possibility of a set-up, because she wouldn't screw me over like that.

The barbie looking one points and says something to the other. My eyes follow her extended hand and that's when I see a black-on-black charger. Parked near the employee's entrance of the club, got to give the guy his props it's a nice car. Shame about the asshole that comes attached to it though. A horn blaring fills the cold night air as all eyes including myself looks for the person responsible for it. I find Maverick idling, with a big shit eating grin on his face, as he beckons me over.

"You want a lift?" He shouts through the passenger window; I grin at him as I hop in. I don't need to be asked twice, plus saves paying for an uber and my ass freezing out here.

"Cheers, Rick! I owe you one," I say as I slink down into the leather seat. The heat is blaring, a welcome feeling from the cold outside.

"No sweat, gorgeous." He grins as he pulls out and takes off. The drive is silent as my brain processes everything that has happened over the last forty-eight hours. Before I know it, we are pulling into the lot of the garage. Turning the engine off, Rick turns to look at me.

"You ever gonna let me take you on a date, Ry?" He grins as he leans further into my side of the car.

"Rick. Every time you ask me that the answer is the same. No. We fucked a few times. That's it." I grouse, I'm not in the mood for his weird obsession he has for me.

"We're good together." He whines only proving my point. This is why I throw their asses to the curb if they catch feelings.

"The sex was great but that's all it was. I don't want to date," I growl.

"What you mean me or you don't want to date anyone?" He asks sheepishly, his hand runs through his hair.

"Nobody." I snap, I should have walked home. "I fuck that is it, anything to do with emotions and the feely shit. Wrong woman."

The smile drops from his face, as he runs his hand through is hair. The movements are more aggressive than they were earlier. I kind of feel guilty for being a bitch, but after tonight I can't deal with anything else. I've got too much to work through as it is. Jumping out of the car, I throw a wave over my shoulder and head upstairs without looking back. Screeching kicks ring out as the gravel kicks up behind his car as he takes off like a bat out of hell.

I plop my ass on the bed and look up at the ceiling. I'll be having words with Alexander when I get my hands on the fucker. But Kane is another thing altogether. An unknown. Ideas pop into my head of ways to send a message that I don't take shit lying down. They always get a warning and if they heed it, then great. If not, well that's when the fun shit starts to happen. Hitting him where it hurts is the only way a man like that will pay attention, Bimbo from the toilets is out of the question. He clearly doesn't give two shits about his women. Nope, I need something else. As my eyes drift closed it hits me. That's it, it's perfect. Chuckling, I drift off into a deep sleep.

6

REIKA

Black leggings, black hoodie, and a backpack of goodies, I have to hold in my snort as I stare at myself. For the first time in a long time, I had a full night of unbroken sleep, so my ass is refreshed this morning. I bounce down the stairs in excitement at the plans I have for today. I'm on my way to talk to Tom. Having a best friend who own's a garage has its perks. He fixes my bike when it needs it. "Morning, Tom!" His eyes shoot up to see me standing in the doorway of his office.

"You piss the bed or something?" He grins as I bounce into the office.

"Ha, you cheeky shit. No, I haven't. I need to ask you something." I fumble through the words in my excitement, causing him to quirk a brow at me. Hopefully, he has the info I need, or my day will be a lot harder. He narrows his eyes, as he leans back in the office chair, "What you need to know?"

"Have you ever worked on a charger that's black with black rims?" I ask in my friendliest tone, with a sweet grin on my face.

He snorts a laugh, moves forward so he's leaning on the

desk with his forearms, his eyes rake over my outfit. "What are you up to, Ry?"

"Nothing." I blurt, my cheeks flush at the fumble, "Have you worked on it before or not?" He eyes me suspiciously, not saying a damn word causing my anxiety to peak as he just stares. My foot starts tapping the floor as my impatience grows.

"Yeah, it's been in a few times. What about it?" He cocks his head to the side. *Play it cool Reika. If you don't, he's going to know.* Then it won't be possible to bullshit my way out of this.

"You have the address to where I'd find it?"

"Ry, what are you planning?" Trying to keep eye contact with him is hard, like seriously hard, he knows when I lie.

My unease grows as he locks his gaze with mine, "Nothing."

"Bullshit, you can't even look at me. You're full of it." he growls, as he stands rounding the desk. Instantly he's in my face. I really should tell him; thing is, Tom would react very badly about the whole thing. But family is family. You don't lie to them.

"Don't freak, okay?" The high pitch to my voice lowers as I continue, "But I need to talk to him, then I've got to have a talk with Alexander." His eyes narrow at the mention of Alexander. I spot his jaw ticking, a sign he's about to flip his shit.

"Look before you start with the hundreds of questions, I'll be straight with you, but don't freak out. I mean it Tom." All this stress over one simple question. I just need an address. My eyes are pleading. Thankfully he stays quiet and motions with his hand for me to continue.

I take a deep breath "Alexander sold me to the g…"

A crash echoes around the room. "What?" Tom's bellow follows, as I watch the remains of a chair drop to the floor.

"Shut it and listen before your head explodes," I snap, as he paces up and down the floor like a wild animal. Clearly this was not the best way to tell my friend that I've been sold like a transaction, for a reason I don't know, to someone I don't know. But fuck, I can't exactly sugar coat this to make it sound any better.

"I overheard two guys talking last night in the club. The guy who owns the charger is the one who bought me off Alexander. I don't know what is going on, but he needs to know I will not stand by and let him think he owns me. So, I'm going to send him a message." My grin is savage as I watch Tom's anger deflate slightly. He knows I dole out punishment that fits the crime, after the customary warning, of course. It will be perfect.

"Ry, do I want to know?" My grin widens as I channel my inner Harley Quinn. *Nope, not a chance.* Tom shudders at the look on my face.

"Nope. I don't want to know. What you're looking for is in the records cabinet, over there." With a nod, he's out the door. Clever on his part. If someone comes asking, they can't pin anything on him. Taking a quick look to make sure the corridor is empty, I head over to the cabinet. It looks like this will take a while as there is no order to the records and the stack is huge. I start flipping through the stack.

"Nope. Nope. Nope. Gotcha!" Matte black charger with black wheels and detailing. Owner name, check. Address, check. This is probably going to kill me, but if he has a brain in between his ears he will listen to my warning. I'm out the door, whistling to myself in excitement. It's going to be a good day.

First stop, the store to get a few supplies. Oh, how I would love to be a fly on the wall when he sees what I have planned. Call me a psycho or a crazy bitch, but the adrenaline is building, giving me a warm and fuzzy feeling inside. I look like a crazy person walking through the aisles. God, I love this town. Everything is so easy to find. Grabbing what I need, I head to the till to pay.

"Doing some DIY?" the older guy behind the counter questions as he scans my items through. "You could say that." I grin at him.

One. Two. I am coming for you. Three. Four. Better lock your door.

Kane

Thump! Thump! Thump! Shit my head is killing me. The thumping starts again making me groan. It feels like a jackhammer is going off in my head; this has to be the worst hangover ever. Everything from last night is a blur, but the bruises and cuts to my hands say that it must have been one hell of a night. Do I want to know what happened? When I saw Marcus and Liam this morning, while on the hunt for caffeine, Marcus just laughed and Liam shook his head. Yeah, they were a great help as I sit in my home office with the curtains drawn and sunglasses on to try and ease the pain. "How the hell did this happen?" Marcus's voice booms in the corridor. What has him so rattled? I head out to the hall to see what all the noise is about, and find Marcus with a grunt pinned to the wall. The guy stutters something as my brother snarls like a savage, gnashing his teeth at the guy. "What the hell is going on with all the shouting? Marcus drop him!"

All the guys in the house have looks of sheer terror across their faces. Something has happened. Not one of them will make eye contact with me. Fear rolls of them in waves some of the rush out of the corridor.

"You're going to lose your shit, Kane, but we will find who did this!" I can see the demons behind Marcus's eyes, dancing freely wanting to come out to play. What? "Is no one going to tell me what's going on?"

"Y-Y-Your c-c-car, Boss." His words hit me with the force of a freight train. My fucking car! I take off running out of the house.

Rounding the corner, I freeze. What the hell? My car is destroyed. I don't mean little bits of damage here and there; no, I mean destroyed, like an aircraft carrier has landed on it. Some fucker has destroyed my baby. Who the hell has the balls to come after me? Everyone knows that my car is my baby. I treat her better than the women I fuck. I've had her for years.

"Holy shit!" I glance to my side and see Liam gawking at the remains, as Marcus strolls casually up to my side. I look over the damage and see three tires slashed to shreds. My windows are nonexistent, mirrors and lights are gone. All the paintwork bubbled up and melted away. All the panels are distorted, like something you would pull out of a crash or scrap yard.Some bastard has thrown paint stripper and battery acid all over her. Inside is just as bad. All my seats are slashed as well as the console. There's garbage and a vile smell coming from the floor.

"Find the bastard who did this." I snarl, causing all the guys hanging around to jump. "I want him found!" My eyes scan over my baby as I think over the price whoever has done this will pay.

Marcus is looking all over, as if he can't believe what he's seeing. Something like this really should be trivial, but it feels like a personal attack on me. Our rivals didn't come at us head on, didn't come after our businesses or anything else. The only thing they damaged belongs to me. It has nothing to do with our dealings and business, it is just mine.

"Kane." Marcus calls my name. "This wasn't a guy."

"Piss off. It's obviously someone trying to make a name for

themselves or something." Liam retorts to his twin. I listen as they bicker between themselves.

"What the fuck?" Marcus bellows, turning my attention him. He stares at something on the roof of the car. "*I can't be bought. I will not be owned* is sprayed in grey paint on the roof." I rush to his side my eyes zeroing in on the words and a weird looking picture of something in the corner.

"What is that?" I ask him pointing at the picture, trying my hardest to work it out. "I spend time with each of my girls and none have said anything. I can't have pissed them off." I wrack my brain; this is full on psycho shit. Did I fuck someone and they're pissed I didn't call? If that's the case they're shit out of luck. I never call if I pick someone up at the club, never will. My phone rings in my pocket, the caller ID shows it's Alexander. What does this cocksucker want?

"Marcus, get this shit dealt with and start looking for the person responsible." I slide the answer call button.

"What?" I snap at the little cretin.

"Just couldn't keep your fucking mouth shut could you, asswipe." He screams down the phone at me, so loud I have to move the phone away from my ear.

"Watch how you talk to me, Alex." I warn. "What are you going on about? Did the store run out of your favorite pads or something?"

"I've just had the beating of my life from a scary as shit, pissed off woman. Actually, pissed off doesn't even cover her mood! You told her about the deal." he bellows again, coughing filters throwing the line as he wheezes.

"Reaper?" My words come out slowly, between gritted teeth.

"Who else, dipshit! Took my door clean of its hinges saying I don't own her and she won't be sold! Next thing I know I'm waking up on the floor in a pool of blood." How the fuck does she know?

I look to Marcus, whose ears have perked up. I nod my head for him to follow as I head back to the office. She doesn't know. How could she know? She left last night when I was kicking the shit out of that guy and only four of us know about it. Lust roars to life in my veins. She beat Alexander for his part in the deal. Fuck me, that is hot. I can't wait to get between her legs and see how wild she is in the sack.

"So, your ego is dented cause you got your ass handed to you by a woman?" I chuckle darkly as his breathing is labored over the phone.

"Woman? She's as scary as Satan himself when she loses her shit. Who have you been running your mouth off to?" He barks, then the

coughing starts up again. His voice is distorted like she squeezed the life out of him.

"The only people who know are you, me and my brothers. We haven't said anything to anyone. So, the question is, Alexander, who the fuck have you been running your mouth off to?" The cheek on this asshole, honestly, we have not said anything. We saw her last night and obviously she didn't have a clue then.

"Yeah, well someone has. After this shit, I know for a fact I won't be able to deliver her to you on Friday. She will go off grid until she gets bored." he hisses.

"You saying she's going to run?" No, no, no. If she runs, it could take years to find her. I need her in my collection. Hysterical laughter crackles over the phone, causing another hacking session. Seriously, it's like he's just heard the funniest thing ever.

"Shut your mouth. Why the hell is that so funny?" I

command, losing patience with the fucking idiot. His laughter turns to snorts.

"One sec, while I sort myself out. That was funny. HA! You really don't know what you've got yourself into, do you?" He chuckles.

"Meaning?" The growl builds in my throat at the disrespect of this lowlife.

"Oh, shit, Kane. Really? You didn't get any idea of how she is?" He muses over the phone.

"No." My reply is instant. Some of the growl has disappeared as uncertainty settles into my veins

"Not even when she stood in front of you and your brothers in my office telling you to get out? You haven't figured it out?" I really wish he would just spit it out.

"In all the years I have known her, she hasn't run from anyone. She takes holidays, as she calls them, to recharge her psycho ass." He chuckles again. Leaving me wondering if he's high? She's a woman. Yeah, she's a damn good fighter, but what sort of damage could she really do?

"Are you listening?" Alex questions. I didn't realize he was still talking. "Yeah." I reply.

"That's why I wanted to deliver her without her knowing about the deal. If she knew, she would flip, like she has. The only good thing is she doesn't know who you are."

"Kane." I forgot Marcus was in the office with me, realization on his face. "She knows."

"What was that?" My eyes bug out of my head at the expression on my brother's face. Oh fuck.

"My car was destroyed sometime last night or this morning. The tires were slashed, windows smashed with paint stripper and battery acid poured all over it. It was her. There was a message sprayed on the roof." Now it makes sense.

"What did it say?" His tone has lost a lot of the hysteria he had in it.

"I can't be bought. I won't be owned." Shit.

"Oh, shit, Kane, that's a warning. If she's done that already, you don't want to see what she is capable of. Trust me." Alexander stutters through the words. I know if I was in the room with him fear would be rolling off him in waves.

"I'm not scared of some silly little girl throwing a tantrum." I growl at the stupidity of it.

"You should be." Then the line goes dead. I drop my phone on the desk and look to my brother, who is watching me intently. Pretty Bird wants to play...let's play.

7

REIKA

A whole week of just eating crap and watching Netflix. This is a state of bliss. No stupid ass men thinking they can run my life, tell me what to do or how to do it. Own me, really? That is the funniest shit I have ever heard. I do not give a crap about most people. It really isn't in my nature to care unless they are my family, but I really do hope he likes the message I sent. Honestly, I wish I could have seen his face, but after doing that and then having my conversation with Alexander, I high tailed it out of there and headed up to Tom's cabin out on the lake. Most people would say that I was running as I was afraid of the backlash. Thing is, I am looking forward to it. The lake is my Zen area where I can think, recharge my batteries and decide things. He isn't going to take this lying down. Now that is a thought. Me, him, a bed.

I must have fallen asleep out on the deck as the sun is setting and the temperature has dropped. Still dazed, I realize my phone is ringing. Running my hand along the floor hunting for the damn thing, I eventually find it after it stops ringing. No caller ID. Huh, if it's important they will call back. What the hell? There are seventeen missed calls from Mel and twenty messages all asking me to call her, when my phone rings again.

"Mel, I'm fine. You don't have to worry." I reassure her as soon as I answer the phone, my words are met with silence.

"Mel?" Again nothing, my unease grows at the silence continues.

"Dammit, talk. I don't find this funny." What the hell? All I can hear is breathing down the phone line.

"Tut. Tut, Reaper. That wasn't very nice now, was it?" a gravelly voice says, my muscles lock up.

"Who the fuck are you? Where is Mel?" I'm frozen from fear. This isn't right. Where is she?

"Pretty girl is spending time with us. She is very beautiful." The voice coos, as muffled noises come through the phone.

"Who the fuck are you?" I scream down the line. I look at my phone screen to double check the name and there it is, Mel. My heart sinks.

The voice barks out a laugh "You know who I am, I've been watching you for a long time... to make you mine. Make no mistake, Reika, you are mine." Coldness shoots down my body. That bastard. That motherfucker.

"I want to talk to her." I seethe. The edges of my vision begin to tinge with red. This bastard took Mel because I destroyed his car. Who the hell does he think he is?

"That's not going to happen, sweet." My phone pings, telling me there is a picture message. Opening it, I find a picture of Mel passed out on a bed, she looks peaceful and in one piece. But that does nothing to calm me.

"If you hurt her, I will rip your head off and scream down your throat." He's a dead man, no one fucks with my family.

"Now, now, no need for threats, sweet. She is perfectly safe. All you have to do is find me something." He wants me to do something for him, I will. She's my family. He doesn't need to know I've already thought of hundred different ways to kill him.

"Find what?" I try to get the words out as calmly as possible.

"Daddy dearest hid something he shouldn't have. I'm here to

collect on our deal."

"My Dad is dead. You fucking idiot. How the hell am I supposed to find something that I know nothing about?" What sort of shit was my dad into?

"You will find it. I don't need to tell you the consequences if you don't." His tone crackles the line, like static.

"Fine." My words are calm. "But if you hurt her…" It must be him. This is a seriously messed up way to get revenge for me fucking with his car.

"We will be in touch." The phone goes dead.

He kidnapped my family, because I fucked his car up. Running into the cabin, I grab my things and head out to the truck.

Before I know it, the town comes into view. Lights and stop signs mean nothing as I barrel through them, not giving a shit, while angry honks and cusses are thrown at me from other drivers. But that is the furthest thing from my mind, at the moment. Pissed off is an understatement for how I feel. Screeching to a halt, I realize I'm outside Kane's house and I still have my workout clothes on. Fuck it, that's a good thing; I don't mind ruining them. I throw my hair up into a bun, jump out of the cab and head across the road. There are people everywhere. I couldn't care less until some asshat blocks my path.

"Whatcha ya doing, doll face?" he grins at me, I smile sweetly in return.

"Huh, don't talk much?" He chuckles "You want to play

with me, baby?" Fucking men, they think because I'm a woman I can't do shit. He's looking me up and down with excitement in his eyes. Widening my smile, I take a tiny step closer. Men are so fickle; he thinks I'm taking him up on his offer. Such a silly boy.

I lash out so fast I connect with his throat and kick him above his knee. His eyes go wide as he grabs at his throat and falls to his knees, struggling to get air into his lungs. Yells come from behind me. I step over the piece of shit and head into the house. I check the lounge and kitchen, nothing. I see a corridor to the right of the hallway. I'll hunt him down all day if I have too.

There are more people down here. I can hear voices at the end of the corridor. I throw doors open to check each room, not caring if anyone hears me. It will be a bonus if I find Mel in one of these rooms. A door further down opens up and out steps the one I call Cheshire. His eyes widen in surprise.

"What are you doing here, Hellion?" He looks up and down the corridor.

"Where is he?" I spit the words like a poison dart. I'm not standing here for a picnic and to talk about the weather. He either tells me where he is, or I'll find the bastard myself.

"He's busy at the moment." He shuffles from foot to foot, looking uncomfortable. I stride down the corridor towards him, as I make my way past, he grabs my elbow. I spin so fast he doesn't expect me to throw him over my shoulder and his ass lands on the floor. Before he's back on his feet I'm at the end of the hallway with a door in front of me. There is noise coming from the other side of the door.

Grabbing the doorknob I hear, "I wouldn't." That's all he gets out as I throw the door open and see big man with his cock buried in blondie. He has her bent over the desk, moaning. His eyes widen at seeing me in the doorway, but he doesn't stop fucking her. Heat roars to life in my veins. Seeing them, I have to admit the guy looks like he's packing between his legs.

"You enjoying the show, Pretty Bird?" He grins as he watches me. God, what a cocky asshole. I don't say anything, just watch as he pounds into her. Cheshire grabs my elbow and starts to pull me out of the office. "Sorry, bro. She got past me."

"Get the fuck off me. I'm not going anywhere until me and bunny over here have a little chat." I snarl in his face. He can try and move me but the same thing will happen to him like the guy outside.

"If you want to talk, TALK." Big man commands from the desk, my eyes connect with his and he grins in triumph. You're messing with the wrong sort of woman, asshat.

"Where is she? Hand her over and you can keep fucking blondie to your heart's content. She looks to be faking, anyway." Blondie screams as he thrusts so hard her hips smash into the edge of the desk.

My comment clearly pissed him off as he picks up his pace, the desk banging into the wall.

"Who?" Seriously, he's going to play stupid? The moans are getting louder, my underwear is getting soaked just from watching. Moving further into the office I sit my ass down on the chair right in front of them. He clearly didn't expect that and licks his lips, looking down at me. Blondie rears back trying to get away from him, so he grips the back of her neck and forces her to stay put.

"He's yours, remember?" I wink. The look she throws my way is unsure.

"Explain?" He looks between me and his companion. Is he for real? I don't think so, asshat.

"Nothing that concerns you." I smile at the other woman. "If you took her as payback for your car, you fucked up."

"I haven't got a clue what you're on about." His brows

pinch together as if he's deep in thought. Fuck this, let's make this a bit more fun shall we.

"Bullshit, I know you took her just like you bought me from Alexander."

"What?" Blondie screeches and tries to get out from under him. "Stay where you are." he growls at the struggling woman. His palm lands on the back of her neck, pressing her into the desk.

"Yes, sir." she mumbles the best she can in between moans. Wow, what a pathetic little bitch.

Running my tongue across my lips, I follow the wetness with my thumb and trace a line down my throat to my collarbone. Back and forth, his eyes track my movement. Shifting myself lower so I can slide down into the chair, I slowly widen my legs. His eyes widen just a touch.

"I don't have Mel." His words are barely above a whisper, as his eyes track every single movement I make. I hold back the snort. Yeah, of course you don't.

"I find that hard to believe." My voice is breathy, as my chest rises and falls rapidly with growing excitement. Sliding my hand down to my chest, I grab my nipple and pinch.

"Oh." I groan at the flash of pain, mixed with pleasure from how hard I pinched. I widen my legs even more so one of my legs is over the chair arm. My fingers continue their exploration as they slide under my boobs, in an imaginary pattern towards my stomach. I don't know what's come over me, but seeing him dominate her like this has my panties soaked and my clit throbbing for attention.

His eyes follow my hand down, over my flat stomach. While I bite my bottom lip, I slip my thumb underneath the waistband of my shorts and work it side to side. Teasing him and myself with the possibility of me stopping. Looking up into his eyes all I see is surprise and lust. He doesn't know what I'm doing, but it's clear he wishes it was me underneath him, not her. I grin sweetly as I push my hand under the elastic band of my shorts. Making my way to my clit that is throbbing and swollen, begging for release. Two birds with one stone, why not?

As soon as my finger skims over the top of it pleasure shoots up into my body sending tingles everywhere. My head drops back to rest on the chair. "Damn." The words come out in half moan and hiss. A grunt has me opening my eyes. As I keep the pace with my fingers, I find Kane looking at my hand, as the noises he makes and the pounding of the desk into the wall has my nerve endings alive. The look he is giving me. There aren't any words to describe it. He looks

like he wants to eat me, while he fucks me. That look has another shot of lust rushing through my veins. I pick up speed with my hand, and he picks up his pace to match. Faster, faster... shit, my veins are on fire. I'm so close to cuming just from playing with myself, but this weird situationjust adds to the hotness of it all. I move even faster. Sparks are running over my body at the speed of light. His moans get louder. Everything explodes at once. "Fuck," I whimper as the bursts of light continue to explode behind my eyes.

"Don't stop," he orders, I obey the command. The first orgasm hasn't passed yet and my fingers pick the pace up again. Faster and faster, I circle them. I can tell by his face he's close, his movements are frantic, as he fucks brutally.Our eyes connect, I wink, and pull my hand out of my shorts. My fingers are covered in my orgasm. His eyes widen and he licks his lips at the sight of it. I keep our eyes connected as I slowly suck each finger into my mouth as I stand up, then step toward the desk.

I lean to him over the desk and run my tongue from jaw to ear. He tastes amazing, like smoke and how the forest smells after a rain. Lips touching his ear I slightly moan again to encourage him and he shivers. "Give her back." My voice rasps against the shell of his ear causing another shudder from him.

"If you don't, I will fuck your life up." His eyes widen as he pulls back to look. He doesn't say anything. I lick the last remnants of myself off my fingers with a grin. He's immobile as he just stares at me. Throwing him the deuces, I spin on my heels and walk my ass out the door with my middle finger thrown over my shoulder.

I get halfway down the hallway when I hear, "Get the fuck out." roared out into the open, followed by the crash of things smashing to pieces. Blondie comes flying out of the room, tears streaming down her face, and she rushes down another corridor I hadn't noticed earlier. Chuckling to myself, I take a step forward to find Cheshire grinning at me like I'm his new favorite person in the world, eyes full of joy and mischief. As I enter the next hallway, I can still hear yells and things being thrown from the office, surely there can't be much more to break. With a smile on my face, I turn the doorknob and step out onto the porch.

Kane

Watching her hand as it moves under her shorts sends all the blood straight to my cock. I am shocked she didn't falter at the challenge, but instead turned the goddamn tables. Hearing her noises is driving me wild, fuck she was made for me. She moves her hand faster and I pick up my pace. I hear nothing other than her, the keening noises she makes as her body trembles, or the way her breathing dips as she

shudders. My brain is telling me it is her beneath me, driving my cock harder and harder. How it would feel with her walls gripping my cock. I have never been this turned on. Her movements are getting faster. Jesus, I feel like a teenager again, the tingle starts in my balls and works out all over my body. I am so close.

"Don't stop," I order.

Fuck my life, she picks up even more speed.My hips are frantically moving to keep up with her, I want to cum at the same time. I'm dumbstruck as she lifts her hand from her core, her fingers glistening with her wetness. What the fuck? She sucks a finger into her mouth, her tongue eagerly lapping up the liquid on them. She winks at me pushing my lust to a whole other level as I watch her continue to clean herself. She stands up and steps toward the desk. Leaning over, a breathy moan flutters across my ear. She runs her tongue from my jaw to ear, which sends a shiver over my whole body. My cock so hard it's painful.

Her lips touch my ear with a heady moan, "Give her back. If you don't, I will fuck your life up." Then she's throwing me the deuces and walking out the door with her middle finger in the air. My blood turns to ice. "Get the fuck out," I roar, picking up the laptop from the desk. I throw it at the wall, then swipe everything off my desk. How fucking dare she touch herself like that, like I am the only man in the world, then walk out like nothing fucking happened.

"Argh." Flipping the table my breathing is heavy, as my rage coils in the center of my chest like a snake waiting to strike. She killed my hard on in a matter of seconds. Ripping the condom off my now limp dick, I throw it into the pile of destroyed shit. What the actual fuck? And what the hell did she mean? "He's yours, remember?"

"One hell of a woman." Marcus stands at the threshold, grinning at the destruction before him. A growl builds in my throat. I am just about to tell him to fuck off when a whimper catches my attention. What's her name stands at his side shivering, whimpering as she wipes erratically at her tear tracked cheeks.

"Marcus, I'm not in the mood. If you want to fuck it, you're more than welcome to." I've just kicked her ass out of here. Why the hell has he brought her back?

"Thought you should know a few things." I snarl as he looks down at the blonde at his side.

"One, Reaper's real name is Reika. Two, she throat punched one of the grunts getting in here, he's in the medical room." My eyes bug out in surprise. "Three, Dianna had a run in with her last night in the club." What the hell, last night?

"What do you mean they had a run in?" My tone is flat as I flick my gaze between my brother and her.

"You want to tell him?" He chuckles as he shudders again.

"I - I, saw your reaction to her dancing with that guy. I thought you were bringing her in as another piece. So, I..."

"You what?" I growl in a menacing tone. Marcus grins as she whimpers, stumbling back a step. Oh shit. If she opened her mouth to Pretty Bird about her and the others and fucked up my chances, shit.

"I followed her to the bathroom, told her I was your favorite, and you would be done with her after you had her but…"

"Stupid bitch. You aren't my favorite." I bellow the words.I fucking knew it. She's being trying to keep me to herself for a while, but it never bothered me before now.

"She said she didn't give a shit and if I was happy to share you with others it's my choice, and that she doesn't want you. She said if I went after her again, she would fuck me up." Her eyes turn steely at that, I watch as she pulls herself up straight. Pulling her disheveled clothes back into place.

"Get out!" I roar. "Get them all out now." All of them are gone, I don't give a crap. I want them all out of my house; none of them are like her. The defiance, stubbornness, spirit - everything about her draws me in.

"You sure you want them all gone, bro?" Marcus frowns at me.

"You heard me. And find out where the fuck she lives. She WILL NOT run from me again."

8

REIKA

P *ick up, pick up! C'mon answer the goddamn phone.*

She needs me. I have to find her. How has this week ended up as crazy as a whore fucking themselves with a prickly dildo? I can't catch a break. Why do people always seem to drop off the face of the earth when you need to speak to them? He is the only person who might know what shit my dad was into, and hunting his ass down will take too long. "Fuck!"

"What do you want?" an angry voice barks down the line.

"Pete? Pete Marshall?" My voice is unsure. Please be him.

"Who wants to know?" The deep timbre sounds like its vibrating the line.

"My name's Reika Martins, I think you knew my dad." I'm pacing so bad I think I have worn a hole in the carpet.

"Little Reaper? Is that you?" he whispers the question in disbelief. Oh, thank God.

"I haven't heard that name since…" My words break off as a sharp pain tears through my heart. "I need to talk to you. Can we meet up?"

"Everything ok? Are you sick?" His tone turns panicked.

"No, No. I'm fine, I need to talk to you about Dad." I

reassure him. Hopefully, this is the thing that will provide me with answers and point me in the right direction.

"You remember the barn? Be there in thirty."

"Yeah, I'll see you soon." The phone goes dead. Grabbing jeans and a hoodie, I head to the bathroom.

Pulling up outside the old barn, I'm hit with a sense of deja vu. I haven't been here in thirteen years. It still looks like the same shithole it was back then.I look at the clock on the console and see I'm ten minutes early. I'm chilling in the truck when a shadow catches my eye on the left side of the building. Side to side it moves almost like it's unable to stay still. The saying curiosity killed the cat comes to mind, but I have never been one for superstitions. The shadow stills at the sound of the cab door shutting and takes a step out front of its hiding spot.

"Jesus, Pete! I nearly had a heart attack." I snort as I find my hunting knife firmly in my grasp. My heart is racing uncontrollably, his eyes widen as he spots the knife.

"Sorry, Reika." He mutters, eyes still on the weapon "You mind putting that away?" I chuckle, sliding it back into its sheath "I haven't seen you since you were little. What's up?"

I take a deep breath, gathering myself for my next words. "Be straight with me, Pete. What sort of shit was my dad into?" Anticipation burns through my veins. Shuffling from foot to foot, my unease grows as he looks everywhere but me.

"Little Reaper, don't go hunting for answers. You won't like the picture they paint." His voice sounds pained, as he stares at the ground.

"I have been following your fights in the underground. Your

dad wanted things to be different for you." He has a gleam in his eye.

"Dad should've thought of that before he turned me into a monster as a child." I snap, my heart sinks a little as the smile drops off his face.

"Pete, don't bullshit me. My friend has been taken and the people who have her say Dad kept something from them. If I don't find it, they will hurt her." I plead with my father's oldest friend. I feel sick at the thought of Mel being in their hands.

"Leave it alone, Reika." He growls, turning away from me.

"Fuck you! She's my family!" I scream, striding towards him. "You will tell me. If you don't, we both know I can make you."

"Don't threaten me, little girl." My muscles tighten throughout my body, at the venom in his voice.

"You will tell me one way or another, old man. She is everything to me."

"I promised him I would keep an eye on you." His voice booms. "That I would protect you from the shadows, so you could have a better life." His voice breaks at the end of his confession. What is he talking about? Not a single person other than Mel and Tom have had my back, since my life turned to shit.

"Better life? Are you for fucking real right now?" I demand. My eyes narrow on him. "I was shipped to a boarding school for psychos by my foster parents. How is that any better?"

"You were out of the way." He starts muttering stuff, as he spins around so he is no longer facing me. "You could have been anyone you wanted to be Little Reaper. It was a fresh start."

"What do you mean out of the way?" My teeth grind with such force a sharp pain spreads through my jaw. There's more to this than I thought, his voice is nervous.

"Leave it alone, please." He words come out strangled. His eyes meet mine and I'm taken aback by the tears filling his eyes. Flashes from my childhood play behind my eyes. All the times Dad disappeared and Mom telling me he had problems at his work.

"You say you're protecting me from the shadows. What are you really protecting me from, Pete?" My heart aches from the guilt I feel, but I don't know why I'm feeling this way.

"I...Fuck!" he screams into the air, throwing his hands up in defeat. "You aren't going to leave this alone, are you?" My jaw sets and I know my eyes are cold as I stare at him. "Nope."

"Your dad wasn't who you thought he was. He was involved in some very shady dealings." He rubs his eyes, with a huff. What the fuck was my dad into?

"Like what?" Dread fills my body, everything is about to change, I can feel it.

"I can't tell you too much, but look into the Damned Crew leader and ask questions about The Butcher." The Butcher? What the hell? That name strikes fear into the hearts of everyone, that knows the stories of him.

"Why The Butcher? What does a psychotic assassin have to do with my dad?" I move closer, grabbing hold of his wrist. His eyes dart to mine. I take a deep breath...

"They were friends at one point. Reika," My hand trembles as his words sink in "Be careful who you talk too."

"I've heard of the Damned Crew but nothing more than that. Who is the leader of it?" The Damned Crew are infamous in this small town, as well as The Grimm's the other crew in the area. They are constantly at war with each other. The streets run red when their wars break out, even the police turn a blind eye to it.

"Malcolm Southbourne. He's a ruthless bastard, so you need to tread carefully." His hands squeezes mine. "There have been rumors he is taking a back seat and his son is more involved now."

"Is that all?" He nods. "Thank you." I release my grip on his wrist, striding back to the truck. I have some ideas where I can start looking for more information. Why the hell my dad was friends with a psycho and involved in dodgy shit? I need to regroup and work out how I'm going to get what I need. I grab the truck's door handle. "Reika."

Looking over my shoulder I see fear clearly written over Pete's face.

"Please, be careful. Knowing to much could get you killed."

Emotions war within me on the ride home. Annoyance at the limited amount of information. Confusion, I feel like I didn't really know who my father was. Uncertainty, how the hell am I going to get Mel out of this? From everything today, I feel emotionally exhausted. A shower and food are needed, and loads of beer.

What the hell am I doing here? There are lights from the building in front of me, the colors splitting through the darkness like a kaleidoscope. The truck idles as I stare at the doors of The Den while people laugh and joke outside the club, just going about their lives. A woman trips in front of the truck, in a drunken state. My lip curls in disgust at the state she's in, she giggles as she spots me through the window. I pay no attention to her. I sit for a couple of minutes deciding whether I should go in or head home, when I notice the guy trying to keep the drunken woman on her feet as she giggles like a school girl. A light from the roof spins my way, blinding me for a second, when... Motherfucker! He was the one Mel was with last night.

He helps the woman off the floor and she is all over him. What the actual fuck? The red veil drops over my eyes, as I watch the woman trailing drool all over his neck. What a complete asshole. They stumble away, her stumbling and him smiling at her. I watch them both head into the club, and my control snaps. He was with my best friend last night and now he is with another woman? Fuck this shit! He was the last one to see her. He must know where she is. Checking my reflection in the mirror I hop out and head over to the club. I look like utter shit but it's worth a try. Luckily for me, there aren't a lot of people outside now.

"Hey, pretty lady." Following the voice, I notice the bouncer at the door from last night.

"Hey!" I mumble, walking through the gap in the crowd he cleared for me.

"Where's Mel?" He chirps looking over my shoulder in search of her.

"I'm not her fucking keeper." I snap at him, moving closer towards the door. I don't want to be standing here talking to him.

"Wow, being a bitch much?" His words have me snarling. I manage to stamp it down and press forward, when his arm blocks my entrance.

"You gonna let me in or what, asshole?" I narrow my eyes at him as he looks me over quizzically.Breathe, Reika. If he turns you away, you're screwed. Plastering a sweet smile on my face, I relax myself the best I can, "Shit! Sorry man, crap day and all that. I kinda turn into an asshole."

"Yeah, I get it. No worries." He is looking at me, like someone would look at a caged wild animal at the zoo.

"Thanks, dude. You're the best!" I pat his peck with a huge grin on the way past. I'm sure I heard him gulp just as the doors closed.

Inside it's a lot quieter than last time I was here. There aren't as many people and the music isn't trying to blow my ear drums out. I head to the bar to grab a beer, and wander around a little to see if I can catch a glimpse of them. That's when I notice there are different people working. Ordering a jack and coke, I start my walk round, dodging creeps that try to catch my attention. I've made it like halfway around when booming laughter and squeals catch my attention. Following the sound I find him, with a woman pressed up against the pool table. Neither of them have a clue that I was standing watching them, along with a couple of other people, that look seconds away from jacking themselves off.

"Can you play?" A whisper dislodges the hair behind my ear. My heart stutters. Shit, I never heard anyone approach. I turn slightly to
my right.

"Yeah, can…" Shit. Cheshire stands to my side. Eyes glued to the couple. "Let's play." He grins as starts to make his way to the pool table.

"Maybe later. I need to have a word with fuck boy over there." I grin savagely, his eyes widen just a touch.

"Bonzo!" he barks. The guy growls.

"Can't you see I'm busy, man?" Bonzo fires back instantly. His eyes land on Cheshire and he freezes. Quickly stepping away from the woman, she whines her annoyance. As he brushes her hand off his arm, "Shit, sorry, man. I didn't know you were here." Who the hell are these guys?

"Reika here wants a word." How the fuck does he know my name?

Bonzo looks me up and down, licking his lips.

"Put your eyes back in your head, dude. You were all over my family last night." My voice is menacing, as I watch this fucker grab his junk.

"Don't know what you're talking about baby. I was on my own here." I growl. This fucker thinks he can bullshit his way out of seeing Mel. I don't think so. I move fast, gripping his shirt. I yank him forward, knocking the woman on her ass. She screams and he snarls at me as I snarl right back. With all my strength I swing, a dark chuckle slipping between my lips at the ouch he hisses as the plaster gives way behind his back.

"Reika." A smooth voice tries to chastise me.

"What the hell, man?" He gulps as he looks over my shoulder for help, while wriggling in my hold like a worm on a hook. He's trying to get out from under my arm.

"Listen up dickhead. You were all over my friend, Mel, last night when I left. She hasn't been seen since." Cheshire and what's his name look at me with confusion on their faces.

"What do you mean?" Cheshire rumbles at my side. I stare into the guy's eyes still wriggling in my grip.

"Where the hell is she? You were the last one to see her."

He violently shakes his head. "I don't know, we got into it and she left. I don't know where she is." He either doesn't know, or is one damn good liar. I apply more pressure, his nails claw at my arm as I block even more of his airway.

"You best not be bullshitting me. I have a habit of getting stabby when people lie." I pull my knife out of the sheath, turning it so the lights catch the metal, causing a pretty twinkle of light on it.

"I'm not lying!" he screeches as he looks at my baby in terror. Dropping the fool on his ass, I look over to my shadow. His eyes twinkle with mischief as a scowl lines his features. "'Sup Cheshire?"

"My name is Marcus, not Cheshire!" he growls, repeatedly rubbing the back of his neck. I chuckle as his cheeks flush slightly in annoyance.

"Ok, what you staring at, Marcus?" Sarcasm drips from my voice. I'm in no mood to play.

"That's the reason you came to see Kane?" he muses as he looks off into the distance.

"No shit, Sherlock." I grouse at the stupid question. "Simple statistics. I fuck his car up, then Mel disappears. What would you think?" Honestly, am I even speaking English right now?

"We don't have her, and you threatening one of our staff isn't going to go over well." I shrug, like I give a flying fuck.

"Yeah, well, what would you do? She's family." My emotions are in chaos. I don't know why I'm talking to him like a friend, but I feel comfortable with him.

"You want a drink?" he asks.

Marcus

Reika isn't like I expected her to be. Yeah, she is a badass on the outside. But talking to her, it's obvious she is more than that. She has so much hate towards anything and everything, but she's broken. Anyone can see that if they are willing to look close enough. She's laughing at something Cam has said. The shitbag came to talk to me about an issue at the front door and hasn't left since. Watching him trying his hardest to flirt with her is funny. It's like watching a bunny trying to make friends with a mountain lion, you just watch and wait for the lion to strike and swallow the fluffy bunny whole. Kane's interest in her worries me. He says he wants to own her, but his reaction to her dancing with another guy was more than that. He isn't going to admit this to himself, but it is more of an obsession, a need. He likes control in all things, no matter what it is. The demons from our past have shaped us to the people we are today. He's volatile and unpredictable, he doesn't like it when he can't control everything in his life. My gut twinges again, telling me to keep an eye on her. If he breaks her too much with the stupid games he plays, I know she will never be the same again. My senses fire off. I should have known he would be watching.

Kane

Standing here for the last four hours watching Marcus and Pretty Bird together has been pure torture. Watching Cam talk shit, like he's the man's man, and her laughing has me grinding my teeth. I want to rip him away from her and take her to the office to teach her a fucking lesson. I want her on her knees begging me to fuck her. Marcus just watches like it's the funniest thing he has ever seen. Fuck this shit. I storm over to their table. Cam is the first one to spot me, the color drains from his face. Marcus has a smirk on his, while she isn't bothered by my sudden appearance, continuing to drink whatever she has in her glass.

"We need to talk." I rumble, her head tips up to me. I have to steady myself internally as storm grey eyes bore into mine.

"No, we don't. I'm having a good time now. Fuck off." Oh, hell to the fucking no.

"Yeah, we do. Now, I'll ask once more. Don't try me, Pretty Bird." She stands and throws a wink to Marcus and rounds the table. "I said, no."

Bending down, I throw her over my shoulder and march for the office. She's turned wild trying to get out of my hold, a crack fills the air as my hand connects with her ass cheek. Marcus's howls start to fade as I climb the stairs to the office. She fights me more with each step I take. The door slams shut behind us, and I drop her to her feet. She snarls savagely, as I grin at her. My palm pushes to her chest and her back hits the wall. I push my knee in between her legs and I smile as I wrap her slender neck in my hand. I can't look away, seeing the defiant look in her eyes sends all the blood to my cock. Fuck me.

"You fucked with my car." I apply a little pressure to her neck. She hisses in the back of her throat.

"You deserved it, asshole," she sneers. Damn, her eyes are beautiful. Kind of a smoky-grey color with a black ring around them. Like clouds rolling in at the beginning of the storm.

"You fucking bought me like a piece of meat." I should've paid more attention to what was happening. She punches me in the jaw, and I stumble backwards. Fucking hell, she packs one hell of a punch. Looking at her with rage burning in her eyes and chest heaving, I can't think straight. The deal, asshole. She knows. That's why she fucked your car up.

"Either I bought you or Alexander was selling you to Andre." The thought of him having her has my darkness drawing closer to the surface.

"What the fuck? Why the fuck did he sell me anyway?" I can see the emotions running across her face: anger, betrayal, annoyance, confusion.

"He borrowed money from me, saying the fight was an easy win." I explain everything that went down with that piece of shit.

"Yeah, I was supposed to lose, then Mason fucked himself over." Rage shows itself on her face.

"How?" My interest spikes at the venom in her voice.

"It doesn't matter. I won't be owned like a piece of

property."She throws daggers at me, her expression flat as she looks me up and down. This is jumping to a whole other level. She is pissing me off with her attitude.

"He sold you to save his own ass."

"That's not my fucking problem, asshole. I don't owe you anything," she screams, taking a step closer.

"You belong to me," I roar, stepping into her personal space. The atmosphere is charged with all the emotions flaring between us. When is she going to get it through her head? I will not stop until she is mine.

"Fuck you! I belong to no one." Everything explodes, my lips are on hers. The kiss is brutal, our teeth are clashing together.

9

REIKA

This is insane. We are both fighting for dominance. I don't know what's worse, that he kissed me first or that I'm kissing him back. He pushes me harder into the wall, his hands are everywhere, touching, teasing. A guttural moan slips out of my lips and Kane growls in return. He grinds himself against me, the pressure from my jeans rubbing on my clit is so fucking good. Kane traces patterns across the top of my boob with his finger, slowly making his way to my hard nipple.

"Fuck me." The pain from the pressure as he pinches ant twists my nipple, sends a shot of heat straight between my legs. Tingling bites down the side of my neck sends my need into overdrive.

"You like pain, Pretty Bird?" I was born out of pain.

"This doesn't mean I like you," I mumble against his lips, which causes him to grind his cock harder. My body is burning like a forest fire.

A rumble of a chuckle leaves his lips. God, this fucker is so sure of himself. He smirks as his fingers run down my stomach to the button on my jeans. With a flick it opens, slowly he unzips them.

There's a challenge in his eyes. I don't have to like him to fuck him.

Placing my feet flat on the wall I push my hips forward, which makes him stumble and release me.

"Chicken shit," he says. I smirk at his words. Silly, silly man.

Stalking forward, I say, "Chicken shit? I don't think so." I press forward. He hasn't realized my steps are forcing him backwards until he lands on the sofa. Straddling his hips, I grind my pussy onto him while running my tongue across his jaw. He shivers. I run my hands down his stomach and slip them under his T-shirt so my hands meet flesh. Dragging my nails across his abs, he throws his head back and moans. Fuck me, he's ripped. Just feeling them has my pussy wet. Our lips meet and I suck his bottom lip into my mouth and bite down.

"Ah. Fucking hell." His eyes are as black as midnight lost in lust.

"What's the matter, Kane?" I purr, looking down at this giant beneath me.

"Say it again?" he groans. "What?" I cant my head to the side.

"My name. Fuck Pretty Bird, say it again," He groans as I grind myself down harder. "You want to fuck me, Kane?"

A growl tears from his throat. Before I notice what he's doing, he has me pinned on my back with a hand around my throat to keep me in place. I lift my head in challenge, so he adds more pressure. My breathing hitches as my airway is cut off. His eyes widen as he notices the change, releasing the pressure a touch. I wrap my hand around his and push his hand down to the pressure I like. With a smirk, I wiggle my hips side to side, taunting him.

"What's up? You forgot what to do?" My voice comes out a

little croaked, but I can't help it. Either he fucks me or I will find someone else who will.

"Fuck you." He pulls me up by my throat, then throws me forward, hand to the back of my neck. My jeans are ripped down to my knees. Without warning, he slams into me. Oh my God, he's fucking huge. My pussy is filled to the point of pain. It feels so damn good the sounds falling out of my mouth are deep. He pulls back and slams into me again.

"You are made for me." His thrusts need to be faster; I don't want cozy shit. I leverage my forearms on the arm of the couch and slam my hips backward, which pulls a deeper moan from his lips. I look over my shoulder to see him.

"Fuck me like you mean it." Slamming myself back on his cock is the only invitation he needs. He's thrusts into me with so much force the sofa is moving, but I don't give a shit. I need more.

"Yes." I pant, his grip on my hips is painful. I fucking love it. I'm definitely going to have bruises tomorrow. The thought of being marked has my walls clamping around his cock with everything I have.

"Say it," he grunts while picking up speed. I move further over the arm of the sofa so my clit is between is against the leather. "Fuck you." I snarl, the best I can between moans from the pounding he is giving me.

Wrapping my hair around his hand, he pulls with so much force I am bent like a human pretzel. He is fucking me so hard I think he's trying to split me in two. My clit is rubbing against the leather, my body is alive. I'm building. I can feel it coming. His breathing is becoming harsher, his pace more frantic. He's close. I feel it. This is primal, this is dangerous and I fucking love it. Pushing my hand between the sofa arm and my body I rub frantic circles against my clit, which causes my inner walls to clamp down around his cock again.

"Fucking hell. Keep playing with yourself," he rumbles. It's not enough I need it to hurt.

"Fuck me harder. I'm not going to break." He slams into me so hard the sofa moves further across the floor. I slam my hips back, meeting him thrust for thrust. Yanking me up by my hair he wraps his hands around my throat. Holy shit he's everywhere. I'm so fucking close.

Heat builds in my clit and roars outwards to all my limbs in my body, we are both dripping in sweat. I arch my back slightly, and his grip tightens so I can take him at a deeper angle. It sends my building orgasm to new heights. My legs start to shake violently, then my stomach, until my whole body is one giant shaking mess. I clamp my pussy walls down harder which pushes us both over the edge. White lights burst out in front of my eyes. Everything is light. Tingles and aftershocks roar in my veins, keeping me in a state of bliss. Holy shit, another orgasm rips throughout my body, tearing a scream from my throat which is joined by a distant roar.

Falling forward, I feel a heavy weight holding me in place. I try to get my breathing under control and bring movement back into my limbs. I wiggle my way out from under his body, and throw my ass down onto the sofa. I look over at Kane who is leaning back with his arm thrown over his eyes. My eyes are drawn to his cock. Holy shit, his cock is huge. Grey sweats, that explains it. Pulling my underwear and jeans back into place, I can feel his cum running down my thighs.

"Where do you think you're going?"

"My ass is going home." He best not start his macho bullshit now. "No, you're not. I want you here." What the actual fuck? He thinks because we hate fucked, he has a claim over me.

"We fucked, Kane. That's it. Don't mistake that for

anything else." My tone is like ice. Before he realizes my ass is out the door heading to my truck. God! What a fucking asshole.

Kane

She fucking left. What the fuck? Just walked her ass out like nothing had happened. How did she even manage it? My legs are still like jelly, my energy is zapped. The thought of moving makes my limbs turn to stone. I said before she was mine, but now she will never get away from me.

"Why the fuck does it smell like a brothel in here?" Liam, looks around the office."Fucking hell, man. Put your dick away." Can't I catch a goddamn break.

"You got a problem with it, get the fuck out. It's as simple as that."

Lust starts coursing through my veins again, as my skin tingles at the memory of what we have just done. I want her again. No one else will touch her.

"Heard you threw the girls out? I'm guessing you found someone else that took your fancy?" Liam grins at me.

"Damn right he did. He went all caveman on her ass." Marcus chimes in gleefully as he strolls through the door. Fucking kill me now.

"Caveman?" he quirks a brow at me in question. I look to my other brother, who is grinning his ass off.

"Yeah, Kane threw Reika over his shoulder and stormed off with her. She looked like a pissed off alley cat." Marcus tries to goad me into a reaction. "How pissed was she when you spanked her ass," he cackles.

"You fucked our fighter? What the fuck is wrong with

you?" Liam bellows, throwing his arms up. Honestly why the fuck is he so pissed off anyway, it isn't like he wanted to fuck her. Screw him and his high and mighty shit; he has been this way since we were kids.

"What do you want?" I demand, changing the damn subject, I really hope he's here to tell me I can fuck some shit up.

"Oh yeah, some fucker has burned down the lot next to headquarters," he blurts, like it's the furthest thing from his mind. My sweats are pulled back into place and I'm out the door with an inferno burning in my veins.

"Who was it?" I snap, as I charge down the stairs in the main floor.

"We don't know but they fucked shit up. You think it was The Reaper getting revenge?" I stop short, how the hell can he think that? She was with me; it isn't like she could sneak off to torch stuff while we were fucking. "Don't be a fucking idiot, Liam. She was here, so it wasn't her."

"How do you know? She could have had this shit planned, Kane." Liam retorts, his jaw set. Anger and something else roll off him as he throws daggers my way.

"Before she fucked Kane, she sat in the club with me for hours trying to find out what Bonzo knew about Mel." That explains why she was here for so long, but why didn't she come to speak to me?

"Because when you two are in the same room together, bad shit happens." Marcus chuckles as I just star. Fuck I must have said that out loud. I can't deny Marcus's way of thinking. Making my way to the lock up I order, "Gear up." My voice echoes throughout the club. Every person nearby can hear the order, they all scramble to get their stuff. I will not let this shit slide. I can't have bastards thinking they can steam roll me and get away with it. Time to make everyone remember who the fuck I am.

Myself, Marcus and Liam with about 20 guys from the crew stand staring at what remains of the building and its contents. The place is destroyed. Nothing is left. All the furniture is burnt to a crisp. The cops aren't likely to stop by, they know when it's one of our buildings to leave it the fuck alone. It's easier than having to make up bullshit excuses. It really does pay to have some dirty cops in your pocket. "Has anyone found anything yet?" A string of replies of 'No Boss', make my ears want to bleed. Whoever has done this is starting a shitstorm for themselves.

"Kane. You need to see this." Following the voice, I find Liam at the end of the corridor which leads to the store room.

"What?" I scan the area. Oh shit! Sprayed onto the wall is the tag for The Grimm's. I should have known they were behind this.

"What do you want to do, bro?" My mind fires off trying to make sense of this, they have never come after us like this before. What is their reason? A motive?

"Set up a face to face with De'Marco now." There isn't anything I can do here, so I head to HQ to see what I can dig up. About an hour later my brothers come into my office. "You get a hold of the little shit?"

"De'Marco wants to meet in an hour., but he says you can only take

one other person with you." Liam grumbles at the severity of it. My gut tells me we could be walking into a trap, I know what he will be expecting. "Marcus, you will come with me."

"Why the fuck should he go with you? I'm your second for fuck's sake." Liam spits, his eyes land on his twin who is grinning at the tantrum he is throwing. This is one of the reasons why because, he's a hot-headed twat, and more likely to splatter his brains everywhere.

"Because you need to set up a fight for Reika and start to get money rolling in." I snap.

"Whatever you say, boss." The door slams behind Liam, his mutterings can be heard down the corridor. Goddammit, he's going to be an asshole for the rest of the day.

10

KANE

Walking into the boathouse restaurant, my body tingles in warning. I don't like this. The occupants aren't the regular types you would find somewhere like this. Guess the one-man rule doesn't apply to himself.

"Are you Mr. Southbourne?" A blonde server asks sweetly.

"I am! Where is De'Marco?" Like hell am I playing games with this clown. "Please, follow me Sir." She smiles at Marcus as she takes off towards the back of the restaurant.

Following the blonde, I notice she has your typical girl next door vibe, with a willingness to do right. My usual type. Normally my brain would be running away with me, thinking of all the different ways I could have her on my cock. She'd be begging for forgiveness, but there's nothing, not a damn thing. What the hell is wrong with me?

"Doesn't that type get your motor running anymore, brother?" he cackles. "Piss off, Marcus," I mumble so only he can hear.

Oh, look at his lordship himself, sitting at a six-chair table at the far end of the restaurant out of view. Wow, he really thinks he's the shit. Why this bozo thinks he is better than anyone confuses the life out

of me. He's a street kid, just like we were. We grew up together. He was as close to me as my brothers. Now we can't be in the same area as each other without it turning into bloodshed.

"Ah, Kane. Please, sit down." De'Marco grins as he smiles between the smarmy tone he's using. *Is it too extreme if I pluck my fingernails out with pliers?*

"Cut the bullshit. You and I both know that voice is a load of shit."

"I can see your attitude hasn't gotten any better," he smirks. He sits

in his seat waiting for me to take mine. The bastard doesn't even stand to show some respect.

"No shit, Sherlock. Why would it for a bottom feeder like you?" His brow twitches. Nah, I should pluck *his* nails out. That thought alone brings a sadistic smile to my face, clearly making him very nervous. I can see the sheen of sweat start to build on his hairline. What did he expect, me to come here and ask him nicely why he torched our property?

"No need to be a sarcastic asshole. I mean Kane, we were close once," he coos, trying to smooth over his insult.

"Yeah, we were, then you threw it all away for some cash and power. It's either Southbourne or Soulless to you." He tuts at me, causing a snarl to build in my chest.

"Now, what the fuck do you want, Grimm?" Spotting Marcus stepping closer, I side eye him and with a slight tip of my head I give him the signal to tap the button on the device in his jeans pocket. We both clearly have the same thought. This meeting is going up shit's creek real fast.

"Word on the street is you guys have bought a new fighter?" he declares with a triumphant grin. Goddammit!

"Maybe we have. Maybe we haven't," I answer. "What's it to you?"

"Don't insult my intelligence, Southbourne. We know you bought The Reaper."

Kill him, end his life right now. Pull your knife and do it. Yeah, it will turn into a war, but with this fucker out of the way...

"So, what if we have, Grimm? She belongs to us. She is our fighter." I try to keep my facial expression as cold as possible. I can't let any emotions slip through or he will take full advantage.

"Me and a few other heads are having a little competition in three months. We want your fighter on the card." Shit. He can't be suggesting what I think he is. "You mean the Battle Royale?"

"Damn right I do. Her reputation is legendary. She's a ruthless fighter. We want her in." Has he been snorting shit? Honestly, why the hell is he asking this? It's a deathmatch and the last woman that was invited to one of these events was torn to pieces in the first match up.

"What are the stakes?" Marcus growls at my side. I know he and Reika have formed a friendship of sorts.

"Well, I'm surprised. It hasn't taken as long as I thought it would to catch your interest." He muses, rubbing his thumb across his chin.

"You haven't, Grimm. Curiosity at its best, that's all. Why do you want her on the card? Be honest." From the set of his shoulders and the way his jaw ticks at the questions Marcus and I throw out, there's another reason he wants her. Let's see if he has the balls to admit it.

"Let's just say a few of the fighters have a score to settle with her." His eyes shining in delight.

"So, you want me to send her in to be slaughtered?" I'm a

sick fuck at the best of times, but Jesus, this isn't a competition. This isn't a game. This is for sport. Something for the rich bastards to get their rocks off, watching the lowlifes battle it out.

"She won't be slaughtered, if she survives." He grins, his goon chuckles.

"There is a reason why you don't have female fighters, Grimm. It's suicide." Marcus argues.

"Ah, you don't have faith in the girl I see." He grins. What the hell is he grinning for?

"I do have faith in her skills but I am not lining her up for your slaughter." I snap, like fuck will that happen. Spinning on my heels, I start to walk out of the restaurant with Marcus behind me.

Deep rumbling laughter follows us. "C'mon, Southbourne, stay for a drink. Let's discuss this like adults." He claps his hands like a king, the server from earlier comes rushing in with a tray of drinks.

"It is a damn shame she won't be on the card but if you don't agree, that's fine."

Reika

My normal fifteen-minute walk to the store, has taken me double the amount of time. My emotions are still at war with themselves. On one hand what went down with me and Kane was amazing, and I want to jump his bones again. The knobhead gets under my skin and rattles my insides. On the other hand, I have never wanted to punch someone so much in my life.

God, can't this shit just piss off for a little while and let me chill out. All I want to do is watch shit TV and eat crap. If I pray, do you think God will give me a break from running into Kane's stupid ass? Yeah, right. God has never been on my side.

"Hey, yo." A voice calls out. They can't be talking to me. "Yo! Reaper, we want to talk."

"You got me mixed up with someone else buddy." They're little boys, Reika. Be nice.

My back hits the side of a parked Lexus. What the fuck? The guy who was shouting has his arm under my chin. *Breathe.*

"Wow, he never said you were this fine." What the hell is this idiot on about?

"Dude, I don't know who the fuck you are, so just piss off." He leans in and runs his nose up the side of my face.

"You smell good." This twat sniffed me like a dog. I'm momentarily shocked at what he's just done.

"De'Marco wants a word with you, Reaper," one of them hisses.

"Who the fuck is that? I don't know what you're going on about."

"Come on." Limp dick starts dragging me toward the blacked out van he and his boys were standing against. How the hell didn't I notice the kidnapper van before. What the fuck?

"Roan, tie her hands and legs you fucking idiot," one of the others says to limp dick.

"Nah, man. De'Marco is wrong. You boys think he will let me play with her?" My vision blacks out without any warning. Muffled screams come through to my ears, but it's not a normal sound. It's like it is being filtered through cotton wool. Suddenly everything comes back all at once, like a veil has lifted. The sight that meets me is horrific.

There. Are. Bodies. Everywhere.

Kane

One of Grimm's guys comes flying through the door, whispering something into his ear. The color drains from De'Marco's face. Hmmm, I wonder what's caused a reaction like that? I look at Marcus and give him the thumbs up. He knows what I'm wanting, so he excuses himself. "Trouble in paradise, Grimm?"

"Fuck you, Southbourne." Something has definitely happened. De'Marco's hands are shaking, knuckles white. I clear my throat to catch his attention.

"What's the issue? I told you she will not be doing the Royale. So, if that's all you wanted to talk about, then we're done.

"But make no mistake, Grimm. If you or your boys come at us again, I will gut you like a pig." Standing up, I make my way out of the restaurant. Grimm didn't say anything about me leaving. He normally protests like a two-year-old. Where the fuck is Marcus? My fingers grip the doorknob.

"After the shit today, Southbourne, The Reaper is in the Royale." I step out onto the sidewalk, not bothering with the fucking idiot. I find Marcus propped against the SUV, cigarette in hand. "Thought you gave up on that shit." I haven't seen my brother with a smoke in his hand in years.

"I did, but after the talk I just had with Liam, I need it." What is going on around here? Is there some drug in the air or something?

"It's bad, Kane. Very bad. Grimm will want her head for this." Without another word, he climbs into the driver's side and waits. Grimm's reaction and parting words send unease into my veins. What the fuck happened?

In no time, we screech to a stop outside HQ. Crew members are everywhere. Some wear expressions of fear while others look sick to their stomachs. Marcus hasn't said a word to me on the drive back.

"Will someone tell me what the fuck is going on?" I roar from the side of the car. Liam comes striding out covered in blood. Shit! What has he done now?

"Before you ask, I ain't done a damn thing." His movements are choppy, I have never seen him this agitated before.

"Where the hell is she, Liam?" Marcus asks in a cautious tone. Ok, I am definitely missing something here. Liam nods his head in the direction he has just appeared from. Marcus takes off like a bat out of hell, I take off after him. When Liam's arm shoots out to halt me in my tracks.

"You really don't want to go in there, brother," he says, shaking his head. "Why the hell not? You gonna tell me what happened?" If someone hurt Pretty Bird, I will tear their soul from their bodies. He gives me a rundown of what's happened. Unable to move, I can't believe what I am hearing.

One of the boys was walking past the store and saw Reika being attacked, or so he thought. My brain can't process anything Liam is saying. Repeating over again in my head are the last words he said. *She practically tore them to pieces with some type of hunting knife. It was a bloodbath.*

11

REIKA

W hat have I done? Rocking back and forth, there are screams in my head, my head pounds with the force of them as I cover my ears to try and block out the sound. Why can't I remember anything? It's been years since I've had a blackout. A broken sob escapes me as the door opens. Why won't they leave me alone?

"Hellion?" Marcus. Some of the tension leaves my body. But it isn't enough, the voices have started again.

Worthless.

You aren't good for anything.

Broken.

Who would want something as damaged as you?

Useless.

You couldn't save them.

What makes you think you can save Mel?

Death.

You bring death to everything you care about.

Monster.

I desperately try to shut my mind down. I can't do this. It's true, what they are telling me is right. "I'm a Monster." Broken screams come from somewhere in the room. Whoever it is best piss off.

"Hellion, it's ok. I'm here." Cheshire's voice reassures me for some reason. I don't freak out when he pulls me into a hug. The wails start up again, and I realize the noises are mine. I can't speak. Even though Marcus is holding me trying his best to comfort me, I can't. If I see the look in his eyes that everyone else has, I can't bear it.

You let them die.

"Reika, talk to me," he pleads, running a hand up and down my back. "I, I, I killed them, Marcus." I start sobbing uncontrollably. I can't get enough oxygen into my lungs. I can't breathe, the room feels like its closing in on me. I start clawing at my neck to make space to allow airflow.

"Hellion, stop." Gentle hands tug my clawed ones away from my throat. "Breathe for me. You're safe. I won't judge." He will judge me when he knows. Everyone judges when they find out.

"They tried to take me. Something about someone wanting me." I shudder as the bodies littering the floor come to mind.

"Who? What was their name?" He presses gently for an answer as he rocks me side to side. His hand still running a trail up and down my back. How should I know? I can't remember much.

"I'm not sure." I think back. It's like my memories are fuzzy, like they are fading. I can hear my thoughts through a filter. "D, the name starts with D." I mumble into his chest.

"Is that all you remember?"

"Look at me, Marcus. I look like I've taken a bath in blood." Looking at my clothes and hands, my stomach turns. How can he stand to touch me?

"Tell me everything you remember." He releases me from the bone crushing hug, allowing me to shift so I'm in a more comfortable position. Then I dive into telling him what I remember.

Marcus

All I can do is stare at her. Hearing what happened outside the store, fucking De'Marco, it had to be his goons. Looking down at Reika, I can't understand how she survived the bits she has just told me. The voices in her head telling her she's a monster. Telling her she couldn't save them. She was a child, for fuck's sake. She is even more broken than I realized.

She killed De'Marco's men; it was a massacre. He will want her in the Battle Royale now as payment. From everything Liam said on the call, she has a chance to survive. Possibly. I have to help her any way I can, because whatever happens she needs to come out of this alive.

"She asleep?" Looking over my shoulder, I notice Kane is standing in the doorway, his eyes fixed on the girl asleep with her head on my lap.

"Crashed out after telling me what happened. She doesn't remember much. It's like she blacked out." I tell him, as my hand strokes through her hair.

"You know who tried to take her?" I can see the bloodlust written across his face. He cares for her.

"All she said was D."

"De'Marco?" he asks. Bingo. Realization runs across his face. He was desperate for Kane to agree to his demands, then someone tries to grab her. It's too much of a coincidence for my liking.

"Step out, I want to talk to you."

"What about her?" He definitely cares. Kane can deny it all he wants, but he can't bullshit me.

"She will be out for a while, I think." Slowly getting to my feet with her in my arms, I gently place her on the sofa and turn to face my brother, who looks like he's about to tear me apart.

"You're lucky you're my brother," he growls, his eyes never leaving her. "Do I need to remind you she is mine?" Is he serious right now?

Leaving her in the office, I nod toward the kitchen. He either follows or he doesn't, either way I need to be as far away from the office as possible. One of the guys sits at the island when we get there. "Get out!" He jumps a mile, wide eyes turning to Kane and I. His complexion pales in an instant and he's off like his ass is on fire. Taking the seat he vacated, I calm myself a little for what's next.

A growl from my side has dread pooling in my gut. He's so anxious he's pacing the length of the kitchen. "Kane, sit down!" I bark, dark eyes meet mine. Shit this is going to end badly.

"Don't speak, just listen. And don't lose your shit." Taking a deep breath, I tell him everything Reika has told me. I don't want to break her trust, but he needs to know he can't keep playing these stupid games with her. She deserves more than that. Normal people would crumble under the pressure of a life like hers.

Kane

I'm speechless. What the fuck do I say? My body is like ice, emotions warring within me. Knowing what I know now, it's as if everything is clear. I can understand why she pushes back so hard. She is the one who has to pick herself up from the ground and dust herself off when life turns to shit. The number of times she has had to do it alone guts me. After digging into her history, I know she has people in her life who are like family; Mel and a guy called Tom.

Shit, Mel. She thought I had her, that's why she came to the office that day, searching for her. The venom in her warning makes sense. She will do whatever is needed to bring her family home. I'll do some digging and find out what happened to Mel, it's the least I can do. I know if I offer to help she will turn me down, but if she doesn't know, she can't. I grab my phone and hit call on a number we haven't had to use for a while.

"Well, well, well. If it isn't the infamous Southbourne brother ringing me."

"Cut the crap, Fox. I need you to find out what you can about a missing person." I snarl into the phone. Fox snorts on the other end of the line, "Fucking hell, Southbourne. You're into kidnapping now?"

"Not me, smartass. Mel Jacobs is a friend of mine and she has gone

missing. I need you to find all the information you can." I forget how much of a prick he is. If he wasn't as good as he is at finding shit out, we would have dropped him long before now.

"Usual fee stands. When do you want the info by?" he drawls.

"Yesterday. You'll get it when you deliver." I cut the call, and head back to the office. After our talk, Marcus went back to keep an eye on my Pretty Bird; we were uneasy about the state she might wake up in.The doors open when I get there, my eyes land on her, she's still out cold.

"Has she woken up at all?" She looks so peaceful asleep. Marcus sits behind the desk staring into space, not answering my question, so I know he is lost in thought. I make my way over to the desk. The sound of a hammer being cocked has me throwing my hands up.

"Easy brother, I just came to check on her." His eyes are dead as he aims the hand gun I keep hidden in the desk drawer at my forehead. His emotions are all over the place, eyes blown wide, but he has a slight tremor to his hands. Shit, he's close to taking his own trip down memory lane.

"Before you go all nuclear on my ass, you think we should take her back to the house? It's safer there than here." I say the words without my usual growl, trying to calm him. His eyes flutter close. When he opens them again, some of the darkness has receded.

"Yeah. Um. Sure. Good idea." He makes a move, towards Pretty Bird.

"It's all good. I've got her." As gently as possible, I scoop her up into my arms.

It's not long before, I'm heading down the corridor to my room with her in my arms. I can't take my eyes off her. I accidentally jolt her body trying to grab the door handle, she groans in her sleep. To my surprise she doesn't wake, but snuggles closer into my chest and falls back into a deep sleep. Without turning on a light I make my way to the bed and place her down. I stare at her laying there sound asleep, while my emotions war with what I know I have to do and what I really want to do. Fuck it. I strip off my shirt and crawl into the spot beside her. I just want to keep an eye on her. Her soft snores and even breaths relax me and I start to feel the pull of sleep. Marcus knows to come wake me up in a couple of hours.

Reika

So much heat. I feel like I'm hugging a furnace. Why is it so goddamn hot in here? Wait where the hell am I? My thoughts are jumbled. What the hell is going on? I know I didn't turn the heat on. As I shift to get my bearings, an arm pulls me closer. I freeze. Oh crap! What the fuck did I do? Peeling my eyes open, they begin to sting like I've scraped them along asphalt. Ouch! I notice an arm wrapped around my stomach. Oh no. I follow the arm from my stomach to the elbow. Tattoos? I continue to follow the arm to the shoulder. *Holy shit, this dude's stacked.*

My eyes land on the owner of the arm. Fuck! What the actual fuck? Did I fuck Kane again? Slowly lifting the covers, I find I am still wearing my clothes from yesterday. Thank God. Something scrapes along my neck. As gently as I can, I reach to see what it is. I really can't deal with this asshole. Nope, not happening.

Hellion!
Be nice to him when you wake up.
He wouldn't leave you or let anyone else watch you.
Don't try to murder him!
Marcus.

Be nice. He's got to be shitting me. I would rather pick a fight with a porcupine. Why the hell wouldn't he leave me? I can't stand his ass and I thought the feeling was mutual.

"Stop moving, Pretty Bird." Is this guy like the dude from Candyman? Only when you think about him too much, he appears.

"You gonna let me go, asswipe?" Ugh, I really need coffee.

"Nope, we're staying put, I'm comfy." What the fuck? Did aliens come down and brain probe him or something?

"Very funny, asshole. Move." Thank God I am calmer than I was last night, but what is the deal with him? As mum used to say, *"Man up, buttercup. Make the most of an unexpected situation."*

"Not gonna happen, Pretty Bird," he grumbles, with his eyes shut.

"You keep saying that, fuckface. Why won't you let me move?"

"Because I'm comfy and you're warm." Yeah, because that makes perfect sense.

"Why wouldn't you leave me last night?" His body tenses. Let's see how honest he's willing to be.

"You're in my bed. I wasn't sleeping on the floor," he grouses, rubbing sleep from his eyes.

"Bullshit! You could have easily tossed me in any other room. Why didn't you?"

"Because, I didn't." Now *this* is the guy I know. He's angry, growling with each question.

"What's up, baby? Cat got your tongue?" I ask, my voice dripping with sarcasm. I really can't help myself sometimes, and ruffling Kane's feathers is just too much fun.

"Fuck you." Aww, someone's too easy today.

"Ooooh, someone's in a pissy mood." Did I hit my head last night? I'm talking to him like I would someone I actually like. Clearly, I must have, but fuck it. Seeing his face as I torment him is so worth it. I'm find myself pinned beneath him. Huh? What? When did this happen?

"Kiss me." I'm shocked.

"Huh?"

"Kiss me, Pretty Bird." Has he got a split personality

disorder or something? "No." I grumble, how can he even think I would want to?

His lips crash down on mine. Motherfucker! My body takes over even though my mind is still trying to figure out what the fuck is happening. His kiss is brutal, erratic even. I can't help myself. I match him in his brutality. With a groan, he presses me further into the mattress, his cock grinding on me. Stop! You have to stop this! My brain is screaming at me to stop, but I'm at war with myself, head against body. Fuck it, what harm will it do? I don't even realize I'm now half naked beneath him. Our skin touches as he grinds even harder. Fuck me. When did he lose his jeans? The heat between us is growing by the second. Lifting my hips, I manage to roll us both over. The shocked expression on his face is priceless. Leaning forward I start kissing my way down the side of his neck to his collarbone.Leaning back, I grind myself harder. I get a good look at him, eyeing his tattoos, I can't make out what they are but they're amazing all the same. He isn't going to go all caveman on me this time. It's my turn to be in control.

"Don't move." He looks at me like I've grown a second head. A

glint of something under his pillow catches my attention, reaching forward I grab it. My palm curls round the handle of a knife. Sweet. I rip it out of its hiding spot and hold it against his throat. His eyes widen even further.

"Don't fucking move, Kane." The sense of power running through my veins is such a rush. Having this beast beneath me, not daring to move, is like a drug.

Circling my hips, I draw a groan from his throat.

"Babe, what are you doing?"

"Stay still. How goddamn hard is that? And for fuck's sake, shut up. I'm running the show." Picking up from where I left off, I kiss across his collarbone, then make my way down toward his chest. I keep going, and as I get to his stomach he shivers. Lifting my eyes to his, I realize I worked the knife in my hand down to his chest. Well shit, that's a turn on. I pass his belly button, exploring his body further, my kisses venture above his hip. I bite down and his upper body wrenches up on the mattress as a roar tears from deep within him. His whole body shakes with need as he lays flat again. Smirking to myself, I slide the knife further down his body, causing another shiver within his body. I lick my lips at his rock-hard cock. One of my hands is on his hip, the other keeping the knife in place. Opening my mouth, I swallow his cock as far down my throat as I can.

"Jesus." I hum with approval causing vibrations in my throat.

"Fuck, Babe, suck my dick before I blow my load." Such a cocky fucker. Not able to resist the temptation anymore, I pick up my pace so my head bobs faster and faster on his cock. His groans and thrashing drive my need insane. I'm burning with the need to touch myself. Just as I'm about to reach down to relieve some pressure...

"Open wide," he orders with a growl. Playing nice, I do as he says.

He grips my hips and spins me. Before I have a chance to process this new position, his mouth is on me. Holy shit. His tongue, fuck me, his tongue. He's eating me out like I'm his favorite meal. Flattening his tongue, he licks from my clit to my asshole. A muffled moan tries to leave my mouth, but his cock still down my throat it causes us both to tremble. This is a war in itself. It's a war I'm going to win. Widening my legs, I drop further onto his face. I swallow, taking his cock deeper in my throat, past my gag reflex. Muffled sounds come from under me.

"Fuck, fuck, fuck." My orgasm is building fast, so I start to hum one of my favorite songs. This is torture of the best kind. We're wild and violent, but damn if this shit isn't amazing. Fuuuuuck. Kane bites down on my clit, sending a shock wave through me. With his cock still in my mouth, I scream as he roars his release. I swallow every last bit of cum down my throat, then lick every last drop from him. He shudders again. Whack! The bastard just slapped my ass. With a grin, I roll myself to the side. Fuck me, for such an asshole, he can do some amazing with his mouth.

Waiting for my body to come back to reality, we are both still wrapped up in a mass of limbs and my emotions are a jumbled mess. The fucker is starting to grow on me. What the hell? Yeah, I've had a couple of mind-blowing orgasms from him, but seriously, me and him can never happen.

I really wish I could talk to someone. Shit! Mel.

12

REIKA

I'm such a shitty fucking person. How the fuck could I forget about her? I try to untangle myself from his legs. "Pretty Bird, what's going on?" Concern fills his face, which makes me feel even worse.

Frantically kicking my legs to untangle ourselves, I accidently kick Kane in the junk. Oops! Without another thought, I'm off the bed, trying my hardest to pull my clothes back on a few seconds later.

"Babe, talk to me. What the hell is going on?"

I can't believe I forgot about her. I am such an asshole.

"You're not an asshole, Reika."

Is he a fucking mind reader or something? "What the fuck? How did you know I said that in my head?"

"You didn't." Fucking great. Finally, I have my clothes in place and I'm off like a rocket out the door, charging full speed ahead, not paying attention to my surroundings. I don't see the person step out of another room until it's too late.

"Watch where you're going, you stupid bitch." Frosty glares at me with hate filled eyes. What's his damn problem?

"Sorry, man. Didn't see you there."

"Aww, has my brother finally kicked the Pretty Bird's ass to the curb?"

I really don't want to be dealing with an idiot today, but his words get under my skin.

"Listen up, Frosty. I don't know what your fucking problem is with me. If you have something to say, spit it out." I snarl at the fucker. I am not dealing with his shit today.

"I don't like you. My brother has taken a shine to you for some reason. But mark my words, darling, your ass will be out of here soon." His words remind me of Blondie's.

"Wow. What do you want me to do? Cry just because you don't like me? I don't give a shit, and me and Kane have fucked once. That's all it is." This is really adding to my sour mood and I find my mouth has taken full control.

"You can't control who he fucks. So, what of a couple rolls in the sack? Don't worry, I ain't trying to steal your brother." He steps closer to me with his nostrils flaring.

"He will get rid of you, but if he doesn't, I will make him. Blood is thicker than water, bitch. Remember that." I can't help myself. I laugh in his face at his attempt to threaten me. Seriously, do men assume just because I have different equipment that I'm going to be scared of them? Fucking idiots, the lot of them.

Still chuckling to myself I head in the direction of what I am hoping are the stairs to take me out of this place.

After God knows how long searching this place, I finally find the front door.

"So, you didn't kill each other?"

"Clearly not since I am standing here. What do you want, Marcus? I got shit to do!" I'm trying my hardest to cut the conversation short.

"What are your plans for today, Hellion?" He grins at me.

"I told you, I have shit to do. See you around, Marcus." I make a move to leave this damn place.

"We got things to discuss, Hellion. I'll join you." He can talk all he wants, doesn't mean I'll be listening.

We're heading out of town and surprisingly he hasn't uttered a single word yet. I can't help but side eye him, it doesn't make sense. Seeing the garage, I know I'm going to catch shit from Tom if he spots me. I can't tell him about Mel. I manage to make it inside without being noticed, Marcus on my heels. He's like a lost puppy that won't piss off and leave you alone.

"Make yourself at home. I need to get changed and find my phone."

A smirk comes across his face. "Here." Dropping my eyes to what he just pulled out his pocket, I see my phone.

"You stole it?" What a prick, bet the nosey little shit tried to have a look through it too.

"I didn't. I picked it up off the floor," he says.

"Huh. Ok, sorry." Did I just apologize? My emotions are a bit all over the place at the moment. *Why have you just told him that?* Even my inner voice is pissed off with me.

"You and Kane?" Why do people think there is anything going on between us?

"No, I've got shit to deal with that's all," I spit through gritted teeth. I suppose this as good a time as any to ask my questions?

"Marcus, can I ask you something?" He looks at me, "Sure."

Here goes nothing. "Do you know anything about The Butcher or The Damned Crew?" If he's lived here a long time surely, he will know something. I need to figure out what they want.

"Why are you asking, Hellion?" I can't put into words how

he's looking at me, but he definitely knows something about one or both of them.

"I've been hearing stories, that's all." A girl's gotta do what a girl's gotta do, and if that means I have to bullshit my way through this, so be it.

"The Butcher is a psycho assassin of sorts. The Damned Crew, never heard of them." He shrugs.

"How come? Everyone has heard of The Damned Crew," I ask.

"I don't know. My brothers and I have worked since we were teenagers to build what we have today. Plus, we don't listen to gossip," he retorts.

"Huh. So, you guys don't sit around knitting sweaters and talking shit then?"

"No, Hellion. We sit around with a beer in hand and talk about who

we fucked the night before." He grins at me, watching me closely. Would Kane shoot the shit with the guys about me? The thought alone makes my stomach turn.

"Are we gonna get started on the shit you need to do, as you put it?" Grimacing, I head off for a shower and change of clothes. My mind is still working over how I feel about Kane possibly talking about me with the guys. Back up bitch. So, what if he does? It's not like you want anything more from him, is it?

Giving myself a mental shake, I put my big girl panties on and say fuck it. I don't want anything more with him. Just because I get butterflies when I see him, it means nothing. Feelings are overrated.

"You ready, Hellion?" When I make it back into the room, I see Marcus pacing. "What the fuck took you so long?"

"You sure you want to come, Marcus? I'm having my hair done." The look on this face is priceless. "Hell no. I'm not coming to a hair appointment with you." I honestly couldn't have thought of anything better to get Cheshire off my case. I don't want him coming with me. I need to track down my boy, Rick, and see what he can find out. Marcus flies out the door like his ass is on fire. Chuckling to myself, I follow him out. Hang on. He came here with me. How is he gonna get back?

"How you getting back, dude?" He shuffles his feet. Neither of us thought that far ahead. Don't be an asshole, Reika. "Get in, I'll drop you off on the way. I'm heading out to Dead Man's Bay."

"Huh. Why there? We've got perfectly good salons around here."

"My girl, Becca, is amazing at doing hair. I won't allow anyone else to get their mitts on me." I grin at him.

"My brother has," he smirks. Brilliant, Reika, you walked straight into that one, didn't you?

"Keep talking, dude, and your ass is walking. You get me?" I growl.

"Yeah, yeah I hear you, Hellion." He's definitely going to be a pain in the ass for the foreseeable future.

I drop Cheshire off, and thank fuck for that. I definitely would have stabbed the little asshole if he had made one more joke about me and Kane. Hopefully the drive out here isn't for nothing, or my stabby mood will not be improving.

Come to think of it, why haven't I been in another match up yet? I'm not surprised I haven't heard from Alexander. I did beat his ass and all, but still. Something isn't right about this whole thing and not having a match up since they acquired me shall we say. It doesn't make sense I'm meant to fight to pay my way. What they don't know is why I need a fight with my emotions being all over the place.

If Rick isn't at the hollow, I'll head on down to Andre's;

TATUM RAYNE

two birds, one stone. My phone starts vibrating on the
passenger seat so I pull over.

Unknown Number:

Meet Langdale Lane
    30 minutes

What the fuck! Who the hell is asking me to meet them? Like
hell, I don't fucking think so.

Unknown Number:

We know what you are planning.
    Meet us to have a talk about our plans
    and your friend!!

What I'm planning? Any normal person would just call the
cops or something, but I'm not normal. Screeching to a halt, I
check the glove compartment for my 9mm Glock and knives.
Checking the magazine is already in; it's full, thank fuck. I
know there's another one around here somewhere. Rummaging
around the cab, my hand touches something under the seat. I
pull it out to check. Bingo! I spot my leather jacket in the
footwell too. Strapping a knife to my ankle, I check it doesn't
show through my jeans. Next, the other knife tucks onto my left
hip. The knife strap is a thin supple leather that's virtually

undetectable under clothes. Tucking the Glock into the back of my jeans and putting the other magazine in my jacket pocket, I'm ready to fuck shit up.

Pulling up to Langdale Road I scan the area. They're not here yet, which works well for me. Checking the time, it's been 29 minutes since the message. Where the fuck are they? Getting out of the truck, I look either direction to try to spot any vehicles coming this way. Nothing. My body is starting to get jittery; I got a bad feeling about this. I'm standing in the middle of nowhere, on a dirt road, surrounded by forest. Nobody in their right mind would put themselves in this situation. *Mel, you're doing this for her.*

Now I'm getting pissed. Why do people ask you to meet them then not turn up? I was hoping to fuck some shit up today.

A whistle comes from somewhere behind me. Fucking games, I fucking hate games. Following the noise, I notice someone standing between two large trees.

"You The Reaper?" The guy in dark clothes shouts from the tree line.

"Yeah. Who the fuck are you?"

"Follow me." He walks off after his command. I have to run to catch up to him. We've been walking for about ten minutes. I am just about to ask him if he is planning on killing me, well, he can try, when we step into a clearing. How didn't I know this was here? It's beautiful.

Bringing my senses back, this isn't a time to be daydreaming, I notice six other men standing around the area. Looking them over, it's pretty obvious they're goons for someone. But who? All eyes are on me, some with smug looks on their faces, while others are staring into space like they would rather be anywhere else.

Just as I'm about to open my mouth two impeccably dressed guys walk into the clearing. Both of them are suited and booted up to the nines. They must be the ones who run this show.

"Ah, how nice to finally meet you, Reaper," says one of the men, walking right up to me, like we're old friends. There's such a thing as personal space, asshole. I can't place his accent, it's definitely not from around here.

"You got me here. Now who are you?" Unease stirs under my skin. He walks around me in a slow circle, looks me up and down like someone would a cow at a cattle market.

"You, my girl, are not what I expected. I have heard talk of the notorious Reaper."

"Well, you can't please everybody I guess." Is he hoping to offend me? If that's the case, he needs to try harder than that.

"Well, this chit-chat is pleasant and all, but we have business to discuss," the man says. Yeah, like why the fuck I am here and where is Mel?

"Yeah, we do. First, where is she?" He turns to face the man behind him and clicks his fingers. Another bastard with a God complex! Fucking great. The grunt obviously understands what that command means, as he heads out of the clearing.

"Have you made any headway with what your dad kept from us?" Motherfucker! This is the prick from the last phone call. Anger roars through my veins. If they have hurt her, every single one of them dies. *Keep calm! Find out if she's ok first.*

"No, I haven't got a fucking clue what shit you're on about." I try to keep my tone even, and not show the apprehension I am feeling at being left in the dark.

"Your dear old daddy made a deal with us years ago. Saying I would have what was owed to me when the time was right."

"I don't know anything about a deal. I was a child." This dude is two planks short of half a brain. His personality reminds me of Dory from Finding Nemo.

"You really don't know anything about your dad, do you?"

Grunts and groans from the far side of the clearing catch my attention. Muffled screams follow the groans. No! No! The guy that left earlier comes back into view, dragging a body that can barely stand. I can't believe my eyes. Mel's in a terrible state, her clothes torn to bits. Her body is covered in grime and shadows that look like bruising, from this distance. White light bursts behind my eyes. He lied. Charging forward, I'm instantly in front of her as she drops to her knees. Wrapping my arms around her she starts to scream. *What have they done to you?*

"Mel," I whisper close to her ear. Please let her hear me. Violent shakes rack her whole body, as muffled screams try to escape her mouth, but can't because it's duct taped shut. I forgot about her. How could I? Guilt races through me, how could I? Seeing her like this, I hate myself.

"Mel, sweetie. I'm here." The shaking starts to slow, her eyes land on mine. The pain I see there breaks my heart in two. I failed her. Her body is riddled in bruises, her once bright eyes, dead. There isn't any light behind them anymore. Mumbling something behind the duct tape, she gives a slight nod in agreement.

"You said she would be fine." The red veil I know so well descends over my vision.

"Well, unfortunately she got a bit wild. We had to put her in her place." The smug expression that graces his face pisses me off even further.

"Word on the street is, you're in the line-up for the Battle Royale."

"The what?" What the fuck is that?

"The Battle Royale." He steps so close we are nose to nose, his eyes flick between mine searching for something.

"I haven't got a clue what that is or what you are going on about." A deep sigh escapes my mouth.

"You don't know? Alexander has a plan for you."

"What the fuck are you on about?" People and their fucking secrets are starting to pluck at my last nerve.

The fucker takes great pleasure in telling me all about the competition itself, but it's obvious he doesn't know everything. There are holes in this story. He thinks Alexander has entered me as his prize fighter. It sounds like a giant free for all where men can measure their dicks, and see who is the ultimate badass.

A hand wraps around my throat. Whoever has hold of me is around my height, if the tightness of his grip is anything to go by. He is trying to assert his dominance. The main man himself seems delighted by this as a hungry gaze shows behind his eyes.

"You are going to fight, Reaper, but you will lose." What is it with everyone asking me to throw a goddamn fight? It's not in my nature.

"Why? What's in this for me?" I sass, as I assess my surroundings.

"All you need to know is that you will fight and you will lose," he says. Before I have a chance to respond he continues.

"Since your name was added to the roster, ticket sales for the event have gone through the roof." He squeals like a child, clapping his hands together.

"Ticket sales? I'm an underground fighter. It isn't something that is really broadcasted all over the place."

"Doesn't matter. People want to see how you fare with the big boys, darlin." My life has been so quiet until recently. How has it turned into a shitshow so fast?

"Are you trying to be a cryptic asshole? Or does it just come naturally?" My chest rumbles as the fucker behind me tries to cut of my oxygen.

"I'm just an asshole, baby." Is he gonna get to the damn point? Pulling teeth would be less painful.

"You're going to fight. Then I will collect what is owed to me."

"What do you mean, what's owed to you?" I've got a bad feeling about this. I feel numb, my body is frozen to the spot. What did my dad do that got me into this mess? Fuckface here is all laughs and smiles expecting me to agree to this. Has everybody gone insane? I'm still trying to process everything, when Mel starts to scream as one of the goons starts pulling her up from the ground. Everything slots into place, why they took Mel. What he thinks he is owed from a deal made twenty years ago by my parents. Why they've hurt Mel like they this.

"Mel," I roar, as my body moves on its own. Good girl, she hits the deck as I throw my head back, hitting goon one in the nose. Running behind the nearest tree, I check to make sure she's safe. All the men are standing around in shock. They weren't expecting me to react like this. Taking advantage, I pull my gun and start firing.

One down. I run for cover against another tree. Lucky for me the tree line is shaded by the sun's glare, giving me the perfect hiding spot to disorient them. The goons are firing at the spot I just left. I fire off another four rounds. Four goons drop. Checking for Mel, I see she managed to get herself into the tree line. Five down, three to go.

"Who the hell are you?" The last goon screams into the air. I pull the knife from my ankle.

"The Reaper." I inhale deeply, I fire. Before his body even hits the ground, I am out of my hiding spot. With a flick of my wrist, the knife I was holding sails through the air and hits the one who dragged Mel by the neck. One left. The fear on his face sends a pleasant shiver throughout my body. Yeah, Dude, you fucked up.

"Wait. Wait. Please," he pleads, as snot mixes with tears and grime. What a sniveling little rat. Not so cocky now, are you?

Stalking forward I allow a sadistic grin to form on my face, which ramps up his fear even further. He's running for his life, well, the best he can considering he's doing it backwards. Clever man, not taking his eyes off of me. It hasn't become clear to him just yet that he won't be leaving here alive. He trips and lands on his ass. Looking down on him, I pin him to the ground with a foot to his chest.

"My dad may have made a deal with yours..." I lean more weight onto the foot holding him, slowly crouching down.

"You kidnap my family, then tell me I am supposed to become your wife." Venom pours from my voice.

"I will not be owned, like an object. I will not kiss anyone's feet." The asshole starts stuttering so badly his words don't make any sense at all. I've had enough of this shit.

Bang!!

Watching his shock disappear as the light dims in his eyes brings a sick sort of satisfaction to me. He got everything he deserved for hurting my family. Now the hardest part of all, helping Mel through this.

13

REIKA

No emotions filter in from what I've just done. Honestly, he died too quickly for my liking. Still standing over his body, I hear a muffled sound. Grabbing my knife out of the other guy's throat, I wipe the blood from it on his suit jacket. I cautiously walk over to the tree Mel's hiding behind, my heart breaks at the massive tears rolling down her face.

"Shhh. I got you girl. I'm gonna take the tape of your mouth. That ok?" The fear rolling of her is disorienting. It's causing waves of nausea in my stomach. Now, crouched down in front of her, I get a better look. The person staring back at me is even more broken than I am.

"I'm sorry. If I pull this off slowly it's gonna hurt more. Ok?" Mel gives me a slight nod of her head, and I tear the duct tape from her mouth. She's trying her hardest to pull deep breaths in. I sit on the ground and start working on the bindings on her wrists and ankles.

Once she's able to move, violent sobs tear from her throat, and her shaking becomes a whole-body tremor. What the hell do I say? Not knowing what to do with myself, I sit quietly rubbing my hand up and down her back. Just wait, Reika. That's all you can do.

Watching the closest thing I have to family break apart in front me is the worst feeling ever. I can't decide if I want to cry with relief that she's here, or cry because she is a shell of the person she was before. I won't push her about what happened, her bruises tell me enough. Without warning she launches herself at me, hugging me so tight I can hardly breathe. I can't hear what she's mumbling into my shoulder as she holds on for dear life. Hugging her close, I wait until the shaking subsides and her sobs have become quieter.

"Mel, Sweetie, I am so sorry you got dragged into this." My voice breaks as the guilt consumes me.

"Y–Y–You came for me," Mel stutters. The surprise in her tone is like a knife straight to the heart.

"Always. I'm so sorry it's taken so long." My voice trembles under the pressure I'm feeling. She's so lost now. What if it had taken me longer to find her? *No, Reika. Stop that thought.*

"You killed them?" she whispers.

"I, um..." What do I say to that? It's not exactly like I can say, 'Yeah, of course. It was fun!'

"Thank you." My heart breaks a little more.

"Mel, I–I'm so–I'm sorry they hurt you. I'm so goddamn sorry." The doors on my emotions fly open and I break down into tears, which of course sets Mel off again. We cling to each other like we'll fall right off the earth if we let go.

Mel's shaking pulls me back to my senses. I don't know how long we have been sitting on the ground but she's frozen to the core. I get to my feet. She grabs my calves, not wanting to release me. Then I bend down and scoop her into my arms. With her arms wrapped around me as tightly as she can manage, I head in the direction of the truck, whispering into her ear, "Don't look." I don't want her to witness the bloody scene around us. There are bodies everywhere; it's bad enough she had to see me cause all this.

Good thing Daddy taught me well. I always complained when I was younger about why I couldn't be a normal child and play like the neighbor's kids. I had martial arts training before and after school every weekday and firearms training three times a week. *You never know when you might need to use your skills, Little Reaper. They will keep you safe.* I never tried to understand my dad's words, because I hated them. I always hated the way he said things. If he really believed that, why didn't his skills save them?

Making it back to the truck, I hear a noise coming from the foot well. I get Mel seated in the cab, and fumble around looking for whatever is causing the noise. My fingers brush my phone as it goes onto voicemail.

"One sec. Lock the doors if you want too." Nodding again, she pulls her legs into her chest.

15 missed calls - Unknown Number

20 missed calls -Marcus

25 messages - Unknown Number

10 messages - Marcus

10 missed calls - Tom

. . .

15 messages - Tom

What the fuck? The fucking pyscho put his number in my phone? How did Marcus even unlock it? What the hell is wrong with these people? He must have used my thumb print at some point while I was out of it. Fuck it, I'll deal with this shit later. Swiping all the notifications off the screen, I scan my contacts for the number I need, hitting dial as soon as the number pops up. I pace listening to the line ring.

"Billy here, what can I do for you?" So fucking formal, clearly didn't save my number like I told him too.

"It's Reaper. I need you for a clean-up." Thank God he hasn't changed his number. Now, I know what people would think if they knew the sort of people I know, but as a teenager, I did some very shady shit for some very shady people trying to cure my constant anger.

"Fucking hell, Reaper! What did you do?" he screeches.

"Doesn't concern ya ass, Billy. Can you do the clean up or not?"

"Yeah, yeah. Usual fee applies though, girlie." Does it now?

"You sure on that one? You owe me for helping with your shit few years back."

"But..."

"No buts! You owe me, so what do you say?" I snap, not having the time to arguing with this idiot. "We square after this?"

"Yep." He doesn't respond. The line is silent for ages. "Where? How many?"

"Clearing on Langdale Road. Eight." My tone is void of any emotion.

"Eight!" he screeches down the line. Fucking hell, is he trying to make my ears bleed?

"Yeah, eight. I'll make it nine if you screech in my ear like that again." The warning works as the high pitch of his voice give ways to anger.

"You're a psychopath. Get out of there. We're on our way."

Not needing to be told twice, I shut down the call and make my way to the driver's side of the truck. Unlocking the door, a blood curdling scream hits my ears. I jump in without thinking and Mel nearly jumps out of the window. "Shit, Mel. I'm so sorry."

"I'm taking you to my place." Shaking her head so fast, it looks like she's trying to snap her neck. "No. No. No. No, they'll find us," Mel whispers frantically. Shit! She's breaking down again. Think, Reika. That's it!

"Mel, I'm gonna head to Tom's cabin. Is that ok with you?"

"D–D–Does he–Does he know?" I shake my head in answer and she sags in relief at my words.

An hour later we pull onto the track that leads to Tom's cabin. This is the perfect place to keep off the radar for a few days. Tom doesn't know, but I've hidden a few things around here, just in case. Mel doesn't want to get out, so I offer to carry her, which she accepts. Shifting her weight to unlock the door, I head to the living room and place her on the sofa.

"I'm gonna go look for a change of clothes for you." I head off on my search and send a message to Tom to let him know we are safe.

Me: Hey, sorry missed your calls. Can't talk. We are safe!

I need you to bring me and Mel a few changes of clothes to the cabin. If that's ok? I'll call later to explain as much as I can x

. . .

Tom: What the hell, Ry? I'll grab you guys some stuff, but I need to know what is going on. Kane and his brothers turned up here yesterday looking for you.

See you in a couple hours! x

For fuck's sake, can't I catch a break? Kane's attitude is really starting to piss me off. He and his brothers can stew for all I care, but we need to have some words about this fucking Battle Royale thing. Finding some of Mel's spare clothes in the laundry room, I head to the bathroom and pull out her favorite shower gel, shampoo, and conditioner. I lay out fresh towels and turn the shower on, then make my way back to the living room to find Mel still in the same position I had left her in.

"The shower's running, Sweetie. I've laid out fresh towels and your favorite shower stuff." She just nods.

"I'll make us some food, while you're in there. You want a coffee?" She nods again and slowly gets up from the sofa. Watching as she heads down to the bathroom, my emotions run away with me. Tears well in my eyes. How can I help her through this?

My hunt through the fridge is worth it as I find bacon and eggs. I give them a sniff to check they aren't going to give us food poisoning. From where I'm standing in the kitchen, I can hear the rumble of an engine heading our way. Shit. He must have floored it. As I wash my hands, I see Tom's recovery truck come out of the lane from the woods.

"Mel, I'm just going for fresh air." Not waiting for a reply, I head out to meet him. I wait for him out on the porch, and my brain just switches off.

"What the hell, Ry?" he shouts as soon as the door slams.

"Shhh! Keep your voice down. I'll tell you what I can, but please stay calm."

Taking a seat on the porch swing, I take a deep breath and start to tell him about everything I can. The story falls out of my mouth like word vomit. As I tell him everything I know, he repeatedly asks if she's ok. But what can I say? Once I finish, I look up and meet his eyes to find tears rolling down his cheeks.

This guts me even more. Tom has always thought of himself as our protector, a savior, and I know he feels guilty he couldn't protect her. He's not cussing me out or anything, yet, but if anyone is to blame for this it's me. My past has come to bite me in the ass. I know one thing for sure, whatever my dad got into all those years ago is making waves in my life now. I really need to distance myself from everyone once I help Mel deal with her trauma. I wish I could've prevented what happened to her. I won't continue to put people I care about in harm's way.

"You can't blame yourself, Ry." His words barely above a whisper.

"I am to blame for this, Tom. If it wasn't for me and my fucked-up past, this wouldn't have happened." The three of us have always been close since I met them as kids, but if I am truly honest with myself, Tom and Mel are closer to each other. They were friends when we met and I kind of wedged myself in so two became three. Now someone I love has been hurt because of me.

"You always said your dad was a good man, Ry." Uncertainty is thick in his tone.

"I was wrong. My dad made a deal with some man that I would be his son's wife."

"You're saying..." His voice breaks off as his eyes widen. "Yeah, the guy who took Mel took her to get to me. She was hurt because of me, and I can't forgive myself for that."

Wallowing in self-pity isn't going to make this any better. Shooting to my feet, I turn to head to the door when I notice Mel standing there.

The look of defeat and sadness across her face tips me over the edge and a tear escapes my eye. Slowly I approach her, waiting for a slap or some kind of anger.I wouldn't blame her. Instead, we stand staring at each other until she wraps her arms around me. How can she hug me after everything?"You saved me, Reika," she whispers into my ear.

"I'm so sorry." She heads to chair next to Tom and motions for me to take a seat. "What happened Mel?" With a tearful look at us both, she starts to tell us what happened while she was being held. I didn't think it was possible for my heart to break any more than it already had, but hearing what Mel has been through shatters it further. I can tell she isn't telling us the whole truth, but I won't force her. After a couple of hours talking, we realize that we haven't eaten yet. Tom heads inside to cook dinner, and that's when I realize the sun is setting and night is coming in.

14

KANE

"What you got for me, Fox?" He better have found her. She's been gone for three weeks. Three goddamn fucking weeks and nobody can find her.

"Nothing on Reika yet, Boss, but I do have info on the people who took her friend." His face looks haunted for some reason.

"What about them?" She must be hunting down Mel, it's the only thing that explains her being unreachable.

"They're dead," he says.

What the fuck? Marcus enters the office as Fox tells me this, and his eyes widen in surprise. Nodding to the seat in front of me, I hit the speaker so we can both hear.

"What?"

"Yeah, they're dead. Nothing about the girl though."

"Find Reika." Ending the call, I look at Marcus, who is cracking his knuckles. Where are you, Pretty Bird? Everything that has happened over the last month flies through my head. *Shit, De'Marco.* Grabbing my phone, I find the fucker's number and hit dial. It rings and rings then goes to voicemail.

"De'Marco. It's Soulless. My fighter is missing. If you have

143

taken her, you are a dead man walking. Do you get that?" I end the call.

"You think he's taken her?" Marcus has struggled to come to grips with Pretty Bird being gone. I hadn't noticed before how close they had become.

"I'm not sure, but I wouldn't put it past the little twat." Just as Marcus opens his mouth to answer, my phone rings. I look at the screen and see De'Marco's name flashing across it.

"You little prick, how dare you threaten me," he snarls down the line.

"Cut the shit. My fighter's missing. You did say at our last meeting..." He cuts me off from my rant.

"Yeah, I know what I said, but I haven't taken her Kane.But you need to find her, The Royale is in two months." I look at Marcus who has the same expression on his face. We have to find her before shit hits the fan. Where could she be? If I find out she's shacked up with another guy, I'll kill them both.

Reika

The past three weeks have been absolute torture. Mel has hardly slept, waking up constantly screaming and thrashing around. I sit with her most nights and try to comfort her the best I can. Tom has tried to do the same, but her reaction to him getting close, guts him every time. It's been a couple weeks since Tom's doctor friend came to check on her and confirmed my worst fears.

Mel was tortured and raped constantly while she was taken, and there were traces of high amounts of sedation left in her system. The doctor pleaded with us to take her to the hospital, but Mel refused saying she just wanted to forget about it. We do the best we can to support her when the nightmares wake her and reminding her to eat. That first day on the porch she seemed ok, less broken. I knew she was holding back, but nothing could have prepared me for the truth of what happened to her.

I stare out the window in the kitchen while I wait for the kettle to boil. My body is currently running on zero sleep and being fueled by caffeine. My brain function is sitting at zero. I spot my phone on the kitchen island. I really should turn it back on, but that's not likely to happen after the string of ranting messages I received from Kane, demanding to know where I am. Marcus has sent loads of worried messages as well, begging me to get in touch and telling me to ignore Kane' because he's an arrogant ass. A throat clears behind me and I turn to find Tom. He has massive bags under his eyes and his complexion is almost white. A slight beard has grown, and his hair sticks out all over the place. Bless him, he's trying his best. He has been supporting me as I try to support Mel for the both of us. This is the first night she has managed to stay asleep for more than half an hour, so I take the chance to catch up on things. I'm in great need of coffee and a bath.

"I'm gonna grab a bath. You mind checking on Mel in about an hour?" I ask Tom.

"Sure, no problem! Grab a bath, Reika. You need it." His smile doesn't even reach his eyes as he tries to joke about my lack of personal hygiene.

Taking my coffee with me, I head off. The bath in the cabin isn't spectacular, but it will do the job. Luckily, it doesn't take forever to fill. I throw a big blob of bath bubbles in, strip out of my clothes, and step into the tub. Exhaustion hits instantly and my eyes start to drift closed. My muscles loosen the longer I lay here. It's a blissful moment.

A shiver comes over me. I must have been laying here longer than I thought, because the water is freezing. Pulling myself up, I am just about to step out of the tub when screaming starts from down the hall.

Frantically trying to get out of the tub, I catch my foot on the side and nearly face plant the floor. I manage to get my feet under me and grab my t-shirt. Yanking it over my head, I run toward the screams. My heart starts to race, then it drops straight to my stomach. The broken sound that meets my ears is filled with so much pain. Tom stumbles backward, hitting the wall. From Tom's reaction, I know what I'm about to find is bad. Cautiously stepping over his legs, I turn to the open doorway and look inside the room.

"No! Oh, God, no!" I run to the kitchen, grab a knife from the drawer and run back to the room. Climbing to where she is, I cut the dressing gown belt keeping a firm grip under her arms. I cradle her to my chest and make a run for the door.

"You're ok! You're gonna be ok." I make it outside, with her curled in my arms, then I stop instantly. My legs give way as realization sets in on me. Fat tears roll down my face and I slump to the ground. This is too much. I pour all my anger, guilt, sorrow and pain into a ball inside myself. Lifting my eyes to the sky, I scream.

Kane

Marcus has managed to track Pretty Bird down. We should have known she would be with the other friend. If anything has happened between them, I will kill them both. We are driving down the road to his cabin when a broken scream comes from behind the trees. The sound is tortured, so full of pain, that emotion fills my body and brings moisture to my eyes.

"Floor it." Marcus puts his foot down. The truck breaks through the trees, charging across the grass to the cabin. Marcus slams the brakes, his hands shaking on the wheel. Following the direction he's staring, a sharp pain stabs me in the heart.

Reika is on the ground, screaming into the sky with a body laid across her lap. Tears well in my eyes. The tortured expression on her face is painful to look at. Glancing at my brother I see the same expression mirrored on his face as tears stain his cheeks. I slowly make my way over to her. I hear Reika's mumbled words, but I can't quite make them out. Her voice is low and raspy, so unlike her. She is completely broken. The girl I first met in the warehouse is so different to the girl in front of me now. I search for her strength, her defiance, the fire in her eyes that makes emotions cloud my brain. Fuck it, I admit it. I love this girl. She's the spark in the darkness, my beacon and she will feel whole again.

"Pretty Bird?" I try to catch her attention as I kneel at her side, but now I can understand her words.

"I'm so sorry, Sweetie. This is all my fault." She repeats the words over and over, growing more hysterical with each repetition, until her sobs are all I can hear.

"Pretty Bird, what happened?" I ask tentatively. I hate to push her, but we need to know what to do.

Violently shaking her head, she refuses to answer, and her sobs grow louder. I don't know what to do.

Marcus is silent with a horrified expression across his face. He has grown close to Reika; seeing his friend like this must be hard. But what's worse, is he knew Mel too.

Footsteps catch my attention. I turn in the direction of the cabin and spot a man slumped on the porch. This must be Tom. His expression tells me all I need to know - he was here when this went down. Hopefully he can answer my questions, and then we can contact emergency services.

Looking back to Reika, I am hit with a stab of protectiveness. This feeling is definitely new to me. With a nod to Marcus, he knows I'm asking him to watch her.

"Hey, man. You okay to talk?" I don't know what I'm supposed to say in this kind of situation, but to my surprise he answers, "Yeah." He slowly pulls himself from the ground, and heads back into the cabin. I follow him into the dining room.

"Sorry to have to ask this, but what the hell happened?" I never thought I would be walking into something like this, when I found Reika. Honestly, I expected her to deck me again.

"Has Ry said anything to you?" Hearing him call her Ry sends jealousy racing in my body. Calm the fuck down, asshat.

"Only when she thought I had taken Mel, but that's it." Fox has really failed me on this. If he had found the info I asked for sooner, I could have prevented this.

He sits down on one of the dining room chairs, takes a deep inhale, then tells me everything he can. Ten minutes into his story and I have to take a seat. Hearing about everything that happened makes me feel sick. Who the hell is my Pretty Bird? The amount damage she can inflict on a person isn't normal. Tom doesn't go into the full details of what she did to bring Mel home, but from Fox telling me that the kidnappers were all dead and Tom confirming it, I can only imagine. Her words outside make perfect sense now. She did what she had to do to bring Mel home, and then this happened. No wonder she's blaming herself. Just as I am about to ask Tom another question, Marcus comes into the cabin with a defeated look on his face.

"She won't let her go. Kane, what do we do, man?" I take a minute to process everything.

"We have to ring the police. She can't stay like that." Shutting my emotions down, I stand up and head out to where my broken bird is.

I step out onto the porch, making my way over as her sobs fill the night. I try to figure out what the hell I'm going to say to her. Nothing comes to mind. Based on my research into her background and discovering what happened after the death of her parents, nothing seems good enough. She was mute for close to a year after her parent's deaths, and during that time she started to lash out and become destructive. The reports say she started to come out of her shell when she met Mel and Tom. After the painful loss of her parents and now Mel, God only knows what is going to happen.

Kneeling down beside her, I place my hand on her shoulder to comfort her. I'm shocked at how cold her skin is. Sitting on my ass, I move so I am sitting behind her, scooting my body forward so her ass is between my legs. I lean and engulf her in a hug trying to bring warmth to her body. We sit like this for a while as I quietly tell her it will be okay. Pretty Bird starts moving frantically trying to break from my hold, so I slide backward so she has enough space to move. She jumps to her feet and moves away from Mel's body. Suddenly, she screams into the air, but this scream is different. It is raw, animalistic. This isn't sorrow or guilt. This is hatred and emotion in its rawest form.

Hesitantly I say, "Baby?"

"Do not call me baby!" she screams in my direction, her body trembling.

"Pretty Bird, we need to talk." Violently shaking her head side to side, she wraps her arms around herself.

"Why are you talking to me? It's my fault she's dead." Stretching out my hand I take a cautious step toward her.

"Pretty Bird, Tom told me what happened."

"You need to stay away from me, Kane. Everyone who gets close to me dies." She really believes this is her fault. Well unlucky for her, I'm not going anywhere. We belong together.

"Too late for that, Pretty Bird. You're stuck with me." Confusion clouds her features, which surprises me.

"You hate me, Kane. I'm a means to an end for you. A way to make money with the fights." Seriously, she really thinks that?

"Pretty Bird, we will talk about this later, but we need to call the police to get Mel, baby." Emotions run across her face, from anger, to guilt, to heartbreak.

In her current state, she's like a wild animal that has been caged. If I'm being completely honest, she is kind of scaring me. I know how hard this chick can hit. At the mention of her friend, she shakes her head, muttering, "No," under her breath. Taking a step toward her, I try to make myself as approachable as I can. I *need* to comfort her. I am just about to take another step in her direction, when she launches herself at me. I brace for the assault of fists bound to follow, but it doesn't. Pretty Bird grips my neck so tight she has likely drawn blood as she sobs into my chest.

Lifting her into my arms, I expect her to protest, but she doesn't. I head toward the SUV, with meaningful strides. Just as we make it to the car, noises from the cabin grab my attention. Placing an exhausted Pretty Bird into the front seat of the car, I look toward the commotion. I find Tom and Marcus staring in our direction, chatting to each other. Marcus waves me over. Leaning back into the car, I whisper in her ear, "I'll be one sec, Pretty Bird." She doesn't reply. Then my ears pick up the sound of soft snores.

With hurried steps I head over to my brother, I want this over with as quickly as possible. "What are you doing, Kane?" Should have known that would be the first thing Marcus would ask.

"She's asleep in the car. I'm taking her back to the house." Neither of them will argue with me on this. She is coming home with me, and once she has managed to sleep, I will try to talk to her about the next steps for her friend.

"What the hell are we supposed to do?" Tom asks. How can he expect her to be here when the police, ambulance, and whoever else turns up?

"She's so emotional. If she's here when the police arrive, which

they will, she is likely to tell them how she got her friend back." Does anybody use their fucking brain around here? Granted emotions are running high for everyone but still, I don't want her in a jail cell.

"Call Norris. Tell them about Mel being taken, that you found her on the side of the road or something like that." I feel like an asshole not doing right by Mel, but I need to keep my girl safe.

"Fine. I'll make my own way back. Oh, and Kane, keep Liam away from her." I really need to talk with Marcus about his issues with Reika and Liam being in the same room.

"Will do. No one is getting near my girl." Laughter bursts from Marcus as Tom looks horrified at my statement.

"We will talk about that statement another time, Kane." Wow, he is a nosey little shit. Honestly, he just wants to grill me on my feelings.

Shaking my head as I walk back to the car, I have to chuckle to myself. Marcus's reaction was better than I expected, but Liam is going to be pissed. He can go suck on a dick. I'm not running from this. The last three weeks without her was torture. Now I just need to convince Pretty Bird this is a good idea.

15

KANE

She looks so beautiful laid out in my bed. I've been watching her sleep for the last several hours. Her in my bed, black hair spilled all over my pillow, lips slightly parted as she sleeps, I want to see this for the rest of my life. Finally finding the motivation to move, I kiss her head and get up. I check my phone and notice a few messages from Marcus. Looking back over my shoulder, my eyes linger on her gorgeous body. I somehow manage to pull myself away.

As quietly as possible, I close the bedroom door and make my way to the kitchen. Rounding the corner, I see Marcus with a coffee cup in his outstretched hand. Liam is sitting on a stool looking angry. That could be because I told him to fuck off last night when I got back with Reika.

"So, are we gonna discuss your feelings, bro?" He's grinning like the Cheshire Cat, and I really want to throat punch him.

"Piss off, Marcus. I haven't had my coffee yet." I can't be bothered to deal with his shit stirring. Before he can utter another word, I ask, "What happened with emergency services last night?"

Liam mumbles something under his breath and slams to his feet,

sending the stool flying across the kitchen. His mood has been off the charts recently. I can't figure out what his problem is.

"Liam. What the fuck?" I need answers. I can't deal with his drama on top of everything else.

"Yeah, I got a problem," he roars, as he steps into my personal space. Marcus steps back, moving out of the line of fire should fists start flying.

"Well, what is it? I am not having you walking around in a mood when she has just lost a friend," I seethe, advancing on him. We're now standing nose to nose. His chest rises and falls rapidly.

"When did you start giving a shit about a piece of pussy?" Hatred is written across his face, either for me or Pretty Bird. If it's her, me and him are definitely going to have a problem.

"That has fuck all to do with you, but you best get fucking used to it real quick, brother. She isn't going anywhere." The look he gives me gets under my skin. Who does he think he is? It's like he doesn't know who is standing in front of him.

"You're shitting me, right? Has the whore got some magic pussy or something?" His words bounce around in my head. "Maybe I should have a go with her once you've finished, brother."

The fog lifts from my eyes, and I realize I just punched Liam. I'm shocked that I don't feel any guilt. How fucking dare he?

"Motherfucker," he roars, blood pouring from his nose down between his fingers. Shock flashes across his face along with other emotions I can't figure out.

"Stay the fuck out of my way, Liam. I don't want to see you until you sort your shit out." Liam storms from the room, ranting under his breath. I walk back into the kitchen, then over the stool on the floor. I pick it up, and put it back in its spot at the island. Sitting my ass down, I slump forward. Nothing is making sense at the moment. On one hand, Pretty Bird is a puzzle piece that I need to figure out. On the other, Liam's unpredictability worries me. We have enough going on with De'Marco playing his games and other unknowns trying to move in on our territory. We need to show a united front from all sides. With a huff, I sip a mouthful of my coffee. Ugh, I hate cold coffee.

"He will come around," says Marcus. I shake my head slightly in answer to his comment. I have never seen Liam like this.

"We have never seen you get attached to someone before. It's strange for the both of us." It is for me too, but I am sick of fighting these feelings. God, it gives me a headache.

"Yeah, I get it. I'm only just making sense of this myself."

"My brother's in love," he chuckles, with a massive smile on his face. He's enjoying this.

"Very funny, Marcus." We need to get the ball rolling on everything, and hopefully, I can have a talk with Pretty Bird.

"We sorted it out with the police and paramedics. Plans need to made for the funeral." This is going to hit my baby hard, but I need to keep her from falling into a pit of guilt.

"I'm gonna make a few calls and catch up on stuff from yesterday. Then I will have a talk with her."

Reika

"Faster, Reika."

"But, Daddy, it hurts." Standing on the edge of the garden

of my parent's house is surreal. What the hell is going on here? Why am I watching this?

Watching my younger self training with my dad is freaking me out. I don't remember a lot of things I did with Dad, but I do remember the bruises and breaks that came along with it.

"It's meant to hurt. How are you going to become stronger if it doesn't hurt?" Hearing my dad's tone as I see the younger me on her knees on the ground covered in blood, cuts and bruises, guts me. Seeing the nearly eleven-year-old me terrified to move because my father's punishments were far worse than the training itself, makes me want to run over and hug her, just to give her a little bit of comfort. "Daddy, I want to stop, it hurts so much." I knew then I shouldn't have said that, but it was too late to take the words back.

The landscape shifts - instead of the garden, we are now in the basement, under the garage. This has to be a memory and dream together. Screams come from further in the basement, or "the lair" as I called it as a child. Slowly making my way toward the noise, I see myself hanging from the ceiling in chains.

"What do we do if people want information from us?"

"We don't say a word." My father picks up a knife and slashes my side with it. My younger self screams out in pain and shock.

"What did you do wrong there, Sweetie?"

With a shake of her head, she doesn't answer, bringing a smile to my father's face. Seeing the torture he put me through as a child makes me hate him. He always passed it off as lessons to make me a stronger woman. To be the best I could be. Now, I know he just trained me to do his bidding.

"Good girl. We are going to speed up your training." Fear fills her eyes. My heart breaks. She doesn't know it yet, but not long after this she will become what her father made her to be.

I'm instantly awake and launching myself off the bed. Tears streaming down my face. I still ask myself how a father could torture a child, his child, like that? Shakes wrack my body as the dream slowly starts to fade. Then everything hits me from the night before and my legs give way. I'm sitting on the bedroom floor, wallowing in self-pity when I am suddenly ripped up from the ground.

A hand wraps around my throat and my body slams into the wall. Opening my eyes, I see Liam in front of me, glaring down at me with pure venom in his eyes. He looks like he wants to squeeze the life out of me. He can for all I care. I don't give a shit anymore. Pulling me forward so our noses touch, he growls, and slams me into the wall again with so much force it rattles my brain.

"What have you done to my brother?" Staring at him, I don't even bother with an answer, because I don't have one to give him. This seems to piss him off. He tightens his grip around my throat, my oxygen is limited. My breathing comes harsher. Most people would be fighting for their life right now, but I don't care. Everyone would be better off if I wasn't here.

"Why aren't you fighting back, Pretty Bird?" he says with a smirk. My face is void of all emotion. I lift my eyes again to his and just stare, showing him he could kill me now, and I would welcome it with open arms. Confusion enters his eyes; he obviously wasn't expecting this reaction.

"Kill me," I whisper in a hushed tone.

"What?"

"Kill me!" I scream in his face. I am so fucking sick of people threatening me. If they are going to threaten me, they best fucking do it. He lets go of me and I land on my ass. I watch as he paces up and down in front of me. I can't bring myself to care. There is a dark void inside of me just begging me to fall into it. I am sick and tired of destroying everything I care about.

Pain roars through my ribs. When I look at Liam, he is pulling his leg back to kick me again. Welcoming the pain, I laugh out loud.

"What the fuck is wrong with you?" he bellows.

"Do it again," I say, hoping he will.

"You're nuts." He runs his hand through his hair, as his eyes dart around the room.

"And you're a weak-ass little bitch, stuck in the shadows of his brothers."

Whack!

He lashes out with his fist. Pain flashes across my jaw, bringing

a smile to my face.

"I bet it's a real pain." I sneer. "Everyone respects Kane because of his aura, he's a leader. He commands a room and demands respect." A range of emotions dance across his face. Good. Now let's see if I can get him to truly lose his shit.

"Then there's Marcus. The happy-go-lucky psycho with an amazingly charming personality. All the women want to be around him, to fuck him if they get the chance." Wow, that hit a nerve. Liam's whole body vibrates with anger.

Punches rain down everywhere - my face, my body, my stomach. My forehead splits open with the force of the last hit. Laughter bursts out of my mouth, I can't stop it. I think I've finally snapped. Liam takes the opportunity to continue beating the shit out of me. Under the force of his brutality, I feel a snap in my side. All I can do is laugh.

Wrapping his hand in my hair, he drags me up off the floor. Pain floods my body. Blood spills from my mouth, as I cough from the pressure of trying to expand my lungs. Using the height difference between us, he drags me forward so I'm eye level with him.

"Get out of my brother's life, Reaper. If you don't, I will make you." Slamming me to the floor, Liam strides from the room as I cough violently from the impact.

Dragging myself up from the floor, a bout of dizziness hits me, causing me to wobble on my feet. Best get cleaned up. I make my way to the connecting bathroom. I stop when I see my reflection in the mirror. Shadows line my right cheekbone. The cut on my forehead stretches from between my eyebrows up to my hairline. It isn't too deep, unfortunately. My ribs, injured from the fight with Mason, have been rebroken. Blood from the cut drips down my face in small rivulets, but what really draws my attention are my eyes. The girl staring back at me is defeated, broken. There is nothing in her eyes, just an endless void. I stare in the mirror for what feels like hours, when I realize I need to hurry and get cleaned up. If Kane or Marcus see me in this state, they will ask questions I don't want to answer.

Looking around the state-of-the-art bathroom, I find a full-length shower with three heads, a sunken bathtub, and his and her sinks. Without thinking, I throw my fist into the mirror, shattering it. Emotions start to build within me again at losing another part of my family, at losing Mel. In a blind rage, I tear through the bathroom destroying everything in my wake. Smashed glass lays like deadly rose petals all over the floor. The shower doors are also in pieces on the floor. The destruction before me fits my injuries perfectly.

"What the fuck, Hellion." I spin to face Marcus, who's leaning against the door frame with a shocked expression on his face. I feel fresh blood dripping off the end of my nose. I move to wipe it off, but my movements draw his eyes to my face. With a horrified expression he rushes towards me.

"What did you do?" Looking at him, I don't say a word. I just lift my shoulders with a slight shrug. He grabs my arm and drags me from the room, screaming for Kane as we go. He doesn't even stop in the bedroom, as he continues to drag me out the door, and down the hallway to the kitchen. He propels me toward the stools around the island, and pushes me down to take a seat, chastising me like a small child the entire time. Not paying attention to what he is blabbering about, when commotion down the hallway catches my attention.

"Where is she?" Great, so Kane heard Marcus screaming for him like a little girl. God, why are they being so dramatic? It's just a little blood. With a huff, I wait for the thousand questions I'm sure are about to start. Charging into the kitchen, like he's about to tear the house to pieces, Kane heads straight in my direction.

"What did you do?" he asks, gently touching underneath my eye. His eyes study all the marks on my face, then he engulfs me in a bear hug. I try not to make a sound, but a hiss escapes my lips. Slowly releasing me to arm's length, he studies my body. He notices I'm leaning to one side, so he drops his hand to my ribs and gently touches them.

"Motherfucker," I roar. Fucking hell! The pain from his light touch brings tears to my eyes. Fuck me, that hurts.

"Get everyone in here now!" he screams to Marcus while, as gently as possible, he wraps his arms around me and pulls me into his body.

Men start filing into the kitchen from all over the house, waiting like good little dogs for their master to speak. Last to enter is Liam, still with a pissed off expression on his face. Our eyes briefly meet, his widening a little at the marks all over me. Releasing his hold on me, Kane paces up and down the line of men. So much anger radiates from his body, everyone he passes steps back in fear.

"I will ask this once. Who laid their hands on my woman?" His anger ignites further, as he surveys the room. Murmurs break out like shockwaves among the men until they are all mumbling to themselves and turning to look at each other in suspicion. I'm just about to tell Kane I did it to myself, when Marcus joins his brother in front of the line-up.

"Whoever it was best own up to it. Because if you don't, my brother is going to tear you to pieces." They panic. All of them start talking at once trying to tell the brothers that none of them had anything to do with the marks on my body. Liam is still looking in my direction when both Kane and Marcus spot him standing at the back of the crowd.

"Was this you, brother?" Kane asks as his chest rises in fast movements, his anger growing to a whole new level.

"Wasn't me. I can't stand the bitch. Why the fuck would I want to touch it?" At Liam's answer, Kane's whole body starts to tremble with suppressed rage. Striding toward his brother to get in his face, he cocks his head to the side. I can't see his facial expression from where I'm sitting, but his body language is enough to tell me Liam is in deep shit. Everyone takes a collective breath and holds it, waiting to see what is about to happen between the two titans standing toe to toe.

The noise quiets down to silence, not even a breath can be heard in the room. Kane acts so fast, no one sees him move until his forehead has already connected with Liam's face. Liam's legs give out from under him from the power of the blow. Kane steps back to address the rest of his men, who are wide eyed, heads flicking between me and Kane.

"Listen up. Reaper here is my woman. If any of you show her disrespect, I will take great pleasure in making you wish you were never born. You got that?" his voice booms.

"Yes, boss!" rings out around the kitchen from the men, acknowledging Kane's words.

My usual violently negative reaction to someone laying claim to me doesn't come. "Can I talk now, asshole?" I say, loud enough so he can hear me, but others at the back cannot.

"Not now, Baby," he says, looking over his shoulder at me. The man, who has just scared the shit out of all the men in this room, looks at me with such devotion in his eyes. I feel the wall I have built up around my heart start to crumble a little. Still, I can't stand and watch him rip these guys to pieces for something that has nothing to do with them.

"I destroyed your bathroom. The marks are from me losing my shit," I say meekly to the room.

"Bullshit, Hellion," Marcus says, while begging me with his eyes to tell the truth.

"Piss off, Marcus. You have seen what happens when I black out, when things get too much?" I will continue my rant until they see sense and let the poor bastards out of the room.

"I don't deal with emotions well. I woke up from a nightmare and then everything came crashing back. I just lost it." I turn to look at Kane. I see concern in his eyes, and another emotion I don't have a name for. "Sorry, dude." I don't know what else say.

Catching Liam's gaze, I see surprise written across his features. He fully expected me to tell his brothers what went down.

"Fuck off," Kane shouts over the voices of the men talking amongst themselves. I catch a few talking about me. Who I am and if I will stay with Kane? How did he find someone like me? How much of a psycho am I?

I sit watching as he barks orders to get someone in to fix his bathroom and other things he wants done. It causes butterflies to swarm in my stomach. In the midst of all the activity, I can't help but admire how his jeans fit his ass perfectly, as people hurry off to do his bidding

"I see what you're doing, Hellion," says Marcus. Does this stalker just watch to see my reactions constantly? He really is becoming a pain in my ass.

With a chuckle I just shake my head at the trouble maker. The pain throughout my body is starting to dull allowing my thoughts and emotions to drip back in. Guilt makes itself known. My hands start to shake in my lap and my breathing becomes heavy. I try to take deep breaths to calm myself, but it's useless. My whole body starts to shake again, as moisture fills my eyes. Arms wrap around me from behind, with whispered words. I am unable to hear them, but my body starts to relax. Spinning me on the stool, Kane's arms wrap around me again, holding me as tight to his body as he can.

"I got you, Pretty Bird. I'll help fight your demons when you want me too." A lump forms in my throat. How can he be so nice to me after everything he's seen and heard? Thoughts of the night before make me realize I haven't seen Tom yet. I don't know what happened to him after we left.

"Where's Tom?" I mutter against Kane's shoulder, not expecting anyone else to hear me with the death grip I have on him.

"He's coming by later to talk." Unease grows in my stomach. I am not sure what his reaction will be. Flashes of Tom in the hallway come to the front of my mind, bringing a choked gasp from my throat. Kane begins to make shushing noises to try and calm me, which helps a little.

"Where is she?" I whisper. What did they do last night? All I know is Kane brought me back here and that's it.

"She's at the funeral home. That's why Tom is coming, to discuss funeral arrangements." What the actual fuck? Rising to my feet I start pacing the kitchen.

"How?" I am lost for words.

"How what?" Kane asks me, grabbing my wrist to stop my pacing.

"How did you sort it so fast?" I can't, I am not ready for this.

"We told everyone what happened. My buddy down at the home owed me a favor. We have two days to get everything sorted." How the fuck do they think I will be ready to do this in two days?

My heart breaks again at the thought of saying my final goodbyes to Mel. It was never meant to be like this. I keep thinking she will walk through the door at any moment and tell me this was all a prank. Tears fall from my eyes. Two days and I am going to bury another piece of my soul. Arms surround me once again; this hug is different from last.

"I'm sorry we weren't there for you, Hellion," Marcus says, his voice breaking with emotion. I work to calm my own emotions, preparing myself to see Tom.

16

REIKA

This waiting game we're playing is driving me insane. My emotions are on a rollercoaster again. I don't want to be here discussing what to do for Mel. Normal people would know their family's wishes, I haven't got a clue. There's a knock at the door as I'm still trying to figure out what is the best way to honor Mel. Nerves settle into my bones, causing my hands to shake slightly.

Noticing, Kane comes to sit next to me and tucks me into his side for support. I hear voices coming down the hallway, and a sick feeling turns my stomach. Standing up, I start pacing. I need to move. After the funeral is done, I am going to have a talk with the guys about getting back in the ring. The beating Liam gave me helped dull the pain, but the numbness is gone and I don't like the emptiness inside.

Tom comes around the corner and I freeze when I see his face. His eyes are dull and lifeless. The other half of my family unit isn't there. He isn't the same person. His expression is cold and unfeeling. I have never been unsure how to act around him, but I am now. I want to run over and tell him how sorry I am, but I can't.

"Hey," I say in a meek voice as I take a step toward him. He turns his eyes in my direction and his look stops me in my tracks.

"Hi. We going to decide what needs to be done? I have things to take care of." Ice runs through my veins.

"T, Tom, can we talk?" I reply, stuttering the words.

"I'm busy, Reika." He called me by my name. He hasn't called me by my name since we were kids.

"Tom, please?" I'm not past begging. I can't lose him too.

"I will call you later, okay?" A tear escapes my eye. He lost his family too. He needs time, the least I can give him is time.

"Yeah, sure." I take a step back to where Kane is sitting on the sofa. He pulls me back into his side and kisses me on my forehead.

The whole time Tom is here, I'm lost in my own head. Childhood memories play like home movies in my mind. The first time I met Mel and Tom. Me and Mel having sleepovers, stealing snacks to hide under our beds for later. Mel telling me about her first kiss, or when she lost her virginity to her jock boyfriend. The first ever time we went to a nightclub without Tom knowing, and I vomited all over the floor of our room. Dragging Mel to martial arts training and her complaining because she broke a nail.

Tears roll down my cheeks as the memories continue. Every fun thing we did together, and the not so good ones. It all reminds me she won't be here to talk about what's happening between me and Kane. Hugging myself, I try to keep quiet so no one notices.

"Pretty Bird, you okay?" I open my eyes and make eye contact with eyes so dark they look like there isn't even a pupil. Kane is kneeling in front of me with a frown on his face.

"Sorry, I must have zoned out." Looking around, I notice Tom and Marcus are gone. It's just us in the living room.

"Where'd everybody go?"

"Plans have been made, Baby. Tom went to do his errands and Marcus has gone to the gym." Guilt consumes me again. I am taking too much time from the guys because they feel sorry for me. God, I am such a selfish prick.

"I need to go home." Standing up, I head to the stairs in search of my phone. I'm sure I left it on the bedside table.

"You're staying here." His tone tells me not to argue. I don't want to fight with him, but I want my own things. Turning to face him, I bump into his rock-solid chest. Slowly, I lift my eyes to his.

"I really appreciate what you both have done for me, but I need to go home." My heart is terrified at the thought of leaving Kane, for some reason he makes me feel safe. But my head reminds me it's best I go. I need to put space between us, to think about everything going on.

"Please, stay here. I need to know you're safe." His eyes plead with me to agree, but I can't. I need time to process everything alone.

"You and Marcus can check in on me. I just need some time, Kane." I hope he can see on my face that I need this. It's the only way for me to cope.

With a huff, he gives a slight nod of his head. Relief comes over me. I honestly thought he was going to fight me on his. I continue my journey upstairs in search of my phone. It was where I left it, along with my keys. Looking around the bedroom floor, I spot my jacket. Grabbing the rest of my things, I head back downstairs to where Kane is waiting. When I get there, Marcus and Kane are having a heated talk. I clear my throat to catch their attention. Marcus turns toward me, "You're staying here. End of discussion."

"I'm going, Marcus. Simple as that." Fucking control freak.

"No, you're not, Hellion. I will tie you to the bed if I have too." Both me and Kane say, "Not a chance," at the same time. Marcus continues telling Kane all the reasons why I shouldn't be going home. I make my way to the front door, leaving the guys to argue amongst themselves. I need food, a shower, and my own space.

As I walk toward Kane's SUV, all the guys I pass say hey or give a nod of the head. Huh, that's weird. I turn to lean against Kane's car when I see him making his way over. With a nod of his head, he gets into the driver's seat to take me home.

The drive to my place is quiet, both of us listening to the radio. Once we pull up outside, I feel kind of nervous. Kane is gripping the steering wheel so hard his knuckles are white. Just as my fingers brush the door handle, he speaks.

"You sure about this, Pretty Bird?" With a slight smile, I lean over the center console and kiss him. I pull back to see shock on his face, I give him a quick nod and get out of the car. Trying not to think about what the hell I've just done

Kane

Striding up and down the hallway, impatience is all I feel. It's the day of Mel's funeral, and I am waiting for Pretty Bird to message me that she's ready. The wait is driving me insane. Two nights ago, driving away from her apartment gutted me. I nearly turned around halfway home and went back. I didn't want to leave, but the look on her face when she told me she was going home spoke volumes. Reika mainly had to rely on herself, and then Tom and Mel. I can't blame her for wanting to be on her own. Marcus didn't speak to me once I got back. He thinks I should have put my foot down and forced her to stay. But I know that would have done more harm than good.

Thinking of that night, the thing playing in my head over and over is my Pretty Bird kissing me, not because we were both horny and it was convenient, but because she wanted to. I've thought of nothing else.

Since being home, Reika kept in contact like she said she would. We spent a lot of time talking on the phone, which is new to me, but the strangest thing of all was the fluttery feeling I got in my stomach seeing her name flash across the screen. If I'm being honest with myself, I kind of like it.

"Where is she?" Marcus grouches from my side. I hadn't realized I stopped pacing. Just then, my phone beeps with a text from her saying she's outside waiting. What the fuck?

Marching from the kitchen, I head outside to find Pretty Bird on the front grass. All I can think is how beautiful she looks. She is dressed in a classic black dress, her hair high in a ponytail with zero makeup on. My baby is stunning. A smile spreads across my face at how uncomfortable she looks. My favorite part is she managed to stay true to herself, wearing her leather jacket over the dress and her biker boots on her feet.

"I thought I was coming to get you?" I huff.

"I got nervous. If I'd stayed put any longer, I would have talked myself out of going."

"We best head out," I say.

We all walk over to the car; I get in the driver's seat. She goes to get in the back, but Marcus shakes his head and jumps in, chuckling to himself. Settling herself into the passenger seat, I notice she is fidgeting uncomfortably. I can't help the smirk that pulls at my lips. The drive to the cemetery is silent. Pretty Bird's emotions are all over the place. Even Marcus doesn't say anything stupid.

We manage to make it to the cemetery with enough time to

search for Tom and find out where he wants us. Keeping an eye on her, I notice her movements are sluggish, her hands shaking. It guts me watching her struggle. You can tell from her face she would rather be anywhere else but here. Tom spots us from a few feet away and gives a wave to let us know we can come over. There is another man with him who must be performing the service. We all shake hands, and with a nod to Reika, Tom turns and heads off with the other man.

The service passes in a blur. I have Pretty Bird tucked into my side, supporting her weight. She is trying to stay strong. I only hear the

occasional sob leave her throat.

Marcus holds her hand in a show of support. Listening to the words Tom said for Mel made nausea turn in my gut. Unease still sits there, for some reason. Everyone slowly starts to leave as the coffin is lowered into the ground. I am just about to ask Reika if she would like a few minutes alone when I see Tom heading our way. The dam breaks inside Pretty Bird and she launches herself at him, sobbing uncontrollably.

"I never want to see you again," Tom says, the words filled with so much venom I'm rooted to my spot. She pulls herself back to get a better look at him. From where Marcus and I stand, I can only see the back of her head. I can hear his words, but I can't hear hers.

"You should be in the ground. Not her!" he screams in her face as his chest rises and falls rapidly.

"Get your shit out of my apartment. You are dead to me." At his words, she stumbles backward. My mind clears from the initial shock, and I rush forward to catch her before she hits the ground, gently placing her down.

"Tom, please, don't do this." she begs in a broken voice.

"I want you gone today." After this final statement, he leaves.

I look down at Reika, she's hysterical, mumbling incoherent words to herself. I look at my brother, who is just as confused as I am. I toss him the keys to the car. As Marcus leaves to get the car, I kneel down so I am face to face with my heartbroken girl. Her drawn features tell me all I need to know. She believes she is the cause of all this. She was only a child when her father got involved in whatever shady crap got him and his wife killed, and she is not responsible for Mel's death. I will not let her believe she killed her family. She is stronger than this hand she's been dealt.

17

REIKA

Despair. Hatred. Guilt.

These emotions hammer through my body. My inner voice tells me to stop causing people misery. Everyone I care about dies because of me or hates me because of the damage I've caused. On my knees in the cemetery, I want to end it all just to get rid of this heartache and leave everyone in peace. Through tear filled eyes, I see Kane kneel in front of me. Why is he still here? He must have heard everything Tom just said to me. The name from my past repeats in my head. *I am The Reaper.*

"Baby, listen to me." I shake my head. I don't want to hear what he has to say. I want to be left alone. Weakly I try to push him away.

"He's wrong. It's not your fault. You can't blame yourself for this." That's where he's wrong. My parents died because I couldn't save them. Mel died because of past came looking for me. Tom is right to walk away, so he doesn't end up hurt, or worse.

Not acknowledging his words, I shuffle backward trying to get away, but he stalks forward, following my movements.

Doesn't he get it? If he stays around, he will die. Gripping my arms, he lifts me from the ground. "You didn't cause this," he spits into my face with intense emotion.

"You are stronger than this." His eyes are looking at me, but he is so lost in his rant it looks like he doesn't actually see me. "Pick yourself up and become who you are." He grinds his teeth with the force of his words.

"Find out what the hell happened to the people in your life. Why? They have been taken away from you." His voice grows louder. People close by must be able to hear him now. "Then you fuck their world up, Baby. You are the fucking Reaper!"

A new sense of purpose flows through my body. He is right. I can't be blamed for the shitty hand life has thrown me.

"We will find them and make them pay." Anger and lust combine in my body at his words.

My father always told me to control your own destiny, and Kane's words have reminded me of just that. I can't change what has happened, but I can make damn sure it doesn't happen again. My father has done things still impacting me today. I will find out what the hell he started. Clearly things have been hidden from me in the past, but for what reason? It's time to find out who the hell I really am. If anyone gets in my way, they will pay in blood.

Kane

There's my Pretty Bird.

Watching the fire ignite in her eyes has all my blood flowing to my cock. I really shouldn't be feeling excitement right now, but seeing her eyes brighten with a spark as she stands taller than she has in weeks, makes my body thrum with anticipation. I know she will have moments where she starts to crumble again, but I will be there to keep her standing. She needs answers about her past, about who she really is. If I'm being honest with myself, I want those answers too. Dropping a single white lily into of Mel's final resting place, Reika strides toward the car with a newfound purpose. Just as I am about to open her door, she turns to me with a puzzled look on her face. "I'm homeless."

"No, you're not." With a scoff she shakes her head at me.

"Tom wants me out, Kane." Shit, I forgot he said he wanted her gone today.

"Yeah? Well, you're with me now. We may as well make it official." I'm grinning like a cat that got the cream.

"Make what official?" Marcus gets out of the car with a shit eating grin on his face.

"Us." A smirk works its way across my face.

"Us!" she screeches, like it is the most horrifying thing ever.

"Yeah, us. It's happening, Baby. You just need to catch up with the script." I can't stop myself from teasing her. Looking over at my brother, his eyes are twinkling with amusement and a look that says, God help you.

"I want my own room. And there isn't an us." Her voice doesn't sound so sure as she chews her bottom lip.

"Keep telling yourself that Baby, if it makes you feel better." I chuckle as I get into the car. The room is a moot point as she will obviously be staying with me in mine.

We head back to the house. I will send some of the guys over to grab her stuff. Maybe accidentally lose something that I can put in my wardrobe along the way. Pulling up outside the house, she jumps out of the car before it even stops and takes off across the lawn like her ass is on fire. "I'm going to pick a room!" she shouts over her shoulder while disappearing through the door.

"When are you gonna tell her, brother?" Marcus chuckles like this is his new favorite TV show.

"Don't know what you mean," I say, sarcasm dripping from my voice. My brother falls to the ground, full on belly laughing, tears start streaming down his face

Chuckling to myself, I head in the house to find out where my Pretty Bird is hiding. Lost in my own thoughts, I am suddenly shoulder checked from behind. Marcus can be such an asshat at times. I look up and see him charging toward the house with a huge grin on his face. Just as he enters the front door, the little shit throws me the bird over his shoulder.

Reika

Running down the landing, I pass Liam's room, then Marcus's. Kane's room is the master at the end of the hall. I don't know where my feet are taking me, but I end up skidding to a halt a couple of doors down from Marcus's room. I brush my fingers over the doorknob. Why the fuck have I agreed to this?

"I had a feeling you would pick that one!" Looking over my shoulder I find Marcus leaning against his door frame with a shit eating grin on his face.

"Oh, yeah?" What makes him so sure? I might not like it once I'm inside.

"Check it out. Then meet us in the office when you've finished." Nodding to him in agreement, I turn and face the door. Butterflies are having a house party in my stomach, bringing nausea to the party with them. Just standing here is strange. For some reason I can't bring myself to open the door. I take a deep breath, pull up my big girl panties, and turn the knob. The door swings open to reveal a bedroom the size of my old apartment. The place is massive compared to what I'm used to.

The walls are all different shades of grey with white and black artwork lining the walls. There is a contemporary, but dark feeling to the room. A wide smile spreads across my face. I love it. A corner sofa is off to one side with a huge flat screen TV. The other side has a built-in wardrobe that runs the full length of the wall. Drawing my attention from the wardrobe is the massive, super king size bed in front of the window with a pale, grey comforter. Squealing like a schoolgirl, I run and dive bomb into the bed. I am spread eagle and my hands and feet don't dangle over the sides. "This is amazing."

It's perfect. This room is just me. Rolling off the bed, I realize there is a door straight across from the bed. Curiosity gets the best of me. It can't be a bathroom because Marcus told me their rooms are the only ones that have en-suites. Opening the door, I step into a huge en-suite bathroom with a full length shower, sink and freestanding tub. It's bigger than my last bathroom. The same dark contemporary color scheme from the bedroom decorates the bathroom as well.

My phone beeps in my pocket. I pull it out, hoping to find a message from Tom. It's just an email about becoming a better you. Shit. I've been in here for an hour and half. I was supposed to meet Marcus in the office. Crap. Running full speed out of the door, I jump down the stairs two at a time, and make it to the office door quickly. It opens just as I am about to grab the handle.

"Took you long enough, Hellion. We thought you had fallen asleep." A blush spreads across my face from embarrassment. I can't believe I got so carried away.

"Oops." With a sheepish grin on my face, I make my way over to the desk. Kane is staring at me. His gaze cause's heat to travel around my veins. I wiggle slightly in the seat I've just taken, trying to distract myself from the feelings his stare is causing. Staring at each other, neither of us break eye contact. Lust may be roaring throughout my body, but I won't look away.

"We need to talk." Well, that sounds sinister. I can't stop the chuckle that escapes my lips. Kane's brow furrows, "What about?"

"There's a big knockout fight coming up." Ah crap, my stomach turns as flashes of that day play in my mind. "The Battle Royale?"

Both guys rear their heads back with horrified expressions on their faces. "How do you know about the Battle Royale?" Marcus asks with a worried tone to his voice. My memories overwhelm me as guilt courses through my veins at the reminder of what happened to Mel. Realization hits that we only buried her today. Tremors start to work their way through my body as I feel further guilt for enjoying my new bedroom.

"He wanted to know the plan for it. He thought Alexander had entered me." Realization dawns on them at the same time which man I'm talking about. I didn't leave this out when telling Tom what happened that day, and he told Kane everything he knew. This shouldn't be news. Kane and Marcus move to the other side of the office. Whispered words are thrown about rapidly. With both of them distracted, my mind continues to race with all the emotions I am trying to keep locked down.

18

REIKA

Loud voices draw my attention back to reality. Following them, I find Kane and Marcus having a screaming match. They're arguing about how to deal with some guy to get me out of the Battle Royale. Memories of my beating from Liam flash to the front of my mind. The pain helped keep my emotions at bay. Maybe the Battle Royale is a good thing after all.

"I'll do it." I speak into the room, hoping the sound of my voice will stop their argument. Their voices continue to grow louder with every word. "I. Will. Do. It!" I scream.

Silence. I turn to meet their astonished expressions. Marcus is so pale he is almost transparent. Kane looks at me like I've lost my mind. "Hellion. This isn't your typical underground fight." Marcus's eyes plead with me to take back my words.

"I'm not your typical fighter, Cheshire!" If this is some sexiest bullshit, I am going to be pissed.

"Women don't fight in the Royale." So, this *is* some sexiest bullshit. Oh, hell no. What the actual fuck? They should know me better than that by now.

"What's up, Cheshire? You don't think I can hang with the big boys?" Annoyance bubbles under my skin. It really pisses me off how female fighters get pushed aside purely because of their gender. Seriously, we aren't in the fifteen hundreds, or whatever era had sexist pigs in control of women's rights. Any female fighter with the right sort of training can be the deadliest person in any room.

"We know you're a damn good fighter, Baby." Kane says with a placating tone, slowly approaching me. My nostrils flare as my annoyance ramps up to an even higher degree because of the tone he's using.

"I want to do this, Kane. I need to do this." Confusion and concern filter across his face. Marcus is cussing up a storm, mumbling to himself that I have lost my damn mind. Kane is studying my face, looking for something hidden within the depths of my expression.

"Ok." With a slight nod of his head, he grabs hold of my hand and pulls me into his arms.

"Are you out of your mind?" Marcus screams in our direction. Stepping out of Kane's embrace, I walk over so I can take a good look at him. Worry and fear dominate the look he gives me. Engulfing me in his arms, Marcus squeezes me so tight my already injured ribs protest at the pressure; but I don't want to say anything. There's a lump in my throat and tears well in my eyes.

"Ivan and Mateo will train you." Kane informs us, which gets Marcus to release his death grip on me. The names are familiar to me from hearing them in the fight rings, but that's all I know. Confusion must show on my face. "They are the best in their styles. You're going to need the extra training for the Royale." Unease starts to settle into my gut. What have I got myself into?

"I'll make the call." Kane grabs his phone and leaves. I look to Marcus for some reassurance, but he just gulps and shakes his head.

"I'll make some food. Do you want anything in particular?" His whole demeanor sends my unease through the roof.

With a shake of my head I say, "I'm gonna go wash up." I head off to my room to process my thoughts.

Scorching hot water cascades over my body. It feels so good on my aching joints. My ribs are black and purple again, my shoulders feel like I lifted a Mack truck over my head. I've been standing here for a while, trying to remember my father's training regimes for hand-to-hand combat. Since I was little, he had me train in Kickboxing, Karate, and Taekwondo. When I turned eleven, he decided it was a good idea to add Krav Maga into the mix. Memories of pain flare to life all over my body, remembering how I used to feel after his training sessions. I always left battered and broken. But even when I seriously hurt myself from one of his exercises, he would still make me train the next day. People might think I am a glutton for punishment, but I am looking forward to the aches and pain that will come with training. Finally deciding to pull myself out of the shower, I find some pajamas on the sink.

Huh? One of the guys must have put them there. The thought of Kane being so close while I was naked in the shower has heat pooling between my legs. Kane all wet with water running over his body? Holy shit, that would be a sight to see. Throwing on my clothes, I make my way down to the kitchen. A delicious smell hits my nose, making my mouth water in anticipation and my stomach growls in response. The sight that greets me isn't what I expected at all. Marcus is standing in front of the stove, each ring filled with pans. It's so strange seeing him play house. I chuckle lightly to myself, then he spins with a grin on his face. My eyes land on his apron which says *Suck My Dick and Make Me Happy* with a naked body on it. I burst out laughing as he wiggles his hips side to side, causing the cock on the apron to wiggle with him. "I don't want to know."

Honestly this guy's mood swings could give somebody whiplash

with how quick they change. One minute he's funny and charismatic then he looks like the world is about to end in the next.

"What's cooking?" My stomach chooses that moment to rumble again. When was the last time I ate something? The smell wafting from the stove has my mouth watering even more than before. Lifting his finger, telling me one minute, he starts grabbing plates from a cupboard and puts them on the island. The big, cheesy grin on his face has me grinning right along with him. Kane strolls into the kitchen just as Marcus starts to dish out the food. His eyes land on me and a huge smile comes on his face.

"Hey." My veins tingle at the look he's giving me and the butterflies from earlier show up again. Seriously what the hell is going on with me? I couldn't stand the sight of not that long ago, then we fucked out of lust, but this? *You like him.* Just great, you had to pipe in now, didn't you? *I don't like him. It's a normal reaction to someone being nice to you.*

Good. Why does my inner voice have to speak up now? *You do. You like him.* I've officially lost the plot. I'm sitting here in a room full of people and I'm arguing with my inner voice. *Stop hiding what you feel. He likes you too.* Ughh!

"Everything ok?" Kane's question pulls me out of my inner argument, which I am glad for. It never works out well, when I argue with myself. One of us always ends up in time out.

"Yeah, sorry. I kind of zoned out there." A plate drops down in front of me, and my attention zones in on it.

The plat is filled with a roast chicken breast covered in some sort of sauce with veggies and weird looking pulp stuff. With a frown, I look at Marcus as he chuckles to himself. Is it rude if you ask what the hell the baby food on the plate is? Handing a plate over to Kane, he then serves himself.

"Lemon and garlic roasted chicken, with sweet potato mash and honey glazed roast veggies." My eyes almost pop out of my head at how smoothly he gives me a rundown of everything on my plate. Now that I know what everything is, one, I know it's safe to eat, and two, how did he learn how to cook like this?

"How? I wasn't that long, and this looks like it belongs in a five-star restaurant, not a kitchen island." Rumbling laughter meets my ears from my side and from the master chef himself. I give Kane a death glare and he instantly shuts his mouth, but his body still shakes with silent laughter.

"You were a couple of hours, and I got the urge to cook." He shrugs his shoulders like the effort he's gone to doesn't mean anything.

Grabbing my fork, I dig in. All the different tastes hit my tastes bud in an instant. I moan in appreciation as my taste buds are caressed by the food orgasm in my mouth. This has to be the nicest food I have had in a long time. It's normally ramen noodles or frozen pizza for me. A yelp rings out. I look at Kane when I realize it was him. He moves away from the island a little, adjusting his cock in his jeans. His eyes are filled with lust, drilling holes into my face. I can't help but smirk. With a wink, I empty my plate in a matter of minutes. Both of them are wide eyed, staring at me as I push the last mouthful in. I lift an eyebrow as they both start laughing at me. What? Have they never seen a woman enjoy her food before? Seriously, Marcus is a fantastic cook.

Current mood, I'm in a food coma. My eyes start drooping as I listen to the guys talk over business stuff. How has Kane managed to keep everything going while spending so much of his time with me? They need to concentrate on their own things instead of worrying about me all the time. I think now is a good time to take my ass to bed.

"The fuck is she doing here?" Liam sounds like a pissed off grizzly bear, but I haven't got the energy to look in his direction, and I sure don't have the energy to listen to his crap again. Heading to the sink, I to rinse off my plate and head on up. I leave the three of them to their guy drama. I hear their raised voices drift through the house. I head up to my room, face planting on the bed as soon as I reach it. Exhaustion takes over, and I feel my eyes drift shut.

Kane

"What is your fucking problem?" I ask Liam as we step into the office. I am sick and tired of his attitude. He's never been the friendliest person in the world but his attitude with Pretty Bird is off the damn charts, even for him.

"I want her out. She doesn't belong here." He snaps, throwing daggers at me.

"Tough shit. She's with me and lives here now." His eyes glaze over at my words and his face becomes bright red.

"So, you guys are official? What happens when you get bored and fuck something else, brother?" Taking a step in his direction, I'm fighting with the urge to pull my brother's head off. Actually, that's wrong, it's not an urge it's a need. How fucking dare he question my choices? She is with me, not us.

Seeing the intent in my eyes Liam steps forward in challenge. Marcus darts between us, holding his arms out.

"Fuck's sake man, chill out." Marcus's nostrils flare, hinting at how pissed off he is. He may be playing peacekeeper at the moment, but I know he is just as affected by Liam's comments as I am.

"Liam, they're together, kind of. He's happy. Leave them alone for Christ's sake." Marcus turns his gaze to me. His eyes asking me to understand Liam's reluctance at adding a woman into the fold. None of us have allowed feelings for a woman to creep up on us after the loss of our mother. As soon as anything started to get serious, we cut that shit out like a disease. With the upbringing we had at our father's hand... our mother's promises were the only thing that got us through. Promises she didn't keep.

"She will destroy us. She hasn't been here long, and there's already a divide between us." The look on his face makes my anger subside. He really believes she's coming between us, that he's losing us.

"I love you, brother, but I want to be with her. You are the one causing the divide." Watching his face fall at my words, I feel like the shittiest person alive. I don't want us to be divided, but I will not walk away from Pretty Bird without finding out where this will go. Without answering me, Liam is out of the door, slamming it so hard the whole door frame rattles like it might splinter apart.

With a huff, I take a seat and start pulling out all the paperwork I need to catch up on. Tomorrow is going to be a busy day. Pretty Bird is starting her training. I know she's in capable hands, but it doesn't mean I have to be happy about it. I would rather she wasn't involved in this shit show, but she said she wanted to do it. After watching her and talking it over with Marcus, we figure this has to be how she copes with her emotions. It's an outlet of sorts. I'm so mentally drained after the last few days. Lost in thought, I completely zone out the worry that consumes me about the Royale. I know she would do it with or without us, and I understand her reasons, but the thought of anything happening to her feels like a knife to the heart.

"I'll keep an eye on him. Go up to bed. You look like shit." Even attempting a laugh at Marcus's words is too much effort. The paperwork will have to wait until morning. With a fist bump, I head up to my room. Walking in a daze toward my bedroom, muffled cries catch my attention from Pretty Bird's bedroom. Putting my ear to the door, I listen. I don't want to disturb her if I don't have to. She needs to sleep.

Agonized screams reach me. Without another thought, I throw the door open to find Reika thrashing around on her bed in the middle of

what looks to be a nightmare. I climb onto the bed while trying to avoid her legs, which isn't the easiest thing to do. *Ow!*

Fucking hell, her legs are lethal. The kick to the gut has just nearly knocked me off the bed. Managing to get around her thrashing limbs, I place my hand on her chest, trying to keep her in place. Her movements start to slow a little.

"I got you, Baby. It's just a dream," I whisper against her ear. I'm not leaving her like this, so I make myself comfy laid out on the bed. I pull her into my side, and my breathing stills as she snuggles in further. Her hand snakes across my stomach, as she pulls herself over onto my chest and nestles herself there. She hums to herself and her movements stop completely.After deep inhale and she hums again. My muscles are locked in place. I'm not in a comfortable position, but listening to the sound of her breathing become deeper, I easily fall asleep.

That tickles. The movement happens again, slowly bringing me out of my sleep. Tingles run down across my stomach. Opening my eyes slowly, I find her tracing patterns there. The room is in darkness. I'm only able to make out her features because the moonlight is shining through the windows. Looking down at her in this light, her features glow giving her an ethereal look like a goddess. All I can do is stare; my body becomes alive under her touch like an electric current is zapping around my veins.

"You were having a nightmare," I mumble my reason for being in her bed, with a shyness I've never felt before.

Her eyebrows draw together in a frown, but she doesn't say anything. She continues tracing patterns on my stomach, the sensation going straight to my cock which starts to get hard. Her eyes work down from her hand to my hard on and her eyes glaze over. She meets my eyes once, then suddenly her lips land on mine and she swings her legs over me, straddling my hips. My brain fogs as lust devours everything in my body; it's like a volcanic eruption and all I can see is her. I respond to her as her mouth moves with chaotic, demanding, forceful movements. This is brutal and raw, it's us. She moves slowly down my body trailing a path of kisses down my stomach, then lower to my waistband. She grabs hold of my jeans and flicks the button. Yanking on them, she practically rips them off in one go. I lean forward, grabbing hold of her throat and growl. She stops, her eyes flick up to mine.

"Stop," I growl in her face. I enjoy the gulp she swallows down with wide eyes, staring at me like I am the only thing on the planet.

"Do you trust me?" Everything depends on her answer.

"Y-yes," she whispers, diverting her eyes from my gaze.

Happiness explodes inside me. I know it's taken a lot for her to admit that, and I didn't think she would this soon. But knowing I've proved to her I am trustworthy is amazing. Now it's time to take care of my woman. Placing my finger underneath her chin, I force her eyes back to mine. I see lust burning in them, but behind that I see the demons plaguing her thoughts from her nightmare. Dropping my face to the crook of her neck, I take a deep inhale, causing her body to shudder. I lick her from jaw to ear.

"I want you to feel. Don't hide away from your pain. Own it, adapt it, use it." Her eyes widen in fear at my words. Violently shaking her head, she tries to pull my hand away from her throat.

Shifting our positions, I apply the slightest little bit of pressure to her neck to limit her air. Most people would shit themselves in this vulnerable position, but not my baby. She leans back allowing me to push her into the mattress. The urge to kiss her, claim her, ruin her for anyone else is too much. With more ferocity than I realize, my mouth is on hers, demanding, claiming. She moans into my mouth, and the sound is like music to my ears. I need more. Sliding my hand down her side, I grab her shorts, bunching them tightly in my hand.

Her shorts tear under the force of my grip and she gasps. I can't stop my smirk as I continue my journey with my hand. Without any further obstructions, my hand brushes over her pussy. Another shudder passes over her body. With my index finger, I start making small, light circles on her swollen clit. Watching the fire in her eyes ignite further, I add more pressure and speed to the circles, making another moan spill from her lips. Her words come out jumbled, I'm struggling to understand them. Her hips rise off the bed in perfect sync with my finger. I think she's begging me with her words, but the cues from her body are enough for me to pick up the pace. Using my finger, I push into her continuing to work her clit with my thumb. Her warm heat makes me groan. My lust turns wild. I don't know how long I can keep this up.

Thrusting my finger back into her, she moans, so I add another. Her hips are rising and falling faster, begging for more as she tries to fuck herself with my fingers. I apply pressure to the point of pain on her clit and add another finger inside her. Picking up the pace, I thrust in and out until her body violently trembles under my hold, her moans filling the room.

"Kane, please. Please, I need you inside me." Hearing her beg makes my cock so hard it's painful. I can already feel precum on the tip.

"Not yet," is my only reply.

"Please," she says as a moan is ripped out of her throat by my hand. I turn my eyes back to the show. I am finger fucking her so fast my wrist is starting to ache from the force of thrusting into her. Her walls tighten around my fingers in a death grip, trying to pull them further into her. Fuck, she's so responsive.

I add more pressure to her clit. She screams as her orgasm hits and tremors roll through her body. To my amazement, she comes hard as she squirts all over my hand and the sheets. I remove my hand, settling myself between her legs as I watch the aftershocks of euphoria on her face. I enter her, thrusting forward so fast she screams from my intrusion. Pulling my cock back so just my tip remains in, I thrust forward again with a roll of my hips. The moan that leaves her throat makes tingles run through my bloodstream. I set the pace alternating hard thrusts that make her scream with to slower pumping movements sending her body into overdrive. Her moans are wild and guttural. I feel my orgasm building. Her eyes glaze over in a sex induced haze, and I feel the walls of her pussy tighten around my cock so hard my movements become erratic.

I thrust harder, faster, leaning my elbows at the side of her head.

"Say you're mine." I whisper into her ear. Her moans filling the room from my violent thrusts are the only thing I can hear. Slowing my pace to shallow thrusts, I repeat, "Say you're mine."

"I'm yours." Reika's words are breathy as she continues to moan.

"Only mine. No one else's."

"I don't want anyone else." At her words, my pace becomes frantic, my thrusts almost brutal. Building up momentum, our emotions soar. I set a pace that will have us both coming together.

Faster, harder, deeper. I'm fucking her like a mad man possessed, her body responding in kind. Her moans are so loud the whole house is probably listening to us at this point. Reika's walls start to tighten hard as her body shakes, her legs vibrating, her eyes wild. Tingles spread from my balls all over my body like static electricity.

Reika screams and I roar my release along with her. Once the shockwaves stop, I open my eyes to the most gorgeous pair of grey eyes staring back at me with a look that says she doesn't regret anything. Rolling off of her onto the mattress, I pull her into my body. We're both breathing heavily, but the feeling of contentment passing through me brings a smile to my face. Her breathing changes, and I look down to see she has fallen back asleep. Kissing her forehead, I move into a more comfortable position on my back, pulling her with me so her head is on my chest. I feel sleep starting to pull me in.

"I got you, Pretty Bird. Always."

19

REIKA

Opening my eyes slowly, I stretch out all my aches and pains. Not the bad kind though, my body feels satisfied. God I'm so comfortable, I don't want to get up. Kane isn't in bed; he must be catching up on work he's missed. The thought of him reminds me I'm meeting Ivan and Mateo for training today. Oh shit! Jumping out of bed, I get tangled up in the sheets and fall face first to the floor. Luckily, I manage to get my hands out before I face plant. I start laughing hysterically, I can't believe I just did that. Running to the bathroom at lightning speed, I quickly flip on the shower and dig out my shorts and sports bra. Hopefully the guys don't want to talk too much today.

Excitement and anticipation spring to life in my veins. The feeling is new to me. No, everything is new to me. Kane asked me to be only his last night, and I agreed. We need to talk about this at some point. I want him to know that I meant it when I said I'm his. Running back into the bathroom, dropping my clothes on the counter, I strip off my top. Thanks to Kane ripping my shorts last night, my shirt is the only piece of clothing I'm wearing. I'm in and out of the shower in five minutes.

As I'm walking down the hallway to the main area of the house, I get a creepy feeling there isn't anybody around. This place is too quiet. The last few times I've been here there have been people everywhere.I get downstairs and head to the kitchen for a coffee. I notice a few people in the living room, but none of them are who I will be looking for after I've had my caffeine fix. Every time I see the kitchen, I'm taken aback by how pristine it is. The modern take on the room is gorgeous. I search the cupboards looking for everything I need. I find the coffee, milk, and sugar, take them out, then hunt down a cup.

"Holy shit. Who's she?" Turning to the sound of the voice, I spot a couple of the guys from the living room standing at the end of the kitchen, staring. Smirking to myself, I don't acknowledge the asshat's statement.

"I dunno dude, but damn she is fine." Do all men have their brain in their pants? What a set of idiots.

"You do know I can fucking hear you right?" I snarl at the pair of them. They both smirk, eyes roaming over my body. One of the little shits licks his lips. Be nice Reika, it's not a good idea to stab someone this time in the morning.

"I could fuck her all night long," one of them says. "I bet she's a screamer." Okay, now *that* fucking pisses me off. I spin back to the douche canoes, ready to tear them a new asshole.

"You wanna do what to my girl, boys?" All the color drains from their faces - well this is awkward, but damn if this isn't the funniest thing I have seen in a while. I can't help the smirk that tips the edge of my lips while staring at the two guys and a pissed off Kane standing behind them.

"Boss! We. Um..." This shit is better than daytime TV. Kane's gaze lands on me. The corner of his mouth lifts slightly in his own smirk. He's enjoying watching them squirm. I burst out laughing, scaring the shit out of the guys as their eyes flick from Kane to back to me.

"Hey, Babe. What ya doing?" The smile that sweeps across his face completely changes his features. Holy shit, he's even more gorgeous when he smiles. My ovaries notice too.

Shaking his head at me, he finally looks at the poor guys about to piss their pants. Kane cocks his head to the side and they are off like hundred-meter track stars. I'm still laughing as I turn to continue my search for a damn cup. Seriously, what does a girl have to do to get coffee around here?

"Where the hell are all the cups hiding?" I grouch out loud. Arms wrap around me from behind. A kiss lands on my shoulder, making a shiver run down my spine.

"Cupboard on your left," Kane says, with laughter in his voice. *Huh, playful Kane is hot.* "I got it. How do you like it?" He gently moves me to the side so he can take my place.

"Strong, two sugars and a dash of milk." With a side order of you, please. The thought brings another smile to my face. Hmm, Kane and coffee. I wonder if we have time.

The smell of coffee wafts under my nose, making my mouth water. I grab the cup from him and take a sip. Damn that tastes nice, better than my usual cheap instant brand.

"Thanks." Staring up at him, I have to crane my neck a little. This is the first time I have paid close attention to him like this, and fuck me, the guy is huge.

"You ready for today?" I see the hesitation in his eyes. My nerves should be kicking in by now, but they aren't. To be honest, I thought it would be a bit awkward between us, but it isn't.

"Yep, I was born ready." I laugh at the stupidity of my words. It draws a chuckle out of him too.

Taking hold of the hand that doesn't have a death grip on my cup, Kane leads me out of the kitchen, and down a corridor toward the gym area. Once inside, I'm surprised at the amount of high-tech equipment here. There's a weight area and a martial arts area with a cage. Seeing the cage, my eyes light up. I can't wait to get my ass in there. It's so shiny, and I bet it doesn't smell like shit. Squealing in excitement, I almost throw my cup at Kane, before charging toward the cage with a shit eating grin on my face. I'm bouncing up and down like an excited child. I can't help it.

Laughter rings out around me. That's when I notice Marcus standing next to Kane, shaking his head at me with a grin. Marcus is laughing his ass off.

"You must be The Reaper?" Turning to the voice behind me, I have to immediately duck to avoid the fist headed straight for my face.

"The fuck, man?" Another fist flies in my direction. I step out of the way and throw a counter punch to his ribs that he manages to block at the last second.

Keeping my guard up, I watch every movement of this guy's body, including every twitch of his fingers. Reading body language has become second nature to me.

Shit! Stop daydreaming. Seconds before another fist slams into my face, I drop to my knees. A three punch combination to his knees makes him wobble. Jumping back to my feet, we circle each other, neither of us taking a shot. Fucking hell, I thought Kane was big. He lunges forward, making me shift my position. Annoyance shows in his eyes, and with a huff he shifts his weight between his feet. Going on the attack he throws everything he has at me; I'm barely managing to avoid his attacks.

He lands a punch to my face, and my brain rattles in my head from the power of it. Fucking hell, that hurt like a bitch. Stumbling backward, I try to shake off the fog in my head. Blackness creeps in from the corners of my eyes. I hear shouts from somewhere nearby. With a growl, I take a deep inhale and give my head a shake to force the darkness back. Finally, my vision returns with only a slight blur. I realize then that I'm on the floor at the other side of the cage. Something wet is running down my face. I lift my hand to examine it - my nose is bleeding. There is blood dripping out of the corner of my mouth, and ribs are screaming at me to stop.

I hear a loud commotion, and turn to see Marcus trying to hold back a pissed off Kane, who looks at my attacker like he's planning his death. Shaking my head again, I stay put a few more seconds to get my bearings. Then as quietly as I can, I stand back up. Marcus's eyes widen, and now Kane looks like he wants to murder me instead.

Hulk. Yeah, that's this guy's name from now on. The Hulk turns to see me back on my feet, his eyes widening slightly. I spit the blood from my mouth, and bring my hands up to cover my face. Hulk's face is an open book, asking me without words if I want to continue. I give a slight nod, and he charges again. I switch between defensive and offensive moves, not sticking to any one fighting style. Hulk manages to maneuver his arms undermine with his hands locked behind my head. It's taking him significant effort to from him to keep me in the air like this while I flop around like a fish out of water. Kane screams at me from the side of the cage. A bloody grin spreads across my face. I shoot a wink to Kane, giving him pause. I immediately drop my weight and slide out of the hold. Before Hulk realizes it, I'm kneeling on the floor, and spinning around land a punch straight to his junk. Bellowing, he falls to his knees. I launch off the floor with an uppercut, connecting with his jaw and knocking him flat on his back instantly.

Kane

. . .

Seeing Pretty Bird standing over Ivan with blood dripping down her face, pride swells in my chest. The guy is an absolute force of nature and she took everything he gave her, and put him on his ass.

"Ah shit," Marcus mumbles beside me, realizing Mateo is standing behind her and she hasn't noticed.

My entire being begs me to warn her, but I can't. I've had to bring them in to help her train for the Royale. Not warning her is killing me. All I can do is watch as Mateo starts his attack, knocking Reika all over the ring. She's already been injured by Ivan and is trying her hardest to keep her ribs covered. Ivan picks himself up and goes back on the attack. My brain flips a switch at the brutality of it all. Marcus's grabs me around my waist, halting the step I've just taken forward. I watch in horror as both fighters set upon her. Hearing her grunts and moans of pain guts me.

'Aaaargh," she screams from another injury. She has blood dripping from almost every part of her body. God, I feel sick to my stomach.

"Brother, if you can't watch her training, you won't be able to stomach her fighting." I know what he's saying is true, but I am at war within myself. They continue their assault on her for thirty long minutes. She's bloodied and bruised, wobbling on legs that look like they'll give out any time.

Getting put on her ass again by a kick from Mateo, she's lying face down on the floor. Ivan and Mateo look at each other, and turn toward the door of the cage. To my horror, Reika pulls herself back on her feet agonizingly slow and brings her hands up, ready to go again. What the fuck? How does she keep doing that? Most people fighting these two would have been out cold long before now. I don't know if it's pride or stubbornness that keeps her getting back up.

Clap. Clap. Clap.

Marcus grins slightly while clapping because Reika is on her feet again. He isn't fooling anyone. I see the pain in his face at having to stand back and watch the horrific beating she is being subjected to. Nausea still turns in my stomach. Both Ivan and Mateo are staring in my direction. Surprise washes across their features seeing Marcus clapping at my side. Turning to see what has Marcus's attention, they find Pretty Bird on her feet in guard position, ready to go again.

"Stand down, Reaper. We have seen all we need to see." At Ivan's words, I almost sag in relief to the floor. Thank God they've called an end to it. I couldn't stand back and watch anymore. I am in front of Pretty Bird just as her legs give way and she collapses, before anyone even noticed I moved. Wrapping her arm around my neck, I help her stay on her feet. She wouldn't want to show weakness in front of these two. We slowly make our way over to where the guys are standing.

"You're good, Reaper. You may just survive this." Ivan's words send unease swirling in my gut again.

"Be honest, Ivan. You're pissed she put you on your ass." Mateo says, chuckling to himself.

"You would be too," Ivan shoots back. I can't help the chuckle that slips past my lips at their banter, causing Marcus to burst out laughing.

"We have training to discuss, Kane." This may be true, but my concern, at the moment, is getting Pretty Bird to her room and having a doctor check her over.

"Let me just sort her out and then we can talk." I am just about to set off with an exhausted Pretty Bird, when she steps out of my grasp and straightens herself, looking around at us all. With a nod, she slowly turns and makes her way out of the gym. I watch as her steps hardly falter, but I can tell that it's taking everything in her not to show how much she hurts. This, right here, is why I love this girl. Even in her current state, she will not let any weakness show.

Reika

Making my way up the stairs towards my room is agonizing. It's slow going, but I'm determined to get myself there. I finally step into the bathroom, the beating I received finally taking its toll as I nearly collapse in agony. I examine myself in the mirror, looking at the horror staring back at me. Memories begin to surface of training I underwent with my father. I remember one time I was beaten so badly I couldn't walk properly for weeks. The next morning, I didn't have the energy or strength to drag myself up from my bed. But my father wasn't having that, so he dragged my ass out of bed and all the way to the training grounds. My screams fell on deaf ears.

Shaking off the memory, I turn away from my reflection and flip on the shower. I gingerly remove my workout clothes, trying my best to avoid the bruising on my ribs. These injuries will take a while to heal, but I don't have that sort of time. My only option is to push through the pain so I can continue training. I need to prove to myself and everyone else I can make it out of the Royale alive. Toweling myself off, I head to bed.

I wipe the sleep from my eyes. It must be the middle of the night, if the moonlight streaming through the bedroom window is anything to go by. Pain flashes across my side, reminding me of training earlier that day, as movement catches my eye. I find Kane in bed next to me. How did he manage to get in here without me knowing? Another round of pain hits me like a freight train. As carefully as possible, I slide out of bed. Painkillers and water are on the bedside table with a note.

Left these out for you in case you wake up.

Kane must have left them. The gesture has a tingle running down my spine. Well, I am not going to be able to sleep now. I take the painkillers with a sip of water and make my way over to the window. Staring out of the glass, I can't help but admire the tranquility I feel even while everything is in shadows, points glowing from the light of the moon. My mind wanders. What will be in store for me in the next two months? Watching the leaves fall from the trees, I know no matter what happens I have to make it through.

20

REIKA

Looking at myself in the mirror of the changing rooms in the arena, I can't believe the changes in my body over the last two months. I have always been lean with a small amount of muscle showing, but now everything is more defined. My abs are clearly visible, my arm muscles are cut. Damn, I look good. My hair is pulled back into Viking braids, and I have on black shorts with a matching sports bra. My knuckles are wrapped up in my lucky purple hand wraps. I'm ready.

The Battle Royale isn't as high class as I thought it would be for all the money folk that will be here. It's a four-fight match up. As they call it, the last man standing round robin style, starting with four fights. Winner from each fight moves on until the last two standing are left. The first group of fights are win by knock out or tap out. Then in the semi-finals a win is a knock out or until the other person can't continue. Broken bones are expected. In the final, I haven't got a clue, but there is buzz around the arena that the final will be bloody with a big surprise in store for the guests. I never get nervous when I'm waiting to be called for my match ups. I always do my research on my opponent. But right now, a ball of nervousness is building in my gut.

Kane has tried to talk me out of this so many times I've lost count.

Our relationship has progressed further than I ever thought possible. We haven't actually said we're a couple, but everything is going great. Honestly, I am starting to fall for the big goon. It's strange thinking about how we first met and where we are now. He's more than I expected him to be, and he has stayed true to his promise. Once this is over with, we will start looking for answers about who I really am. The roar of the crowd reaches down to the changing rooms, adding to my nerves. There are definitely more people here than I'm used to.

"Get ready bitch. You're playing with the big boys now." I was wondering when of these fuckwits was going to open their mouths. The other fighters threw a tantrum when they realized a female fighter was on the cards, but they soon got over it when they recognized my name. I don't even bother to acknowledge the idiot; I am not about that drama tonight. I need to survive, that's it. Whatever gets said back here is fuck all to what I'll be dealing with out there. People are expecting me to quit and walk out of here. Slowly my mind blocks out all sounds and noises so I am in my own world. Nothing can enter my bubble.

"You ready, Baby?" Bringing my eyes back into focus, I see Kane standing behind me, in the mirror. He's nervous, it's written all over his face. I haven't seen Marcus yet. He's probably keeping Liam company. Fucking Liam. I hate that fucker with a passion. We've had loads of fights and disagreements over the last two months.

"Have I been called?" I can't answer his question because I'm not sure if I *am* ready or not.

"Yeah, you got Viper." Me and Viper have a long-standing

rivalry. He's still pissed Alexander dropped him after the last time I beat his ass.

"Looks like I will just have to beat his ass again," I chuckle to myself. Checking my wraps are tight, I spin on my heels and make my way to the corridor.

Security lines the walls on either side. I haven't got a clue what for. It's not like one of these rich suits will be starting shit with fighters from the wrong side of the tracks. They must be here to keep the audience safe from the likes of us. The walk to the doors is a short one. I have been lost in my own world. A hand on my lower back scares the shit out of me. I manage to hold back the scream rising in my throat. *Smooth, Reika.*

"Give 'em hell, Baby." A soft kiss lands on my shoulder, sending a shiver down my spine.

"Let's go" by Trick Daddy blares out through the speakers. With a deep breath, I make my way to the cage. The crowd goes wild when they lay eyes on me. I usually get a mixed reception from spectators. Some cheer like I am a damn celebrity, while others boo or shout abuse in my direction. Viper is already in the cage throwing daggers my way. Yeah, he is definitely still pissed. Well, this should be interesting... tap out or knock out.

Looking at my opponent, I study his movements as he hops about like he has a cactus stuck up his ass. Right leg, knee issue. He isn't putting a lot of weight on it. Left shoulder is dropped slightly further than his right. He has either broken it before or it was recently dislocated and not set back correctly. A wide smile spreads across my face, my breathing calm and even. That's all I need to do; I don't jump about like this idiot does. The announcer finishes his introductions for the fight, and gives the spectators two minutes to place their bets. I would be surprised if Viper and I aren't evenly matched. We are pretty much the same height. His build is slightly larger than mine, but I am packing more muscle than he is.

"Fight." Game on bitch. Viper charges forward trying to use speed to his advantage. I step out of his left jab, and he falls face first onto the cage. His nostrils flare, and I can't help but chuckle. He charges at me again, and I laugh at the stupidity. I keep the game of cat and mouse up for about five more minutes.

"You're dead, bitch," Viper screams. I'm grinning like I've won the lottery, then I smirk at him. He charges again. Fuck this shit. I set my stance and wait. *Thump*. With an uppercut to his bottom jaw, he's lifted off his feet before landing flat on his back with a sickening thud. He's out cold.

"Your winner ladies and gentlemen. The Reaper!" The announcer screams my victory through the microphone. The crowd goes wild. My brain is in a haze from the atmosphere. It is nothing like the fights I'm used to. Blinding lights blaze down from the ceiling as the spectators are sitting around massive circular tables drinking champagne. The cage, however, is what I would have expected. It is just as grim and dirty as the one from the warehouse. Stepping down the steps, I head back to the changing room with Kane and Marcus walk just behind me on either side. When we arrive, Liam blocks my path.

"Nice fight. At least that's something you're good at." With a wink, Liam wanders off in the direction of the cage.

Kane

"Sorry, man." Ivan blocks my way at the door of the changing rooms.

"What the fuck? Get out of the way. I want to be with my girl." Who does this fuckface think he is, blocking my path? Pretty Bird shocked the whole audience putting Viper on his ass like that. Her training with Ivan and Mateo has been brutal, but it clearly paid off. Fucking hell, she was dangerous before, but now she's downright lethal and she's all mine. I can't wait until this is over, so I can get her home. We haven't had much time to spend together, and I am dying to get my hands on her.

"Let her chill out before the next round, man. If she gets through that, I will let you in."

"What do you mean if she gets through that?" Is he starting to second guess her? I can't believe this piece of shit. His eyes dart around as he rubs the back of his neck. "You'll see. She will need you if she makes the final." What the fuck have they organized for the final?

Unease settles in my stomach; I have a bad feeling about this. But if we pull her out now, shit with De'Marco will escalate. He backed off after he watched a training session between the guys and Pretty Bird. He's been quiet and not a giant pain in the ass.

"I don't like this, Marcus." Looking at my brother, I see he has a scowl on his face.

"Me either, bro. We will deal with whatever it is."

We head back to our seats to watch the next round. The guys in this match up are almost as tall as me and my brothers. The fight lasts longer than hers did, but the winner is The Deviant. He's good, scarily good. He's definitely had training with people on par with Ivan and Mateo. A sick and twisted smirk spreads across his face as he looks at his opponent who has blood pouring out of his nose and mouth. He makes his way out of the cage. Instead of heading to the changing rooms, he heads towards our table. The smirk he had on his face when he left the cage, is replaced by a stone-cold expression. Pulling the seat out across from me, he sits down like we are old friends.

"Your girlfriend is dead, Soulless. Get ready to pick her flowers out." Lunging across the table, I grip his neck and pull him over back to my side. Marcus tears me away from the bastard who is now on the floor laughing his ass off.

"Calm down, Kane. Fucking hell." Spinning so I'm face to face with my brother, my whole body is vibrating with anger at his words.

"Calm down or get out," Marcus says, in a hushed tone. I know he's right, but having to see all this, that bastard's taunt pushed my unease over the top.

"Kane, can you hear me?" His words are muffled. I see that he's talking to me, but I can't understand what's being said. It's as if cotton wool is stuffed in my ears, blocking my hearing. He waves to one of the guys we brought with us.

"Get him outta here. I'll call you when you can bring him back." My body won't move. I can't tell Marcus to fuck off because it feels like my mouth has been wired shut.

"I've got her, Bro. Be ready to celebrate." With that, I'm dragged me out of the arena, toward the car.

21

MARCUS

I should've known it wouldn't take long for Kane to lose his shit. All it took was one waste-of-space fighter pushing his damn buttons. We knew this would happen with the other fighters. The men in this world don't take kindly to a woman that can do things better than them, especially when that thing is kicking their ass.

Liam has gone AWOL too. I don't have a clue what's wrong with him, but the tension between him and Hellion is off the charts. Thank God he came tonight to show a united front to the other crews. If they see so much as a blip in our armor, they will pounce.

"Now, ladies and gentlemen. The last semi-finals match up. The Reaper verses The Destroyer."

How the fuck did I miss the last round, for fuck's sake? I need to start paying attention. Kane will fucking gut me if anything happens to her. I spot Hellion looking around the tables for us. When she finds me, she looks worried that Kane isn't sitting here with me. Quickly giving her a thumbs up to let her know everything is ok, the tension leaves her body. I fire off a quick message to Kane letting him know she's up and I will keep him updated. I manage to send the message without looking at the screen. I watch intently as they size each other up. I'm really fucking glad Kane isn't here, because he would be having a seizure at the size difference between these two. But Hellion isn't fazed one bit.

Kane:
Please tell me she's ok?

Me:
Bro, they haven't even started yet.

Kane:
Let me know she isn't hurt!

Me:
Chill out man! Girl means business!

The roar of the crowd draws my attention back to the cage. Quickly putting my phone on silent, I watch as she moves around the cage like a pro. Watching her train with Ivan and Mateo was hell, but damn, I have to admit they did train her well. I'm amazed at how fluid her movements are, but her signature savagery is still there. I nearly choke on my drink when she dick punches him, and he drops to the floor screaming like a bitch. Hellion looks down on him and pounces. She puts the guy on his front with his left arm twisted behind his back, and her knee resting on his shoulder. A maniacal laugh flows from her like this is her favorite thing. She applies more pressure, and his shoulder gives way under her with a sickening crunch.

He screams, making Hellion laugh more. Security rushes in, dragging her away from The Destroyer. She grins as they pull her away, the crowd silent as she laughs her ass off. Security removes her with everything they have, and she just continues to laugh like a psycho. The Destroyer hasn't moved; I think he has passed out cold. They manage to get her out of the cage and drag her toward the changing rooms. I go to follow, but Mateo stops me in my tracks.

"We need to talk about your brother."

"Which one?"

"Liam."

Reika

"Get your fucking hands of me, clown!" I roar at the bastard man handling me. It's not like I'm putting up a fight. I just found the whole thing hilarious. The changing room door swings open, then I'm flying.

I hit something with a thud, I yelp as the pain from my injuries scream in protest. Some motherfucker just tossed me on my ass in the changing room. What the actual fuck? Adrenaline pours through my veins. I can't believe I have made it this far in The Royale. My whole body is a live wire with zaps of electricity tingling all over. I can't stand still. Pacing up and down quiet the locker room, there is nothing to dull my buzz.

Suddenly, the changing room goes pitch black. I hear the women in the crowd screaming. Something is going down. Leaving my bag, I head to the door to find out what's happening. Peeking my head around, I see bodies running in different directions.

"Hey, what the fuck is going on?" I shout to a security guard as he runs past like his ass is on fire. He doesn't even bother to answer me. The screams and shouts are growing louder out in the main arena. Everyone is in a panic. Cautiously walking down the corridor, I head off to search for Kane. Maybe he knows what's going on. My body comes alive again, something feels off about this. I make it to the doors leading to the main arena, when something is placed over my mouth. My body goes into fight mode as darkness starts to creep in on me, my body going limp in my attacker's arms. My inner voice screams at me internally. *Fight Reika!*

22

REIKA

A weird noise rattles in my head. Shit! Why do people have to make so much damn noise when you're trying to sleep? Is there any courtesy anymore? Slowly the fog in my brain starts to lift. Opening my eyes, I try to shake the black spots from my vision, but nothing. I try a couple more times before my brain catches up to my surroundings. I am in a dark room lit up slightly by a single lamp, on the other side, next to a chair. A clink catches my attention. Pain rips across my shoulders. Lifting my head, I'm suspended in the air from a pipe by chains around my arms. That explains the pain. What the fuck happened? Where the hell are the guys? This makes no sense. Trying my hardest to remember what went down at the Royale, I get lost in my thoughts.

"Welcome home, Reaper," a deep gravel-filled voice says from the darkness.

"Home? Are you smoking crack dude?" I scoff at the voice. Honestly, home? It's don't expect the Ritz, and don't get me wrong, I kind of like this kinky shit, but I really don't think Kane would be down for this. I chuckle at the thought; the perfect image of his horrified face comes to mind.

"You are home, Girl. Well, you will be, once you accept your fate." The voice doesn't as sound so gravelly. It's more robotic sounding now. My fate? What is he, my fairy godfather or something? Because if he is, I really got the shit stain of the bunch.

"You seem confused, Sweetie. You want me to enlighten you?" The echo has me grinding my teeth. I am so fucking done with this creepy shit.

"What I want is for your stupid ass to unchain me."

"Not going to happen. I'm not that stupid," he laughs, although it seems forced. "You belong here with me."

"You? Dude, you are definitely on something. I am not yours. Plus, I'm with someone." Did I hit my head? I must have and landed my ass in a different dimension.

"Ah yeah, Kane." He steps into the light so I can see his face. Well, I could see his face if there wasn't a creepy as shit mask covering his face.

"You actually know who he is?" If they do, then why the fuck would they risk taking me? "You know what? I don't give a shit. They will come for me. I know they will."

Well, I know without a doubt that Cheshire will. Kane is still an unknown. I do have feelings for him, which I wanted to tell him after the Royale. I can't be the only one who feels the spark between us. Cheshire wouldn't leave me here, and I'm pretty sure he would make Kane find me too.

Laughter breaks out around me, bouncing off the walls of the room. Pain to rushes through my head as my existing headache grows. The look in my captor's eyes turns manic. Gripping my face, he squeezes so hard I feel like my jaw will to crack. Flicking his eyes between mine, "You really think he gives a shit about you, don't you?" Confusion layers his voice. From what I can make out now, he's closer to me.

"Yeah, I do. He's very protective. I can't wait to see what he does to you." Fucking stupid ass. When the guys realize I am missing, they won't stop until they find me.

Pain radiates through my jaw from the blow he delivers. I can't help but laugh. The chicken shit decked me while I am dangling from the ceiling. Such a bitch move. My laughter only antagonizes him further, and he doles out blow after blow until pain is radiating through my whole body. I can feel the blood running down my face and ribs. My chin rests on my chest, and my wheeze can be heard across the room from my labored breathing. Exhaustion is radiating off me. I am so tired. My arms are killing me. This fucker thinks he can beat on me? My brain scrambles trying and work out how long I've been here.

"Are we going to keep this up, Reaper?" He can go take a long walk off a short pier, for all I care. The guys must have noticed by now that I am missing. I can't bring myself to reply. The beating picks up again. When he finally decides to stop, my eyes start closing on their own. No sound has passed my lips since he began pacing in front of me, ranting to himself. My eyes drift shut, and sleep pulls me in.

Red hot pain shoots across my stomach just above my belly button. I am instantly alert to my surroundings.

"Motherfucker!" My scream echoes around the room, joined by a laugh that sends chills down my spine.

"Look who's awake. Was I boring you?" the voice jokes.

"Fuck you!"

Everything hurts so fucking much. My throat feels like there is cotton wool stuffed down my it, with razor blades hidden inside. My eyes sting from the grit and blood running into them. My shoulders feel like they're about to tear off any minute. I don't know how much longer I have before I pass out from the pain again, but I can't do that.

"He will come for me." My voice is barely a whisper, I

struggle to even hear them leave my mouth. But, whoever this asshat is doesn't miss my words.

"You really think he will come, don't you?"

"I know he will." When I get out of this, I need to be honest with Kane about my feelings. The asshole starts shaking his head while tutting, striding out of the light. I hear a door slam across the room, and my body relaxes slightly.

Suddenly the door slams open again and I hear excited voices. The asshole shows his masked face with two other guys, wheeling in a TV on some kind of trolley.

"His name is Kane Southbourne. Leader of the Damned Crew." Shock renders me speechless. No, he has to be lying. Surely, they would have told me who they were. How could I have been so stupid?

"Their dad ordered the hit on your mother and father." Rage boils under the surface of my skin, all the pain and fatigue I feel is pushed to the back of my mind.

"You're lying," I scream at him, my emotions are all over the place. Nothing makes sense.

"He doesn't give a shit about you!" he screams back at me. He starts mumbling to himself. I can't wrap my head around any of this. Why would they lie about who they are?

Exhaustion presses in on me. How the fuck I missed who they were? I so blinded by the feeling of being one of them that I didn't question anything. I completely missed that they are the ones I've been looking for. A TV screen blinds me as the asshole turns it on, my eyes are glued to the screen as a gritty video begins to play.

"You really think any of them give a shit about you?" His words only just register. I'm horrified by what I see on the screen. My heart starts to beat erratically at his words, unease building in my stomach. A malicious smile spreads across his face.

"That shit won't work on me, asshole." How fucking stupid does he think I am? Laughter fills the room. He seems to find this hilarious if his deep belly laugh is any indication. My guys wouldn't set me up like this. I know they wouldn't.

"Look at the bottom left corner."

My eyes drift to the bottom left-hand corner of the screen, where I see the date and time stamp of the film. My head and heart are at war. My heart starts to crack as everything slots into place, but my brain refuses to accept that he would do this to me. I don't want to believe this. Kane did tell me to trust him, and I said I would. Strength and determination pour through me. This madman is just playing games with me; he is concerned about Kane for a reason. There has to be an explanation about my parents' death and why they haven't told me they are the Damned Crew. I lift my head slowly with a grin on my face, looking this motherfucker in the eye.

"You stupid girl. You are nothing to them." He strides toward me, his intent clear in his eyes.

Everything turns to background noise. Pain radiates throughout my body as he gets another beating under way. Suddenly, the screen is switched to another video. This video is clearer than the last. My eyes widen at what is happening on the screen. Screams tear from my throat as I violently shake my chains to get free. The attack from the man in the room escalates as I try to free myself. A noise reaches my ears, halting my movements. Small fissures start to crack through my heart. Ice builds in my veins. I feel nothing except the all-consuming pain of my heart shattering into millions of little pieces. My head drops to my chest in defeat as a tear slips from the corner of my eye. Watching it fall through the air and mix in with the blood on the floor, the million shattered pieces of my heart turn to dust.

23

MARCUS

"Where is she?"

Standing in the meeting room and watching the devastation on my brothers face because absolutely guts me. Hellion hasn't been found yet. Kane and I have both been hit hard over her disappearance, but I wasn't prepared for this. Slowly, Kane has lost control of his inner monster, and his sanity along with it. He has become unpredictable and volatile, a truly dangerous combination. Fights are breaking out within the crew because they are starting to question his leadership. We cannot afford to appear weak, especially with everything else going on. Looking around the room at the terror on the crew's face, we must find her and fast and get Kane back to himself.

My jean's pocket starts to vibrate, startling me from my despair. I pull my phone out and look at the caller ID. Fox's name flashes at me.

"Man, you best have some fucking good news for me." I have everything crossed that this is the call I have been desperate for. Kane tears through the room like a man possessed, his demons riding him hard as his control slips further. Liam being AWOL isn't helping either. Seriously, why now? What could possibly be more important than family?

"You're going to hate me for this, man. But my lead went cold." My whole-body freezes. My heart stops. I'd swear this was an out of body experience if I wasn't living this hell. How can she drop off the face of the earth like this? Someone has her. She wouldn't run from us. Would she?

"Marcus, you still there?"Fox's voice comes through the line with a little unease.

"Yeah. I'm still here. I need you to get your ass into the office ASAP."

"What for?" his tone comes out high pitched with surprise.

"Don't fucking question me. Just get your ass here." Ending the call, I turn to face the direction of the noise echoing around the room.

All the crew members are frozen in place, each wearing a mask of fear or desperately trying for indifference. How do I tell my brother our leads are cold?

After the Royale, when Ivan and Mateo realized Reika was gone, we argued between us over who would tell Kane. Unfortunately, word spread faster than our ability to make a decision, and Kane turned up in the arena like a madman, tearing through the warehouse looking for her. He interrogated anyone working The Royale for information. But when they had nothing of use to tell us, the night ended with bloodshed and a pile of bodies to get rid of.

"All members. Get out!" my voice booms across the room, so loud some of the them duck. Not needing to be told twice, everyone runs out the door like hellfire itself is on their ass. I give myself a moment to prepare. Fuck, I need to get my head straight. This is going to go down like a lead balloon.

"Please tell me they have her?" Kane asks. Slowly lifting my eyes to my brother, I try to hold my emotions in check so nothing shows on my face. I've had a lot of practice at wearing this mask of indifference recently. The town wouldn't survive another manic episode from Kane. He's standing so close to me; I hadn't realized he'd moved into my personal space. I can see every emotion playing across his features as he tries to keep the darkness at bay. Hope and fear are the two most potent, burning brightly in his eyes. Betrayal as well, but to be honest, I have that at the forefront of my mind too, though I'm constantly doing my best to dismiss it.

"Fox is coming into the office." These are the only words I can bring myself to speak. Kane's whole body looks like it's vibrating, like a ticking time bomb ready to blow. His look of defeat has my own emotions in turmoil.

Looking up at the sound of something hitting the floor, I find my brother on his knees, his head on his chest. Gently placing my hand on his shoulder, I bring myself down into a crouch so to meet his gaze. Well, I would meet his gaze if it wasn't glued to the floor. He is so lost in his despair that all I can hear is a mumble of unintelligible words leaving him.

Wrapping my arms around his shoulders, I pull him into a bone crushing hug. Kane is the strongest man I have ever known, but he is falling to pieces in my arms. I'm not sure I'm strong enough to hold the both of us together. I think it might be time to call the doc in and have him sedated. He desperately needs rest. Then it's time I hunt down my twat of a twin to see what part he had to play in this. His absence speaks volumes. I don't want to believe he had a hand in this, but the facts don't lie.

"Bro, I need you to get up." I plead with Kane, as he remains on his knees.

"Why did she do this. This is the reason I don't care. It hurts too much." Kane whispers and my heart breaks for him. He finally lets someone in, and this happens. My brain can't come to terms with the broken man on his knees. This isn't my brother.My brother is strong, a fighter; he doesn't fall, not ever. But this man before me is only a shell of the man I have known all my life. His shoulders collapse in on themselves as he mutters to himself. Searching for answers to questions not even God himself has answers too. I would love to ask the bastard myself why things had to unfold this way. Our family has never been religious, but fuck me, if it would help repair the damage to my brother's heart, I would go to church all day, every day.

Kane's broken mutterings draw my eyes back to him once again. His arms are wrapped around his body as he rocks back and forth asking the question, "Why did she do this?" My anger grows not only for how broken he is, but the fact that he blames her for what's happened. I don't believe she ran. She would not do that. My self-control snaps.

"Get your fucking ass up, Kane. She needs you." My anger burns under my skin, and I can't seem to stop the words from pouring from my mouth. He flinches at my tone, but I don't stop.

"She could be fighting with everything she has to get back here." With a shake of his head, he turns away from me. Is he really that blind, or has he just given up on the world already?

"She fucking loves you! Anyone who watched you two together could see it." Grabbing hold of his face, I force him to look at me and see the truth in my eyes.

"You said she was yours, Kane. So do what you have to do to bring her home." Slowly standing back to my full height, I bring my gaze back to my brother's slumped body on the floor. Everything in me is screaming for him to pick himself up off the floor. *Be the man I know you are, brother!*

"Get up, Kane," I growl, my fury burning white hot through my veins. "Get your fucking ass up off the floor!" I scream at him. Where has his fight gone?

Nothing. No reaction at all. I can't understand how he's allowed himself to become so defeated. I know he fears she ran, I do to, but I won't accept that until she is standing in front of me and tells me so herself.

"If you want to feel sorry for yourself, I'm done, you're on your own. I will find Reika. Then you can explain to her why you weren't there." Spinning on my heels, I stride toward the meeting room door. It's time I get things in motion and do what my brother can't. No matter how hard it is, I will not give up on her. On him. On them.

REIKA

"Wake up, bitch."

That voice could put the fear of Satan into anyone. It haunts me in my sleep and well into the daylight hours when my mind tries to play tricks on me. It has to be that time again; I try not to acknowledge the voice, pissing him off even more. Honestly, what does he expect? That today will be the day I break? I'm not certain how much time has passed because the days and nights blend together, but one thing he will not make me do is break.

"Aww, the little princess doesn't want to play?" God, this guy's voice grates on my nerves, it's like nails scraping down a chalkboard. If I wasn't as malnourished as I am, I would kill this motherfucker without a second thought. On second thought, a quick death is too easy for someone like him. Covering him in petrol and burning the bastard alive sounds like a better idea.

I haven't even got the energy to pick myself up off the dirty floor my blankets are on. So, the murderous thoughts I have on the regular are just that, thoughts that get me through the isolation. My new home is a dank, disgusting room with no windows. A single steel door at the end is the only entry point. I turn myself away from the asshole. I really can't be bothered with his shit today. Since the first night I was taken, I have only seen the man in this room twice. He asks me if I have decided to be his, I answer 'No,' and he tells this other fucker to 'break me.' Guess what? He is still failing, much to his master's annoyance. Searing hot pain radiates through my scalp. Before I can even react, I am being dragged across the hard concrete floor.

"Listen up, you stupid little whore."

I'm frantically trying to get some traction on the ground with my feet. My unease grows as he snarls down at me every now and then and spits at me. Something's off. He's always been a hostile dick, but this is different. The anger in his voice and look on his face are more hostile than usual. I notice a few new injuries and scars on him. I guess his boss is pretty angry this piece of shit hasn't broken me. Finally, I spot something I can use to my advantage.

Sticking my heel in a divot on the floor, I use the last of my energy to push myself into a turn, causing the asshole to stumble, releasing his grip on my hair. Pulling my knees up to my chest, I pray that in my debilitated state I will have enough power to do some damage. Once the asshole gets his footing, he comes charging at me like a pissed off bull. I keep my legs up, and wait until he's close enough. With all the power I can manage, I kick out with both my legs and connect with his chest.

My eyes nearly bug out of my head when the asshole is thrown a couple of feet away from me. Not wanting to waste any time, I scramble to my feet as fast as I can and take off running toward the door. Not having any weapons is a nightmare, but a girl's gotta do what a girl's gotta do, and my ass is getting out of dodge, no matter what.

Stepping out into the dimly light hallway, a groan reaches my ears. I look over my shoulder and realize the asshole's waking up. I make a run for it. Another door to comes into view at the end of the corridor. My legs move as fast as they can as my muscles scream in protest. I make it to the door. Praying it's unlocked, I give the handle a tug. The door clicks open and my heart rate reaches a whole new level, excitement thrumming in my veins. What the fuck? I step out into another dimly lit hallway with doors on either side; this place is like a fucking maze. This must be the main building. I strain my hearing to try and pick up any movement nearby. I haven't heard an alarm or anything yet, so that has to be a good sign, right?Not wanting to push my luck any further, I don't hang around. I push through the door and take off running again.

"Well. Well. How did you get out, you little bitch?" Fear courses through my veins. I quickly throw a look over my shoulder and I notice he is standing a couple of doorways down from me. With my heart rate reaching the pace of a runaway train, I push myself faster to put distance between us.

Static reaches my ears. It's just my luck that jackass would have a radio on him. I need to get out of here, and fast. The end of the hallway comes into view, splitting to the left and right. I take a breath and turn left, praying my gut decision hasn't screwed me over. My lungs feel like they're about to explode, my legs feel heavy like weights. It's sheer determination to get out of this shit-hole that keeps me pushing forward. I'm fighting my body every second as it feels like it's about to give out on me.

A stream of light bursts through the gloomy hallway, like a beacon of hope. I push myself harder. Flicking my eyes up, I see a women step into the corridor. I throw every last ounce of energy I can muster into my muscles. If I can just make it outside, I can steal a car or something. Thank God, she hasn't even noticed me charging at her. Just as we are about to collide, she screams like a banshee and jumps out of my way, leaving the door wide open.

Fresh air slams into me, a mixture of scents assaulting my senses. It's heaven after inhaling that dank oxygen in my cell. My eyes finally adjusting to the brightness outside, I look around realizing I am in front of an office building with a driveway. Getting my bearings, I search the area looking for a car or motorbike, even a goddamn bicycle would be awesome right about now. The sunlight bounces off something to my right, hidden away at the side of the building. I throw a look over my shoulder to check that no one is following me, when I hear commotion from inside. Heavy footfall thunders from inside, headed in my direction, while a gruff voice barks orders. Fatigue weighs me down as I run as fast as I can to the side of the building.

I spot a silver Mercedes parked there. My breath whooshes out of my lungs and excitement starts to bubble in my veins. Stepping to the back window on the driver's side, I prepare myself to break the window. I would usually pad my elbow to stop my skin from being torn to pieces, but in my current clothes that is not an option. A door slams shut at the front of the building, and I hear several male voices arguing amongst themselves. Bringing my elbow to the angle needed, I take a deep breath and force as much power into the blow as possible.

"I'm sorry."

My knees give way, as pain roars through the back of my skull. Laying face first on the gravel, I see the shoes of the person who hit me. My eyes grow heavy as I feel myself being pulled into someone's arms. I want to fight but my limbs won't cooperate. *I was so close.* My thoughts trail off as the darkness pulls me under.

Pain radiates through my head like shock waves as I groan. My mouth is as dry as the Sahara Desert, and it feels like I have razor blades shoved down my throat. The words 'I'm sorry' are playing on repeat in my head. What did my attacker mean by that?

Someone clears their throat, catching my attention, but I can't look at the person responsible because it feels like my eyes have been glued shut. My memories flicker in and out in a hazy mess. That must have been one hell of a hit to mess me up this much. Whoever cleared their throat decides to do it again, a bit more forcefully this time. I don't even attempt to reply to the mystery person, because considering the only suitable response in this situation is 'Fuck off, asshole,' my mouth is likely to get me into trouble.

"You just have to cause trouble, don't you, Reaper?"

Feeling starts to return to my limbs. I try to lift my arm, but I can't move it more than about an inch. I hiss as pain roars through my muscles. Damn that shit hurts! Prying my eyes open to look down, I find I'm tied to a chair-bound by my wrists and ankles. I was expecting to be back in my cage. I should have known once they caught me, they wouldn't put me back there, but I still expected the usual torture chamber. Nope, I currently find myself in a room I've never seen before.

Huge floor to ceiling windows line one entire wall, while a sleek black desk takes pride of place in front of me. The desk the only color in the room, everything else is the purest white. Four men stand in the room. Three have strategically placed themselves between the door and the man standing behind the desk, like the lord of the manor. Haven't these douche canoes realized yet? I'm not impressed by their macho bullshit. Like seriously, c'mon guys, up your game for fuck's sake.

"Reaper. Oh, sorry, my bad. Reika," he snickers. "What are we going to do with you?"

I meet his gaze, not breaking eye contact as I give a slight shrug of my shoulders. I would have opened my mouth to reply, but I am not sure I would be able to manage words right now. Exhaustion drags through my veins. Running like I did wasn't the best idea for my battered body, but the opportunity came, so why wouldn't I take the chance? Frustration flickers across his features, pulling a strange sounding chuckle from me. I can't help it. I grin as wide as possible. I'm sure I look completely insane, but it just feels right.

"Do you not realize how much your defiance is hurting you?" Scoffing at his words, I keep my gaze on him and twist my neck just a bit to try and release some of the tension.

"Defiance? What did you expect, really?" The sarcasm drips from my words as he glares at me causing another chuckle to bubble up in the back of my throat "Did you think I was going to get tired and do as the lord commands?" He snarls at me, annoyance replaced by anger. "You've had me locked up for God knows how long. You've starved me, and you want me to be compliant? Fuck you!"

He roars, launching himself across the space between us. He grabs hold of my face and squeezes. From this close, I can see he's seething.

"Say yes to taking your place at my side, and all the pain stops." He tightens his grip further. My teeth start to ache under the pressure. Any sane person in this situation would keep their mouth shut. But I never said I was sane. I lower my gaze and prepare myself for the consequences of the actions I'm about to commit.

Lifting my gaze up slowly, I allow a smile to spread across

my face. Keeping my voice as low as possible, "I…" He leans in to better hear me, and I lash out with my head, hitting him square in his nose with a satisfying crunch.

"Argh!" A chorus of shouts from the other men ring out in the room, like music to my ears.

My brain didn't have enough time to register that I'd been hit until now. I'm on my side on the floor. An ache across the left side of my jaw. This fucker just pimp slapped me. What the fuck? Anger burns through me like super-heated lava. These bastards have to starve me and keep me chained, because they know if I was at full strength, they would die very slowly by my hands.

Growling to the other men, Fancy Pants starts pacing around the room. Every now and then his gaze drifts to me and his growls turn thunderous. One of the others leaves through a door I hadn't noticed behind the desk. When it closes, I realize why - it looks like a fucking wall. Ha that's kinda cool. The pain in my already battered body increases, pulling a hiss from my throat. The man returns to the room through the secret door with a black pouch in his hands. Fancy Pants perks up at this, smiling. I'm sure he means it to intimidating, but really?

"Pick her ass up." His snarls as he gently, almost lovingly, places the pouch on his desk. In perfect view of me, so I have to watch as he slowly unwraps it. God, clearly this asshole is going for a dramatic reveal.

A snort leaves me at this thought which draws the attention of all the men in the room.Two of them grab hold of my chair and yank me back into an upright position. The speed with which they do this causes my stomach to roll.

"Let's see how funny you find this, bitch." My head is still fuzzy from everything that's happened, and I don't even bother to lift head it from my chest. Honestly, I think I might throw up at any moment.

"Do you still hope they are going to come for you?" His eyes dance like he has fire flies in them, while he whistles a tune to himself.

An animalistic growl rumbles from my throat. Ever since I saw the videos, any mention of them turns me feral. Father would be so angry with me for showing emotion, but I'm not gonna lie, what was in those videos cut me deeper than anything else ever has.

"He never wanted you... He was the one that gave us the go ahead to take you."

My heart stutters at his words. I don't know why. What I do know is nothing surprises me anymore. I was just a gullible sap who opened her legs for an asshole who played the game better than I did. This is the last time I ever allow anyone to get the upper hand on me.

"They knew who you were as soon as they saw you in the cage. They lured you in and you fell for it. Hook, line and sinker.

"Speak! Reika, I want to know what you're thinking?" he growls.

"You talk too much, asshole." My body jolts in my seat as manic laughter fills the room. You know that strange state of mind you go into when something terrible happens? Like your mind is trying its hardest to catch up with your body, but instead you fall down the rabbit hole into oblivion? The laughter increases in volume, the hysteria grows making Fancy Pants and his goons uncomfortable, looking around the room at each other.

It's then that I realize the laughter is mine. My brain finally caught up, and my body is in shock from a big-ass hunting knife sticking out of my thigh. I must have truly snapped, because I don't feel a damn thing. I just continue to laugh at this shit show I've found myself in. I must have a manic expression on my face, because Fancy Pants takes another step back.

"Aww, what's the matter, fuckface? Am I too crazy for you?" My laughter builds even more, at the looks of uncertainty on their faces. It's like their staring at their worst nightmare. In reality, it's just little old me strapped to a chair, making them shit themselves.

My father's favorite song comes to the front of my mind, and I start to hum the tune. My humming continues until the words for the song start to flow from my mouth.

"One, two. I'm coming for you. Three, four. Better lock your door." I repeat the start of the song over and over. The room is silent apart from my song. Which I find hilarious, so I take a break from singing and burst out laughing, loving the sound of it echoing around the room.

Pain radiates through the back of my skull once more and darkness bleeds in from the corners of my eyes. The last words I hear before unconsciousness welcomes me once more are,

"It's definitely her."

25

MARCUS

"What do you mean your lead went cold?"

"Exactly what I said. Nobody knows where she is," explains Fox. Pondering Fox's words, I turn to look at Kane. I can't stop the flood of emotions rising inside me. Liam had something to do with this. He has been MIA since the night of the Royale. It's too much of a coincidence that he disappeared after Hellion was taken. As much as I hope he isn't the reason behind all of this, I can't shake that feeling of foreboding that surrounds me every time I think of him.

"Find Liam." I look back to Fox, so my eyes aren't on Kane. I see the horror my words cause in Fox's eyes, clear as day, while his face is frozen in shock.

"You think he had something to do with this?" Fox takes a step back, eyes wide.

"He made it clear he hated her and Kane together. I wouldn't put it past him." A deep growl fills the room, Fox's face slowly turns ashen at the ferocity of it.

Kane is close to losing his shit again, and I don't have the time to deal with another mammoth clean up if he does. With a nod to Fox, he knows it's time for him to leave. He's off, leaving dust clouds in his wake. I turn to my brother, "Get some sleep, will you?"

"How do you expect me to sleep. I need her, Marcus." His voice is shrill as he rings his hands together.

"I know and I am doing everything in my power to find her, but I need you in a functioning state, Kane."

I've been through this with him too many times since that night. If he's going to bring her home, I need him at his best with a clear mind and the level of ruthlessness only my he has. I pull my phone out of my pocket and scroll through the contacts in search of Doc's number. He answers on the first ring. Before he has chance to speak, I say, "Doc, it's time."

The line goes dead, and I'm left staring at the phone in my hand. I have put off ringing Doc because I know Kane will refuse sedation out of fear of becoming like Mother. He has never forgiven himself for the night she disappeared. No matter how many times everyone tells him he isn't to blame, he never believes us. He's determined to punish himself for things that were out of his control.

I walk over to where he's sitting on the couch and notice his eyes glazed over from exhaustion, not really focused on anything. There is a slight tremble to his arms. I'm not sure how much longer his body can keep up like this. "C'mon, bro."

Hooking his arm over my shoulder as gently as possible, I help walk him up to her room. He hasn't stepped foot in here since she disappeared, but honestly, I think it's what he needs to feel closer to her. His legs are barely keeping him up and our pace is slow going. If I don't get him into a room soon, I'm likely to end up on my ass. Fuck me, I forgot how heavy this bastard is. Finally making it to Hellion's room, I move us both as quickly as I can before he collapses.

The fact that he hasn't uttered a word about where we are is concerning. I have no idea where his mind is right now. I gently place him down on the mattress when, thankfully, Doc walks through the door. With a quick nod from me, Doc rushes over to where Kane is lying and jabs him in the thigh with an injection before he can protest.

"Motherfucker!" He roars as he lurches off the bed. Yeah, if you haven't guessed it already, my badass, big brother is terrified of injections. Normally I would rib him about it. It doesn't take long before his breathing evens out and his body relaxes.

"Thanks, Doc."

"Marcus. You need to do something. I don't think there is enough sedation in the world for when he utterly loses it." His eyes move in every direction but don't land on me once. I know the fear he feels.

"I know."

I spend five minutes watching my brother go into what I hope is an undisturbed sleep. Now that I don't have to worry about him for a bit, I can sort shit out within the crew and get things back under control.

Kane

What the fuck is going on? *I am currently standing in my childhood bedroom.* Shit this is a trip. What the fuck did the doc put in that syringe?

"Kane. They're at it again." I turn to the voice and see Marcus standing at my doorway talking to my younger self. I watch intently, call it the masochist in me. I remember what day this memory is from.

"It's ok, bro. They will kiss and make up soon enough, you

235

know what they're like."

"I don't think so, it feels different this time."

"What do you mean?" My younger self cocks his head at the words.

"They are arguing over your marriage."

Horror spreads across my face. "What do you mean my fucking marriage? I'm sixteen for fuck's sake."

"I know, Bro. But that's what I heard."

Screams ring out around the house from my mother. I watch in horror as me and Marcus charge toward the noise. It's as if I'm a glutton for punishment as I follow.

"You can't do this to him, Malcolm!" My mother screams at my father.

"They are my sons, Amelia. I will do with them as I please."

The teenage me and Marcus are hiding behind the corner of the corridor looking down the stairs at my parents below.

"Malcolm, you promised we would never get involved with them."

"Amelia, the Grimm's are stepping up their attacks on our territories."

"I don't give a shit, kill all of them if you have to, but please, not this."

"We have tried that and they come back like fucking cockroaches."

"The Butcher. Call in the fucking Butcher Malcolm!"

"This deal with the Russians will make the crew more powerful, you stupid bitch."

"Bitch! How fucking dare you. I am your wife!"

"No, you gave me heirs, that's all. Why do you think I have fucked everything and anything other than you for the last 5 years?" Watching my mother drop to the floor at my father's words causes my stomach to churn uneasily.

"Kane will marry Mila Drago when he is eighteen, and that is it!"

My mother runs out of the room at his words. I stand and watch my reaction, seeing the horror on mine and my brothers' faces. They don't know what I do, that the marriage never goes ahead because a year later Mila commits suicide, but it's not her that has tears gathering in my eyes. My younger self heads back to his room in anger and disbelief at his father's words.

A few hours pass as I watch my younger self pacing the room. When my door opens, my heart sinks.

"Baby?" My younger self looks up to find my mother in my room.

"I know you heard what your father said just then."

"Yes, mother."

"I won't let him do this. I am going away for a couple of weeks, then I will come back and get you and your brothers."

"Where are you going?"

"I have a plan. Keep your brothers safe for me?"

"I promise, Mother."

With a kiss to my head, she leaves my room. The smile that spreads across the face of my younger self is gutting. His face is filled with so much hope. He has dreams to get out of this shithole life. But what he doesn't know, is that this would be the last time he ever saw his mother again.

26

LIAM

Everything is muffled. I don't know how long I have been here trying to drink my feelings into oblivion. I do keep going back to check on my brothers, but I can't bring myself to approach them when I get there. That night plays on repeat in my head like some broken old-fashioned black and white movie. I really thought I was doing the right thing. But seeing my brother's reactions as they tore through the warehouse looking for her, my soul crumbled piece by miserable fucking piece. I never meant to break them. She was trouble, or so I thought, and now I have to make things right. Even if that is an impossibility, I must try to right my wrongs, or else they'll never forgive me.

"Earth to asshat." Slowly lifting my gaze to the bartender, I see frustration on his face. He must have been trying to get my attention for some time.

"What's up?" I ask him, annoyance layering my voice. Can't he see I don't want to be disturbed?

"Time to pay up and get out." Throwing a stack of bills on the bar, I down the last of my Jack and Coke. I decide to head back to the motel I've been staying in and figure out my next move.

Back in the dingy room, I force myself to stay awake as exhaustion and guilt try to pull me under. I pick up the files and have another read through to see if I've missed anything. All the information I've gathered on Reika and her family is limited at best and practically useless at worst. It's as if she never existed up until seven years ago. There is one name that repeatedly shows up on the paperwork, a Pete Marshall. Tiredness overwhelms my body, and my eyes start to droop on their own as they give in to the silent command. I really should get some sleep. Tomorrow looks like it could be a better day, hopefully.

Groaning at the sunlight assaulting my eyes even through my closed eyelids, I turn over to check the time. Dragging my ass up off the bed, I make myself a shitty tasting coffee and grab a shower. A knock on the door has me alert. Who the fuck is that? Making my way to the door, I slide the curtain to the side to take a peek. No one knows I am here. I've been paying cash for the room, so no names have been used. Well, real names anyway. Fuck! The last person I expect to see is here.

"Open the door, Liam. I know you're in there." I flip the locks, swing the door open and come face to face with Fox.

"Should have known they would have you looking for me." I grumble at my own stupidity. I should have known one of them would send him.

"You gonna let me in or what?" he demands. I spin on my heels and head back into the godawful room.

"Lay it on me. Has my big brother ordered a hit?" I

wouldn't put it past him, in all honesty. After our mother left, he was never quite stable in the mental health department.

"Not a hit. Marcus sent me. It's bad, Liam. Kane's completely lost it." Guilt swirls in my stomach. I was hoping she was just another piece of ass. He would get her out of his system and then she was out of the picture.

"Liam! The crew is falling apart. People are questioning his leadership." I have no words. How have things gone so far into left field since that night? My brain is running so fast, everything else is background noise.

"Are you listening to me?" his voice booms.

"What?"

"He slaughtered all the staff at the Royale after his interrogations turned up empty." Horror fills me, as my stomach turns. What? Why? They weren't together that long to warrant a reaction like this.

"They've had to sedate him to keep him in check. Marcus needs you." I scoff, God how fucking wrong can someone be?

"Marcus is going to tear me to pieces. He was close to her too. He even had a nickname for her."

"Yeah, I know, but he's had to pick up the slack on his own." The unspoken end of that sentence hits me in the face like a house brick. 'Because you're not there' is the bit he didn't say, but I can tell by the way he throws daggers at me he's definitely holding it back. Dread fills me. I thought my guilt was bad before, but now? How could I do this to them? How did I fuck things up this epically? Clearly, I didn't look that closely at the dynamic of their relationship. Kane has always been ruthless, but he has never acted unnecessarily before. Cold and calculated has always been his game, but now this… it won't be long before our father shows his face, and that's something none of us want.

"Fox, I need you to find someone for me." My brain works overtime as a plan forms in my mind. Yeah, this could work.

"I work for Marcus." He snarls at me through gritted teeth.

"Cut the shit. You work for The Crew and I am one of the three." My tone is calm, with authority lining the command.

"You left them, Liam."

"Can you blame me? I destroyed my brothers. I have to fix this, or at least, I have to try." My words break off, it's the least I can do.

"So, you were involved." Disgust fills his face, his eyes full of judgment, not that I can blame him.

"Yeah. I hired a couple of guys from the city to grab her and drop her off in another city."

"Which one?" Fox snaps, pulling out his phone. The tap-tap of his fingers across the screen has me grinding my teeth.

"I don't know. I was going for plausible deniability. I never wanted to know where the drop was. But that doesn't sound so great right now." I start pacing up and down the room as I process everything.

I didn't want to know where she was taken so I couldn't give them a place to start looking. I don't know the guys I employed. They were from an outside source, a shady-as-shit guy called Diego. But what if they didn't take her and someone else did? Fuck, how did everything go to complete shit so quickly?

"Fox, find me Pete Marshall." I pull my phone from the nightstand and call Diego.

"Liam, my man. I…"

"Did the job happen?" I hope my tone clearly tells him that if he doesn't give me the answers I want, I will feed the fucker alive to the gators.

"Well... We… Umm…" stutters Diego.

"Answer me!" I yell, setting all my anger free.

"No. Someone got there before us."

That's all I needed to hear. Ending the call, I turn to Fox to see a horrified expression on his face. My temper is burning. I'm pacing like a wild lion that has been locked in a cage; a cage that won't be able to contain me much longer.

"Why are you looking for Pete?" Fox's voice is meek, laced with nervousness.

"You know him."

"Everyone knows him." Relief runs through me. I honestly thought I would be searching for him for ages.

"Let's go." Without a backward glance, I am out of the door and heading to the car.

27

KANE

"Wake ya ass up!"

"The fuck." Unsticking my eyes, I see Marcus charging through my room like a man possessed.

"Get the fuck up!" He screams at me as he dashes out the door, barking orders as he goes.

Rolling over, I grab my jeans and pull them on. Shit, man. My brain is seriously groggy from whatever Doc gave me. The house is in absolute chaos. Grunts are charging up and down the hallway. I can still hear Marcus ordering men about somewhere in the distance. Stuffing my feet into my boots, I head to find out what the hell is going on.

"What the fuck is going on?" I say to a grunt as he runs past.

"Marcus thinks he found her, Boss." My heart stops. I'm down the stairs in record time. I find my brother with most of the crew in front of him. I don't want to hope. Everything we have tried so far has been a dud. I'm not sure I can survive one more dead end.

"Marcus?" All the crew turn wide eyes to me and freeze in

their tracks. I should feel awful at the fear that shows in their gazes, but I really don't give a shit. I need my girl home.

"We have a lead. Warehouse down by the old mill." His face doesn't betray any of his emotions, but I know we are both praying she's there. Murmured voices break out from the crew. I know they are hoping we find her just as much as me and my brother.

"You heard him! Get moving!" I roar above all the noise in the house. The crew swarms out of the room; they all know their jobs. I head over to my brother.

"Bro?" My voice is low, it feels like my throat is trying to close in on itself.

"I don't know what we'll find. It could be nothing, Kane."

Not bothering to reply, I spin on my heels and head back to my room to get ready. She has to be there. I won't survive another dead end. I will tear the world apart to bring my girl home. Then we need to have a serious talk, because she won't be going anywhere without me again, ever. I will chain her to me if I have too. Ten minutes later most of the crew members are loading up into the vans.

"Bro, what's Doc doing here?" Doc's loading a bag into the back of the SUV, while Marcus keeps an eye on the crew. His face is set as stone, a perfect mask hiding every emotion. "Just in case, brother. We don't know what state she will be in."

My whole-body freezes. If she is hurt, they will wish to meet Satan in hell because I will butcher them slowly. Everything they did to her will be delivered back to them tenfold. I know she'll want to deliver her revenge herself, but she's a part of me. If she's hurt, then I'm hurt; if she bleeds, then I bleed.

"Kane, we need you to keep as calm as possible. Please?" A growl builds in my throat. How fucking dare Marcus think I would fuck this up? "If she is there you need to get her out, and I will deal with the rest," he says.

"I want the people responsible, Marcus. You are not cutting me out of this!" His face tells me everything without him saying a word. He will fight me on this, but he has to understand I can't allow anyone else to handle them. Someone took what is mine, and that is not acceptable.

My body feels like a live wire. I can't help the waves of animosity seeping from my pores, as a growl starts to build in my chest. Marcus hasn't even acknowledged me, which pisses me off even more. I will fight him over this. I always said I would never turn on my brothers. Family first. But after what happened with Liam's disappearance straight after the Royale, I don't know what to believe anymore. We have always had each other's backs no matter what. It has been drilled into us since we were kids that blood is thicker than water. You never turn your back on family. But, how can I let people believe it's easy to allow a family member to fuck you over, especially like this. I'm lost in my own thoughts, trying to get control over my emotions. I'm no use to Pretty Bird like this.

"Roll out!" orders Marcus. I look to my brother who stands with a cold, calculated indifference.

"Move, Kane, or you stay here." Without even a backwards glance, he climbs into the driver's side of the car. Taking a deep breath to calm my nerves, I jump in and pray. That's saying something because a praying man I am not.

Marcus drove us here in record time. I think we went through every red light, but I'm glad he did. The outside of the warehouse is horrendous, the building falling to pieces. All the windows are smashed in and the brickwork is crumbling off with huge cracks all over the place. The worst thing of all is the putrid smell that reaches my nose, causing my stomach to roll. Fear strangles my heart in a death grip. If this is where she is, the state she could be in is unimaginable, if she's even alive. The thought of her not being in the world anymore has me frozen to my seat. My breathing starts to pick up, and the interior of the car feels like it's closing in on me. I look at my brother. I can see his mouth moving, but none of the words reach my ears. All I hear is a disorientating static. Violent trembles start throughout my body, as fear slams into me. I have never felt like this in my life. What the hell is happening?

Marcus grips my shoulders spinning me toward him. His mouth is still moving. I shake my head the best I can to try and tell him that I can't hear him. Gripping the back of my neck, he pushes my head in between my knees. The movement causes my head to spin, darkness starts to invade my vision.

"Kane! For fuck's sake, Kane. Breathe!" The fear in Marcus's voice shocks me slightly out of my stupor, but not enough. The feeling that I am about to die stays in place.

"Breathe in through your nose and out your mouth." Slightly turning my head so my gaze clashes with his, I am shocked to see pure terror across his features. Trying to do what he says, I take a massive breath into my lungs and slowly breath it out through my mouth. After a few times doing this my body starts to slowly relax, breathing becomes a little easier, and the weight on my chest is lifting.

"You good, bro?" Marcus asks.

"W…What. Was. That?"

"Looks like you were having a panic attack." A fucking panic attack. I've never had a panic attack in my life. What the actual fuck? Still breathing in and out, my mind and body clear. I lean back in my seat and keep my eyes looking out of the window. I can't even look in his direction. I know he will have a pitying look on his face.

"Kane! Look at me." I can't bring myself to do it. My teeth ache with the pressure as he grips my face, yanking my head in his direction. I see fire in his eyes, not the look of pity I thought would be stamped across his features.

"We will find her." His tone dares me to argue with him. He has been so strong throughout this. I know he cares for her differently, but where I am falling to pieces because of her loss, Marcus has stepped up with such ferocity. I am proud that she has him in her corner.

"Repeat my words Kane."

"We. Wi...."

"Now!"

"We will find her." My voice doesn't even sound like mine, it is so defeated and flat.

"Say it again. Like you mean it."

"We. Will. Find. Her." Looking through the windshield, I notice the crew standing around waiting for orders. Nodding my head at my brother, I climb out of the car.

"You all know why we are here. Someone took Reika from me, and that isn't just an attack on me, that is an attack on the whole crew." Mutters break out throughout the crowd.

"Some of you know her, some of you are still getting to know her. But do we allow someone to hurt one of our own?"

"No, Boss!" the crew yells.

"Will we search every corner of this town and surrounding areas until we find her?"

"Yes, Boss!" Looking at Marcus I see the corner of his mouth hooked up into a slight smirk and his eyes tell me, this is what he wanted to see from me.

"Let's bring my Pretty Bird home. If she is here, cut down anyone who stands in your way. Do. You. Understand?"

"Yes, Boss!" every man roars to the sky. So much for a quiet arrival. But honestly, if they are here, I want them to know that I am coming for my baby, and hell is coming along with me for the ride.

Marcus starts barking out orders to different groups what their jobs inside the warehouse will be. We have five groups. One will be providing cover outside, while the rest of us break off to search the warehouse. Determination courses through my veins, the fire in my heart burning stronger than it has in what feels like years. Rounding the back of the SUV, I leave Marcus to make sure everyone knows what they are doing. I open the trunk and start strapping my weapons onto my hips and leg. A mix of guns and knives will do nicely. I can't wait to paint the floor red with the blood of those who think they can take what's mine. After placing the last hunting knife on my hip in its sheath, Marcus steps to my side loading himself up with his go to weapons.

"Nice speech there, brother."

"Ha, very funny, you snarky twat. You were right." It pains me to admit this to him, but...

"Excuse me!" he gasps at me, being as dramatic as ever. With a hand to his chest covering his heart, he continues, "Did the great Kane Southbourne say someone else was right?"

"Yeah, I did. Don't get used to it you fuckwit."

"Oh my god!" he squeals like a twelve-year-old schoolgirl. I bark out a laugh, I can't help it. He can be such a dickhead at times, but he always has your back no matter what. After today, we really need to have a talk about Liam, I know he's just as pissed as I am over everything. I wouldn't put it past Liam to do some shady shit, but I hope he didn't have anything to with this. I wouldn't be able to forgive that, no matter if he is family.

My men have questioned my leadership since she's been missing. Honestly, I can't really blame them. I need to do right by them, but most of all I need to do right by her. I'm lost in my thoughts as movement catches my eye. Groups are splitting off in different directions to do the jobs they have been tasked with. Making sure all my weapons are secure, I head over to Marcus as he leads a group toward the main door of the warehouse.

Every single one of us is on high alert as we enter through the main door. The hinges creak as we open them. The groups break off, some going left while the go right. Me, Marcus and a few others take the route forward. As I look around, I realize I recognize this place. We used to play here when we were younger, avoiding our father's wrath. It's the old slaughterhouse. The air is putrid as the stench of death still lays heavily within the ground and walls. My stomach rolls. I force myself to breathe through my mouth, so the smell doesn't reach my nose.

Silently moving through the corridors, we check every room. We find nothing. There isn't a hint of anyone having been here in years. With the direct route we've taken, we have to be somewhere in the center of this place. The other teams haven't picked anything up yet either, if the radio silence is anything to go by. Marcus and I clearly have the same emotions running through our systems. His shoulders are set, and the further we move and find nothing, his aura grows increasingly hostile. The guys with us have moved further away, trying to put at much distance between them and us as they can. I know they're waiting for one of us to blow.

Crackle. Crackle.

"Err, Boss." I freeze as a voice crackles over the radio. The frequency must be being disrupted, because the words are coming through disjointed.

"We got something." the voice says.

"Where are you?" My heart starts beating at a frantic pace. We all look to each other waiting for the position.

"Holding pen."

That's all I need; I charge down the corridor like a man with hell hounds on his ass. The thump of footfalls behind me tells me the others aren't far behind. Erratic breathing reaches my ears. Looking to my left, I see Marcus keeping pace. Before long, we are heading down the corridor to where the pens used to be based at the rear of the property. I'm finding it hard to breathe. My lungs are screaming at me to slow down; not enough oxygen is reaching them. But, I can't. The fear coursing through me won't allow me to slow the pace. I have to know, I have to see her, no matter what.

I haven't realized I'm through the doors, until I plough into one of the grunts and knock him flying. Skidding to a halt the best I can, I spot Bonzo and three others blocking something from view. Pale faces stare back at us, horror shining in their eyes. My heart starts to crumble in on itself, and my hands start to tremble.

"B…Boss. Don't." Bonzo says as he and one of the grunts block my path. I didn't even realize I was moving forward.

"No." My brain fog lifts enough for me to see Marcus looking at whatever they're blocking me from. He turns in my direction and the look of defeat and horror across his face has dread rearing itself inside my veins. I feel a darkness ready to consume me like nothing I've ever known before.

Cracking Bonzo in the side of the face and shoulder checking the grunt, I rush forward to see for myself. I stop short and horror fills me. On a desk is a laptop with a video. The image on the screen has bile burning my throat as my stomach churns and an ice cold sweat runs down my neck. Pretty Bird is hanging in chains. Her feet are barely touching the floor. What has horror filling me is the state she is in. Blood covers her body like a deadly veil. Bruises litter almost all of her skin, barely concealed by the blood, the cuts and wounds that mar every surface of her body... my eyes to fill with tears. There's a sticky note on the left side of the screen with that says,

Play Me!

My right-hand shakes violently as I move it over the laptop to click play. The screen comes to life just as I feel mine is about to end.

"Well, well." The sound echoes throughout the room. It sounds so loud because there is no noise coming from any of the men with us, as everyone collectively holds our breath.

Someone steps into the shot with Reika wearing all black clothing, gloves, and a ski mask with goggles. Nothing distinctive shows of the person to give anything away.

"You're not so scary, Reaper." A robotic sounding voice says. The person's face is covered, I can't tell if they are speaking or if it's someone else.

"I'll give you this though, you were a tough bitch to break." A robotic cackle sound out through the speakers, echoing around us on a continuous loop.

He walks around the back of Pretty Bird. He yanks her head back, causing a scream to tear from her lips. My heart and soul crumble to dust. Leaning forward the video zooms closer to her face. Her eyes slowly open to the camera and my heart stops. There's no fire, no defiance. Just acceptance. A flash of silver lights the screen. A knife is against her throat.

"Loving you killed me." My knees give way at her words as they start to run the blade across her neck and the video cuts off.

Horror. Hatred. Disgust.

They all fill me. Marcus violently shakes me. Anguished screams fill the room as tears run down my face. I did this. This is my fault.

I killed the person I love.

28

LIAM

"Are you sure he will be here, Fox?" My body is jittery as we wait for our meeting.

"He said he will meet us here. He's not happy that you're here, but he agreed," he mumbles as he checks our surroundings.

"Why? I don't even know the guy."

What the fuck is this guy's problem, seriously? I'm glad Fox is here at this meeting with me or I would likely slap the twat. Fox won't tell me anything about him. The only thing he has said is he isn't the sort of person you want to get on the wrong side of. Well, that makes two of us, buddy.

Nervous energy runs through my body. I just want this meeting over with, then it's time to go and face the music with my brothers. Thirty minutes pass, and my ass is starting to go numb.

"Fucking hell, man. What's taking him so long?" I am not the most patient person in the world. I try, but this is an absolute joke and a bloody insult. Patience. That's more of Marcus's forte. I would rather get shit done instantly. I don't like waiting, and this fucker is taking his own sweet time.

"There," Fox says.

Looking in the direction Fox points, I see someone step out of the tree line. The dude is either paranoid or clever, wanting to meet in this deserted place. It could go either way at this point. Climbing out of the truck, I round the hood. Fox needs to hurry his ass up. Man, come the fuck on. Finally, he climbs out and we start walking over.

"Drop your weapons." How the fuck did I not notice this motherfucker had a gun in his hand? Pulling my Glock from the back of my jeans, I put it on the ground and kick it to my right so it's close if I need to make a dash for it. Fox does the same, but takes longer than I did. I can't believe the shit he's pulling off himself. If he pulls a weapon out of his ass crack, I'm done. That's shit about another dude you don't need to see.

"Pete Marshall?" I can't help my surprised tone. He isn't at all like I expected him to look. Pete is around the same age as my father, but has laugh lines on his face. He doesn't look too dangerous, but I know better than anyone, don't believe what you see.

"Don't talk to me, boy. I will speak with Fox. You can listen." I'm gearing up to argue with this bastard, but I stop when Fox looks at me, giving a slight shake of his head. In Fox language, don't be fucking stupid.

"Thanks for meeting us, Pete."

"Yeah, well, I wish you didn't bring a damned leader with you. But…"

"Yeah, well, I needed to. You need to talk with him."

"Is he a prick like his old man?"

"He's standing right here, fuckwit!" My father used to talk about us like we weren't even there. It pissed me off then, and even more so now.

"So what, boy? Are you just as bad as your father?" Who the fuck is this guy?

"How do you know my father?" I ask.

"Oh, we go way back, boy."

"My name is Liam, Old Man, not fucking boy!"

The crazy bastard starts laughing, like seeing me get pissed off is the funniest thing he has ever seen. He's a fucking weirdo, man. How the fuck does he have any connection to Reika? If he's her guardian, no wonder he packed her up and shipped her off.

"What do you want, Liam?" Pete asks.

Here goes nothing, I guess.

"I fucked up. Bad shit has happened since then, and I am looking for information on Reika Martins." He goes wide eyed and rigid on the spot. How does he know her?

Ring. Ring. Ring.

Yanking my phone from my pocket, I see Marcus's name flashing on the screen. "Bro. I'm…"

"Come home, Liam. Please." My heart stills at the emotion in his voice. I have never heard him sound so broken. Dread fills me. Has Kane done something stupid?

"Marcus…."

"She's dead, Liam."

What the actual fuck? My legs start to tremble, and my breathing increases in pace. It's not possible, she wouldn't let anyone off her like that.

"No. You are trying to make me feel guilty."

"Kane is out of it. He hasn't spoken to anyone since we got back."

"You?" I know Marcus was as close to her as Kane was. If they are both out of it due to Reika being dead… I don't know how…

Manic laughter fills the air, my eyes dart to the sound. What the actual fuck!? Pete is doubled over laughing like he is high on laughing gas. Looking back to my phone, Marcus has cut the call.

"What's so funny, old man?"

"God, you boys are as thick as pig shit."

"What the fuck are you talking about?"

"I just heard what your brother said." Another bout of laughter breaks free from his lips. How can he find the heartbreak my brothers are going through so damn fucking funny? My temper reaches boiling point. Lunging at him, I grip the idiot by the throat.

"They fucking loved her!" I scream in his face, satisfaction spreads through me as spit lands on his face.

"You fucking idiots. You don't know?"

"What?" I've had enough of this. I need to get home.

Spinning on my heels, I march towards the truck. What a fucking idiot. What information did Fox really think this twat could give us? Just as my fingers brush the door handle, I hear Pete speak up.

"I know she has been kidnapped. I know your brothers think she is dead."

I can't help but turn my head in his direction.

"She won't be dead," Pete says. If she's not dead, why do my brother's think she is?

"How the fuck do you know that?"

"Because without her there is nothing. She is too valuable."

Why is she so important? Who the fuck is she? Has she played everyone?

"Fucking riddles, old man."

"I will find the truth. If she isn't alive, you best find God, boy, because you aren't prepared for what will come."

"Who the fuck is she?"

He doesn't even bother to answer me. He just takes off

walking the way he came. My brain is racing trying to process what he means. I'm leaving with more questions than answers. Unease prickles in the back of mind. A healthy dose of dread is there too. I've got a bad feeling about this.Is she using him?

29

LIAM

"Who the fuck was that kook? Honestly, he made me look kinda sane." Fox snorts at my words. We are back at my motel room after that shit show of a meeting, and I am kinda stalling heading home to come face to face with my brothers. I can't see Kane heartbroken. After mother died, he wasn't the same, but now, I don't know what he will become.

"Do you think Pete's right? That she's not dead," Fox questions.

"You rang Bonzo to find out what happened! Her throat was cut open." Seriously, is he stupid. Nobody could survive that. What a fucking idiot.

"C'mon, you heard Pete. She's too valuable to be offed like that."

"How the fuck is an underground fighter that valuable. Really? C'mon, Fox, she isn't the fucking queen." Not bothering to listen to his answer, I storm out of the room and walk for five minutes to clear my head. My soul is tired, and I'm just utterly exhausted. You know that deep ache you feel when everything gets on top of you, and it would be so much easier to close your eyes and never wake up?

Buzz. Buzz.

Pulling my phone out of my pocket, I'm too chicken shit to read the

message. I take a deep breath, and slide open my phone to see what shit Marcus has decided to throw at me now.

Unknown Number:
   Tomorrow 9pm Stockton Hold Lane
   Behind the run-down bookstore
   You best be there.

                                           Me:
                        Who the fuck is this?

Unknown Number:
   The fucking boogey man
   Be there and come alone, dickhead.

                                           Me:
                  Fuck off you prick. I don't know
                  how you got this number but don't
                             message me again.

Unknown:
   Just fucking do it Southbourne….

                        •   •   •

What the actual fuck makes whoever this is think they can talk to me that way? I've gutted people for less than that. Fucking hillbillies trying to make a name for themselves again. I don't even bother to reply. Childish arguments over text messages annoy the fucking life out of me, and I'm not in the mood.

"Liam!"

"What?" I bark back at Fox. How hard is it to just get a moment of silence around here? Fuck me, when did everything go to utter shit?

"Marcus just rang." My heart skips a beat at that.

"Do I wanna know?"

"He says you can't go to the house tonight. Kane is on a rampage."

"What kind of rampage?"

"He's tried to kill a few of the crew grunts, and has now locked himself in the office."

Yep, my ass isn't going anywhere near him while he is like this. I know it's a chicken shit thing to do, but who could blame me. Even Satan would tuck tail and run if he came face to face with Kane on a murder spree. A violent shiver runs down my spine at that thought alone. The unbearable weight of guilt sits on my shoulders. I caused all of this. I set the wheels in motion.

"Liam!"

"For fuck's sake, man! I just need a fucking breather! This conversation doesn't need to be shouted across the fucking parking lot!"

Heading back to the room, I find Fox pacing like the weight of the world rests on his shoulders. "Fox, I've just had a weird message."His ears perk up at that. I tell him about the message and he gives me a complete run down on what's happening back at the house. We seriously need to sort this cluster fuck or daddy dearest will show his face. That is literally the last thing anyone needs to happen. I wouldn't put it past Kane to kill him just for shits and giggles. Fox agrees that whoever sent the message is a brave son of a bitch, but he thinks we should go find out what it's about. My gut is telling me shit is about to hit the fan. I hope that this someone can tell me who has Reika, because I can't figure out for the life of me why someone else would kidnap, torture, and kill her just to get back at Kane, unless they want to start a war.

30

MARCUS

"Kane! Open the fucking door, man." My heart breaks for him at the loss of Reika, I feel it too. He has never cared like this for anyone before. He has always been a hit it and quit it type of guy. But with Reika, Kane's eyes showed so much emotion when he looked at her. It was like having my real big brother back, not the one who was shaped by all the punishment and torture my father dished out to discipline us. My brain starts to lose itself.

"Liam, have you seen Kane?"

"Yeah, Dad wanted a word with him for something that went on at school."

My heart sinks. Fuck, Dad knows about the beating I put on the mouthy little shit who was trying to feel up my latest fuck piece. My anxiety hits. If Kane is talking to Dad, he is going to take the blame for this. I can't let him take the punishment. He randomly started getting tattoos. He thinks we are stupid as to the reason why, but we know it is so he can hide the scars littering his body. Father has beaten Kane with whips, bats, anything he could get his hands on to punish him with. His favorite is to stub his cigarettes out on him.

265

Running out of Liam's room, I head to the office as fast as my legs will carry me. I nearly wipe out on the stairs as I trip over my own feet. Just as I hit the bottom step, a scream echoes around the house. Vomit hits the back of my throat, burning as the bile slowly sinks back down. This is all my fault.

Trying my hardest to hold my stomach, I charge to my father's office. Crashing through the door, I stop horrified at the sight in front of me. Kane is pinned to the chair in front of my father's desk by the knives sticking out of each hand. How can he be so cruel to his own sons? Me and Liam don't get as much as Kane. Kane tells us he takes it because it's his job to look after us. He is still trying to keep that stupid promise to Mom.

"What do you want, boy?" Father growls at me.

"He didn't do it." At my words his eyebrow raises.

"Marcus, shut up." Kane growls in my direction.

"It was me. I fucked the guy up. Not Kane! If you want to beat on anyone. It's me you need."

"Bahahaha. Silly boy, you're gonna wish you never admitted to that. Your training starts now."

My father looks over his shoulder to the guard standing behind him. Dread fills me as he starts to walk in my direction. Kane is thrashing around in the chair trying to loosen the knives in his hands. Roaring like a pissed off lion, he hurls abuse in our father's direction. What has me frozen to the spot is the manic gleam in my father's eyes.

The click of the door unlocking brings me back to the present. Reluctantly, I walk into the office. I am hit with a strong scent of whisky.

"Jesus. It smells like a fucking brewery in here, bro."

The only response I get is a grunt, as he drops back down into his seat behind the desk. Dark rings circle his eyes. He looks old, like he has aged twenty years over night. He clearly hasn't slept; losing Reika has fucked him up so much. The guilt is clearly eating at him. He blames himself for her death.

"She wouldn't want you to dwell man. Hellion wouldn't..."

"Don't. Say. That. Name!" he bellows.

"For fuck's sake. Get a grip on yourself! You weren't the only one to lose her."

I know my brother is hurting, but I lost her too. Reika became a part of my family, my sister. My life before her was so cold. Yes, I looked like I was full of life and loved having fun, but on the inside, I was dying. Having to keep up that false persona was fucking draining. Then Hellion stormed in bringing chaos with her and I found myself laughing and smiling because I was happy. Actual, real emotions warmed my cold, dead heart. Anybody that spent time with her felt it too. Her snarky comments and one liners would have you choking on laughter. She was true to herself and didn't take any shit. She would call you out in one breath, then have you in hysterics the next. My heart grows heavy at her loss, slowly shutting off again, but I know she will want us to skin the bastards alive that did this to her.

"What do you want Marcus?"

"We need to get things sorted, and tell Tom what happened."

"He disowned her. He isn't getting told shit." His face is set in stone. This is the person everybody fears. He's locked his feelings down and plans to hide from them. Refusing to acknowledge his pain while it eats him from the inside out.

"I'm going to get hammered, then I'm going to bed since all this shit is finally over with," he says.

"How can you say shit like that?"

"She was a piece of pussy that got her ass murdered. Not my problem, bro." He glares at me, not a flicker of anything on his face and I lose it.

"Fuck you." Storming out of the office, I slam the door with so much force the pictures on the walls crash to the floor. I hear the glass shatter, making me look back toward the closed office door. With a shake of my head, I head to my bedroom. Today can fuck off and so can everyone in it.

31

LIAM

"What time is it, Fox?"

"A minute after you asked last time, dude," the snarky shit chuckles.

"Why the fuck is it dragging, man."

"Chill out. Fucking hell, man, you're giving me anxiety."

"Something isn't right, man." Nervous energy flows through me. I'm on edge. My gut is playing havoc, giving me a bad feeling about this. I don't know anyone who would be brave enough to demand a meet like this. What if it's a bloody ambush?

"What time is it?"

"Fuck this, man. Ask once more and your ass goes alone."

"Fuck you, asshat. You're telling me you don't have a bad feeling about this? We could be walking into a trap, Fox."

"Nah. They would go after Kane, not you, man."

Fucking prick. I wouldn't envy any stupid twat that tries to take my brother on, at the moment. Honestly, I'm a little terrified at what he might do if someone triggers him.

"Time to roll out, man."

"Fucking finally."

Doing my best Flash Gordon impersonation, I shoulder check Fox on my way out. I jump into the car, as he shouts asshole after me. I can't help the chuckle that falls out of my mouth. Luckily, I don't have to wait too long for him as he climbs in the car, and we're off. My anticipation and anxiety grow the closer we get to the meet up point. I can't figure out what the fuck we are doing here. Before I know it, Fox gives me a dig to the side to let me know we are five minutes from the old bookstore.

"Park near the back, I don't want whoever it is getting the jump on us," I say.

We take a right onto a side street, then continue, pulling up a couple of stores down. My palms are starting to sweat, and my body feels like it has a million bees in it. Fox fidgets in the driver's seat. He has to be feeling what I am too. Thank fuck I'm not alone in it.

Ten minutes is all we had to wait until a truck pulls down the other side of the back street and stops behind the store. I wait as the headlights dim to a low level, one shadow gets outs and rounds the hood.

"Showtime." Jumping out, I head over to the newcomer.

"Didn't think you would show."

"Who are you?"

"That is none of your concern."

Huh? Who the fuck does this guy think he is? He is my height. I can't tell the color of his hair or build because he has a hat on his head, and wears baggy clothes.

"What. Do. You. Want?"

"Before I tell you, I need you to keep your shit together."

He doesn't even give me the chance to answer, just spins on his heels and heads back to his truck. Unease rolls through me, so I pull my gun from the back of my jeans, and flick the safety catch off. He looks to me and waves me forward. Cautiously I head over to where he is standing. The sight that greets me has my heart dropping into my stomach.

"S...She's dead?" Reika is passed out in the back of the cab; she is a mess. Fumbling for my pocket with my phone in it, I manage to wrap my hands around it and yank it out.

"No!" He snatches the phone out of my hand and throws it into the footwell.

"What the fuck do you mean, no? My... My..."

My chest grows tight, I can't breathe. My lungs are screaming for air and my eyes are streaming with the effort of trying to catch a deep enough breath. My legs tremble under me.

"Liam! What the fuck?" Fox yells. He must have seen me land on my ass.

I can't make the words I want to speak pass my lips. I still can't believe what I am seeing. Lifting a trembling hand, I point to the back of the cab. Leaving my side, he looks in the back and starts cussing enough to make a sailor proud.

"Who the fuck are you?" Fox asks the newcomer.

"Dude, I know he must be in shock but do you guys have a safe house?" His words jolt my brain back to functioning on all cylinders, and I jump to my feet.

"I'm taking her home!"

"You can't, fuckface, that is the first place they will come looking for her."

"Who the fuck are you?"

"Paine Anders."

"Well, Paine! You can't stop me." I take a step toward the cab, and he steps into me to block my path. I'm gonna gut this motherfucker if he doesn't move. Why does everyone think they can walk all over me?

"They'd go there for her. We need a safe house, and you can't tell your brothers!"

"Why not? They are both destroyed thinking she's dead." I can't believe she's alive and here.

"Because, you fucking idiot, she will be dead if they find out where she is," he snarls at me, hostility shining in his eyes. He tracks every movement I make, which has my own anger growing.

"They are broken by her death," I roar at the idiot in front of me. "I need to tell them she is alive."

Indecision flashes across his features, as he rubs the back of his neck. His eyes keep moving back to Reika in the truck. Her breathing is shallow, but I can see the rise and fall of her chest letting me know she is still breathing. "They can't know." His words turn my blood turning to ice.

"Do you know what they will fucking do to you if they know you have her and haven't told them?" I can't believe I'm trying to reason with the dick, but desperate times call for desperate measures.

"Liam calm down." Fox mutters over my shoulder. A groan from inside the truck has both our eyes turning in that direction.

"There is too much at stake here, Liam." Paine looks me dead on, his jaw ticking as he grinds his teeth. My temper boils over.

"Why the fuck does everyone keep saying that? What is she the lost princess of some foreign country?" I step closer to the new guy as Fox shouts obscenities behind me.

"Fuck this," Paine says, turning on his heel and heading back to the driver's side of the truck. My brain scrambles to piece everything together as I charge towards him, knocking the pair of us onto the asphalt.

A huge fist smashes into the side of my jaw, as we roll around on the ground. His movements are fluid, and he continues to land blow after blow. I'm doing everything I can to block, when Fox yanks the fucker of me by the back of his collar. Paine spins rapidly connecting with his jaw. Fox is launched off his feet and rolls to a stop in front of our vehicle. Fuck me, he's out cold. Scrambling to my feet, my roar fills the night sky as I charge the goon once again. Something shines half a second before I get there. Pain radiates through the left side of my head, and I'm falling to my knees. Black spots dance across my vision, as I try my best to ignore the call of unconsciousness. A clang of metal rings out, as a bar drops to the ground in front of me. I feel the drip of something down the side of my face before my body gives up the fight, and I fall to my side. The darkness closes in on me.

"Fucking idiots, the lot of you."

My vision starts to fade further as a shadow steps in front of me. Pain flashes through my jaw, as my head is yanked up to look up at the guy glaring down at me.

"All of you think you are so important. That the town revolves around you. That you are all gods." He spits on the floor in front of me. "Well, I'm sorry to enlighten you, asshat, but you and your brothers are fuck all in the ocean that is this town. The sharks are out for blood. I will not break a promise because you are too dense to see what is really going on." I don't have chance to block the blow, as darkness creeps in faster and swallows me whole.

32

REIKA

My body screams in agony. It feels like I am on the spin cycle in a washing machine. Everything feels heavy as I try to unstick my eyes. The sound of someone singing fills the air as all my senses switch back on. "What the fuck," I groan, as I try my best to roll onto my side.

Leather creaks underneath me, as I manage to get my bearings. Pulling myself up, I find myself in the back seat of a truck. A huge tattooed guy is bouncing in the driver's seat, singing away to the music on the radio. "Glad to see your finally awake, Little Warrior." His voice has a deep gravelly undertone that sends shivers down my spine.

"Who are you?" The words come out scratchier than I would have liked. Looking out the window, I notice the forest moving past us at warp speed. My eyes blur as they try to pin point something to tell me where we are. "I'm a friend," he says, as he resumes his rendition of "Down with the Sickness".

Not once has he taken his eyes off the road to see what I'm doing. Either this guy isn't fazed by anything, or there are no weapons close by for me to beat the shit out of him with and make a run for it.

"There's nothing around for you to hit me with," he chuckles darkly. I just stare at the back of his head.

"Erm, are you a mind reader or something?"

He chuckles again. "Nah. It's just the first thing I would do if I woke up in a strange vehicle." The rumble of his voice sparks something inside me. I'm pretty sure I've heard it somewhere before. I rack my brain trying to bring up the memory that seems to be buried deep in the recesses of my brain. My brow furrows as I try to will it into existence.

"I got you away from Fancy Pants," he says, as he continues to hum the tune of another song. Relief floods me as his words sink in. Thank God I'm not anywhere near that bastard.

"What happened?"

"How about we grab a coffee?" He points out of the windshield at a diner further up the road.

"Is there food involved?" My stomach chooses this moment to growl. He laughs, and I feel mortified at the sounds coming from my stomach. I have to admit, I'm surprised I'm not panicking about being in some random weirdo's car. I feel safe, but I will fight if I have too. The truck stops and he jumps out. Testing my muscles to see how much they hurt, I realize my range of motion is limited.

The back door swings open, and he stands there grinning with an extended hand. "Yeah, dude, not happening. I can walk," I growl. Laughter lines show on his face as he chuckles. Shaking his head, I'm taken aback as I get a proper look at my hero. Fuck me, this guy is gorgeous. I should be freaked that I don't know his name, but honestly, I'm past caring about anything anymore. All I want is to get payback for what happened to my parents.

I slide out of the back of the truck. My legs only just keep me upright, trembling as I try to take a step away from the truck. My legs crumble and I yelp as the gravel gets closer.

"Easy there. You're not as strong as you were." My companion shakes his head again and slides his shoulder under my right arm to prop me up. My steps are tiny as we slowly make our way to the door of the diner.

I snort as I see the interior décor from outside. Are we in a horror movie? I'm pretty sure I saw this place on an episode of *Bates Motel*. A bell chimes as we get through the door, and the waitress' eyes nearly pop out of her head as she takes a good look at us. I try to reassure her with a smile, but I'm pretty sure it was more of a grimace as I hobble towards a booth. I flop down on the cracked PVC covering my seat, and groan as my joints scream at me. Cutie takes his seat across from me, sparks dancing in his eyes. He picks up the menu.

"What can I get you both?" a chirpy voice says. My eyes land on another waitress who looks to be around the same age as me. She has the girl next door vibe going on with her blonde hair tied up high on her head. The pink and white uniform hangs on her tiny frame perfectly, the name Kay scrawled across her apron.

"Can we have two coffees please, and whatever my friend here wants to eat?" His smile is wide as he looks at her. A blush spreads across her face as she stares at him. I think I can see a bit of drool at the corner of her mouth. I start laughing; I can't help it. Panicked eyes dart to mine as she looks between me and my dinner partner. I can see the cogs in her head turning, causing my laughter to turn hysterical.

"Don't panic, sweetie," I say to calm the look of terror on her face. "Check him out all you want." I chuckle deeply as he rolls his eyes and grins at me.

"Oh, thanks, Little Warrior. And here I thought you liked me?" The poor girl's face pales even further as her eyes dart over my face and body. I'm still in the same clothes I was in, at the Royale. I don't need to look at myself to know what sort of state I'm in. A folded napkin drops on my lap. Keeping it below the edge of the table, I open it to find *'Do you need help?'* scrawled across it in pretty handwriting, I look back to her, and see her eyes brimming with tears.

"I'm fine, sweetie. No need to worry," I smile as sweetly as possible. Some of the tension slides out of her shoulders. She seems more relaxed, but now daggers are being thrown my way from the other side of the table. I snatch the menu out of his hand, grinning as he curses me. While my eyes scan the menu, my stomach rumbles again. "Can I have the cheeseburger and fries, please?" She frantically scribbles down my order.

"Make that two."

She's heads off, taking our order to the kitchen. "So, who are you and what do I owe you?" I throw the question that has been rattling around in my head for a while out in the open.

"Nothing, Little Warrior."

I'm caught off guard by his quick response, and scoff at the stupidity of it. No one does anything for free, and definitely not taking on whoever the hell that was back there.

"Do you think I'm stupid?" My words come out with a savage snarl.

"I know you're not stupid. But I am keeping a promise to someone," he replies coolly, picking up his phone that just pinged on the table.

"Promise to who?"

"I can't tell you at the moment," he shrugs as he carries on, tapping away on his phone. My anger grows when he doesn't say anything more. I'm just about to lose my shit when a plate slides in front of me. The smell of food hits my nose, and I groan. Leaving the conversation for the time being, I dive into my food, devouring the whole burger in seconds. Pain flares in my stomach as I stuff the fries into my mouth like a cave man. The waitress' eyes widen as I groan while I stuff my face, barely taking a second to breathe.

I lean back, my plate is empty, my stomach bloated from the food. Even still, I'm eyeing the burger on Cutie's plate that is calling my name.

"You want it?" he asks with a smirk, tipping up the corner of his mouth. I reluctantly shake my head. I'm starving, but I know better than most, when you have been treated as I have, you have to be careful how much you eat at first, until your body gets used to food again.

"So, what happened?" I ask as I swirl the coffee in my cup. "You said you took me from Fancy Pants. Why?" He shifts sheepishly in his seat as he looks everywhere but me.

"I'm not going to stop asking until you answer me," I demand.

He takes a deep, painful sounding breath, closing his eyes. Sweat gathers on the top of his brow. He eventually opens his eyes and guilt shines clear as day in his eyes. "I'm sorry it took me so long to react, but I had to time it perfectly." He mutters pulling his arms into his stomach.

"I managed to get in touch with Liam before you woke up, and we met up," he says. White hot rage flashes across my mind. "What the fuck do you mean Liam?" My fist slams into the table as I fight to keep myself in my seat.

"I know the guys were hit hard about everything, so I got in touch with him to see if they had a safe house." His face pales as I growl at the fucker, slamming my palms down on the table. I stand up on shaky legs, gritting my teeth. I slowly get out of the booth, stumbling as I try my best to march away from this fucker. I fall flat on my face a few times. He rushes over to help me, but I slap his hand away as I use a stool to drag my ass up.

"Get the fuck away from me asshole," I snarl as I head to the restroom.

I can't believe I got to the restroom in one piece. I only fell flat on my face once. I can't fucking believe he rang Liam. Of all the people in this fucking town, he has to ring one of three people I plan on chopping up into little pieces and feeding to the gators. He's a fucking idiot. He has to be.

I splash cold water on the back of my neck from the faucet. Well, if you want to call it water. It looks kind of murky. My rage is potent, but my logical side rears its head, reminding me I'm in the middle of God knows where, with Fancy Pants and his delinquents chasing me. I'm going to have to play nice with the fuckwit until we get somewhere with more people.

I sigh in defeat as my logical side wins out for once. I'm not happy he rang the bastard, but Liam's not here. I won't have to go on a murder spree right now. Nope, that can wait until my strength is back and I can torture them all slowly. That thought has me laughing my ass off. I hobble back out into the diner. Cutie is nowhere to be seen. "He's outside on the phone," the waitress calls to me from the hatch in the wall. Sticking her hand through the gap from the kitchen, she points out the window.

I see him pacing up and down, shouting into the phone by his ear.

The pissed off expression tells me he's definitely arguing with someone, but who? Fuck it, curiosity killed the cat and all that. As I make my way through the door, the bell chimes behind me. I follow the raised voice, and head back to the truck slowly. My legs wobble with every step I take, but the determination to eavesdrop pushes me on. I manage to get to the hood of the truck without him noticing me.

"Yeah, fucking try it asshole, and I'll kill every single one of you," he snarls into the phone. My adrenaline picks up and the sound of the words.

"You and what army? I don't think so," he laughs. "Eat dick."

He cuts the call. Spinning around, his eyes widen a touch as he finds me glaring at him.

"Who was that?" I spit the accusation.

"My uncle," he retorts with a shrug of his shoulders.

"So, you have a habit of threatening to kill your uncle then?" My voice drips with sarcasm as I narrow my eyes further.

"Look he's a prick, and I can't deal with him."

My unease grows as all my thoughts crash together. "Is Fancy Pants your uncle?" I blurt the words, as my chest caves in on itself. How could I have been so stupid? My chest heaves. The feeling of being crushed under a building hits me, like a freight train.

"No. No." Shit, the words sound distorted as my fears come to life.

"For fuck's sake, Little Warrior." The voice calls to me in the darkness, as my body rattles. Trying to shake my mind free at the horrors I know I will be facing again soon. "Reika, listen to me!" The darkness fades, as I find myself flat on my back at the side of the truck with my companion, crouched over me.

The panic roars to life as I try my hardest to scramble away from him, but my limbs are not doing what I want them to. His eyes pinch together at the expression is on my face. He unfurls himself from the crouch and takes a step away. I finally manage to breathe a little better at the space.

"I'm sorry, Little Warrior. I didn't mean to scare you." He grimaces, while chewing on his bottom lip. "Fancy Pants isn't my uncle," he rumbles. His face contours to one of rage at the name. "That bastard needs to rot in hell."

I blink rapidly, my mind conjuring up its own reasons for why the hell he has brought me here. My heat rises in my body as a weird sensation starts in my stomach. For some reason, I'm feeling fully exposed as he stares at me, waiting for a response.

"Who was on the phone?" I mutter the words, praying he is honest with me. The lies and everything else surrounding me at the moment is becoming too much.

"Liam," he snarls, as he starts pacing in front of me. My anger grows. Who the fuck does that bastard think he is? "Why the fuck would he be calling you?" I hiss, pulling myself up onto my feet. His eyes shine as he turns to look at me. I can see he's sweating all over now, and not because of the heat blaring down on us.

"He wants me to take you back to the safe house he has," he mumbles, moving stones around with the tip of his sneaker. "Before you blow, I'm not going to do it. He wanted to tell the others where you were, and I can't have that." He mumbles to himself as he tugs on the neck of his t-shirt "No one can know where you are, there is too much at stake."

"What the fuck are you babbling about?" I'm getting headache from all the Riddler shit. "What do you mean there's too much at stake?" His head snaps to mine like he forgot I was there, then he looks away again. I notice he's closing and opening his fist repeatedly.

"I really wish I could tell you," he starts, a growl builds in my throat. "Before you try and pull my head off, I plan to tell you as soon as you are up to it. You will find out, but there are too many moving parts, at the moment."

I hate this. I fucking hate being kept in the dark. But the look on his face tells me I'm not ready to know what is really going on yet. How the fuck has everything turned into such a shit show? I don't want to be with this idiot a second longer, I have shit I need to do, but I'm not about to look a gift horse in the mouth.

"Look I'm pissed you're keeping stuff from me, but for the first time in my life I need to be logical." I manage to squeeze the words past tight lips. "But I will say this, if you don't explain to me what the fuck is happening, I won't think twice about killing you."

He sucks in a shocked breath, then he looks me up and down. Studying me, his eyes connect with mine. "Are you serious?" He chuckles again.

"I'll tell you something, sweetie," I grumble, using the truck to steady me as I move closer, "I will kill you if I have too." I grin savagely as I watch his Adam's Apple bob in his throat. "I won't lose any sleep over it either."

I spin around with a huge grin as I leave him in his spot with his mouth hanging open. I yank the door open and pull myself into the cab. My chest heaving with the effort it's just taken to get into the truck. Fuck my life, Dad never did me like this. Even when the training was brutal. "Hurry up fuck face," I shout out of the door.

A deep chuckle rumbles from Cutie, and I hear the gravel crunch under foot. His door opens, a huge grin greets me. A shadow passes across his window and my eyes widen as he drops to the ground unconscious. I yelp, scrambling to get across the car, when suddenly I'm yanked back. My hands try and fail to catch hold of anything when a sharp pain on my neck has me roaring in anger. Dark spots quickly cloud my vision. I see a blurry figure picking up Cutie when the darkness consumes me.

33

REIKA

Thump. Thump. Thump.

Ugh! Looks like it's that time again. I force my body to turn, so I can look at my captor. The fuck?

Soft sheets and, if I'm not mistaken, it feels like there is a mattress underneath my body trying to keep me cocooned in its depths. I can't help the groan that falls from my mouth. Damn, that feels nice, I'd forgotten just how nice a proper bed was. You don't realize how much you enjoy things until you don't have them anymore. This has to be a dream. It can't be real. How the fuck have I got here? Raised voices reach my ears, but the voices sound distorted, like when your ears go funny on a plane. Finally, I decide it's best to open my eyes. I am dumbstruck by what I find. The room isn't my cage. There is not a bar in sight or the inside of a truck. The walls are an off white, there's a chest of drawers in the corner and the bed I'm on. My memories are blurry as I try to remember what the hell happened.

Footsteps echo in the hallway, getting closer with each second that passes. I try to brace myself, but excruciating pain tears through my body as it protests my tensing up. Tears fill my eyes with the onslaught of intense pain.

"You aren't going in there!" a voice booms outside the door, I shudder at the ferocity of it.

"Fucking stop me!" another voice retorts, with the same amount of venom.

"You really think I'm going to let you anywhere near her after what you did?"

My heart rate runs rampant, like it's trying to explode out of my chest. I kind of recognize both of the voices. I know I've heard one of them recently, but the other one has dread pooling in my stomach. The bedroom door slams open and horror fills me. I think I'm going to be sick as bile shoots up my throat.

"R...Reika."

Emotions swirl like a building hurricane inside me - anger, disgust, hatred. Frosty stands in the doorway like he can't believe his eyes. Happiness and a look that can only translate to 'Thank God' written across his face. Is he for real right now? There is another guy behind him with a look of surprise. Concern lines his face, and I rub my head, trying to clear the fog and emotions that continue to make me feel sick. Frosty takes a step in my direction, and I slide myself further up the bed to keep space between us. His face crumbles at my reaction, but I can't help the growl building in my throat. If he steps anywhere near me, I will beat him to death.

"Reika?"

Stepping toward me again, my whole body starts to tremble with the pent-up emotions I'm feeling. Trying to keep them under control is a battle, I'm thinking, is worth losing. Cutie comes up behind him, yanks Frosty by the collar of his T-shirt, and throws him into the wall behind him. He then rushes to my side, placing himself between me and the fucker. I can't decide if he is friend or foe, but the defensive position he is standing in tells me I could maybe trust him.

"*What happened the last time you trusted someone, you stupid bitch?*" my inner voice snarls.

Bitch has a point, but still, I need to make alliances. My memories slam back into me with the force of a Mack truck; the sharp pain, Cutie dropping to the floor in a crumpled mess. I realize I'm at a disadvantage, sitting as these two snarl at each other. I slide to the edge and jump to my feet. "Argggh!"

My legs give way, and I crash to the floor. Cutie jumps over the bed and lifts me. My body freezes, and I cringe waiting for the pain to come. His eyes cut to mine and I can't help but flinch at the look there.

"I won't hurt you, Reika." The deep baritone of his voice sends shivers down my spine. I have never heard a voice as deep as my father's, until now.

"What the hell happened?" My voice is so meek compared to normal. Why the hell are we both here? I know he is familiar. They must have taken him too. My body starts relaxing in his arms.

"My name is Paine. I'm so sorry about what happened." I cringe.

"Yeah, I know. Not my first choice, but you should know how random parents can be, with a name like yours." A slight chuckle passes my lips, he does have a point.

"Where are we? And what's Frosty doing here?" Rumbling laughter rattles my head, as Cutie laughs at my words. Flicking my gaze to look at Frosty, I see confusion and anger melding together. But he hasn't tried to approach me again, thank fuck.

"As I said last night, I took you from Fancy Pants." There isn't a word to describe how I feel at hearing that name. "Do you remember me telling you that I contacted Liam about a safe house?" I growl as the conversation repeats in my head. "He must have been tracking my phone when he rang me. I woke up here earlier." He grumbles looking annoyed.

"Where's here?" My voice is scratchy, and it feels like it has been eating sand. "We're at the safe house. I'm not happy about his methods but this is the best place for you."

"I'm not staying with that bastard!" Wiggling myself from his death grip, I land back on the mattress and shimmy to the other side to put distance between us. My body feels cold not having his heat wrap around me, as shiver racks my body.

"Easy, Little Warrior." Cocking my head slightly, I look at him. I feel like a puppy waiting on orders from his master. His voice is so soothing. My feel my anger start to calm a bit. This is strange; I'm not sure I'm ready to examine too closely what's going on here.

"It's safer for you here, and you must stay safe. You're too important for Fancy Pants."

"Why? I don't even know the crazy bastard."

"As I said I will explain everything in time. But now, I need you to stay safe and get your strength back."

"Why? What does anything have to do with me? I'm a nobody." Apprehension fills me. Nothing is making sense anymore.

"That's not true. You want answers, don't you?"

"Yeah!" I snap. Obviously I do. What sort of stupid question is that?

"Get your strength back, and we will find them."

"Thank you for getting me out. I don't know what would have happened if I had been there any longer. I'm sorry it's taken me until now to say it." A hand lands on top of mine as I rub the mark on my thigh where that bastard decided to attach me to a chair with a knife.

"You got a doc?" What the hell? That's a quick change of

topic. I am about to answer no when Paine says, "I'm talking to you, Frosty."

"My fucking name is Liam!"

Paine sniggers at his response and I can't help but laugh at the face Frosty is pulling. I'm in no position to challenge him at the moment, but I am pretty sure Paine wouldn't let the icy bastard anywhere near me. I check him out from the corner of my eye - the dude is stacked. Tattoos are visible over every piece of skin showing. I thought Kane and the guys looked like trouble. Well, Paine makes them look like pussy cats who love belly rubs. The atmosphere between us is strange, like my soul is happy he is so close. I don't know, I can't explain it.

He seems familiar, but I've never met him before. I think I'd

remember if I had.

"Do you have a doc or not?" he snarls again.

"Yeah, we do."

"Get him here to check her. Do. Not. Tell. Your. Brothers."

I can't face Kane and Marcus. I don't know which is worse, Marcus bullshitting me about our friendship or Kane.

"I have too."

Crack

Paine moved so fast Frosty didn't have a chance to brace for impact. Paine lifts him up the wall by his throat. The animalistic growl that leaves him sends shivers down my spine and brings an evil, sadistic grin to my face. Frosty frantically claws at Paine's hands to try to loosen his grip. Personally, I hope he chokes the life out of the bastard. He deserves everything he gets.

"I told you not to tell your brothers. If you do, I will take her somewhere else." The terror on Frosty's face has glee running through my veins.Looks like he isn't the baddest one in the room anymore.

"Reika! Please help?" I flash a cold smile in his direction.

"Now why would I do that?" I sneer.

A shudder runs through his body. Hopefully he can see how much I despise his conniving ass. I can't wait to see him and his brothers burn, to pay in blood for everything they've done. Wheezing greets my ears from Frosty's labored breathing. Paine obviously has a tight grip on his throat. I can't help but enjoy watching the prick squirm, while Paine's eyes show him nothing but his death. My enjoyment is short lived, however, as my stomach growls so suddenly both men lock me in their gazes. My stomach continues to growl, letting everyone know it's still hungry.

"Call the doc. I'll go make her some food." Paine strides out the door. I adjust my head to look Frosty up and down. He rubs at his throat. I can see from where I'm sitting it's red and bruising rapidly, filling me with a sense of satisfaction.

Baring my teeth at him, I adjust the pillows behind me so I can attempt to sit back and get into a comfortable position. My body is in agony. The cuts and bruises aren't causing me too much pain, though the cauterized wound on my thigh looks to be infected and angry. What really hurts like a motherfucker are my tendons. They feel like they have been stretched within an inch of their life. The lacerations around my wrists are deep, because they have tried to heal and been reopened again. They are bright red and puffy with a weird sort of liquid weeping from them.

"What happened to you?" His words break me out of my inspection and I meet his gaze.

"The state I'm in, it should be pretty obvious, don't you think?"

"Don't be a snarky bitch, Reika."

"Oh, I'm sorry! Did you want me to say I feel like running with unicorns because I'm so happy to be here?"

"What is your fucking problem?"

"You. You're my problem, dickhead."

"Why? I didn't do anything!" Is he for fucking real right now? Jesus, does he actually believe the shit he's spouting?

"You're full of shit! You know what you guys did!"

"What are you talking about?" His gaze bores into mine, like he's pleading with me.

I can't fucking believe this! I can't. How can he stand there and lie to my fucking face? My mouth rapidly opens and closes as I try to piece together a response to the utter bullshit this asshole is spewing. Is he that deluded that he really thought I wouldn't find out? They played me. Granted, Liam always made it known he despised me, but they fucking played me like a fool. Well, fool me no more you will.

"Reika?"

I can't bear to look at him, so I lower my eyes to my feet underneath the covers. I try to ignore the daggers he's throwing my way. Hopefully Paine comes back with food soon, because he's right. I need to regain my strength. Then I can get answers to the questions that plague my mind. I can't even escape them when I'm unconscious.

"I didn't know what you liked." I look up as Paine strolls into the bedroom with a breakfast tray filled to capacity. Seeing all the food sets my stomach off again, deep growls and rumbles fill the room.

"Everything ok?" He suspiciously eyes me and Frosty, who looks like someone just ran over his favorite childhood toy.

"What you got?"

"Well, I wasn't sure, so I guessed."

Pushing myself up the bed, a hiss tears out of me as I try to cross my legs.

"Fuck me." Agony has me immobile as my legs throb under the protest of my muscles. That motherfucker. When I get my strength back, I am going to hunt that bastard down and chop him up into teeny tiny pieces and feed his ass to the wolves. I'm sure there must be a pack around here somewhere. If not, bears or pigs will work too. Paine looks like he wants to help me. Frosty looks like he wants to run in the opposite direction as fast as he can.

"I'll put the tray to the side so you can reach."

Gently placing it down on the bed on my right side, he puts the glass filled with what looks like orange juice on the little table at the side of the bed. The smell of actual food makes my mouth water. How can something so simple be so utterly amazing?

34

KANE

Ring. Ring. Ring.

Rolling over in bed to grab my phone, my head throbs from too much whiskey last night. The persistent ringing of my phone makes my headache worse. Without checking the caller ID, I accept the call.

"What are you playing at, Kane?" Dread fills me.

"Hello to you too, Dad," I deadpan. It looks like karma is being an even bigger bitch today than yesterday.

"Cut the snark, boy. I'm not one of your grunts." Like I could forget, the fuckers wouldn't talk to me like that, ever.

"God forbid."

"Sass me once more and I will come to the house." I freeze at his words. If he comes here, the shit show that is already my life will turn into an even bigger cluster fuck.

"Are you even listening to me?"

"Sorry, Dad. We partied a little too hard last night." The lie rolls off my tongue, without a hitch. I was the one that partied too hard in the den last night. Marcus, well he can't stand to be in the same room as me. Stopping that train of thought instantly, I put it in a box to deal with later.

"What's with the talk I've heard?"

"What's that?"

"Your leadership is being questioned by the crew, boy. They don't think you're fit to lead anymore."

I snort at his words. Is he for fucking real? The men in my crew are still throwing a fit over my occasional killing sprees? Seriously, get over it. I didn't kill any of their family members, so what's the issue?

"What's so funny?"

"That the weasels are questioning my authority."

"Do they?"

"No."

"Good. I taught you to be ruthless and relentless for what you want."

"You did. You taught me well, Dad."

"Well, it's needed now. The Grimm's have taken over two of our territories this week."

"What?!"

"So, the rumors are true. You have been preoccupied with a bit of pussy."

"Err…"

"Look, stick your dick in whatever you want, but do not ever allow it to consume you to the point the business falls."

"You don't need to worry about that, Father. The stupid bitch got her ass murdered."

"You'll find another. What have I told you about emotions?"

"They are distracting and make life harder when they are involved."

"Good and what do we do with that pesky little shit?"

"Turn it off."

"That's right. You have two weeks to sort the shit out with the Grimm's or I put one of your brothers in charge."

He ends the call before I can even utter a response to his last statement. Motherfucker! I need a drink. Climbing out of bed, I look around to find a bottle of whiskey. Every bottle in my room is empty. My brain works overtime, I know I have one around here somewhere. Fuck it. I head to the door to go and check the office, hopefully I don't run into that sap of a brother of mine.

"Hey there, baby." A soft touch across my shoulder blades sends an icy chill down my spine. Looking over my shoulder, I find the blonde who was one of my girls with a sickly-sweet smile on her face. What does this piece of shit want now? She isn't worth the effort.

"What the fuck do you want?"

"I heard the news that the bitch is gone." My heart practically jumpstarts at her words, but I stamp the bastard down without a second thought.

"Yeah, so?"

"Well, I was thinking we could pick up where we left off, baby?" She presses her body flush up to my back and grinds herself on me. She reeks of desperation.

"No."

"No!" She gasps like she is hearing things. Slowly prizing her fingers off my bicep, I turn to face her head on. Looking down at her small size my heart tries to jump again, and I give it another slap.

"Did I stutter?" I growl at her.

Ever so slightly, she shakes her head at my question. I drop the hand I had a firm grip of and spin to continue my quest for a bottle of whiskey. Fuck it, let's add tequila too. Rooting through my office, I throw all the objects out of the cupboards and drawers. I know there is some around here somewhere. My frustration is building to an out-of-control level. He moved them! I bet he fucking moved them. The interfering little shit.

The last time I saw Marcus he looked at me with utter disgust, like he didn't know the person who was standing in front of him. I know my words about Reika hurt him, but fuck him and fuck her too. My eyes have been opened now. Dad was right, emotions are nonessential things that cause problems. They won't ever be let back out of the box I've got them locked up in now. Yeah, it's shit she got murdered, but people die all the time. My mother was murdered, and Dad didn't dwell on that fact. He threw himself into the crew and made it what it is today. Honestly, I think I would have gotten bored eventually, she was feisty and a challenge - that is all. Definitely, that's all she was. A distraction that's cost me nothing but time and men.

"Searching for the sauce again?" Marcus stands in the threshold of the door with a judgmental look on his face.

"What the fuck do you want? Can't stand to look at me, can you?"

"Wow. Acting like a child now, are we?" Where does he get off spouting all this shit at me?

"The only one of us acting like a child is you. Just because you're hurt from my words about your precious Hellion."

"Don't. Say. Her. Name." Baring his teeth at me, he steps further into the office. Whoops! Looks like I hit a nerve. I bark out a laugh at the look on his face.

"I know you're hurting, Bro."

"Actually, I'm not, Brother. But please, do continue your speech. I'm just dying to hear it." Sarcasm layers my voice so thickly it could be cut with a knife.

"You heartless piece of shit!" he seethes. Rushing toward me, he grips my arm and kicks me in my shin, knocking my legs from underneath me so I end up in a heap on the floor.

"You loved her. Just as much as she loved you. And now, you're acting like she never existed." I can't help but push his buttons further, so I look up at him with my best heartbroken expression. Emotion flickers across his eyes as he relaxes his grip on me.

"Love! What's love, but an idiot who's just pussy whipped? They are all replaceable, Brother." Throwing a wink at him as I stand, I round the desk and take a seat in the chair. My search for alcohol is totally ruined now. I'll have to snag a grunt to get me some more.

"Now, Brother, you are acting like our father!" he spits in my direction. Then with a shake of his head he leaves me alone once again. Honestly, thank fuck for that. He was starting to annoy me.

Thanks to my brother's words, thoughts of Reika start to flood me. Memories of our touches, and the push and pull that was between us. Stop it! Fuck this shit. I launch myself to my feet, then storm from the office. I head back upstairs to get changed. Another night at the den getting shit-faced it is. Hopefully I can get on top of everything over the next few weeks. Fuck knows I need to, can't have the old man appearing and messing with everything.

35

LIAM

The last six weeks, playing babysitter to Reika, has been a pain in the fucking ass. It's pretty obvious her strength is coming back just by the amount of sass and shit she gives me day in and day out. Paine fucking encourages her, and thinks half the shit she is slinging in my direction is hilarious. Fuck my life he is such a prick. Those two have become as thick as thieves. Reika's whole attitude changes when Paine walks through the door, like she's ecstatic to see him. Doc came and checked her over and prescribed medication for the infections on her wrists and legs. Most of the cuts were superficial, but the damage to the tendons in her shoulders was pretty bad.

Only in the last couple days has she managed to lift a drink to her mouth without pain, or lift any object for that matter. The hell she went through, I still no idea, but it must have been some fucked up shit for the damage to be this extensive. Fox went MIA the day we came here, but he rings every so often give me updates on my brothers. I really wish I could tell them she is here, but Paine smashed my phone to pieces one night because I gave in and picked it up to call them. Fox has mentioned that Marcus and Kane don't speak and avoid each other like the plague. Also, Kane has been drinking his weight in alcohol constantly. He'll have irreparable liver damage at this rate. I thought it was his way of dealing with his loss, but Fox says he doesn't give a shit about that and is having a field day putting the fear of God into the town residents. It was apparently Dad's orders or some shit. I was wondering when that snake was gonna pop his ugly head up again. I can't help but think it'll be any day now when I lay eyes on him.

"Move out of my way asshole!" Reika comes storming into the kitchen, shoulder checking me as she passes. Her attitude is really starting to piss me off. I know I fucked up, but this is some next level bullshit.

"What is your fucking problem, Reika?" I can't stop the bite of my words as they lash out into the atmosphere. But c'mon, enough is enough already.

"My. Fucking. Problem?" Her skin flushes all over and her nostrils flare as she stalks toward me. Being honest with myself, the look in her eyes has my fingers and toes tingling. My eyes flick to the exit out the back door. She looks like an angel of death with the whites of her eyes showing and her body vibrating.

"You are my fucking problem. You and those piece of shit brothers of yours!" she screams in my face with such ferocity, spittle flies everywhere.

Crack.

My eyes widen, as I feel a stream of wet liquid hit my top lip and carry on. I swipe my hand across my lower face, and my closed fist skims my nose bringing tears to my eyes. The pain has my legs shaking. Pulling my hand away, the stream of blood that freely flows through my fingers shocks me. Running my finger from the bridge of my nose to the tip has horror filling me. My nose is bent at a weird angle, and blood pours out of it like someone turned on a tap. She broke my fucking nose! Raising my eyes to look at the satisfied and smug look on her face, I draw back out of striking distance. Prickling starts to spread throughout my scalp, and unease has me stepping further away from her. The gleam in her eyes and the aura radiating of her has me feeling sick to my stomach. It's like she is shrouded in darkness that thirsts for blood and vengeance and nothing else. What the fucking hell happened to her?

Lunging at me, she practically climbs me like a tree and wraps her arm around my neck in a chokehold. The manic laughter falling from her lips would have most people pissing in their pants. Luckily enough, I managed to hook my palm under my chin so she can't get much leverage on the hold and I can easily break free. Trying my hardest not to hurt her, I adjust my stance and throw her over my shoulder trying to limit the force of the impact on the floor. The crazy bitch jumps back to her feet, and with a war cry, charges toward me again.

Fuck this shit! I run for the back door to put space between us. I gulp air in to try and sate the need for oxygen, as I fight to breathe through my mouth since my nose is no longer functioning. Clanking coming from the kitchen stops me in my tracks. Turning to face the door, I open my mouth to speak, but no words come out. Reika is standing on the back porch with a steak knife in her hand. I raise my palms, trying to placate her. I don't want to hurt her. She has already been through enough, more than anyone should ever have to experience. I don't care that Kane won't say it, he still loves her. If I hurt her any more, he will gut me. Slowly backing up I frantically search for a way to put an end to this. She runs at me again.

"Reika!"

She stops so suddenly is causes her to slide across the grass and land on her ass. Paine is standing there with his arms full of grocery bags. His eyes open wide as he sees me with blood still pissing out of my nose, my white T-shirt a lovely shade of red, and Reika who looks like she wants to burn the world to the ground and then dance in its ashes. Slowly she climbs back up to her feet, leaving the knife in the grass. Mumbling to herself, she heads back toward the house, slamming the door with so much force the windows rattle.

"What the fuck happened?" he barks at me.

"You tell me? She went all psycho on my ass while I was in the kitchen!" How the fuck am I to blame for this?

"What. Did. You. Do?"

"Nothing!" Shaking my head, I set off to my truck.

"Where the fuck do you think you're going?"

"For a drive! Before the crazy bitch kills me." He can be on babysitting duty for a bit.

36

MARCUS

I can't leave it like this with Kane, the darkness is consuming him. He can pretend it isn't, but he's my brother, and I can see it pulling him down further every day. I am responsible for pulling him out since Liam is still AWOL. Fox updates me, reporting every time he gets closer to finding him, he disappears again. Determination fills me. Slamming my glass down on the kitchen counter, I head toward the stairs. My mind is a jumbled mess as I work through all the things I can say to my brother that might bring the real him out of the shadows and stamp out Dad's clone.

Reaching the top of the stairs, my body freezes on the spot. Disgust rolls through me as I watch the blonde bitch that approached Hellion in the den toilets slowly buttoning her shirt back up with jerky movements. Turning around, her eyes widen seeing me rooted to the spot. Then ever so slowly, her mouth hooks up into a smirk. My whole body comes to life, buzzing as spots flash in front of my eyes sending my vision into a kaleidoscope of colors. As she struts toward me, I don't even attempt to move out of her way.

"I told that bitch! He always chooses me." I am seething. My body kicks into over drive. Looking at her out of the corner of my eyes, I

see fear flicking across her face, as it should.

"Run." I bite out, the timber of my voice is so low, the words vibrate in my throat for a few seconds. Squealing like the little runt she is, she takes off down the stairs, the situation with her clothes forgotten. I storm toward the bastard's bedroom.

Throwing the door open, I don't even give him a chance to react before I am on him, laying ferocious punches to his face. Something crunches under my knuckles, but I don't care. How could he? How fucking dare he? I knew he was fucked up, but this? This betrayal is on a whole other level.

"What the fuck, Marcus?" he roars, throwing a punch to my chin, sending me off the bed. Hitting the floor, I jump to my feet as he jumps off the mattress. He's looking at me like I'm crazy, while I plan on tearing this fucker to pieces.

I can't bear to look at him. My mind fills with thoughts of Hellion, and the betrayal she would feel because of this. The feeling of a knife twisting in my stomach has me looking down to my abdomen. Nothing. Slowly, I raise my gaze back to the person I always admired as a boy. I shake my head and start to take careful steps backward toward the hallway.

"Wait!" he calls out after me. My heart is pounding in my chest so hard it feels like it will break through my ribs.

I can't. I can't listen to this; I have to get out of here. I spin so fast the movement disorients me and I stumble over my feet. I run toward the stairs, as cursing fills the air behind me. I somehow manage to make it down the stairs without tripping. Luckily, the key rack is open and I grab the first set of keys I find. I'm running for the door when I hear footsteps on the landing. Outside, I hit the unlock button on the fob and the Audi beeps to tell me it's unlocked.

"Hey, Marcus!"

I don't answer. I jump into the car, hit the ignition and the engine roars to life, just as Kane falls flat on his face through the front door. I hope it hurt. My brain is so out of focus that as I reverse, I crash into one of the others cars. Yells sound throughout the crew members as they look on in horror. I throw the car into gear and hit the gas. I need to get out; I need to be anywhere but here.

After thirty minutes of driving around the town, I pull up outside Old Sal's Diner. Fuck it! I get out and hit the lock button on the fob. Nostalgia should be hitting me right now, but thankfully it doesn't. I can't deal with memories from when I was younger after what I just witnessed. Looking up to the sky I snort, she would have gone the other way, dickhead! Looking to the earth I think, I'm sorry, Hellion. I don't know what's wrong with him. The wind blows around me, lifting my hair off the back of my neck. A shiver races down my spine. My brain is playing tricks on me - it has to be. I step into the dinner and I'm hit with the smell of coffee and grease. With a nod to the waiter, I head to the back of the diner to grab a booth. Grabbing a menu as I sit down, I try to read what's on offer, but my eyes are drawn to a figure to my right. Squinting to see into the shadowy corner, I climb to my feet and walk over to sit across from my twin.

"So, this is where you've been hiding?" His eyes lock with mine, as he reaches for the gun he always carries with him.

"What you doing here, Marcus?"

"Could ask you the same thing?" He huffs and leans back to stretch his arms across the back of his seat.

"Rough day!"

"You could say that." He has no fucking idea what I have been dealing with since his disappearing act.

"You?"

"Yep."

Taking a closer look at him, he looks like he has aged since the night of the Royale. Clearly, he hasn't been taking care of himself. His hair is longer. He has a slight beard is on his face, his clothes are crumpled and...

"Is that blood?"

"Yep." He spins the sugar canister between his thumb and finger. It's his go to when he is deep in thought, the same as when Kane has his coin in his hand.

"You wanna talk about it?"

"I can't."

The fuck? We have never kept secrets from each other. He knows every dark detail about me, like I do him. Huffing to myself, I stare off into space.

"What happened?"

Cocking my head to the side I wait for him to continue, because if he isn't gonna tell me what happened to him, then why the hell should I open my mouth.

"Let me guess. Kane did something stupid."

"That's a fucking understatement." His ears perk up at my choice of words, and he leans forward. Fuck it, if I keep this in my emotions are gonna chew me up and spit me out.

"To shorten it up, Kane has been an asshole since Reika was killed. He switched his emotions off and hit the sauce heavily."

"Shit." I nod my agreement.

"He's become Dad's clone. Telling me she was a bit of pussy and acting like he doesn't give a shit." Liam's eyes widen so much it looks like he has dinner plates for eyeballs.

"I went to go and talk to him, but just as I got to the hallway the blonde that approached Hellion was coming out of his room buttoning her clothes back up." Even saying this out loud to my twin has nausea twirling inside my stomach.

He doesn't mutter a word at my confession and I have nothing else to say to him either. Our relationship feels strained, and I don't know if we can ever get back to the way we were. The waitress puts a cup of coffee in front of us both, with a slight smile she heads back to the counter. I fix my coffee just how I like it, as Liam does the same. Nearly an hour passes. Both sitting there, not saying a word.

"Where have you been?" I ask.

"Around." Vague much? It's like he thinks I'm stupid or something. "That's not good enough, Liam. We needed you. I needed you!" My voice raises louder. The customers closest to us throw daggers in our direction until they realize who we are, then they look away so fast I'm surprised they don't snap their necks.

"I've had a job to do for Dad, ok?"

"Why Dad?"

"He knows there have been issues with the Grimm's, and wanted me to case the location of their stash."

"Why hasn't he asked us?"

"Why do you think?"

Shit! Dad would have heard about the crew questioning Kane's leadership, and would have lost his shit over it. No wonder he has Liam running on his own. Kane is a liability at the moment.

"Look, Marcus, I need to go." Unravelling himself from the seated position he was in, he looks down at me.

"Be safe, yeah." I mumble.

For the first time in years, I get the overwhelming urge to do something we have been told is wrong all over lives. Climbing to my feet so I am standing face to face with my twin, I throw my arms around his neck and yank him into a bone crushing hug.

"I'll be safe." Some of the tension leaves my body, as I hug my brother for the first time in years.

"Call me if you need me." Tapping his fingers on the table, he nods and heads toward the exit. Throwing a stack of bills on the table, I head toward the exit to head back to the fuck-up.

37

REIKA

After my meltdown earlier, Paine came to speak with me. Luckily enough, he knows my reasons for reacting the way I do every time I see his face or hear their names. My body gets tense, and then the tingles start, as a red hue descends before my eyes.

'Control the bloodlust, Little Reaper. If you don't, that's when you make mistakes.'

My father's words rattle around in my head. While before they used to bring me comfort, now they make me sick. Thinking of my father has memories of me and that bastard. How his presence used to quiet my father's voice when it got too loud to bear.

'You will know when you find the one, baby. Just like I did when I found your dad, but always remember to trust your gut.'

My mother was a beautiful woman. Her personality was one that would shine even in the darkest of days. After training with Father, she would see to my wounds with tears brimming in her eyes. She would tell me she was sorry she couldn't stop it, but that what I was going through would help me later on in life. She was partially right; I wouldn't have made it through the months of torture with Fancy Pants if it hadn't been for his training.

'It is her.'

I have tried to figure out his meaning behind those words, but nothing comes to mind. My mom used to raise money for charities and my father worked with a friend of his for the logging firm his parents owned. They were quiet people. Why would someone hurt them?

Raised voices reach my bedroom from downstairs. Frosty and Paine must be going at it again. Honestly, I think they need to have an all-out brawl to find out who is top dog so they can stop this pissing contest. Not gonna lie, I would bet on Paine. He is so calm on the surface, but the darkness in his eyes tells you there is something monstrous in the depths of his soul, waiting to be set free. Leaving the guys to it, I grab my shower stuff and go to the adjoining bathroom. I drop my borrowed clothes on the counter. I'm not letting either of those two buy me clothes. They would probably come back with horrendous flowery summer dresses or some shit. I would rather walk around naked than put anything like that on me; I mean I've got standards. So, I'm stuck using Paine's clothes to at least cover myself until we can figure out a way to get my clothes back. Flicking the shower on so it can warm up, I step in front of the mirror and stare at my reflection.

The bruises have faded. The marks left behind from the cuts and stab wounds I received are no longer infected, thank God, but some are still prominent. Little lines here and there cover quite a bit of my body, making me look like a character from Edward Scissor Hands. My eyes get drawn to the angry red lines. The scarring on my wrists and my thigh are disgusting. The burn mark has to be at least four inches long and about three inches wide. I'm a pro when it comes to scars, and my thigh in particular will always be a little darker than the rest of my skin.

My phone pings in the bedroom. I head to grab it and I'm surprised to see a message from Paine. Huh! He got me a burner phone so I could contact him when he isn't here, just in case I go all murdery on Frosty again.

Paine:
Stay where you are! Lock the door.

Is he for real? Telling me to stay put is like telling a wild lion not to eat a fucking zebra. Fuck that. Turning the shower off, I roll the band at my waist of Paine's joggers to keep them in place, and head through my bedroom straight for the door. As quietly as I can, I peel open my bedroom door, carefully watching where I place my feet. In a cabin like this there are squeaky floorboards everywhere, and I don't want to give myself away. At the top of the stairs my heart stops and my breath catches in my throat. Descending the stairs, my palms grow sweaty and the back of my neck heats up. I grab the bowie knife from its sheath on the coat rack, and put it in my jogger pocket. I know, not the best place to put a knife, but fuck it. As I creep along the hallway, shadows move across the walls. Paine has his back to the doorway, blocking whoever it is from getting any further into the cabin. Fortunately for me, Paine's size alone blocks me from view.

Undiluted rage ignites my whole body. My limbs violently start to shake. Cautiously, I run my hand up Paine's back, and wrap his t-shirt into my grip. He stills at my touch, as his body seems to grow bigger. I step to his side. I'm slightly behind his arm, but am now able to see the owners of the voices. Frosty, Marcus and Kane turn wide-eyed gazes on me.

"Hel...Hellion?" Marcus looks like the rug has been pulled out from underneath him. Shock, disbelief, haunted. He's as white as a sheet, like he's seen a ghost.

Cocking my head to the side, I grind my teeth. I can't believe he can stand there and look at me like this. But, Frosty and Marcus never do anything without the say so of the person currently staring intently at the side of my head. Turning my gaze away from Marcus, I look the bastard dead in the eyes and put as much contempt and disgust into my expression as possible. Paine watches Kane's movements so intently it looks like he's about to pop a blood vessel. Both Frosty and Marcus stare at Kane, each of their expressions so different. Marcus looks like he wants to murder Kane where he stands. Hmm, interesting. I wonder what went wrong there? Kane's eye is frantically twitching. Emotions flicker across his face like a human slide show. But what surprises me most, is he doesn't say a damn thing. The rage I'm feeling bubbles up slowly underneath the surface. If I didn't have hold of Paine's T-shirt, I don't know what I would do.

For twenty minutes, Kane stands and stares at me. The atmosphere in the kitchen is supercharged with electricity. Marcus has tried to approach me more than once, but a quick death glare and a tsk has him stopping himself.

"I told you not to bring them here!" Paine glares at Frosty.

"I said fuck all. It's not my fault Marcus decided to follow me after the diner."

"Well, what did you expect? You forget I know when you're lying." Marcus throws at his twin while me and Kane have a stare off.

"Why the fuck did you go to a diner?" Paine asks, annoyance coats his voice.

"Well, if the crazy bitch didn't go all Ted Bundy on my ass, I wouldn't have!" he bellows. The horror that shows on Kane and Marcus's faces, has my lips twitching to move into a smirk. I feel a chuckle start to bubble up inside me, but I squish it down, for now.

"Pretty Bird?" Kane takes a step toward me. I pull Paine with me as I step back to keep the distance between us. The hand holding Paine trembles. A growl builds in my throat at that fucking name. How fucking dare he think he still has the right to call me that; after everything he has done.

"H...How are you here? We watched you die. My soul broke into a thousand shards thinking you were dead." His voice cracks at his own words as tears build in his eyes. Falling to his knees he lowers his head to his chest, his body rocked by tremors as he tries to keep hold of his emotions.

"Why would you try to kill my brother?" Kane turns pleading eyes to me.

I'll give him his due. He is very fucking believable when he lies. I was gullible before, believing his words so easily, because he made me believe he was the only thing I would ever need.

"Because you weren't here." I snarl at him, baring my teeth in his direction. Rage builds and my whole body starts to shake. Wrapping my hand around the handle of the hunting knife, I take a step toward the lying, manipulative bastard.

"Calm, Little Warrior." Looking up into Paine's eyes, my body instantly relaxes. Without breaking our eye contact, I step back to his side.

"You Motherfucker!"

Kane launches to his feet and moves in our direction. My rage explodes like a fourth of July fireworks display. I throw the knife toward his head, but he manages to dodge the flying object. He wraps his hands into Paine's t-shirt, yanking him away from me as the other two stand motionless, staring at them attacking each other with utter shock on their faces. Running forward, I tackle Kane with as much force as I can. The surprise attack does the trick, and Paine stumbles out of the way. I follow his movements back to our side of the room. Kane is spinning, with his nostrils flaring and his chest rising and falling rapidly. He looks like a wild animal as he keeps his gaze on me.

"Why?" he begs.

"An eye for an eye!" I scream. Kane's eyes widen instantly. *Bang.*

Yells fill the room, as Paine yanks on my arm to pull me away from the chaos I just caused. I can't stop the manic laughter bellowing out of me as I see the blood splatter on the kitchen cabinets. Marcus and Frosty are trying to help Kane while blood pools on the floor under his body. Paine scopes me up into his arms, charging through backyard toward his truck.

"The fuck?" Paine asks.

"Shouldn't keep your gun so easily accessible."

I jump into the cab as soon as he unlocks it and strap myself in. I hear yells then a roar come out of the open doorway. Paine is spitting out words so fast I can't understand him. Spinning the tires as he hits the accelerator, I look out of the passenger window to see Kane charging in our direction.

"Fuck! I missed."

Paine slams his foot harder on the gas, and we take off with screeching tires and rocks flying. Looking into the mirror, I watch with a smile as he hits hauls ass.

38

MARCUS

"Kane!" He's lying face first on the grass. I can't inhale properly, no matter how hard I try, air just isn't going into my lungs. What the actual fuck just happened here?

"Why? Why would she do that?" Liam looks at me like this isn't real.

Hellion shot Kane without hesitation, without a second thought. What the hell happened to her? Never in a million years would I have thought she'd do something like this. The horror I felt seeing her with the gun in her hand, pointed at him. Our lives flashed before my eyes. All the moments fun times play like a movie in my head. Watching as her and Kane's relationship grew to see them both happy, then crumble into dust. I froze. I couldn't do anything but watch.

"I don't know."

"Fuck that, Marcus. She tried to carve me up with a steak knife, and now this. I thought she loved him?" Luckily, I'm kneeling down next to Kane, so I hear the words he's mumbling to himself about how this is his fault.

"Who the fuck was that guy?" He calmed her. When I realized she was there, the anger radiating off her was thick in the air. Her body vibrated with it, but I honestly thought it was from seeing us again after so long. Seeing the state she was in, the scars littering her body and the angry red ones around her wrists, made me sick to my stomach. She must have been tortured for weeks for that sort of damage to be done. Evidently, the damage they inflicted on her wasn't just physical. Have they tried to reprogram her? Is that why that man could calm her?

"Marcus." I look to Liam, who is looking down at Kane.

"Ugh!" Slowly, Kane pulls himself into a seated position.

"Please tell me I imagined that?" he manages to say though gritted teeth. I don't know what to say. Liam and I stare at each other, hoping the other one is going to think of something.

"She shot me." His face clouds over with disbelief and several other emotions. But just as fast as they came, he shuts them down.

Oh, fucking hell, no. He isn't turning his back on this shit show, because he can't deal with what's happened. It's time for Kane to man up and face his problems, rather than pretend they just don't fucking exist and boxing his feelings away.

"Who the fuck was that guy?" He bares his teeth as he spits the words out.

"Paine Anders." Both our heads snap round to Liam, who had answered.

"Are they fucking?" asks Kane. Liam looks to me, and I can't help the growl that builds in my chest.

"Are you being fucking serious right now?" I jump to my feet and

pace up and down. How the fuck can he ask that after he fucked blondie and played the whole women are replaceable card? He's so full of shit, I just can't deal with it anymore.

"Oh, shit." Kane moans.

"How the fuck can you ask that!?" Liam and I both scream at him.

"Marcus told me about what happened between you and blondie."

"Guys. I. Feel…" Kane collapses on the ground. I pull my phone out and hit call.

Liam

Pacing up and down the corridor, my body feels restless. Marcus took off like a bat out of hell once we made it back to the house, saying he needed time to think. Doc has been patching Kane up for the last thirty minutes. I'm still in shock that she shot him. I knew she was unhinged before, but I'm not sure if there is any coming back from that. What the hell is going wrong with the world? For us everything. Nothing was meant to be like this. We were meant to be the kings that rule the world.

"Where is he?" No, no, no, FUCK no.

I look to the end of the corridor. Ice runs through my veins as my dad saunters down the corridor, goons flank either side of him. The newer crew members situated in the corridor turn to me with fearful expressions. With the slight nod of my head, they leave the corridor and disappear out of sight.

"Doc's patching him up."

"Tell me, boy. Who was stupid enough to shoot my successor?" The sneer on his face has me wanting to back pedal and get out of this damn corridor. Fuck this shit. Not today, Satan; not today. I need to get out of here now.

"We didn't get a good look at them, Dad."

"We?"

"Me and Marcus were with Kane at the safe house." I try to keep my voice as even as possible. The bastard is like a bloodhound when it comes to sniffing out a lie.

"So, you're telling me all three of you were there and Kane was still gunned down?"

I lower my gaze to the floor so I don't antagonize him further. He steps closer to me. All I can see is the shine of his shoes.

Crack.

My already smashed nose explodes from the force of his back hand. I stumble back, slipping on something on the floor.

Argggh.

I land on my ass, and feel the swelling on my face grow further with blood freely falling again. Looking up to my dad, I can see the gleam in his eyes at having me beneath him once again. Malcolm Southbourne has a God complex, and when we all became bigger than him, he never had the balls to challenge us all because he knew he wouldn't stand a chance.

"Ahem." Looking over my shoulder, I see Doc standing in the doorway to Kane's room. I jump to my feet and rush over to him, without another thought of my dad.

"Doc?"

"He's asking for you and Marcus." I gulp and give a slight shake of my head. Doc looks over my shoulder and his face pales seeing the person standing behind me. Every person in this house will try to stay out of sight because of his arrival. I was hoping to talk to my brother without anyone else around.

"Go," I whisper, so only we can hear my words. Doc doesn't need to be told twice and heads off into another part of the house. I take a deep breath and brace myself for whatever reaction is waiting for me.

Stepping into the room, Kane pulls himself up. He opens his

mouth, but shuts it quickly. I knew he wouldn't wait out in the hallway. Kane's eyes widen, I give a slight shrug to let him know I had nothing to do with this. Them both in the same room is normally a recipe for disaster. Kane won't yield to Dad, and Dad can't stand that Kane won't bow. But what Daddy Dearest really needs to remember, is he had to hand over control of the crew to Kane. Because as soon as Kane started making a name for himself, the crew feared him more than the leader.

"Son."

"What do you want, old man?" The ice in Kane's words sends a shiver down my spine. He may be injured, but by the look on his face, he will beat Dad if he isn't careful.

"I want to know who the hell shot you, boy?"

"Doesn't concern you. I will deal with it." He doesn't even bother to make eye contact as he speaks, but I can feel his gaze burning a hole in the side of my head.

"You had better, or I will step in. Your leadership is already in question. If you fail to do this, then you will be removed from your position." Without a backward glance, my dad struts out of the office with a chip on his shoulder.

"Where's Marcus?" Ah! Fuck. Straight down to business.

I try my hardest to look anywhere but at Kane. How the fuck do I explain to him that Marcus took off straight after we loaded him into the van, and he hasn't been seen since? I know he is having a hard time accepting the fact Reika shot Kane, or I hope he is. I saw anger on his face when he realized she was alive. Fuck me, I have never seen so much hatred for one person, but what is surprising is who it was aimed at. He and Reika have such a special bond. He always said she was like the sister he always wanted. He must be trying to deal with his emotions. He will come back when he has everything figured out, I hope. He fucking better. I know I might have caused some of this shit, but he needs to deal with his so we can all fix this before one of us ends up dead.

"Well. He. Um."

"Well, um what?"

"He kinda did a thing." I can't help but gulp the saliva down that's pooling in my mouth from nervousness.

"What thing?" Kane grits between his teeth as he pulls himself up from the bed to stand before me.

"He took off after the shit at the safe house."

"What do you mean took off?" Did Reika hit something that affected his brain? Nah, she couldn't have, she got him in the shoulder.

"What do you think?"

"He's dealing with seeing her again. I can't blame him, but right now we need to find out how she is still alive. Find her, Liam. Me and her need to have a little talk." My heart skips a beat at the ferocity in his gaze. I can't tell if he's hurt or pissed off.

"Ok, Bro."

39

REIKA

"Are you planning on ignoring me for the rest of the car ride?" The silence is killing me, and making me even more anxious than when that bastard was standing in front of me. I still can't believe I fucking missed.

"I can't even look at you right now."

"Fuck you, Paine!"

The audacity of this motherfucker. How dare he! He knows the shit I have been through because of Kane and his crew. Weeks of fucking torture because Fancy Pants thought I could give him some information on them. All men are idiots. It would be so much simpler if women ruled the fucking world, instead of this constant testosterone pissing contest. I am fuming. I can't believe him. Clearly, his ego is dented. What did he expect me to do, really?

Sitting in silence, my brain stews on everything that happened earlier. I can't believe Kane tried to play the holy shit card. The look of shock that quickly morphed into pure happiness at seeing me alive. If I hadn't seen the truth for myself, I would have fallen for it, but I know it's all utter bullshit. Marcus's reaction is the one that has doubt niggling in the back of my mind. I was so surprised to see the hatred on his face for his brother. I must have been imagining it. *But what if you weren't?* My inner voice snarls. I'm pretty sure I have lost my mind now, because that bitch randomly pops up when her input is not needed.

So, you're saying you weren't happy to see him?

Why the fuck would I be? I know what I saw on the video.

Hmmm, if you say so.

Fucking snarky bitch.

"We're here."

What the hell? I didn't even hear the car stop. I look around and see we're in the middle of nowhere. Trees surround us on all sides.

"Where's here?"

"C'mon, I haven't got time for this."

I wonder if a porcupine crawled up his ass and made a home there, prickly bastard. Climbing out of the car, I look around. What the fuck are we doing here? There isn't anything for miles either way.

"This where you plan on trying to kill me?"

"Trying to? Ha! You're delusional, Little Warrior. I could if I wanted to." Annoyance sparks in my veins at the smug look on his face.

"I wouldn't attempt that, Paine." A deep voice says from behind me. I turn, eyes wide, to find the owner of the voice.

"She would kill you instantly, if she wanted to."

I can't help the smile that spreads over my face seeing my father's friend standing behind me.

"Pete!"

Ok, call me a sap, but I run over and engulf him in a hug. He chuckles at my silly gesture, because he knows I have never really been a hug type of person.

"Good to see you, Little Reaper."

"She wishes she could kill me, Pete." I look over to see a shit-eating grin on Paine's face. Hmmm. How do these two know each other?

"She hasn't got any stuff, but I need to get back before anyone starts questioning shit."

"I got her, Paine. Check in, ok?"

"Ok."

I'm still standing in Pete's arms as I watch Paine climb back into the car and pull away. What the hell is going on around here? I thought we were good friends. He did save me from Fancy Pants. But he just gets in and drives away like I'm nothing.

"Well, he's a prickly son of a bitch, isn't he?" I step away from Pete as I watch the taillights disappear.

"Ignore your cousin. He has an asshole complex."

We both freeze, I can't breathe. Did he just say cousin? Pete looks horrified as I glare at him. The color slowly drains from his face.

"C-cousin? Come again?" It can't be. I don't have any family. My father and mother where the only ones left in their family. They didn't have any siblings.

Frozen, that's what I am. Frozen to the spot as my senses dull around me and my vision blurs. Memories race before my eyes, searching for a time when either one of them might have mentioned they had a sibling. Nothing comes to mind. For years, I thought I was the only one left, but I have a fucking cousin. My breathing picks up and my eyes narrow on the man in front of me. I have a fucking cousin!

My knuckles crack underneath the pressure I'm putting on them. It's a nasty habit, I know, but it's the only thing keeping me from losing my shit at the moment. I can feel myself in danger of spinning the fuck out. How did I not know? Why did no one tell me?

"What do you mean, my cousin?" The words lash out so fiercely, Pete flinches away from me.

"L-little…" He stutters, frantically looking anywhere but at me.

"Don't bullshit me, Pete. What. Do. You. Mean?" I can feel the vein in my neck pulsating rapidly. A cold sweatstarts to drip down the back of my neck.

"He's your cousin. Your dad's nephew."

My mouth drops open at his words, as I frantically shake my head. It's not possible! Dad would have told us if he had a sibling. Every time I asked why I didn't have any relatives, he would tell me his parents died young, he didn't have any siblings, and neither did my mother.

"You're lying!"

"Why would I lie, Little Reaper? I've watched over you for years. You know me."

He takes a step in my direction. I step back to keep him out of my personal space. I feel like a time bomb about to go off at any second. My body shakes violently as I try to get myself under control. Disbelief wars with the anger inside my body. Either he is lying now, or my father lied my whole life. But if that's true, why did I never meet them, never see Paine? I might have dealt with my father's training better, I wouldn't have felt so alone. Why did he keep them away?

"Reika! Don't go down that rabbit hole."

"How can I not, Pete? Either you're full of shit, or my father lied to me."

Folding my arms, I bend over slightly as nausea rolls in my stomach. Did he know? Tears fill my eyes. He can't have known? How could he have left family there to be tortured for weeks and do nothing about it? White hot rage burns through me.

"He had his reasons why, little one."

"W-Who?" The words barely make it past my lips. My whole body is vibrating with such ferocity my teeth chatter together.

"Paine." A growl builds in my chest. He knew and he did nothing!

"He had his reasons? Are you fucking serious?" I seethe.

Stalking my way forward, Pete backs up toward the tree line to keep in front of me. I must have a manic expression on my face to match the emotions playing Russian roulette inside me. Honestly, I don't know which one is going to win. Maybe my head will just explode? This just goes to show that I can't trust anyone but myself. Everyone lies.

"Fancy Pants tortured me for weeks, Pete!" I feel sick.

"I can't make the betrayal any better, but he had his reasons, Reika."

My legs give way beneath me, my hands are in my hair. I can't believe this! Why? He could have told me at the safehouse! My heart feels like a dead weight and the pain hurts like hell. From my heart to my fingertips, it feels like my body is on fire. I can't trust anyone. My body temperature grows as my vision blurs and tears build. My throat is so tight, I can't get enough moisture in my mouth. Stumbling to my feet, they barely hold me up. Pete runs toward me as I stumble away from him.

Stupid! Stupid, stupid, stupid! You should have known this was coming. Everyone has a motive when it comes to you! They all lie!

My emotions flit between disbelief and hurt and rage. Nothing is as it seems. I trusted Kane and his brothers, and look what happened there. Why did I think Paine would be any different? Even Pete kept this from me. Why? I have to get away. I can't stay here!Lies, it's all lies! Everything. Everyone…lies!

"Little Reaper, please don't run. I will tell you everything."

Oh, now he wants to be straight with me? Why do people have to bullshit their way through life? Specifically, my fucking life. Who gave them all the goddamn right to continuously fuck me over? It doesn't matter if the truth hurts. It's still the truth and everybody deserves it.No one should have the world pulled out from underneath them when the lies come crashing down, because believe me, lies always come out. Everyone always forgets. The truth has a way of pushing to the surface no matter how people try and bury it behind a wall of lies. What else have my so-called family lied about? I know the boys will get what's coming to them for the bullshit they pulled. But Pete... He was like a father to me when my real one was gone. Without another thought, my feet start to move, and I'm running into the trees as fast as my legs will carry me.

40

LIAM

Life is one big, massive pile of shit at the moment. Kane is holed up in his room, refusing to talk to anyone. Dad is walking round like he owns the damn place. Well, technically he did at one point, but still… Marcus has been AWOL since the night at the safe house. Word spread like wildfire about Kane being out of action, and the little cretins in town are trying to make a name for themselves. I don't have the time to deal with their shit. The Grimm's are pushing for more territory, and we are constantly having to push them back. Yeah, I am currently more grumpy than usual; I can totally understand why Kane is always an asshole. I have hardly slept or even had a shit without someone having to disturb me because of one thing or another.

"Yo, Liam. We got a problem, bro." Looking to the voice, annoyance fills my veins.

"I've told you before, Bonzo, do not call me bro."

"S-Sorry man. We got trouble." A huffed breath whooshes out of me. I don't know who much longer I can put up with this shit. Seriously, it's like everyone has gone fucking crazy, thinking it's a free for all.

"What?"

"There's a meeting going on." And that's my problem because?

"De'Marco is pushing for back up from other families to take over Damned Crew territory."

That motherfucking cocksucker. I wondered when that bastard would have the balls to show his face again. Honestly, I'm surprised he has with Dad being here. He was always terrified of him when we were kids. Apparently, he isn't anymore. Ha! I wonder what the old man thinks of that.

"Liam?"

Bonzo is still standing in the kitchen, waiting for me to decide what I'm gonna do. I climb down off the breakfast stool. It's time me and brother dearest had words. Heading out, I make my way upstairs to his bedroom. With each step, I swear time slows down making this short walk excruciating. Rounding the corner, I see Blondie walking toward me in the opposite direction with a smile on her face. Honestly, that girl makes my damn skin crawl. We both step in front of Kane's door, her in a half-naked state I didn't notice before.

"The fuck you want Blondie?"

"Kane asked me to come by and make him feel better."

"Oh really? How? By grinding your half naked ass on his lap, I guess?"

"Ha! Liam your so funny. He loves it when I grind on him. Hopefully, we'll be naked for this." The fucking audacity of this girl. What a fucking idiot. There is no way Kane would be that fucking desperate, especially when he knows Reika's alive.

"Are you on drugs?"

"Ha-ha. No. I know your brother is going to make me his Queen soon. We are perfect for each other." I double over, pissing myself laughing. She really is a fucking idiot.

"What's so funny?"

"Reika is alive." The horror on her face sends tears rolling down my cheeks. Before I can rub dirt in the wound, she takes off down the corridor. I enter my brother's room, still laughing my ass off.

"What's so funny?" Kane is sitting on his sofa with Spotify playing, but strangely he has the tv muted.

"Your fuck-piece thinking she will have your attention permanently."

"The fuck you on about, Liam?"

"Blondie was headed this way, pretty much naked."

"The fuck!"

"Chill out, Bro. If you want to fuck it, that is your choice. But don't lie about to me about it." I quickly change the subject.

"Look, Kane. De'Marco has set up a meeting to gather help taking over our territory. What do you want me to do?"

"Why'd you change the subject, Liam? I haven't done anything wrong."

"Look, Bro, dip your cock in whatever you want. I don't give a shit. We need to sort out this other stuff."

He goes quiet, and suddenly looks like he's constipated. He must be thinking. As I wait for him, my thoughts drift to my twin. I wonder where he is? Did he go after Reika? Did she hurt him? I stop my thoughts in their tracks. I know the bitch is crazy, but she wouldn't hurt Marcus. Their relationship was close, and she didn't have a look of pure hatred on her face toward him that night in the safe house kitchen.

"They need to be sent a message. They need to know that even though I am injured, you will step up."

"So, I get free reign?"

"Yeah." Well, it seems things just got a whole lot more interesting.

He turns back to stare at his tv, with the music muted, and I know that's my cue to leave. Heading downstairs without a backward glance, I shoot off a message asking some of the crew to meet me in the office. It's time to fuck some shit up.

Twenty minutes later, seven of the crew are standing in front of me. They're bitching among themselves about how brave the Grimm's have become and wondering who shot Kane.

"Silence!" I bellow at these fucktards. Their heads swivel in my direction, as all eyes focus on me.

A hush spreads over the room, it's so quiet you could hear a pin drop. Some of these assholes really pluck my last goddamn nerve, but they are all loyal which is the thing we need in our way of life.

"One, don't gossip like a bunch of girls. Two, we need to send a message to the Grimm's." Smiles break out across the room. They have all been waiting for something for this, and have been chomping at the bit to stick it to those bastards. Their bloodlust becomes a tangible feeling in the room.

"We could destroy their HQ," one of them throws out.

Chatter breaks out around the room, with different ideas tossed out every now and then. This is why none of them will ever get further up the ranks. They are thinking too small. We need something with an *oh fuck, they aren't playing* message. I lose myself in that train of thought. My brain fires on all cylinders as I work out the perfect message that will make me a legend in my own right. I want to to walk into a room and have it fall silent. I want people to squirm at the thought of me turning my attention their way. I don't know how long I've been lost in my head, but I suddenly realize the room around me has gone quiet and all eyes are on me. A chuckle builds in my throat.

"How many labs do they have on their side of the tracks?"

"Four. Why?" Seriously? Can no one see where I'm going with this? Amateurs.

"Because we are about to cut off their income. I want four teams made up in the next thirty minutes ,with as much explosives as you can get your hands on."

"You mean?"

"Yep, boys. We are gonna blow up their meth labs. It's time to burn it into their memory that they don't fuck with us." I have been dying to do this for some time now. Yeah, our crew deals in drugs, guns and women, but we draw the line at the hard drugs, like meth and heroine. They all break out into a run and head off doing everything I need them to do to prepare.

Grabbing my phone, I try to call my elusive twin. I know he'd be on board with my genius plan. The call rings for a few moments before going to voicemail. I know the bastard has put the phone down on me. I will deal with the Grimm's situation, and Fox can find that little shit.

"What's all the fuss, boy?" Ice runs down my back. I turn toward the voice that could make hell freeze over. My dad stands in the office doorway.

"The Grimm's are causing an issue, so Kane has told us to send them a message."

"Ah. So, he has decided to be a little more productive in the crew, even though he is still sulking about something."

"Yeah. Well, not being funny, Dad, but I don't blame him." Fuck. Shit. I shouldn't have said that.

"Is that so?"

"What the fuck are you doing here anyway? You have never bothered with us before?"

"It doesn't concern you, boy. I caught wind of some rumors flying around that piqued my interest."

"Oh, really. Like what?" He never answers a question fully. He only ever gives half-truths, or answers you with another question. Always so evasive. It's like he doesn't trust anyone, even us.

"Again, not your concern."

"Anything to do with a Pete Marshall by any chance?" His eyes widen at the name. So, the old man wasn't lying when he said he knew my dad.

"How do you know that name?"

"Just do. In your words, Dad, it's none of your concern."

I leave him in the office with an ashen expression, brush it off and head off in search of my teams. I don't even bother to change. I don't give a shit if they recognize me. It's not exactly a covert operation now, is it? Not like you can just subtly blow shit up. Fox is standing just outside the front door as I step outside.

"What are you doing, Liam?"

"Sending a message. I need you to find Marcus."

"What's with you guys running off when you can't deal with shit?" That's the million-dollar question, isn't it? A fucked up childhood will do that to you.

"Ask him when you find him."

Nodding to Fox, I head over to the van that is parked next to a couple of SUVs. My eyes light up at the sight of the back of the van. It's nearly full of explosives.

"What you trying to do, boys? Level the block?"

"Nah, man. But we don't know how big the labs actually are." Fair point!

"Load up!" I shout.

Every man coming with us climbs into their vehicle, and we're off. The drive to the lab located near the Grimm's HQ will take us about an hour. I figured if we hit them at the same time, they won't stand a chance as they'll be too worried someone is gunning for their HQ next. The members in the car are all pumped - laughing and joking about what we're about to do. I can't stop the smile that graces my face. I just wish Marcus or Kane were here to enjoy this moment. I tune them out after thoughts of my brothers start to bring me down. So, I sit back, get myself comfortable for the journey and think about what possible retaliation could come from this. The drive passes quickly. We pull up on the corner down the street from our mark. The other vehicles all broke off in different directions to head to their marks. I wait until everyone piles out and moves into their respective places. They know what they need to do. It will take them about fifteen minutes to get the explosives in place and make their way back to me, if we don't get any trouble.

Watching the men scurry off through the windshield, I take a deep breath and slip my ice-cold mask back on. I know that's the reason Reika calls me Frosty, because my cold look could freeze someone in their tracks. Gun shots alert me that there is an issue. I jump out of the vehicle, making sure my weapons are in place. I take off in the direction of the chaos. I only make it to the metal door, when it swings open and Bonzo with a shit eating grin comes charging out, blood splattered up his face. The other men follow with the same expression.

"What happened?"

"Grimm's."

"And?"

"We dealt with them before we could get everything in place."

"Is it done?"

"You bet, Liam." A whoosh of air leaves my lungs. I loom the team over, and there don't seem to be any injuries.

Just as I am about to ask him to check in with the other teams, his phone bleeps three times and he turns the phone to me.

Site 2 done.

Site 3 done.

Site 4 done.

Showtime! I think, looking at Bonzo.

"Stay out of our territory, De'Marco, or you will lose more than this." With that I press the trigger in my hand.

Boooom'

The building behind me instantly explodes and is devoured by flames. I feel the shockwave hit my face, just as explosions can be heard all around the area as each of the other buildings go up. A smirk hooks the side of my mouth as I look to the phone Bonzo is videoing this on.

"You have been warned."

41

MALCOLM

Annoyance flares through me as I pace up and down my room. How the hell does Liam know about Pete? Nobody should know about that treacherous bastard. Someone hasn't done their job properly. It's bad enough someone had the balls to take a shot at Kane. Now that name pops up? This can't be a fucking coincidence.

"Derek!" My head of security strolls into the room without a care in the world.

"Boss?"

"Find out who the fuck shot Kane. I don't want to wait for the information, got it?"

"Yes, boss."

He leaves. Unease settles in my stomach as a heavy weight descends on my shoulders. There is more going on here than I know, and I don't like it. I always know everything that's going on. I have always been the most powerful, after all knowledge is power. A few of the crew members have been talking about someone my son has been sleeping with. I have a basic idea of who she is, but he told me it was done because she died; and he agreed when I reminded him emotions are for the weak and I made him anything but weak. Fuck this. I head down to the kitchen for a coffee. If I don't stop this, I will end up wearing a hole in the floor from my pacing.

Crew members scuttle out of my way like roaches when they see me in the hallway. It's good to know my reputation still has that effect on people. I have always told my boys you need to rule with fear, not with anything else. Loyalty is a fleeting thing. Fear, now, that leaves a lasting impression. People are only loyal to you when it benefits them, and love is for the weak. I learned that the hard way when their bitch of a mother did what she did. The boys were broken when they found out she died, but it was for the best, cheating tart that she was. I heard the rumors about her fucking some of the crew. When I called her out, she just said I didn't spend enough time with her. She was happy enough, though, to spend the money I made from all the shit that would keep me away. We had an agreement. She could fuck who she wanted as long as I didn't know about it, but I could do the same. What was surprising, was that the night she died, I found out she was having a relationship with the Butcher. It was lucky for her that her car swerved and crashed like it did, or God knows what would have happened. He was one of the people I trusted. I don't trust anyone anymore, and the boys know only what I want them to.

The thing that is still bothering me is, how the hell does Liam know Pete's name? He hasn't been seen for years. I honestly thought he was dead.

"Derek!" Hopefully he's back from doing what I asked. He really should have only been making calls.

"Boss?"

"We need to go out for a bit. Where are my sons?"

"Kane is still upstairs. Liam has just gotten back, and Marcus is in the office."

"So, the wanderer returns, does he?"

"Yeah, boss." I head out to the car. I'll find out what that little shit is playing at afterwards.

Fifteen minutes later, we pull up outside the one place I never thought I would see again. God this place is a shithole. I can't help but reminisce about my life growing up here, the struggle to get to out, and all the bodies I put in the ground to get there. Walking through the door and down the dank hallway, nausea churns in my stomach. This place is disgusting. How it's possible he has managed to keep this going for so long, I don't know. At the end of the hallway is a desk with paperwork scattered across it and a blonde sitting in the chair with her boobs on show and make up caked on looking like a poor excuse for a sex doll.

"How can I help you today, sir?"

Not bothering to answer her, I walk past the desk and head to the door, acting like I own the place. I fling the door open while the blonde hurls abuse in my direction. The scream that meets my ears brings a sadistic grin to my face. A light grip lands on my arm. I turn round and growl at the blonde, who scuttles off like a bug I'd crush under my shoe. The little pissant in the office is still screaming at my entrance.

"Well, well, Alexander. Nothing has changed I see."

"Malcolm. What are you doing here?"

"Aww, have you missed me?"

"Get out!" he screams. I haven't seen this little fucker in a long time.

"Derek? Tie this bastard to his chair. We need a little chat."

Alexander tries his hardest to avoid my security, but he clearly forgets I keep the best of the best around me. Derek is ex-military and damn good at what he does.

"Malcolm. Please?"

"Don't beg, Alexander. You know how much that annoys me."

"What do you want from me?"

"Well, I want to know why one of my sons knows the name Pete Marshall."

"I… I don't know."

"Lies!" How fucking stupid does he think I am? Liam will have heard that name from somewhere.

"I. Don't. Know. Please, Malcolm." Urgh, just quit it with the begging. Why do they always beg? Such a waste of good fucking air.

"Well, funny thing is, he dropped off the face of the earth at the time of my wife's accident."

"So?"

"Why would my son know his name? Has he had contact with him?" My face gives nothing away, but I will leave here with the information I need.

"I don't know. Pete disappeared after your wife did what she did with the Butcher." Ah, so the little shit does know something.

"I know all about the Butcher and my wife fucking. But please, continue." I pace in a circle around Alexander's chair. His anxiety spikes and sweat gathers at the back of his neck. What? Was he not expecting me to know that? A smug grin pulls at my face, knowledge is power. I have to hold all the cards.

"They…they…"

"They what?" Toying with my prey isn't something I normally do, but Alexander's fear filling the room in waves has happiness singing in my veins.

"They weren't fucking," he says. I snort. What an imbecile. Everyone knew how much of a whore she was. She would literally open her legs for anyone with a cock.

"I know they were."

"She went to the Butcher for help." This piques my interest.

"She wanted to leave you and take the boys with her. He was helping her with it, and then the accident happened."

"So, my wife was planning on leaving me?"

"Yes."

"Huh? The bitch had some spunk after all." Alexander's face pales, and I can't stop a chuckle from passing my lips.

"Tell me the truth. Why would Pete be back?"

"I don't know. I didn't even know he was alive."

"Are you bullshitting me, Alex?" His fear ramps up again. Nothing happens in this town without the leech knowing about it, apart from people coming back from the dead, evidently.

"Next question. And think hard about this one." I meet his gaze head on so he can't look away from me.

"Would he go to his usual place if he was back?"

"Y-yes."

Turning my back on him, I head back out to the car. The screams following me down the hallway are music to my ears. Looks like we are hunting down a ghost. Ten minutes later a gunshot rings out from the building followed closely by a second. Derek strolls out of the building with blood splatters on his chest, and quietly gets into the car.

"Where to, Boss?"

"Just drive. I'll direct you."

The car bounces as we drive down the dirt road. This far out in the sticks, you would think wildlife would be the only thing out here. As the car breaches the trees, a cabin comes into view. The screen door opens and out steps the man in question.

"Get closer."

Driving as close to the stairs of the porch as he can, I jump out of the car, gun in hand, aiming it at the man's chest.

"Pete."

"Malcolm."

"Why are you back here?"

"Unfinished business." This bastard is he has such a good poker face. I can't tell what is going on in his head. Normally, people who have guns aimed at them sing like canaries, spilling all their dirty little secrets, but not Pete fucking Marshall.

"Which is?" My anger flares at the flat look on his face.

"Fixing the house up before it goes up for sale." With a shrug he turns his back on me. Gritting my teeth, I storm up the steps, grip his arm and spin him in my direction.

"You're full of shit. I have just had a lovely talk with Alexander."

"Oh, how is the snaky bastard? It's been a long time."

"Cut the shit, Pete. Sarcasm doesn't suit you."

"Oh, no, it doesn't?" He rubs a hand to his chest and places the other in front of his mouth to hold the gasp in, like he is offended at my words.

"He told me some lovely things about my wife." Pete's face pales at that. "Ah, so you do know something."

"Woah. You're a big fella, aren't ya? Did your parents feed you a growth hormone?" Pete questions. Following the line of his gaze, I realize Derek is standing just to my right.

Crack. His legs give way under the force of the punch I give him. My patience only lasts so long. I can't be bothered dealing with his delay tactics.

"Tie him up and put him in the back. He knew the consequences of seeing me."

"Yes, Boss."

Climbing into the car, snippets of the last time I saw Pete come to mind. He tried to initiate into the crew, but didn't have the stomach to follow through with his task. After that, I told him if I ever saw his face again after that night, I would kill him. So, color me surprised that he's so close.

The drive back to the house was horrendous. Pete woke up half way through the journey, and decided to kick up a fuss. So, now I have a pounding headache from all that racket. The boys are on the grass out front, which is surprising. All three of them together. I head over.

"What's going on Dad?" Kane asks, while Marcus throws daggers in my direction.

With a whistle, all of the crew moves toward the front of the house. My gaze meets Derek's, and I signal him to pull our guest out of the car. Commotion from the back of the car carries to my ears. After a few seconds a cursing, Derek comes into sight, dragging a body that looks like a worm on a fishhook.

"Dad?" Looking at my boys confused expressions, I think I need to explain further.

"This, boys, is the person who caused the accident that killed your mother." Gasps spill from their throats. They know another car swerved on the road and collided with her car. The sheriff said it was a drunk driver.

"You're full of shit, Malcolm. I was nowhere near the town that night!" Pete thrashes in Derek's grip.

"No, I'm not. I knew that night it was you. And only a few days after I told you that you were not crew material."

"Stop lying!" A sadistic grin lifts my lips. I have been hoping for this for some time.

"You couldn't complete your hit to initiate, and then you decide to take it out on me by going after my wife!" I roar in his direction. All three boys step toward the bastard, wanting their pound of flesh.

"Put him on his knees." Derek does as I ask. Pete is on his knees in front of me, with his head resting on his chest. Heaving breaths reach my ears. I look to my right. Kane's chest rises and falls rapidly. He looks like a wild beast raging against the bars of his cage.

"Pete Marshall." He lifts his head to meet my gaze.

"You will be executed as a failure and for killing my wife."

His expression doesn't falter one bit. I'm kind of surprised by this, but he has to die and this is the perfect opportunity.

"Do you have anything to say?"

"You don't want to do this, Malcolm." A cool, calm, serenity emanates from him; it's awkwardly unnerving.

"Yes, he does you fucker! It's the least you deserve for what you did to my mom!" Kane bellows from beside me. His anger and rage are reaching a boiling point. I step closer to Pete. I want to be as close as possible to see the light leave his eyes. Pulling my gun from its holster, I flick the safety off and take aim. Pete's eyes gaze at me from underneath the weapon aimed at his head.

"Malcolm?"

His gaze lowers as his shoulders start to move. At first, I think he is showing signs of fear, but then the slight chuckle reaches my ears and continues to build in volume. Raising his eyes back to mine, the humor on his face is out of place for the position he's in.

Tut, tut-tut echoes around the garden. I look for the owner. Who dared to interrupt me? Laughter suddenly reverberates around the yard. The crew turns in every direction. The boys all stiffen at my side. The cold hand of unease runs down my spine making my heart rate spike.

"Oooone. Twoooo. I am coming for you. Threeee. Fooour. Better lock your door."

"No." Fear grips me like a vice and I'm frozen in place.

Manic laughter fills the area as ice slides down my spine. It's not fucking possible!

Boom!

42

REIKA

Shouts and curse words are fired around the yard, while my manic laughter ricochets off every surface. I see Pete on his knees in front of a man flanked by all three assholes. Pulling out the pin of the grenade I toss it under another car, and sprint to the other side of the yard, out of sight.

"It's not possible!" the man yells. My manic laughter goes into overdrive at his words, sending a spike of adrenaline through my system.

Chaos erupts all around as members run in different directions to avoid the debris from the cars that just exploded everywhere, scattering like cowards as they run. Checking I have everything I need, I step out of my hiding spot with my head held high. A sadistic grin splits across my face, as I laugh at the fear on the bastards' faces. Some of the crew freeze, looking like they've just seen a ghost. I chuckle and head in the direction of the three stooges and big papa.

"Pretty Bird?" Kane's expression is haunted.

"Stand up, Pete." Keeping my eyes on the men in front of me I watch for any twitch that will give them away.

"Back the fuck off, Ninja Turtle!" I seethe, as the fucker

who looks like a cat stole his slice of pizza takes a step to grab hold of Pete. His eyes widen at the Glock I have aimed in his direction. Not just a pretty face, don't you know?

Slowly, Pete manages to get his feet underneath him and make his way to my side. The look he gives me is one of a father chastising their child.

"Not one crew member moves a muscle. Got it!" I bellow into the air so none of these idiots decides to play hero. I'd fucking blow their heads off if they did. Moving my aim from Ninja Turtle, I aim at the head of the man in front of me. Gasps echo around me, and the fear on the three stooges' faces has me laughing again.

"Tell them, Kane! I missed once. I won't miss this time."

"Do as she says," he orders the men.

"Hellion. This isn't who you are!" Marcus pleads with me.

"You don't know me, Marcus, just like I don't know you. But I do now, I've seen who you all really are."

Training my gaze on the main man himself I can't help the look of triumph at the uncertainty on his face.

"You like my song, old man?" I snicker at the pathetic look on his face.

"Who the fuck are you, girl?" he spits in my direction.

"Aww. Don't get brave now. Answer the question."

"Pretty Bird, please."

"Ugh! Shut your damn mouth, Kane." I spin, one gun aimed at their dad, another firing a shot into the chest of the crew member that tried to sneak up on me. He stumbles on the spot, and the color drains from his face as he smashes into the ground.

"Reika, he didn't do shit!" Liam screams at me from his position.

"Shut up! This is between me and him. Then, I will deal with you!" Looking at Kane, I see the confusion on his face.

"Pete, you free?"

"Yeah."

Passing my guns to him, he takes aim just as I did before. I step closer to the old man who is frozen in place. Gripping hold of his shirt,I yank him in my direction just as I land a headbutt to his nose. He bellows in pain, and I hit him with a roundhouse that launches him into the middle of the yard. Stalking him as he crawls on his hands and knees, my laughter starts again, then I catch a whiff of ammonia. He's pissed his pants.

"Fight, boss. It's just a little girl!" screams Ninja Turtle.

"They don't know, do they?" My interest is piqued, he must not have told anyone.

Argggh!

My eyes water from the dirt that just hit me in my eyes. My back slams into the ground, as hits start landing all over my body. That's it fucker! "You should be dead!" Spit hits my face as he screams at me.

Lashing out, I catch him just under his Adam's apple making him grab his throat, and frantically try to pull air into his lungs. Jumping back to my feet, I stand over his body while he continues to fight for air. Bracing my muscles, I rain down hell on him. Blow after blow, kick after kick. Bones crunch under the ferocity of my attack. The fucker is bellowing in agony as chaos erupts around us. The crew screams for the well-being of their leader, begging me to stop. I scream, like a banshee, down at the bastard bleeding under me.

"You slaughtered my fucking parents! You're the reason why they're dead!"

Hands grab me all over as I'm yanked from my position. Multiple crew members drag me away from the fucker. I scream in fury at not being able to end the bastard where he lays. The horrified expressions of the three stooges meet my eyes, as Pete meets my eye with a conflicted look. I nod to him, which is all he needs to start firing and running in the opposite direction.

I don't bother to fight against the men dragging me toward the house, landing blows of their own. Doc comes rushing past us to help the bastard coughing up blood on the grass. Good, I hope he chokes to death on it. Peace settles over me at the sight, and I laugh.

The sunshine disappears as I'm dragged in the house. I'm pulled around corner after damn corner, and down hallways I have never seen before. How fucking big is this place? The temperature drops as we get deeper into the house. The sound of metal scraping on metal reaches me. I try to twist to see what the noise was, but another blow clocks me in the side of the head. I latch onto the hand that wasn't quick enough to get out of the way of my teeth, and bite down, sinking my teeth into his skin. The following scream is like music to my ears, as I smile with blood pouring out of my mouth. I'm thrown onto a hard object. Five men keep me pinned in place, while two others grab hold of my wrists. I freeze at the next noise. Metal clinks as my wrists are weighed down and my ankles feel heavier. A cold slice of fear cuts through me. The men get out of striking distance, as I launch myself at them, but I am meet with resistance and propelled backward. Looking down, I see metal cuffs attached to my arms and legs. They fucking chained me! The chains are secured into the wall by massive bolts, which then trail in my direction, up to my cuffs. Voices echo in the corridor as footsteps thunder in this direction. A few seconds later the door is thrown open and in steps the biggest thorn in my side.

"Leave us!" Kane commands the men as he, Marcus and Liam step into the room.

Nobody says a word as the crew depart and leave us alone. I

have three sets of eyes locked on me with different expressions of shock, what the fuck, and murder.

"What the fuck, Hellion?" Looking to Marcus, I lift a shoulder as if to say 'what do you want me to say.'

"You will tell me why you have just nearly beaten my dad to death, Pretty Bird." Kane's voice is coated in uncertainty. He has no idea how to handle this cluster fuck I just created.

"One. I am not your Pretty Bird." My voice is as cold as a winter's night. Before he can open his mouth even to draw breath, I continue.

"Two. You should be glad I am in chains, because I will kill him, then you. All of you." His eyes widen and the others gasp at the venom in my words.

"Three. My name is Reika Martins, the daughter of Thornton Martins. You will know him as The Butcher!"

43

KANE

"What's the matter, Kane?" Pretty Bird sneers in my direction. I haven't heard that name in years.

"Hahaha. Aww, cat got your tongue?" Horror freezes me, the hatred in her gaze is palpable. I can feel it crawling across my skin like an army of fire ants.

"Pretty Bird, I…"

"You what? I know about your vote in the hit on my parents. I also know what you did." Her tone is laced with so much venom, I flinch. Fuck, how did this happen?

"I was young, stupid, and gullible when that hit was made." Hopelessness fills me at the contempt Marcus stares at me with. It feels like a blade driving into my gut and twisting, repeatedly. They knew I had to have a say in some of the votes for the crew when we were younger, but they never knew what the votes were.

"Fuck off, Kane. You're full of shit," she says, with cold words that slice right through me.

"How am I?"

"You know the difference between right and wrong! I was

349

eleven when I watched them get murdered!" The pain in my heart has me sliding down the wall onto my ass.

"Me and my father had to watch while they repeatedly raped my mother, and we couldn't do a damn thing to help!"

Fuck. Bile burns my throat at the image of what she had to witness. Her words hit me like a whip cracking across my body.

"I-I. Didn't. Know." The words stutter out of my lips that refuse to work. Guilt claws through my insides. I feel sick, completely crushed under the weight of her revelation. It explains why she is the way she is, and I had a hand in that.

"Yeah, because you are that clueless you didn't know voting yes to a kill order is exactly that?"

"Pretty Bird. I didn't know it was your parents." Pleading with my eyes I hope she sees the honesty. I didn't know. I had to do what Dad said, or he would beat my mother.

"What else are you taking about, Hellion?" Marcus finally decides to speak. My eyes widen at the compassion he has for her.

"When Fancy Pants took me, he showed me videos while torturing me." I run to the corner of the basement just in time to empty my stomach. They tortured her? Of course, they fucking did. Only an idiot would assume they wouldn't hurt her.

"Hellion, please tell me?" Marcus coos, as he slowly steps toward her.

"That wasn't the first thing I saw. The first video was you fucking someone while I was fighting at the Royale." She doesn't even look at me as the words fall from her lips. What the fuck?

"My heart broke. I thought I could believe what you said. Then I see the video of you meeting someone else." she snarls, gritting her teeth. I notice the slight tremble to her bottom lip.

"Errm. Reika?" Liam pipes up.

"What, asshole?"

"That wasn't Kane, that was me. I kinda set it up so it looked like him from a distance. I wanted you to disappear, but my boys didn't get to you in time." Liam rushes through his words like he is terrified of the outcome. Silence fills the room so thickly you could cut it with a knife. I am shocked by Liam's revelation. He looks like he wants the ground to open up and swallow him. At this precise moment in time, I wish it would.

"Get out. Get out, both of you!" Marcus screams. My legs move on their own, as I head to the door. I so badly want to look back at the girl I love, but I can't bring myself to do it.

Hushed whispers come from the basement, as me and Liam haul ourselves back up toward the house. Neither of us says a word; the silence between us utterly damming. I'm in shock at what she has seen causing her to think so little of me. Liam's confession plays on repeat I my mind along with everything Reika shared, battering my brain and leaving my stomach sick with dread. My brain doesn't want to process anything, it just wants to shut down. We make it out of the basement level and trudge through the house.

"There you are," Doc says, as he steps out of the room where my father is being treated.

"What?"

"It's bad, Kane." His face is pale with sweat beading on his forehead and running down the side of his face.

I walk into the room where my father is laid out on a hospital type bed with wires and things coming from his body. I don't feel anything other than disgust for the destruction he has caused.

"What's up with him?"

"Four broken ribs, a broken nose, gashes and cuts cover pretty much all his body. He has damage to his right hand which needs a splint. Almost all of his body is a giant bruise."

"What does that mean?" I'm not hearing any words clearly. It's like cotton wool has been stuffed in my ears.

"I've had to sedate him to limit his movement and calm him. He was cussing up a storm. He will be out for a while."

"How long will he take to heal?"

"He should be able to do most things between three to six weeks."

This makes me happy. That means I have three weeks to find out what the hell is really going on with this shit show that is my life. To find out the truth buried in all the little lies. Then I need to decide what I am going to do with either my dad and Pretty Bird.

"Bro." The voice barely reaches my ears because it falls so gently from Liam's lips. Uncertainty and fear coat his words. I haven't got it in me to react to his part in the damage. It is just too much. But mark my words, the shit will pay for everything in due time.

"I'm sorry." I step into the office. This isn't a conversation we should be having with members walking around and my father's men here. I park my ass on the couch.

"Why?" My voice breaks slightly at his betrayal. I knew they didn't get on but this? I don't get it.

"I didn't trust her. I thought you would be better off without her." He can't even look at me.

"That wasn't your decision to make, Liam. I love her. I can't stop loving her even after everything. What does that tell you?"

"I was scared, ok. Mom dying nearly destroyed you. I didn't want the same thing to happen with her!" he bellows. Anytime Mom gets brought up we all have the same reaction. She promised she would never leave us, and then she never came back.

"That's my choice."

"Kane, please. She shot you for fuck's sake. You've seen how unstable she is." His last words are barely a whisper.

"Can you blame her? I can't, not after everything, Liam. She watched what happened to her parents, and I had a part in that. I don't blame her at all."

"She will try to kill you again, Brother." His words are the truest words he has ever spoken.

"I know." I rub the shoulder she shot; it still hurts slightly.

"Keep an eye on everything here, I'm going out for a bit." Liam looks like he wants to argue with me, but I don't give a shit. I need space from all of this shit.

44

MARCUS

Numbness. Regret. Guilt.

It's all there playing ping pong on my soul. I don't know how long I have been down here trying to coax Hellion to hold a conversation with me. For all I know, time is standing still. Her replies to my questions are either a growl with her gnashing her teeth in my direction or ignoring me completely. The calm in her eyes is beyond unnerving. But what has a hollowness spreading across my chest is there is no light there, just darkness in her eyes. Her demons have always been what drew me to her. I only ever saw snippets of the darkness that lived within her. Her light would always shine through in her sass and the crazy shit that came out of her mouth. But this... What the hell happened to her?

Learning she is the Butcher's daughter shocked me as soon as the words left her mouth, but I have had time to think and honestly, it makes perfect sense. The Butcher is still a legend in the darkness. The brutality with which he handled a job would scare the shit out of Satan. He was relentless, all-consuming. His song made full-grown men piss in their pants, apparently my dad included. He wanted you to know he was hunting you. My dad used him a lot when he needed something dealt with.

Over the years, I've seen the man himself leaving my father's office, like an old friend. But rumors still circle that The Butcher was killed because he was working for both crews. Now, I know my dad was the one to issue the kill order. But Kane? This guts me above everything, because of Hellion. After being tortured and finding all this out, I'm not surprised she's lost her mind. I don't blame her for hating him, because I do too. She can never find out about what Kane did with that slut. I can't allow her to be hurt any more, especially by him. I know she still cares, you can't just switch feelings off instantly, but she's doing a fucking damn good job of trying.

I won't abandon her again. I will deal with the members who decided to throw punches at her as they dragged her away. There wasn't a command made for it. They just decided to do what they wanted, and that shit doesn't fly with me. It won't fucking sit right with the others either once they've got their heads back on straight and out of their asses either.

"What are you still doing here?" Her voice sounds so tired, yet her strength and resilience is there as strong as ever.

"I'm not leaving, Hellion." Determination fills me. Our trust has been broken, but I will repair it.

"God, what is with you all and your asshole tendencies?" She is glaring daggers at me. I have to smirk at the sass that shows.

"I'm just an asshole, baby." She snorts at my words, then quickly tries to cover it up with a scowl, which has me chuckling to myself.

"Very funny, asshole."

"You can try to cover your laugh as much as you want, Hellion, but I know you really love my stupid ass." I can't help myself, even after everything. She is the thing that makes everything feel normal, Even in our crazy, fucked-up life. She doesn't answer me and goes back to sitting in silence. The uncertain look on her face has me keeping my mouth shut. Some more time passes when her stomach suddenly rumbles.

"You want something to eat?" You fucking idiot Marcus.

"No shit, Sherlock. That's why my stomach sounds like a pissed off T-rex."

Standing up I head over to the metal box located at the far end of the room. I wondered what the stink was in the room, when I see the vomit from Kane. Ughh! That needs to be sorted. Rooting through the box, I grab what I need. As I clip the first side of the handcuff to her wrist, her head shoots up in my direction.

"What are you doing, Cheshire?" My heart rate picks up at the nickname she uses for me.

"You need food, and I need to send someone to clean that shit up." Looking over my shoulder, she grimaces at the sight.

I continue on with my task. Just as I am about to secure the other wrist, I freeze. The mark on her wrist is still slightly swollen and red, but the line that looks like it runs the whole way round has my breathing becoming rapid. Rubbing my thumb over the line, my eyes shoot to hers as she tries to pull her hand free. The look in her eyes has me consumed. She is fighting her emotions, but it's there, sadness, disgust and helplessness.

"What happened, Hellion?" It's barely a whisper, I can't even put to words what I am feeling.

She gulps, and her eyes begin to glaze over as she averts them. Gripping her chin, I force her gaze back to mine as I plead with my expression for her to tell me. I need to know. I can't cope with the answers my brain is supplying.

"They..." she whispers, breathing in deeply and slowly.

Then turning to face me dead on, she squares her shoulders and looks me in the eye.

"They hung me from the ceiling for hours while they tried to get information on the crew." Blinking rapidly as her words bounce around my head, I lift her other hand, finding the exact same marks on that one. Exhaling through my nose, I compose myself the best I can, but my rage is a living thing, coiled underneath my flesh and ready to strike.

"No one will touch you ever again, Hellion." My voice is so thick and determined, her eyes widen in shock.

"Cheshire?"

"No, Hellion. I am sorry. I failed you. When I thought you were dead, my heart shattered. You are family and no one marks my family like this and gets away with it." My breathing is growing rapid again, as my rage continues to build. A gentle touch to my cheek brings my gaze back to her, as the corner of her mouth twitches.

"Did you know about the hit, Cheshire?" Uncertainty fills her voice, invading my senses. Her doubt weighs on my shoulders, causing my stomach to revolt. How has it all come to this?

"No." I say with more certainty than anything I have ever said before.

The chains clink as they hit each other. When my brain finally focuses, I realize Hellion has me in a death grip of a hug. I move my arms to encircle her and hug her back. Her strength still shocks me. But she is here and she is hugging me, so she believes I am telling the truth. This is the start of me regaining her trust and I will have it back no matter what.

"Time to feed you. I'm sorry, but I have to leave the handcuffs on. Is that ok?" I hate having to ask her this.

"It's fine. Plus, it's the safest option, because I might end up murdering your crew." Laughter barks out of me at her words, and she joins in. I shouldn't be laughing, but I know she is telling the truth.

"Let's go."

Reika

The walk up to the kitchen has me feeling like a prisoner on death row about to get their last meal. Every crew member we pass either looks terrified to see me, or takes a step toward me that Marcus shuts down instantly with a look that promises pain. My emotions are in such a whirlwind over our talk. I could see from his face he was being genuine when he told me he didn't know about the hit. Knowing how he felt at the live stream of my fake death guts me. I hurt him so badly.

Then there is all the shit with Kane. My brain doesn't know what to think after finding out the first video was set up by Liam to break us apart. The worst thing of all is Kane openly admitted to voting yes, and I don't know what to think about that. My stomach protests at the lack of food again, which has Marcus laughing his head off. Hearing his laugh with such a carefree feel to it has me laughing alongside him. Thank fuck we are finally at the kitchen. Honestly, I don't know how prisoners walk around with his shit on them; it seriously blocks your movement and makes walking so damn hard. I guess that is kinda the point, but fuck me, it sucks. I am glad they are on though, because I don't trust my reaction to having free rein in the house. Especially knowing Malcolm is here somewhere; me and that bastard have some unfinished business.

"Um. Dude?" Marcus turns to me. I have to smile at his expression, he hasn't got a clue. I lift my hands slightly so the cuffs clink. He cocks his head, still not understanding what I am asking of him.

"Am I gonna have to sit on the floor?" His eyes widen as he realizes what I mean.

"Shit! Sorry, Hellion." He comes over to where I am standing, and gently lifts me so I am sitting on one of the bar stools.

"Thank you." The cheeky smile he gives me has some of my darkness retreating slightly.

With a flamboyant spin, he gets to work pulling different things out of the cupboards. I know how much he loves to cook, and if I'm being honest, the guy is a damn good one. Pots and pans end up on the island while he pulls out bowls and strange looking things that look more like torture devices and puts them to one side.

"Cheshire?"

"Yes." He spins to face me and nearly drops all the shit in his arms.

"What ya doing?" My curiosity piques at all the stuff in his arms.

"I'm going to make you the works, Hellion."

"Dude, I would be happy with a grilled cheese at the moment."

"Really?"

"Duh!"

"Okay, so you want me to make you one?" A smile grows on my face. He is such a mother hen.

"Only if you add Bacon to it."

"Bacon?"

"Yep." He shakes his head and starts to put everything away he will need for grilled cheese. What can I say? I'm a simple person who likes easy meals.

"Coffee?"

"Do unicorns fart glitter?" He laughs at this. We spent enough time together for him to know, asking me if I want coffee is like asking a heroin addict if they want a hit. A few minutes later the smell of bacon has me groaning and my mouth salivating.

"What's she doing up here?" Following the voice, I find Liam staring at me from across the kitchen.

"What's up, Liam?" Sarcasm drips from my voice. Marcus shakes his head as he places a steaming cup of coffee in front of me, and then gives me a look to that says, 'keep your damn mouth shut.'

"Her stomach was growling. She needs to eat." He says with a slight command in his voice, as if he is daring him to argue.

"Kane won't like it."

"Fuck, Kane! I don't give a shit."

"Okay. Reika?" Lifting my gaze over the edge of my cup, I see Liam staring at me so intently, unease swirls in my stomach.

"Hmmm."

"I'm sorry about the video, ok? I thought you would destroy my family and I didn't want to see either of my brothers hurt again over someone." Sincerity flows off him in waves as he watches me, waiting for my reaction.

"From what I can tell, Liam, Kane has done that all by himself." Taking my reply as a conversation starter, he moves to the other side of the island. Thankfully, Cheshire puts the food in front of me and I dive in without a second thought.

"Fuck me!" I shout, wafting my hand in front of my mouth. It feels like I decided to kiss a lava block. Both Liam and Marcus laugh at me. I throw a look at them; they both instantly go quiet but the corner of their lips twitch. You know that look when your parents tell you off and you're trying your hardest not to laugh? Fucking children, honestly.

"Glad you assholes think it's funny," I snipe while lifting the corner of my mouth to let some of the hellfire out of it.

"Reika? I really am sorry." Looking him dead in the eye, I ask.

"Did you know about the hit?"

"No, I didn't. I was in the dark, just like Marcus."

"I believe Marcus, because I trusted him before. He wouldn't intentionally hurt me, but you?" I let my words break off.

"Yeah, I get that. Reika, you have to understand our dad ruled everything growing up.

"We knew he was getting Kane ready for when he had to takeover, but if anything went wrong or we acted out…" He pauses, taking a deep before he continues. "He would beat our mom up to punish us, before she died." Some of my anger toward him thaws a little at his words. I understand better than anyone about losing a parent. She must have been one hell of a person to put up with that bastard and have her sons.

"I am not forgiving you for what you did, Liam, but we can call a truce, if you want?" I really hope this isn't a mistake, but I need people in my corner.

"Yeah. A truce." With a nod he gets up and leaves. I catch Marcus side eyeing me with a smirk on his face.

45

KANE

Hours must have passed after I left the house; I haven't stopped walking since. Pretty Bird's words have been playing on repeat in my head. Guilt claws its way up my throat every time my mind takes me back to the night I voted yes. I wasn't lying when I said I didn't know it was her parents. That night, my dad didn't give me any details, only that they were causing the crew trouble. Everything got buried with the shit that happened later. When my dad came to tell us our mom was involved in a car accident and didn't make it, everything else disappeared as my heart broke.

My mind feels like a typhoon. I'm not shocked Marcus kicked me and Liam out of the room. I was hurt by the contempt she held for me and Liam, but she only held a look of indecision on her face for Marcus. Random things run through my head, like someone else is putting them there. My mind drifts to that night at the safehouse. Who the fuck was that guy? And why did it look like they were close?

Possessiveness roars to life within me at the thought of Pretty Bird being with anyone but me. I don't know how we can come back from all the shit that has happened.

"Kane?" Looking around a street I don't even remember walking down, I see a figure is standing to the side of a rundown store. I don't recognize them from a distance.

"What do you want?" Frost coats my voice. I am not in the mood for an asshole.

"Can we talk?"

"Who are you?"

The figure steps out into the sunshine, and my heart stops as I recognize the guy Pretty Bird let run. A growl tears from my throat as I charge toward him, and grip him around the throat. I slam him so hard into the brick wall, some start to crumble under the force. I watch pieces float to the ground.

"You killed my mother," I spit out the words as spots dance in front of my eyes.

"I didn't. Look, you don't have to believe me. I just need to know Reika is ok." The concern in his voice has my left eye twitching. How the fuck do they know each other?

"Talk!"

"I was out of town when it went down that night. I didn't see your mother. I got a call about what happened to Thornton and Adele, and I had to come back for Reika." *I watched them repeatedly rape my mum.* Shaking my head to dislodge the words, I relax my grip on him.

"I cared for her from the age of eleven, but Kane, I am not the sort of role model a child that age needs. So, I sent her to a boarding school that was more of a reform school. Which ended up being a good thing because she became wild, uncontrollable. At eleven, teachers were already terrified of her. She disappeared after a while, and I had to hunt her down. Then I found her here, fighting for Alexander." I knew some of this already, as Alexander had enlightened me about her randomly turning up one day.

"So, I kept my distance and watched from afar, trying to keep her hidden and safe."

"Why?" Everyone has a reason for the things they do. I wonder why he would go through so much trouble for someone else's daughter.

"If word ever got out that the Butcher's daughter was still alive, every person wanting to make a name for themselves would try to get their hands on her." Realization hits me.

"Is that why she was kidnapped?"

"I think so, yes. She didn't tell me much about what happened there, but I've seen the scars and the darkness that now surrounds her."

"What do you mean scars?" A confused look slips across his face as he studies me.

"Where is she, Kane?"

"Still in the basement where some of the crew chained her."

"Get her out of there." His words grow in intensity, "Kane, she can't be chained again. I don't know what it will do to her. Please, you have to let her out. I will leave with her; we won't ever come back."

"No!" The word reverberates around the alley.

"No?"

"She isn't leaving me again."

"She tried to kill your father. Do you really think the crew is going to let that stand?" His words hit me like a freight train.

"They can deal with it or leave, but she isn't going anywhere. Knowing what I do now, I don't blame her for wanting him dead." My head and heart are in agreement for the first time in a while. The only other time they agreed was when I claimed her as mine.

"She's too important. Nobody can get their hands on her. I need to see her. I have to talk to her." What the fuck is going on around here? Why is she so important? Why is he so concerned?

"Are you going to tell me why she is so important?"

"I can't. Not yet. There is too much at stake." The fear radiating off him is palpable. I can practically taste it on my tongue.

"Look, I can't stay any longer. Just please get her out of the chains. When the time is right, I will come and talk to her, ok?" He starts moving further into the shadows of the alley.

"What's your name?"

"Pete Marshall. Tell Little Reaper I will come for her as soon as it's safe." Then he's gone, running down the alley as fast as he can. What the hell is happening? My thoughts swirl trying to figure it out, but I am left with more questions than answers. It's like everyone has a piece to a puzzle I had no idea needed solving, and everything seems to have something to do with my Pretty Bird.

Marcus

Hellion demolished three grilled cheese sandwiches before saying she was full. I had to laugh because she wanted bacon on every single one of them and drank a full pot of coffee, before apologizing for acting like a starving person. It was clear to me, though, that she had barely eaten since the Royale. I did try to ask her questions about what happened, but as soon as I did, she clammed up and wouldn't look at me. The crew members pissed me off to no end with all their bitching about Hellion being out of the basement. They learned to shut their fucking mouths quickly after I promised a whole load of hurt if they didn't.

Pacing up and down between the door and the adjoining bathroom of Hellion's room, I'm counting my lucky stars Kane hasn't been around all day. He would probably pop a blood vessel from my actions. The basement is dank, and both of us are covered in dust and grime just from being down there the little time we were. I don't care how much he demands it; she isn't going back down there. Kane spent a lot of time in her room after the night I took him there for Doc to sedate him. He found some comfort because all her stuff is still here. He wouldn't let anyone in here, and I couldn't bring myself to empty it.

"Cheshire?" She poked her head around the door to catch my attention.

"Yeah?"

"Can you throw me some joggers and a T-shirt please?"

"Why?" Hmmm, this isn't usual Hellion behavior.

"Um. Because. I. Um. Please?"

"What are you hiding?"

"Cheshire, please just leave it and pass me my clothes."

Before she realizes it, I have moved over to the door and yanked her out into the open. She blushes from embarrassment. I am frozen in place, eyes wide, and it feels like blood vessels are bursting all over my body. My hands tremble, and my vision starts to go black.

"What the fuck?" Both me and Hellion look to the door. Kane is staring at her with a mortified expression as his eyes track over every part of her body. I hold my breath, waiting for something to explode. Hellion doesn't have her restraints on and Kane is here. What could go wrong?

"Pre..." The growl that sounds out in the room is enough of a warning to stop his words.

"Reika. What the fuck happened?" Kane's words are barely a whisper. His mortified expression is still there, and I know my face mirrors his.

With a shrug, she doesn't acknowledge him. His gaze meets mine, silently asking what the actual fuck, but I can't answer him. Seeing the red lines all over her body makes me sick, but the one that sticks out the most is a massive scar in the center of her thigh.

"Hellion. What happened there?" Sitting herself down on the bed with the other leg tucked under her she traces the line with her fingers, as if she's debating if she wants to answer or not.

"They kept me in a metal storage type room a lot of the time. When the goon, as I called him, came for a wakeup call, I knew it was time for a new tactic." Breaking off from telling us anymore, she looks between me and Kane.

"You best sit down for this," she says, looking at Kane. "This doesn't mean I like you." Thankfully, he is too lost to pick a fight with her, and for that I am so grateful.

"Anyway, he would come and drag me off to wherever Fancy Pants wanted me. I would either be hung from the ceiling…" She starts to rub her wrists; Kane zeros in on this and he gulps.

"I tried to escape once, when I realized you weren't coming for me. I knocked the goon on his ass and ran like hell. I even made it outside and found a car until someone hit me over the head." My heart races hearing this, but I have to know.

"When I woke up Fancy Pants was saying all sorts of crazy shit. I was pretty out of it because of the blow, but he kept telling me my defiance was hurting me and I needed to accept my fate and become his." A roar lashes out through the room as Kane jumps to his feet. He sits down immediately at the murderous look he gets from Hellion.

"My answer was always the same, fuck you. This scar is from a hunting knife he decided to slam into my leg. I don't know what reaction he was hoping for, but my mind finally snapped from the torture, exhaustion and starvation I'd endured. My reaction freaked him out. They wanted me to fight in a match somewhere, but it didn't happen. Paine got me out. You know the rest." Tracing the different marks all over her legs, she doesn't say anything more. Kane sits in stunned silence. So do I.

"You're not going back to the basement. I understand why you did what you did, Reika, and I am so sorry for everything." Kane's words are so meek and mild, it's like he has had a personality transplant. He never apologizes, ever, and he has repeatedly apologized to her.

He gets up and leaves the room. Me and Hellion look at each other wondering what the fuck just happened. She's just as shocked as I am. It guts me to have to say my next words, but she looks exhausted.

"Get some sleep, but I will lock the door from the outside. Is that okay?"

"Yeah."

"There's a phone on your bedside table. If you need anything message me, yeah?"

"Okay, Cheshire." Pushing herself up the bed, she gets herself comfy, and releases a sigh of contentment. Looking back at her from the doorway, I smile. She is already asleep.

46

REIKA

"Please, Daddy! I don't want to stay here!"

"You have to. You need to learn."

"Daddy, please!"

Tears roll down my face as he looks down at me in the hole. The smile on his face isn't my dad, he looks angry. But I didn't do anything wrong. I always try to be faster, better, and do exactly what he wants me to do, even when I hurt so much I can't move. My mom's screams echo around the forest as she begs my dad to not leave me here. I don't know if this is another training session or if they don't want me. It's so dark. The glow from my camp light only gives me a bit of light to see. Dad left me with a bag. Opening it, I see a set of clothes and some weapons. I know what this means.

Why does he do this to me?

I am his daughter.

I'm scared.

"What have we got here?" Moving further away from the man, I grab some things out of my bag.

"What are you doing, Xander?" Another voice says. My body freezes as another man stands next to the first.

Daddy will come back.

He will.

Looking around the hole, there is a root behind me. The first man jumps down as I clamber up the root and out of the hole on the other side.

I run. As fast as I can.

I can't see anything. It is so dark. Daddy will be mad I ran.

He always says to stand and fight, no matter what.

He will hurt me for not doing what he says.

My legs are getting tired and I have to force them to keep moving. It is so dark I can't see anything in front of me, but I know the men are still chasing me; I can hear their voices sometimes.

I don't know how long it's been since Dad left. The forest has gone quiet. I stop. I can't breathe properly; my legs are shaking and I feel sick.

Snap!

The sound is so loud. I search for what made it, but I can't see anything. Holding my breath, I listen for more noise.

"Got ya!"

Hands drag me backwards as I scream.

"Pretty Bird?"

Hands are grabbing me everywhere. I'm thrashing my body to try and dislodge their hold on me, I lash out with my head and legs, kicking frantically.

No. No, no, no.

"Reika!"

"Get off me!"

"Look at me!" My vision starts to come back slowly, even though it is blurry. Shock has me frozen in place. Kane looks down at me with a terrified expression as he pins me to the bed. Blood drips from his face from scratch marks over his cheek.

"K-Kane. What?"

"Shhh. I heard you screaming. Are you ok?" My body is still in the after effects of the memory. My whole body trembles from fear, sweat gathers in my palms. I nod my head slightly, I don't want to look at him.

"Nightmare?" I shake my head in answer.

"Memory?" I nod slightly, my body shakes as the voices start to withdraw from my head.

"How did you get in here? Marcus locked the door." My voice sounds so broken.

"He isn't the only one with keys to all the rooms." Why has he come here? "You okay?" I nod again.

Relaxing his grip on my hands, he sits back on his haunches. My eyes widen as realization hits me that he is straddled over my hips. Climbing off of me, he sits on the side of the bed, staring off into space like he is trying to compose himself. With a deep exhale, he climbs to his feet. I grab his wrist, and he turns wide eyes on me.

"Please, don't leave me." I swallow hard at the confession, but his being here is helping me get over my terror. I hate appearing weak, especially to him, but my needs dictate I must.

"I don't think…."

"Please, Kane."

Something in my expression tells him I don't want to be alone. He slowly climbs onto the bed, over me, then settles himself down on top of the covers. I'm dumbstruck; I honestly thought he would leave me at war with my mind.

"Come here." Gentle hands pull me across the bed, so my head is resting on his chest. My body tenses as he holds me in his arms. The echoes in my head start as the screams of the girl I once was reverberate in my skull. Looking up into his gaze, I try to ground myself. My mind is fighting to keep me in a state of terror, while my heart works to fill my body with the feeling of safety. My emotions are a whirlwind. Lunging forward, I smash my lips down on his in a brutal kiss, driving my tongue into his mouth. Shock brings my focus back to the present, and I pull back with wide eyes. Kane openly stares at me with confusion.

We just stare at each other; our chests rise and fall rapidly. This time Kane lunges forward and smashes his lips to mine, and everything stops. His lips move with such ferocity I am fighting to keep up. A growl starts to build in his throat, while he tortures me with this brutal, all-consuming kiss. Flipping our positions without breaking the connection, he is above me. My legs widen automatically to allow him to get closer.

Our teeth clash together as we both fight for dominance and control. Grabbing the bottom of his top I rip it up and over his head as his fingers shred the front of mine, tearing it from my body. Without breaking the contact between us, he slides his hand under the waistband of my sweats and pulls them down my hips, while I unfasten the button on his jeans and slide them over his firm ass. Breaking away from the kiss, my mind is on autopilot kicking my legs to lose my pants. I stare as Kane slides his jeans the rest of the way off with a sexy ass grin on his face. Leaning forward, I yank him back down so our lips can continue their assault.

"Fuck!" tears from my throat, as he slams into my pussy in one brutal thrust, joining us together. We both still at the invasion, staring at each other. My temper flares as a growl grows in my throat.

"Don't you dare fucking stop."

My words have his unfocused gaze meeting mine. Slowly he pulls back so only the tip of his cock is still there. My pussy tries to clamp down to pull him back in, but is met with nothing. Agonizingly slow, he pushes back in before he slowly pulls back out again. He continues this unbearable torture until I lose it.

"Fuck me hard, goddamit!"

A sadistic grin pulls at his lips. He slams back into me with so much force, my eye's roll back in my head and a deep guttural moan leaves me. His lips crash back down on mine, and he picks up his pace, finding the perfect rhythm slamming his cock in and out of me. The pace isn't fast enough for me. I try to wiggle myself a little to change our position, so I can fuck like my body is craving and begging for. A hand lands on my throat. The grin on his face returns as I bare my teeth at him.

"Pussy! Fuck me!"

Tightening his grip around my throat has the masochist in me singing. His thrusts have picked up to a brutal rhythm as my pussy tries to grip his cock as hard as it can. The grunts and groans falling from his lips have my pussy growing wetter by the second. The headboard is smashing into the wall and echoing around the room. Lifting my legs, I hook my ankles together and pull him deeper.

"Yes. Yes. Yes!"

I lift my head so the pressure increases on my throat, tingles start to travel up from my clit, through my stomach, and into my limbs. The force with which my orgasm is building has me chasing my release. I slide my hand across my stomach. Kane's eyes narrow on my hand as he fucks me like his life depends on it. I rub my finger across my clit and another round of moans tear from my throat. Sweat drips from us both as our breathing intensifies. Kane's thrusts become so brutal it's like he's trying to rearrange my organs, but his brutality is exactly what I need. Kane's movements start to become erratic, while I rub my finger across my clit building the fire within me to an inferno.

"Come with me, Baby."

Rubbing my clit faster, Kane's movements reach a whole other level. The sound of skin slapping against skin and our grunts and moans, gather in the air. The fire inside me has my pussy clamping down on Kane's dick with such force, we both explode. White light flashes before my eyes and I lose focus. The lights and tingles start to subside, as fire roars through my body again as another orgasm consumes me. I swear I'm about to black out. The feeling of floating slowly begins to subside. Erratic breathing fills my ears. Something drops onto my face making me open my eyes.

The darkest eyes stare back at me. Kane's breathing matches my own as we both come down from the high. Slowly, he removes his hand from my throat, placing his palms on either side of my head as he just keeps staring. Oh shit! Pushing against his chest, I kick my legs trying to move him off me. Taking the hint, he moves back as I roll off the bed and run for the bathroom. Staring at my reflection, the face staring back at me is haunted. I hate him! Why would you do that? Turning on the tap, I splash cold water across my face to bring my senses back to normal.

"Reika?" Kane says through the door.

"Go away."

"Reika, open the door." his voice is backed with a tone of determination.

"I said go away, Kane!" I scream through the door.

Nothing, the other side of the door is quiet. I look back into the mirror as I try to get my brain working again. A shiver passes over me while I stand in front of the mirror. God knows how long I have been standing here. Listening for sounds from the room, I'm greeted with silence. Grabbing a towel from the rack, I wrap it around myself and open the door.

"We need to talk." I nearly fall over, startled by his voice coming from next to the door.

"No, we don't."

"Yes, we do. I know we have issues, but we can work through them." His eyes lighten as he stares as me.

"Get out." I put as much grit into my voice as I can manage.

"No. We need to talk." Taking a step toward me, I back up to keep space between us. If he touches me again, I don't know what I will do.

"Get out, Kane!"

"Why do you deny this connection between us?" Cocking his head to the side the corner of his mouth twitches, which pisses me off.

"It was a mistake. It never happened. I will forget it and so will you."

"Like fuck I will." He's angry at me.

"I hate you. This shouldn't have happened."

"Fuck off, Pretty Bird. You and I both know there is something between us."

"Yeah, lust, asshole."

"For fuck's sake woman!" he roars as he charges across the room, grabbing hold of the top of my arms. "I fucking love you. Don't you get it, Pretty Bird? I love you so much it hurts to fucking breathe."

My brain explodes, my palm connects with his face with such force he is forced to let go of me.

"There's a difference between love and lust, Kane." I bare my teeth at him.

"I love you and I know you feel the same way, Pretty Bird." I scoff at his words. Wow, the ego on this bastard.

"Haven't you learned anything from when I tried to kill you?" Stalking across the room toward him, I layer my voice with as much venom as I can. "Or how about when I tried to beat your old man to death?" Uncertainty flickers across his face.

"I was in a vulnerable place and you were there. So, we fucked."

"That's not true." His voice isn't as strong as it was.

"It. Meant. Nothing. How could you think I would love you when my hatred for you is so deep the devil himself swims in it?"

"Pretty…."

"You really want to know?" My voice is dripping acid. He nods his head at me.

"We fucked because my demons had a hold of me. I used you to escape them. Now. Get. The. Fuck. Out!"

His anger flares as he rushes me and slams me into the wall. The murderous look in his eyes should terrify me, but I sneer back at him.

"You will never use me as a way to escape again, Pretty Bird. You can hide behind your tough exterior, but I know you. And you hate me for it because I see the girl behind the mask." Quickly releasing his grip, my ass lands on the floor in a heap as he strides from the room, slamming the door as he leaves.

Composing myself, I climb back to my feet. I look around the room to see chaos. Not wanting to think anymore, I head over to the cupboard at the side of the built-in wardrobe, pulling a clean sheet out to make the bed. Slamming to a halt, I grab some clothes from the wardrobe, throwing on a fresh pair of sweats and t-shirt. Like fuck am I sleeping here.

Heading over to the sofa on the other side of the room, I make myself comfy. My mind starts to wander. I grab the remote and spend however long flicking through Netflix to find something to watch. My mind keeps trying to pull me back into the darkness, so it looks like I won't be sleeping at all. Ah! Hell to the yes! Sons of Anarchy. Hmmm, who doesn't love a bit of Jax Teller. That guy is so drool worthy it should be illegal to look like that. I settle myself between the cushions and get comfy ready for a Netflix binge. I know this will keep my brain busy.

47

MARCUS

Something is happening. The house is in chaos. People are running around all over the place. It isn't any sort of special day, so fuck it. I adjust the tray in my hands so nothing falls over as I head up to Hellion's room to deliver my surprise. I balance the tray the best I can with one hand, give up because I'm terrible at it, and put it down. Pulling my keys out I slip the key into the lock and turn. Oh shit! The key doesn't turn. Rushing into the room, I find Hellion bundled up on the couch asleep. I spin around, grab hold of the tray and stand at the edge of the room.

"Hey, Cheshire." She sits up while rubbing the sleep from her eyes. My nose twitches.

"Why does it smell like sex in here? Please don't tell me you fucked a grunt?"

"Nope. Your brother."

Crash!

I drop the tray and everything smashes and spills everywhere.

"Errm. What… Huh?" I'm speechless.

"What?"

"What? Are you serious? What? You fucked him again. Why?" That is not what I expected when I found the door unlocked. If she had gone on a killing spree, I wouldn't be as surprised as I am now.

"Don't make a big deal of it, Cheshire. It won't happen again."

A shit-eating grin spreads across my face, which has Hellion looking like she wants to murder my ass. I can't help but laugh. They are so blind to the fact that they are still drawn to each other like two magnets. Hopefully, Kane gets back to being himself again. My brain starts cooking up ideas to get them to stop denying themselves, and ways to improve her and Liam's relationship.

"Uh oh. I know that look. What are you planning, dickhead?"

"Nothing, Hellion." My grin widens even further. "Nothing at all."

"Yeah, yeah, asshole. Now what did you drop?"

"Ah shit, I brought you breakfast." I say, with a sheepish look. I feel bad. I know she calls me a mother hen, and she's right. She has a surprised look on her face and I'm unsure what she's thinking.

"Go grab a shower and I'll bring you some more up, yeah?"

"Yeah." She says reluctantly, arching her eyebrow, and I'm cracking up again.

"I'm not gonna poison you, Hellion."

"Kane might." We both crack up. She's not wrong there. He is a special kind of strange at the moment. I lock the door on the way out. I feel like an asshole, but I have to for the safety of the crew. I know she won't run off, because she had a chance to last night and she didn't. I'm doing it for the safety of whichever idiot realizes her door is open, then tries to make a name for themselves. Walking into the kitchen I stop short. A cocky grin spreads across my face.

"Next time, Brother, remember to lock the door on your way out." I laugh as Kane's eyes widen and he chokes on his mouthful of coffee.

"She told you?"

"Nope, but the room does smell like a sex pad." He throws me an uncomfortable look and I laugh my ass off.

"What are you laughing at, Bro?" Liam asks.

"Ah, nothing. We were just talking about Kane leaving Hellion's room unlocked after he left last night." Liam's eyes practically bug out of his head.

"What did you do?" Liam questions.

"Me?" asks Kane. Both Kane and I are shocked at the protectiveness in his voice.

"Yeah, asshole." Well, that's a shift in dynamics. I can certainly work with this.

"I didn't do anything."

"Well, unless you count sticking her real good," I add, wiggling my eyebrows at Liam. He looks shocked then bursts out laughing, which sets me off again.

"Fuck you."

"Nope, you got fucked last night." We both look at each other, and I laugh so hard I fall on my ass. This twin thing is great sometimes.

"Grow the fuck up the pair of you."

"You did the growing last night, Brother." Liam says between laughs. Tears roll down my face; this shit is hilarious. Kane looks a second away from popping a vein. He stands to storm out of the kitchen.

"Look, Bro, we're sorry. Okay?" I don't want him running off and hiding again.

"Hmm, you two gonna crack jokes again?"

"We won't, okay. But c'mon, man, you can't blame us for being surprised." Liam says.

"You're right. It's just so damn hard, man." Liam snickers at Kane's words, and I death glare my twin.

"What's the issue, Kane? We know how you feel about her." Liam nods his head in agreement.

"It feels like I'm drawn to her when she's around. Like something is pulling me in her direction." He sucks in a breath "But when we are together, it's explosive. We could want kill each other one minute, and it's pure electrifying passion the next."

"You mean, you don't know if you want to fuck her or kill her?" Yep, Liam has a way with words.

"Yeah. It's fucking exhausting, man." My heart goes out to him. I'm not a mushy feelings kinda guy, but he looks so down.

"Do you love her?" Liam's question has me standing up straight,

waiting for Kane's answer.

"Yeah, I do."

"So, what's the issue?" He looks to Liam with confusion. God, he's dense sometimes.

"Look, Bro. What Liam is trying to say is this. If you love her, why the fuck are you wallowing. Get your ass up there and show her."

"Easier said than done. She hates my guts." I'm surprised he says this. Kane never gives up.

"She has had a shitty life. We all know this." I brace myself for my next words. "She thought we forgot about her. Then she finds out, while being tortured, that our dad was the reason her parents were killed. We all heard what happened that night." Silence fills the room, none of us say anything. My mind drifts back to her words in the basement.

"Marcus is right." My eyes bulge. Liam is saying I'm right! I need that shit in writing.

"Before you open your mouth, Marcus. It ain't gonna happen." Motherfucker! "Dad is to blame, not you. He trained you for your position. The fact that you feel guilty, shows how much you care. So, stop being a sap, and go prove that she's your woman and you deserve her."

Okay, I'll admit that was a damn good speech from his frosty ass. It seems to work though as determination slips across Kane's features and he square's his shoulders. A smile grows on my face.

"Do you trust me?" Kane asks.

"Yeah, I do." Liam says. I don't even get a chance to answer before Kane heads out.

48

REIKA

For fuck's sake, I'm so bored!

Checking the time on my phone again, my annoyance grows further. My stomach has been growling for the last twenty minutes. Marcus left a couple of hours ago saying he was bringing food back. I'm going to shoot him a message.

"Reika?"

"What do you want, Liam?" Can anything else happen today? Asshole number one last night, and now asshole number two comes for a visit now.

"Can we talk before Marcus comes back?" His tone has me curious.

Walking over to the couch, I sit. He looks around with a sheepish expression, his movements jittery. Either someone sent him here or he's nervous. I don't give a shit which it is.

"Look, I know we both got off to a bad start." I grunt my agreement.

"I know what I did was wrong, but I will prove to you I only did it with the best interests of my brothers in mind. I know you are badly hurting and I am sorry about that, more than you will ever fucking know. But you can't blame Kane for

385

what happened to your parents. He was a pawn more than anything else. Our dad just used him to push his own agenda."

"Who fucking cares, Liam. He voted yes!" I don't want to hear anymore. How fucking dare he come in here spouting this shit. I jumping to my feet. I can't sit here and listen to this bullshit anymore.

"Sit your ass down and listen you stubborn bitch!" Shocked I drop back down onto the couch. Damn. Frosty has some fire.

"I'm going to tell you a little story. Then you can decide what to do after that." I nod my agreement; guess I might as well get comfy for this little shit show.

God knows how much time passed since Liam started telling me what life was like growing up with a dad like Malcolm. Throughout his story, my emotions have been running wild. I swear he's given me whiplash. I move from raging anger to tear-jerking sadness, then get smacked with soul-crushing heartbreak. Hearing about all the things they went through growing up was tough enough, but hearing everything Kane had to endure makes me think of him differently. It explains so much about who he is now. He is a product of his environment, just like I am. We were both groomed, beaten and molded into the image our dad's created, although their methods were very different.

To keep him in line like a good little soldier, their father would have him tied down, and force him to watch the beatings he would give their mother, for his defiance. That even had me gulping against the rising bile in my throat. My father was brutal, but outside of training sessions he was the best father I could have ever wanted. He would sit with me at night, read me a bedtime story, and tuck me in or kiss me good night on the forehead. A small gesture that let me know he loved me. Kane, Marcus and Liam they never got anything like that. No affection from their father, and even less after their mother died.

Malcolm wasn't raising children; he was raising soldiers. Frosty even admitted that when he or Marcus did something wrong, Kane would take the blame so they didn't have to go through the beatings as punishment. He protected them, shielded them, with everything he was in the best way he knew how. He also told me about the marriage Malcolm had set up for Kane. My stomach is in knots at this. Malcolm just wanted to use him as pawn to build and strengthen his empire. After hearing about all the times Malcolm had him in crew meetings, forcing him to be involved from such a young age, I can't help the guilt that twists my insides. It's eating away at my resolve, slowly shredding the blame I've held on to. I'm lost in my own thoughts as everything rushes through my mind. There's so much I never had a fucking clue about.

"Now do you see what I mean?" I nod my head. I am shell shocked from everything I have just heard.

"You're not a bad person, Reika. I can see that now. You're good for them both. I want us to get on, you know? Can we do that? Not tear each other to shreds anymore?"

"I think we can manage that, Frosty." I chuckle at his expression. This is one of those moments I wish I could take a photo to laugh at later.

"Why do you call me that?" Oh boy!

"Cause Jack Frost has nothing on you with that cold expression of yours." We both burst out laughing.

"What's going on here then?" We both look to the door. Marcus is standing there in a defensive position.

"Chill out, Cheshire, we've been talking."

"And you're both still alive?" He grabs at his chest like he's having a heart attack, little shit. "Wow."

"Very funny, asshole." Liam smirks at him. The difference between them in personalities was easy to see before but after talking to Frosty they may act differently a lot of the time, but there are definitely some similarities. It's kinda cute, in a weird way.

"Kane needs us." I look between them both as I grab the remote.

"You too, Hellion." What the fuck?

"Me?"

"Yep." Marcus grins at me while Frosty looks just as confused as I am. What the fuck is going on?

Marcus fidgets from foot to foot like he has damn ants in his pants, or a toddler that is busting to piss. It's clear he's fighting some kind of internal battle. Suddenly, he runs over, grabs my hand, and drags me out the door. Frosty busts out laughing at the horrified expression on my face.

"Cheshire! What the fuck, man?" Seriously, I feel like I'm in some alternate reality where everything has been flipped on its head. It's

trippy as fuck.

"Hurry up, Hellion. We don't wanna be late."

"Late, for what?" He doesn't even answer, just keeps dragging me behind him. Frosty follows behind us with a smirk on his face that makes me wanna smack it off.

He drags me down the corridors like an excited five-year-old on Christmas morning; I have nearly face planted several times. He's changing direction so fucking quickly I'm getting goddamn whiplash and I have no idea why. Frosty, the bastard, just laughs his ass off at me as he follows us.

"For fuck's sake, Marcus. Slow the fuck down!"

"Ooooh, she used my proper name. Did you hear that Liam?" Marcus taunts like a damn child.

"I did, Marcus. Ha! You're in trouble." Liam bursts into laughter.

"No! I'm not. Hellion loves me. Don't you?" He looks at me with so much warmth and happiness.

"If you both don't knock it off, I'll knock you on your asses. Got it?"

"Yes, boss." Sarcasm thick in their voices. A chuckle leaves me at the boyish games they're playing. Honestly, it's kinda nice - fucking weird, but nice.

Our laughter fills the hallways as we go wherever Cheshire is leading us. My mind is so preoccupied with our banter that I don't notice anything out of the ordinary until we step out of the front door. I'm faced with a mass of bodies filling the lawn, Kane standing front and center.

"What's happening?" I ask them both as murmured voices fill the area. What the actual fuck is going on? Today's weirdness apparently isn't over.

"Just watch, okay, Hellion?" Erm, okay, like I have any other plans right now.

"Okay."

Anticipation fills me. Some of the crew members throw daggers my way. Guess they're still pissed about daddy dearest. I can't help the crazed smile that spreads across my face. They instantly avert their eyes from me, looking to the two shadows standing on either side of me. I look to them and I realize why. Both Cheshire and Frosty have looks that say *I fucking dare you* on their faces for anyone looking like they want to make a move. The murmurs of the crew grow in volume, and some of them shout out their annoyance at my presence. I'm now waiting for the mob with torches and pitch forks to join them. I hear more raised voices as tempers rise.

"Silence!" Kane booms, shutting down their complaints.

"I've called this crew meeting because many things have come to light that have pissed me off." His voice commands the whole area. The entire crew watch him wide eyed.

"I know a lot of you are wondering why Reika is standing behind me without restraints."

"Yes," rings out from a lot more of the crew than I had expected.

"Well, if you don't like it, fucking leave the crew!" Shocked gasps and cries of outrage fill the air.

"Why! She tried to beat your dad to death?" One member says, stepping forward to stand in front of the others. "You would choose this bitch over your own?" Kane stalks toward the man. From the position I am in, I can't see Kane's face.

"Ah, Lennox. Trust you to open your bloody mouth." Finally, I can see his face. His cold calculating look sends a shiver down my spine.

"You opening your mouth gives me the chance to kill two birds with one stone."

"Why?" My heartrate increases as the atmosphere electrifies.

"You see, Lennox has been caught out."

"What's happened, boss?" A few of the other crew members shout out while others turn to look at the men beside them with confusion on their faces.

"Lennox here, is a traitor." Some of the men look shocked, while others don't seem surprised at this. Lennox on the other hand starts shouting out trying to say he hasn't done anything.

"Bonzo!"

"Yes, Boss?"

"Restrain him." Bonzo does as Kane says, which is lucky considering Lennox tries to run past him. Bonzo takes him down easy enough, quickly secures his hands and drags him onto his knees.

"You have been giving information about our plans and movements to the Grimm's for months! You thought you could get away with it, clearly forgetting the pledge you took after initiation. You know what's coming now, don't you?" Bloodlust roars through me as Bonzo pulls out his gun, takes aim and fires through the back of the traitor's head.

"Treachery will not be allowed here. If you are loyal, you will have a family here for life. If you betray me or the crew, you die. It's fucking simple, really." Cheers erupt throughout the crowd. Blood thirsty bastards.

"You all know the reasons why Reika did what she did. If you can't accept that she is still here, then leave. The crew will give you a head start before we hunt you down." To my surprise only two of the crew members run. I don't recognize their faces so they must either be grunts or something to do with Malcolm.

"Bonzo, bring him out!" What the fuck is going on now? My alternate reality theory is really proving itself right now.

He disappears into the house as silence descends over the crew, a sense of foreboding filling the air, smothering all of us. Nobody makes a sound as we all wait. My eyes bulge and my mouth drops when I see Bonzo dragging someone out of the house with a hood over their head. What the fuck? I hear grunts and groans from underneath the hood, but I realize something more is going on here when a guy I don't recognize comes striding out of the house behind them.

"That's Fox." Cheshire whispers in my ear. I have heard about him before. He is the one they go to for information.

The man puts up more of a fight the further Bonzo drags him. Kane looks around at all the people gathered. When his eyes land on me, I'm pinned to my spot. Sucking in a breath, I am surprised to see the stone cold look on his face, none of his emotions are on show. I'm reeling wondering what is about to go down. My thirsty bitch of a pussy quivers at the dominance pouring off him. This here is the man that runs the Damned Crew, the man they call Soulless, yet he sets my soul on fire.

Bonzo drops the guy in front of Kane. Breaking our eye contact, he looks down as the hood is ripped off his head.

"You have fallen from the path of what this crew stands for, and I will not allow it to be tainted by your vile presence any longer." Kane's words are sharp. Ice slithers through my veins as the man looks up to him, his skin deathly pale.

"You have destroyed something I adore. I will not allow this to stand." Stepping closer to the man, the sheer size difference has my heartrate kicking up a notch. What the hell is happening? A hand grips me to keep me rooted to my spot.

"Consider what happened to you a warning. The truth always comes out.

"You are no longer a part of this family. Someone as tainted as you does not belong here." I finally recognize the man on his knees.

"Malcolm Southbourne, you are no longer known as our father or associated with the Damned Crew. You are an outcast, exiled from the crew."

"You can't do this, son!" Malcom begs in a pathetic attempt to get Kane to take back his decree.

"I will find out the truth of what happened, the whole truth. Run fast. Run far, old man. Because the next time we meet, I won't stop her from dishing out your punishment."

He. Did he just? Just. They. Did they know? Oh my god!

Bonzo unbinds Malcolm's hands. He stumbles to his feet, eyes pleading with the son who has just turned his back on him, on his own flesh and blood.

"Son?"

"Run, old man. You have ten minutes to get out of my territory or I will have the crew hunt you down! I'm sure I don't need to explain to you what will happen when you're caught." Kane looks around at the crew. I'm shocked by the bloodthirsty look on most of their faces. Seems the hatred for this vile waste of air runs deep within the crew. Nice to know.

"Any crew member who crosses paths with him after he leaves is to kill him on sight." A lot of eager faces hone in on Malcolm standing there, looking nothing like the lord of the manor anymore. Without saying anything he turns and runs as fast as his battered old body will carry him. My heart stutters as the three brothers watch their blood run for his life.

49

MARCUS

Cold.

    Indifferent.

Thank fuck.

That's all I'm feeling as I watch the man who I'm meant to look up to run out of the yard, like the hounds of hell are chasing him. Hellion is standing at my side with her mouth hanging open and tears brimming in her eyes. I wish I could read her mind right now. She doesn't know this yet, but he did that for her. He really does love her.

After the talk all three of us had, Liam pulled me to one side and said he wanted to talk to her, to make things right between them. It was about fucking time. I don't agree with the way he went about it, but I understand his reasons, as messed up as they were.

As I was making the food I promised to replace, Kane came back and told me he had an idea. His only words to me were that I had to trust him and he is doing what is best for us all. I was shocked he exiled Malcolm, but I know why he did it. A lot of things don't make sense about the situation with Hellion's family and the night of the vote. The closer we look at it, the more things just don't add up. Unease swirls in our guts, well mine and my brothers, because we know how manipulative our father is. By exiling him, Kane has given us time to find the answers we need. Then, with a bit of luck, we can send a hunting party after him. Some of the crew are still dumbstruck, while others have a look of relief on their faces. When Malcolm led the crew, he caused a lot of unrest throughout the ranks that came to light a year before Kane took over. He was having affairs with crew members wives and trying to fuck their daughters. Not one person dared to challenge him about it, they only stayed because they didn't know any other way.

Kane stands rooted to his spot, staring into nothing. I feel the nervous energy coming off Hellion in waves. The one person I need to have a word with starts to leave.

"Fox!" He looks over his shoulder at me. I nod my head toward the house.

Gently taking Hellion's hand, I lead her in her stunned state toward the house. I didn't think he would be far behind, but I check to make sure Fox is following, finding Liam at his side. Once in the office, I gently push her onto the couch and lean against the arm.

"What's up, man?"

"I need you to look for someone for me."

"Who?" Curiosity coats his voice.

"Hellion?" Looking down at her she looks up at me with rapidly blinking eyelids, like she's pulling herself back together before my very eyes.

"Yeah."

"I need you to tell Fox what you remember about who took you." Her head pings left and right between us. It's time to find whoever took her.

"It's ok, Reika. Just tell me what you know." Fox's voice is so soothing, I watch as her shoulders slump, taking a deep inhale.

"I didn't really see much. They had me in a type of metal room, well

more of a cage really. A lot. But when they had me out of there, it was like an office type of room with windows all down one wall and it was bright. Really bright as the walls were a white color, everything was white. I managed to escape outside once but I didn't really see much apart from the driveway and it looked massive."

"Massive?" Fox asks.

"Yeah, massive like an estate type of thing."

"That all you remember?" he asks.

"Yeah."

"Can you work with that?" I know it's not a lot to go on but it's not like they're gonna drop a location pin for us or something.

"Stupid question, Marcus." Fox shakes his head as he leaves the room. He really is a cocky son of a bitch, but he is damn good at what he does.

"Drinks?" Liam asks us both.

We both nod as he heads over to Kane's secret stash that he thinks we don't know about. Glasses clink around at the other end of the room as I silently watch Hellion. Her face gives nothing away, but I know her enough to know she's questioning Kane's reasoning for sending Malcolm away. Liam comes back over with three glasses and a bottle of Absolut vodka in hand. My mouth starts to water, nothing but the best. Not bothering to measure what he's pouring, he passes the glasses out almost full to the top with vodka. This shit's gonna hurt in the morning, but fuck it, we are celebrating. As I'm about to take a drink, I look to Hellion, snort a laugh and nearly inhale the whole glass choking. She swallowed that whole thing in one go. Fucking hell. How does she do that?

"You want another?" Liam asks. Her hand shoots out shaking the glass in front of him, and a smile tips up the left corner of his lip. I know he's enjoying this, as his laughter lines show around his eyes.

"Easy, Hellion. You don't want to get hammered, do you?"

"Whatever, mother hen. Hurry up and fill the glass, Frosty." She laughs. "You got any ice with that?"

"Fuck off, Reika."

A huge smile comes across my face as I watch the two of them bitch at each other, hurling insults back and forth. The more Liam tells her to stop calling him Frosty, the more she does. It's nice to see them both actually getting along and it just feel right. Like we're a family.

"Can I join?" Liam trips from spinning so fast. Hellion looks like the weird fish from *Finding Nemo.* I'm not surprised in the least.

"Is that ok with you, Reika?" Kane asks her directly. Both me and Liam stare at each other. This is it… make or break.

"Normal you or asshole you?" she asks. I bite my lip at the confused look on Kane's face.

"Umm. Normal me?" Kane looks so confused, looking between me and Liam for help. Hellion bursts out laughing spitting vodka everywhere.

"Sit down, Kane. Fucking hell." I say. He slowly walks to the other end of the couch. We all wait for her reaction.

"Oi! Frosty, fill me back up will you!" Oh shit!

"Whaaaaaat!" Kane roars as he jumps to his feet. Liam runs around the desk to put it in between them.

Laughter fills the room and all eyes follow the sound. Hellion is doubled over on the couch holding her stomach with tears streaming down her face.

"Whoops." Kane narrows his eyes on her.

"Fucking whoops!" That sets her off laughing even more. I start laughing too, because seeing the smile on her face has hope building in my chest. Things might actually work out for the better, for once.

"Pretty Bird?"

"Put a sock in it, Kane."

Thump.

What the fuck? Looking for the culprit. We all find Liam in a heap on the floor, rubbing his ass.

"Ow! Fucking hell that hurt."

We all look at each other and that sets us off in another fit of hysteria. My heart feels complete seeing all the people I care about enjoying themselves together and bonus, no one has tried to kill each other yet. Thirty minutes later the bottle of vodka is empty. Hellion looks annoyed beyond belief by this while Kane openly stares at her with a starry-eyed look that he's not hiding from anyone. Liam is on the hunt for one more drink.

"Ahem! Excuse me." We all jump up at the new voice in the room. A dude in a suit is standing there looking terrified.

"Who let you in?" Kane asks with his don't fuck with me attitude.

"One of the guys out front said I would find Reika Martins here?" The frown on Hellion's face would be funny if Kane hadn't planted himself in front of her so she was out of view.

"Who are you?" she asks while peeking her head around Kane. This makes her look far too sweet and innocent. Ha! If only he knew what she was really capable of.

"My names Nathaniel Jamison, I am Mr. Waines lawyer."

"Mr. Waines?" Confusion is clear on her face.

"You will know him as Alexander. Rocco told me I might find you here."

"Yeah, I know the asshole. Why, what's he done now?" It's clear from her tone how much she hates him.

"Well, you see, Miss Martins. Mr. Waines has passed away, and he named you beneficiary in his will."

"What do you mean?" She frowns, a multitude of emotions flit across her face at his words.

"I have paperwork for you to sign for the things listed."

Slowly he pulls a manila envelope out of his jacket. Walking over to him, she takes it out of his hand and sits down at the desk. Opening it up, she starts reading through the stack of paperwork. Her eyes bug out of her head more than once, putting me and my brothers on edge. What the fuck is in there to cause that kind of reaction?

"Is this for real?" Uncertainty layers her voice.

"Yes, Miss."

"Oh." Looking down to the paperwork, she looks back up and meets my eyes. Then looks to Kane and then Liam, like she's silently asking us what to do.

"Where do I sign?" What the fuck? The lawyer walks over to the desk, passes her a pen he points where she has to sign. For the next five minutes, the scratching sound of the pen is the only noise in the room. The tension level skyrockets. Once she's done, he takes his paperwork and pulls a set of keys out of his pocket, placing them on the desk in front of her.

"Here's all the keys you will need. Everything is explained in your paperwork."

"Thank you."

He spins on his heel and walks out the door without another word. Hellion just sits there, staring at the keys in front of her. None of us says as word, but I am dying to know what the hell just happened. What the hell has the little leech done?

"Pretty Bird. What's happened?"

"Alexander is dead, but he left me… He…H- He left..." Her words break as she shakes her head.

"It's ok, Hellion."

"He left me the warehouse and his house in his will." Huh?

"Warehouse?" Liam asks.

"The warehouse with the fight ring." Her voice is so shocked. Honestly, I am surprised myself.

"What you gonna do with it, Reika?" Liam asks.

"Fuck's sake, Liam. Don't be an even bigger asshole than usual." I scold. I'm sure all he gives a shit about is money.

"Stupid question, Frosty." Looking up, she has a shit-eating grin on her face. "He left me the one thing I've wanted since I started there."

"Thing is, Hellion…"

"What?"

"When the hell did Alexander die, by who and how?"

50

REIKA

uck me! My brain hurts. After the shock of Alexander's lawyer turning up, we decided to continue getting hammered in the office. It was pretty funny. If any of the crew members tried to disturb us, they were told to fuck off, and off they fucked like we'd lit a rocket and shoved it up their ass. We all had a great time. Cheshire kept saying it was a blast because I didn't try and murder anyone. He makes it sound like a little bit of murdering is a bad thing.

My mind is finding everything hard to process. I'm still in shock from yesterday's events. I know Alexander was a slimy bastard, but I don't know who would kill him or what would motivate them to do so. I can't believe the fight ring is mine. I have had loads of ideas since I started and he shot every single one of them down. Now that it's mine, I can make them happen. I would love to upgrade the cage as it's falling to pieces. I'd upgrade the viewing bleachers to draw in a better crowd than the delinquents that currently come in, In turn, higher bets and increased return.

Knock. Knock.

"Yeah?" No one ever knocks on my door.

"Can we talk?" My head shoots up to find Kane sticking his head around the door.

"Umm. Sure." Uncertainty laces my voice, but I can't hide it. Time to suck it up and face this, whatever this is, head on.

He comes to stand at the edge of the bed with an unsure look. We just stare at each other, neither of us knowing how to start off. Honestly, I'm in a bit of a mindfuck. Seeing what I did on those videos fueled my hatred for him in ways I have never hated anyone before. However, after yesterday, my heart is screaming that he didn't have a choice in the vote. Frosty explained everything and the vote does make sense. It's hard for me to swallow, but then I ask myself if I would have done anything differently if the roles were reversed? Probably not, no.

"I. Umm." Nervousness pours off him in waves.

"Sit down, Kane." I almost laugh as his ass hits the end of the bed, hard. He looks just as surprised as me that he followed my command. I hold in the chuckle bubbling up my throat.

"You wanted to talk. So, talk." *Reign your bitch in*, my inner bitch orders me. I can't help the snarky attitude that comes out in uncomfortable situations, it's my fucking coping mechanism.

He stares at me with suspicious eyes, and I don't know why. I'm starting to get annoyed the longer he just stares at me. He came to me not the other way round.

"You gone mute overnight?"

"Look, Pretty Bird, I came here to say I'm sorry." He speaks his words so slowly.

"Why did you do it?" The question comes out without me even realizing it.

"Because I didn't have a choice. If I didn't vote the same as him, he would hurt my mom." He grinds his teeth. Looking in the opposite direction from me, his shoulders hunch as guilt rides him hard.

"I know." He spins so quickly to look at me I'm surprised his head doesn't snap off. I can see the question floating around in his head.

"Frosty told me. What it was like for you growing up."

"I doubt that," he scoffs.

"He did, Kane. I know about the arranged marriage." I try and repress the shudder that takes over my body when I say this. "I know about the torture inflicted on you repeatedly if you didn't do what he wanted, or how he would beat your mom to keep you in line."

"He...."

"I know about you taking the blame for stuff they did, to protect your brothers from the beatings." I shuffling closer so I'm sitting next to him. I thought the rage I felt at first seeing him again would come, but it doesn't. I touch the intricate tattoos that fill his arm. He freezes, he's still as a statue.

"I know the reason you have all these tattoos." The look he gives me, has my stomach fluttering. "You hide your scars beneath them."

Dropping his head into his hands, a whoosh of air rushes out of him. He doesn't speak, doesn't react in any other way. Movement catches my eye. I look up and Cheshire is standing in the doorway with a frown.

'Are you okay?' he mouths to me. I nod my head to let him know I am. 'Is he?' he mouths to me. I lift my shoulder slightly to say I don't know. He takes a step into the room and protectiveness roars to life inside me. I shake my head to stop him from coming any further. The frown on his face deepens as it battles with confusion.

'We need to talk.' I mouth back to him slowly so he catches it. His frown deepens even further and I have to stop the laughter that nearly escapes me. 'You sure?' God, Cheshire is a great person, but sometimes his mothering really pisses me off. I cock my brow at him. 'Fuck off,' I mouth, which brings a smirk to his face. Fucking finally. He slowly closes the door, so I can't see him. I'm glad he did, because I know Kane wouldn't want any of the crew to see him like this.

"I'm so sorry, Pretty Bird." The whispered words fill the otherwise silent room.

"We're products of our environments, Kane. I have done shit that's unforgiveable."

"No, you are..." Grabbing hold of his chin, I force him to look me in the eye. I need to tell him everything.

"Listen to me, okay? Then you can decide what you want to do."

"Okay."

Taking a deep breath, I tell him everything that happened while I was with Fancy Pants. Every little detail of the torture, abuse and mind games I went through. As I talk, the emotions running across his face have me anticipating his reaction. The horror at me being starved, at me being held down while the grunt beat me and I couldn't defend myself; the utter despair hearing about me being chained and electrocuted to extract details about the crew. When I escaped, how I got hit over the head and where I was when I woke up. I spill it all. His whole body vibrates as I speak, but he does as I asked. He listens.

"Fuck, Pretty Bird. I hate myself for not finding you, but we watched a video of you being killed."

"Ah."

"What?"

"Let me finish the story."

"When I saw the video of you fucking someone."

"I..."

"I know, just please listen. Just after I was taken, they had me chained up and were telling me that you set me up, that you had manipulated and used me. That you guys were the ones to hand me over to them, that you never wanted me. I was adamant that I knew how you felt, just as I was certain of my feelings for you. Then they showed me that video and it broke my fucking heart. I have always had fears of never being good enough; that someone would never be able to love me. That I wasn't worthy." I have to cut him off with a look, because if I didn't get this out now, I never would.

"That my demons were too scary for someone to ever want to be with me. That video broke me. Even though my heart was crushed, I wasn't sure if they were spinning a line or not, so I continued questioning everything in my head. Then they showed me the video of the meeting. My heart splintered even further at that. I had put so much trust in you. Not one person has ever gotten under my skin like you did, but that broke my soul and made me thirst for revenge. I hated you. I hated you so much that I am glad you didn't find me soon after I saw that, because you would have been dead. I would have killed you without a second thought." My hands shake, my breathing ragged.

"What?" His voice is so low, I almost didn't hear it.

"Fancy Pants knew the hatred I had after that, and he used it to his advantage. I don't know what his problem is with you, but during a torture session he asked if I wanted to make you hurt. I jumped at the chance, I wanted to make you hurt like you'd hurt me. He had heard that you and the crew were searching for me, and set the plan up for the video. They put one of those special effect blood pack things on my neck to make it look like that. The line I said was his idea. We watched you find the video on a live stream. Honestly, my body thrummed with happiness with your reaction. It felt like I got fucking justice for what you had done to me."

"I'm telling you this because all this anger is too much, too much for me to handle anymore. I know that you aren't to blame for what happened with my parents, but I am not sure if I can forgive you straight away."

"I get it, I do. Can I ask why you didn't make yourself known sooner?"

"You mean at the safehouse?" He nods in agreement.

"Dude, I tried to kill Frosty and shot you. Doesn't that give you an idea why Paine kept me hidden away?" He growls at the mention of his name.

"Easy, asshole. Nothing happened."

"How do you know him?"

"He's my cousin, apparently."

"What? And he works for Fancy Pants? Why didn't you tell us this?" He jumps to his feet and starts pacing.

"I have my reasons. The things that are happening don't make sense, Kane. Surely, you see this too. What happened to Mel. Me being kidnapped. Finding out about you and your dad. Finding out my father is one of the most feared assassins that has ever lived." I count each point off on my fingers. "There is more going on."

"What do you mean?"

"There's more to this, and I need to know what it is. I need answers, Kane."

He stays quiet for a while. I know he is processing what I have just said, because his left eye is twitching. I've noticed that's his tell when he's deep in thought. All this is probably very hard for him to hear, but I had to get it off my chest. I still like him and kinda still have issues with the video, but after spending last night just getting along, I like the idea of what things could be like if I can forgive him.

"I promised you answers before, Pretty Bird. I will help you find them, but I need one thing from you."

"What?"

"Don't over think anything that happens between us?" My heart skips at his question.

"Okaaaaay." I'm unsure about this, but what harm can it do? I guess only time will tell.

"I need to get going, Kane. I'm meeting Rocco at the warehouse."

"Take Marcus with you."

With a slight nod, I head off in search of my babysitter, good thing he's a fucking mother hen. My fingers barely skim the door handle when I am spun into Kane's arms. Shock renders me speechless as his lips crash down on mine in a kiss so dominant my legs start to shake. As quickly as he grabbed me, he lets go and walks out.

51

MARCUS

"So, Grizzly let you out then?" Color me curious as we drive down the road toward the warehouse.

"Yep."

"Did you enjoy your talk?"

"Ow!! What the fuck, Hellion?"

"If you weren't such a snarky bastard, Cheshire, you wouldn't get a smack for running your mouth." Okay, she has a point. But c'mon, I've been dying to ask since I found her heading to the gym with a flustered look on her face.

"What we doing here, Hellion?"

"Gotta meet Rocco and sort out some shit."

Pulling up outside the warehouse, he's already standing there waiting for us. She's jumping out of the car before I even get the damn thing in park. Rocco gives her a hug, which makes me glad I came with her and not Kane, or poor Hellion would be looking for another fight organizer. Climbing out, I walk over and laugh at the shit she is giving him for the house profit being down and him trying to bullshit his way out of it. I watch as they head off through the door.

"What you doing out here?" Hellion asks with her head sticking back out of the door, a smile slips across my face.

"You'll see."

"Uh, what you planning, Cheshire?"

"You'll find out soon enough." With a frown and a shake of her head, she turns back inside.

Twenty minutes. Fucking twenty minutes of me freezing my ass outside waiting for this motherfucker to show up. If he isn't here soon, I will lose my shit. Man, it's fucking cold. It's so bad my cock has shriveled up and hidden itself.

"Sorry I'm late, man," Dax shouts to me as he runs down the road. A growl builds in my throat, he knows I hate fucking waiting.

"You best pull this shit off, Dax, or one of us will be castrated. You get it?"

"Yeah, man. I get it." His eyes have widened, but I am looking forward to seeing what happens next.

Heading inside to search for Hellion, the god-awful stench of piss, blood and vomit fills my nose. How the fuck did she fight here? We go down one corridor after another, searching for them. When we finally make it into the back of the warehouse, were all the bad shit happens, I stop and laugh spotting them in a corner. Rocco looks terrified as Hellion's hands move in every direction. She talks with her hands when she's excited about something. Poor Rocco, though, keeps ducking thinking she's gonna smack him. Showtime!

"Hey, yo, Reaper!" A confused frown meets my gaze as I try not to laugh.

"No fucking way!" Dax screeches from the side of me.

"Who's the girl, Cheshire?" Walking over to me with a judgmental look on her face, she watches Dax.

"OMG! No fucking way!" Dax starts bouncing up and

down on the spot. I'm dying to laugh, especially when Hellion throws a me look saying, *who the fuck is this clown.*

"I'm so sorry, Reaper. But what the fuck? Argh!" Blood drips down my lip from me biting it so hard to stop the laughter bubbling in my throat.

"Dax. Stop acting like a groupie and talk to her properly." He looks to me wide eyed as he realizes what reaction he had. Cracking his knuckles, his face goes from excitement to a yeah, whatever look.

"Sorry. I never thought I would meet you. You're a damn legend, Reaper. Anything you need." Throwing his hand out for her to shake, she crosses her arms over her chest and throws daggers my way.

"Dax here is the man you need for upgrades."

"Upgrades?"

"Well, Reaper, Marcus said you need the full works for an upgrade to the warehouse." Her mouth drops open so far, she could catch flies. It's fucking hilarious.

"What the fuck is going on?"

"You want upgrades, don't you?" I ask.

"Stop acting dense, Cheshire, it doesn't suit you." I smirk at her, causing her to narrow her eyes again.

"Dax, have a word with Hellion." He looks at me confused. "Reaper. Find out what she wants done and bill Kane."

"Are you fucking shitting me?" Screeching, she storms toward me. I run backwards to keep her in sight, nearly ending up on my ass more than once.

"Take it up with him, Hellion."

She blows her cheeks out with a pissed off look that would rival a wild beast stalking its prey. I don't envy my brother for the hellfire headed his way soon. It sure as shit will be funny to watch though.

"Well, if he's paying." The grin that spreads across her face.

Oh, shit! I want front row seats to Kane getting the bill, so my ass can sit back with a tub of popcorn and laugh.

"I need to make a call."

Leaving them behind to sort everything out, I head back out front. I haven't heard anything yet and it's pissing me off. Pulling my phone out, I ring Fox for an update. The call takes forever to connect making my hackles rise.

"What's happening?"

He tells me he is struggling to find anywhere that fits Hellion's description, but he will keep trying. He has a feeling this is closely related to her dad being the Butcher. I know for a fact the guy had a lot of enemies. If that's the case, it could be anyone, which puts the list to a whole load of people we know nothing about. Fuck, when it rains it pours.

"They did it to hurt us, Fox. Look at the video we watched. That isn't a coincidence."

He agrees that it isn't, but not knowing what they look like or anything distinctive about them he is searching blind.

"Look I asked you to help find them, but after talking to Kane he wants them found asap so we can put this to bed. We can't risk anyone trying to take her again."

Another damned excuse comes out of his mouth. I know it isn't fucking easy, but now that Kane and Hellion are getting on, Kane is back to being his possessive self.

"Yeah. Yeah. I get it, but do you want to ring him and tell him that, cause I fucking ain't." Fuck my life. Is it too damn early for a scotch?

"Marcus?" What the fuck now? Looking over my shoulder, I spot the guy my father had on his knees walking toward me. Where the hell did he just materialize from?

"What do you want?"

"I need to talk with Reika."

"She's busy."

"Cut the shit, asshole. I know she's in the warehouse, and if I do other people might know too."

Scanning the area to see if anything sticks out, I can't believe I never thought of that. Neither did Kane. What if Fancy Pants, as she calls him, knows she's here? Don't get me wrong, they would have to get through me to get to her again, but still, I don't wanna risk it. Shouts tear through the warehouse as people scream for someone to stop. Without looking back, I take off into the building. I run full speed to the voices which are growing more concerned by the minute. Rocco and Dax are going head-to-head with a couple of guys, but what has my blood boiling is the two guys that are backing Hellion into a corner. With a roar I charge, slamming into the side of one of them knocking him on his ass.

"Cheshire, don't!" Hellion says, just as I grab the other fucker by the back of the shirt and haul his ass off the floor.

"What the fuck is going on here?" I glare at the fucker that is flopping about like a fish on a hook because his top is bunched up around his throat.

"Drop him, Cheshire." Releasing my grip, he lands on his ass. Before he can even blink, Hellion has her foot resting on his throat. The fucker splutters underneath her boot. Every time he tries to move, she adds a little more pressure stopping his movements.

"What do you want, Mason?"

"This place is mine, you little bitch. I want it." He spits at her, causing my chest to rumble.

Crack.

Blood splatters up her face, as Mason's nose gives way under the force of the punch she just landed.

"Who the fuck are you spitting at, asshole? I'll pull your fucking tongue out of your head and feed it to your friend if you want?" Friend one looks at her horrified, and I just stand there smiling.

Rocco and Dax come cover to join us. The other guy here to talk with Hellion has a massive bloodthirsty grin on his face.

"Hey, Pete." She acknowledges the guy standing to my side.

"What you doing here?"

"I came to talk, Reika, but you seem busy." He laughs and she joins in.

"Argggh!" Mason screams. Hellion pushes even further down with her foot after he tried to take advantage of her being distracted.

"Again. What do you want, fucker?" Her chest rises and falls rapidly. I know she's trying her hardest to keep control of her temper. I'm not sure who all knows here, but the one thing we don't want is Hellion having a black out.

"I want what is meant to be mine, Reaper! This is meant to be mine."

"Dude, get a grip. You got the fucking strip club, no doubt. It's not my fault he left me this place and the house."

His eyes bug out of his head. Whoops! Clearly, he didn't know that bit. He starts to thrash around. The guy, Pete, starts laughing his head off, as I watch stunned while Hellion keels down, placing more weight into the foot that has Mason pinned.

"Now, if I let you up are we going to discuss this like adults, or are you going to keep throwing a tantrum?"

The sickly-sweet smile slowly moving across her face has a shiver running down my back. She looks possessed, and it's fucking scary, if I do say so myself. Banging noises come from somewhere in the building. We all freeze as loads of footfalls can be heard making their way through the corridors.

"What the fuck is going on here?" Kane booms as he strides toward us.

"The fuck you doing here?"

Hellion looks my way and I divert my eyes, so I don't have to see whatever her face is saying. Kane extends his hand to the guy, Pete, as my eyes bug out of my head. What the fuck am I missing here? It's like I'm in an alternate universe, and I don't have a damn clue what's going on.

"Marcus pocket dialed me. I overheard."

"So, what? You came to rescue me." Faking a swoon, all of the men burst out laughing, while Kane just glares at the snarky little minx. I'm kinda regretting calling him now because this could go one of two ways. Whoops!

Crack.

"Who the fuck are you biting, Cujo?" Holy shit! Hellion junk punches the poor bastard. My own balls retreat into my stomach. Tears roll down Mason's face as he fights to breathe and the amount of pain he is feeling right about now. A round of ah's leave all the men in the room as they cringe. Lifting her foot, she starts pacing. Both me and Kane watch for any sign of her losing her shit.

"Don't bother tracking her movements. You wouldn't get to her quick enough." Cocking my head at Pete, I try to get a read on who the fuck this guy is.

"How do you know?" How the hell would he know?

"Because, Marcus, I am a family friend that has seen absolutely everything she is truly capable of, and honestly, that shit is scary." He stares down at his hands as a sigh leaves him.

"What don't we know, Pete?" The sadness pouring off him has me regretting asking my question.

"You will have heard how brutal her father was?"

"Yeah. That's why he got the name the Butcher."

"I've never met anyone who was faster or more deadly than him." Unease grows in my gut. I don't like were this is going.

"Until her. She is faster, relentless in her pursuit of the end game. She's unequivocally ruthless."

"I know this, but the thing is, I have seen first-hand the damage she can do. After the blackout, she was riddled with guilt. She was an emotional wreck."

"That was before. After everything she went through at the hands of her kidnapper, do you really think she came back whole?"

"Don't you?" My voice is so low he has to shuffle closer to me to hear it. We are both lost in this conversation.

"I know the state she was in when Paine brought her to me. Honestly, I think her mind broke during it all." My eyes widen. Oh, fuck.

Hellion is a loose cannon at the best of times. You never know when she's going to explode. But thinking back, she has been more calculated lately in her actions and brutality, like with Malcolm. She could have easily pulled a gun and shot him, but instead she beat him into a bloody fucking pulp. Dragging it drag out slowly and as painfully as possible. I had never heard Malcolm scream like that before, and she did it with *that* scary-as-fuck grin on her face.

52

KANE

Rubbing the back of my neck constantly is starting to hurt, but I can't help it. The look in Pretty Bird's eye has me on edge. She looks like a wild animal that has been caged at a zoo. Luckily, she seems to have forgotten about the fucker on the floor, muttering to herself as she goes. One of the guys he came with him walks over to give him a hand up.

"Don't touch him!" she yells. It echoes throughout the room, and we all freeze at the murderous intent on her face.

"Take the warning. Don't be an idiot!" I warn. He looks at me like I'm talking crazy. I give him a shrug as a way to say, *your funeral*.

What the fuck is Marcus doing? Looking for my brother, I find him deep in conversation with Pete. My stomach knots at the fearful look he sends in Pretty Bird's direction.

"Stupid Bitch! You will give me this." Mason pulls himself to his feet as the words leave his stupid mouth.

I run as quick as I can I manage to catch her before she gets any closer to him. Keeping my hold as tight as I can, she thrashes around in my arms trying get to the bastard.

"You think you're so bad, Mason?" she asks, laughing like a lunatic.

"Yeah, bitch! What you gonna do about it?"

"Put your money where your mouth is then."

"What do you mean?"

"You want the fight club and house that much, fight me for it!" She screams over my shoulder. I stop at her words. She can't be fucking serious?

Laughter breaks out in the room from someone behind me, then a laugh joins in that I recognize. Turning I find both Pete and Marcus pissing themselves laughing. Pretty Bird whispers 'put me down' in my ear. I instantly do as she asks, but stay glued to her side as she walks toward him. The guys with him all have huge grins on their faces.

"You serious, Reaper?"

"Deadly." The grin on her face highlights the darkness swirling behind her eyes.

"You're on."

"Rocco, set it up for tomorrow night. Have it open for the regulars to watch." Turning her back on Mason, his face grows cold at the brush off.

"Dax, once this is done you can start the upgrades on my club."

Without looking back, she walks toward Pete and Marcus, who watch her intently. Pete smiles as she reaches them. Hooking her arm around his she drags him toward the door which leads out to the back of the warehouse.

"You heard her, Mason, tomorrow night. Now fuck off."

They all walk off with that false swagger, making them appear scarier than they actually are. Not taking my eyes off them, I slowly follow behind to make sure they leave through a different door than Pretty Bird. My mind races. He knows he can't win. He's tried before and she beat him. The humiliation of that doesn't disappear overnight. Nah this fucker has something planned. I need to find out what the fuck it is.

"You sure about this, Kane?" I was so lost in my own mind watching them leave, I didn't even notice Marcus sneak up on me.

"Get Ivan and Mateo here, now. They will want to know we found her and she is gonna need to work with them for a couple hours."

"You do know this is gonna end extremely bloody, don't you?"

"I think that's what she's hoping for."

Once the door closes behind the guy who just signed his own death warrant without even realizing it, I head in the direction the others went.

Reika

"Have you got a death wish, Little Reaper?"

My veins still buzz with annoyance and rage. He fucking bit me. I can't stand still. Honestly, if Kane hadn't caught me like he did, I would have torn that jumped-up motherfucker apart with my bare hands and I would have reveled in his blood as it sprayed on my face. I know the bastard is planning something. He agreed too easily knowing he couldn't beat me the last time. No, he's definitely planning on something. But what the fuck is it?

"Hellion, you okay?"

"Yeah, Cheshire. I'm not going to explode, ya know."

"Err, Reika, what we gonna do about this fight?" Rocco

stutters. Seeing my outburst must have scared the shit out of him. He has only ever seen me in the ring.

"Get the word out. Call it a grudge match." My eyes light up as my brain gives me a fantastic idea. Even if I beat him again, he will always keep coming at me for what he thinks he is owed.

"Sure thing, boss."

"Rocco, I'm gonna message you a list of a few things I need, but you can't tell anyone. I don't want it getting back to Mason."

"What you need, boss?"

"It's a surprise." My smile is so wide all my teeth show. Rocco shudders as he watches me.

Pulling out my phone, I send him the list of things I need. The horrified emoji he sends back has me laughing. Honestly, even he won't have a clue what I plan on doing with it. All this excitement makes my blood sing, and the need to set my darkness free is palpable.

"I've just seen the list, Little Reaper. Are you sure about this?" asks Pete. The frown on his face has me wanting to reassure, but I know he will understand my reasoning.

"Pete, we both know I have to end this or he will keep coming back."

"I don't like it, Little Reaper."

The metal door bangs open. Kane and Marcus step out, both eyeing us closely. I have to keep what I am planning a secret, because there's no way in hell either of them will allow me to go through with it. I just hope Pete keeps his mouth shut, otherwise I'm fucked.

Kane

.   .   .

Pretty Bird is planning something. It was obvious when we made it outside and Rocco was gone and Pete giving her a look. When she saw us, she smiled wide and walked over, punching me in the damn shoulder and cussing me out for stopping her from getting to Mason. The other assholes getting in the car with us all laugh, surprised I stayed on my feet. I will not be admitting to any of these fuckers that she nearly wiped me out, because I would never live it down. I have to smile, though, listening to their banter. Marcus pouting every now and then because Pretty Bird shoots him down in flames. The ride back is pure chaos. They fight like rabid dogs while Pete laugh's his ass off and encourages them. I have to admit, it was amazing to see her enjoying herself.

We pull up outside the house. The crew members are chilling out. A grill is lit on one side of the yard and there's a few drink coolers scattered around. The passenger door is thrown open and Pretty Bird's seatbelt is practically ripped off her.

"Motherfucker!" The crew jump to attention at the noise, but with a shake of my head they back down. None of us make a move to get out of the truck.

"I'll rip your fucking head off!" Marcus fidgets in the back.

"Kane, I'm not sure this is a good idea." I agree with Pete, but this needs to be done.

"It's fine. She will be fine."

The crew watch in different states of disbelief. They keep looking to me and all I can do is ignore their stares. It's the right thing to do!

Bracing myself for what's about to happen, I slowly climb out of the car and walk over to the blood bath unfolding on the lawn. Ivan and Mateo tear into Pretty Bird like they are intent on killing her, but she meets them head on, blow for goddamn fucking blow, with a scary as shit grin on her face. Lust roars through me watching her. Manic laughter fills the sky as she lands an uppercut to Mateo and launches him into the air. With more speed than I have ever seen, she dodges Ivan and rips his legs out from underneath him. Before he even hits the ground, she's on him landing blow after blow. He is so stunned, all he can do is cover his face and defend himself the best he can. Mateo finally gets to his feet. She's obviously hurt him badly. He wobbles, struggling to keep his legs underneath him, trying his hardest to get to his friend who currently lays underneath Pretty Bird while she deals blows to any part of his body she can reach.

"Reika. Enough!" Pete roars over the noise of the crew.

Instantly she stops. She looks down at Ivan, who uncovers his face, and pushes his head into the dirt and roaring at him. Slowly climbing to her feet, she steps back and looks around at all the faces staring in her direction. Marcus is frozen to his spot. Pete looks at her like a parent seeing the true person hiding underneath the skin of a child he thought he knew. Mateo manages to get Ivan to his feet and they both sway on the spot. I head over to their side while they both mutter to each other. I'm strain my hearing so I can pick up what they are saying.

"She was lethal before, Kane. This-this..." Mateo's words break off. Ivan mutters something under his breathe with an unreadable expression, as we all watch as Pretty Bird slams through the door of the house.

53

REIKA

"Ladies and Gentleman! Are you ready for The Grudge Match!"

Rocco's words reach me in the office of the warehouse as I get myself mentally ready for what's about to go down.

"We've got a treat for you all tonight!"

My nerves normally cause havoc when I am waiting to fight, but tonight there is total complete calm. A chilling state of mind, but this thing with Mason has to end. Rumors have been circling throughout the underground about who my dad was. A few have made it known how much they want me to be a part of their crew, by any means necessary. Tonight isn't just about putting an asshole in his place, it's also about sending a message to anyone who wants to come at me. Fancy Pants got lucky catching me off guard like he did, but it won't fucking happen again. If anyone tries, there will only be a death sentence.

"You ready, Little Reaper?"

Turning to face Pete, I'm shocked to see all three brothers standing behind him. Liam has an excited look on his face, while Marcus looks extremely unsure of what's about to happen. Kane just stares at me with a murderous expression. Marcus told me how fucked up Kane was after the video, and about the murdering spree he went on. I feel that energy burning through my veins right now. Pete walks over as I lift my first hand to be wrapped. All eyes zero in on what Pete is doing.

"What the fuck is that?" Liam asks.

"It's fine, Liam."

"What are you doing, Hellion?"

"Fucking hell, Marcus. Would you just trust me?" Pete carries on binding my hands, not paying attention to the three assholes throwing daggers over his shoulder.

"Where's your favorite hand wraps, Pretty Bird?" Pete gulps as quietly as he can, but unfortunately, they all hear him.

"I don't want to ruin them." I chuckle at how stupid that sounds even to my own ears.

Pete finishes my hands and grips them while pleading with me, without words, not to go through with this. I know if I hadn't sworn him to keep quiet, he would be singing like a canary to the guys right now.

"Ladies and Gentlemen. I give you, Mason!"

The crowd goes insane as yells of excitement reverberate around the cage and the stomping of feet rattles the walls. As I bounce from foot to foot, I clench my fists to make sure the bindings aren't too tight. I glare at the guys as they all huff, then they turn around and head out to the viewing area. Tightening my ponytail, I circle my shoulders and crack my neck.

"You sure about this? You know once they realize what's happening with that," he points to the bindings, "they are gonna spectacularly lose their shit and try to stop it."

"I'm prepared for that." I have had to plan this perfectly so nothing can go wrong.

"I'll give you five to relax and get your head in the right space before your walk out."

I hear the door click shut behind him. I breathe deeply and slowly, in and out to center myself. I let my mind drift off. Grounding myself before every fight helps me keep my emotions in check. Just like any normal fight, I can feel the darkness in me trying to come to the front of my mind. Normally I would push it back, but I need it brimming just below the surface tonight. The clink of metal brings me back to the present as Pete and some guy I don't know put the boxes on the table. Lifting the lids, the light from the bulbs catches against the contents in one of the boxes while it deepens the yellow tone of the other. Walking over I dip my hands in the first and wait a few seconds before doing the same thing to the second. Mesmerized by the shimmer that is now on my bindings, I smile wide at Pete.

"We need to get done here."

Placing the lids back on, we set off on the short walk that will take me to the doors. Halfway down the hallway, the noise of the crowd has grown so loud my ears vibrate. The door is already open at the end; the hallway is shrouded in darkness so nobody can see. Pete continues to take his place to watch as I stand there waiting. A slight grip on my arm has me standing at attention, as a soft breath moves across my ear.

"I fucked him on more than one occasion, and it will happen again. I am meant to be his Queen!"

Looking over my shoulder, the darkness conceals some of her face. I step further back and the blonde of her hair catches in the little bit of light in the hallway, then I see the malicious grin on her face as a snarl leaves my mouth.

'Ladies and Gentlemen, I give you, Reaper!'

Kane

The crowd roars its appreciation for the Reaper being back in the ring. Me and my brothers are standing in the same place we were when I first laid eyes on her. I can't believe how much has happened since then. A light shines toward Pretty Bird and my heart stutters; the look on her face has a promise of death. The crowd pushes forward, trying to get a closer look at her. The reaction of the crowd at the mere mention of her name tells anyone she will always be their favorite. Her face takes on a colder look with each stride toward the cage. She climbs up the steps without a glance in our direction. Once inside, they size each other up, and the crowd falls silent. The hairs on the back of my neck stand on end, what the fuck? Something isn't right.

"Oh fuck!" Liam gasps, forcing me to look away and stare at him.

"Kane look at her fucking hands!" Looking at the bindings on her hands, I don't see anything out of the ordinary until she moves slightly and the light bounces off them. What the fuck?

"Kane! She has fucking glass on her bindings." My mouth drops open as I look back to her hands and I can see the glint of the glass as the light bounces off it again. Looking to Mason, his hands have the same bindings.

"That's hemp and resin, dipped in glass." The horror on Liam's face roots me to the spot. He is the only one of us that seems to know what it means and judging by the look on his face it's something fucked-up.

"Yeah, so?" Marcus asks.

"This isn't a fucking cage fight, Kane! Only one of them is walking out of there alive!" What the fuck did he just say?

Liam jumps down from his spot trying to push his way

through the crowd to get to the cage. My mind catches up slowly and I jump down, practically launching people out of my way to get my girl out of there. Liam rattles the door as Pretty Bird looks over her shoulder to us and smirks. Liam is cussing up a storm, yanking on the door that won't open. Looking down, I see a lock on the door. It won't open without a key.

"Rocco! Unlock the fucking door!" The bastard saunters over to us like he doesn't have a care in the world.

"Sorry, man. Boss lady says no one gets in until it's over." Gripping the front of his shirt, I yank him forward so our noses are touching.

"Open the door, or I'll tear you to fucking pieces." Pure venom drips from my words as I growl at him, which is echoed by two others. His face pales as he realizes both Marcus and Liam flank me.

Bloodthirsty screams fill the air as the crowd roars their approval. I drop Rocco and look to see what has caused the reaction from the crowd. They are going full out on each other. She barely dodges a kick to the face. Jumping back, she beckons Mason forward with her fingers. Just as he gets within striking distance, Pretty Bird lashes out so quick with a back hand, Mason is torn open from hip to peck from the glass on her bound hands. Mason roars in agony, clutching his chest as she walks around him, taunting him. I don't know what she says, but whatever it is riles him up. He launches off the floor and spears her flat on her back. My stomach somersaults as vomit comes to the back of my throat. Blood splatters all over the canvas from the hits he lands on her.

"Kane, we gotta stop this!" Marcus screams in terror, trying to rip the door off the fucking hinges.

The minutes pass slowly as we try find a way inside the fucking cage. If any of us try to climb over the side one or the other of them knocks us back off it. Neither one of them want this stopped. They go toe to toe, neither of them moving out to even take a breather. It's a fucking blood bath in there. I don't know who is hurt worse, as they are both covered in blood. The glint in Pretty Bird's eye tells me she's enjoying herself. She is a fucking psycho, but I hope she'll be my psycho again.

"Kane, they're gonna fucking kill each other!" Liam screams at me.

"Fuck this!" Marcus takes off running in the direction of the office.

I don't know what to do; I feel so fucking powerless, everything is numb. I spot Marcus charging back toward us with what looks like bolt cutters in his hands. Fuck, why didn't I think of that? He slams to a stop, his eyes bulging so wide they could fall out. I watch as the item in his hand drops to the floor. Silence. I don't hear a fucking thing. What? Terrified screams ring out around the warehouse as the guy to the side of me throws up. Pushing him out of the way, I see the color drain from Marcus's face. Looking over my shoulder the sight has my knees giving way. Fuck no, this can't be happening. As the crowd slowly backs up, I see Mason has Pretty Bird on her back landing blow after blow, with a manic smile on his face.

"No!" Rocco screams as I watch the horror show in front of me. I can't move.

"Kane!" One of my brothers screams as I watch blood explode everywhere.

"She's not moving, she's not fucking moving!" Marcus screams at me. I'm taken back to the sound of Pretty Birds screams the night Mel killed herself, at the brokenness of his words.

"I fucking told this bitch I would have what was mine!" Mason screams into the air. Wrapping his hand around her throat, he stands up and lifts her limp body off the floor so it dangles in the air.

"I'll fucking kill you!" I roar as I run toward the cage, scrambling up the side as fast as I can.

"Watch as I snap your bitch's neck!" The smile he gives me is one of a mad man.

My vision blurs as tears brim in my eyes, this feeling of helplessness is like nothing I have ever felt before. I feel my soul shredding from my body.

"Oh, shit!"

My body sags as I see the one thing that allows relief to pour through me. Mason is still staring at me; he hasn't realized yet. Pretty Bird lashes out so fast into his throat, he drops her. His hands frantically grab at it as he fights for air. Standing to her feet, she looks up and around the room with a smirk, looking like a demon born of blood. Looking down to the fucker who is choking for air, she grins and coos at him. His eyes widen as tears drip from the corners down his face.

Stomp.

Walking away from the now lifeless body on the floor, she calmly heads over to the door and pulls a tiny key out of her sports bra. Rocco scrambles up the stairs as she passes it through the wire. Once the door opens, she climbs down and walks toward the back of the warehouse where Pete is waiting without a word to anyone.

54

REIKA

Walking toward Pete is pure fucking agony. Every goddamn step I take has my whole body is shaking. It's taking all the energy I have left just to put one foot in front of the other. Pete doesn't say a word, just falls into step with me as I walk down the corridor heading straight for the office.

"Pete, get one of them to ring Doc and make sure no one comes into the office. I need to be alone." His eyebrows bunch together at me, but honestly, I hurt too fucking much to answer.

I spin to shut and lock the door as the three amigos come charging down the hallway. I just manage to lock it as all three of them crash into the other side of the door. Blocking out the abuse they are hurling at me, demanding me to open the fucking door, I try my best to walk to the desk on wobbly legs without causing further damage. I round the desk just as my legs give way underneath me. I have to haul my ass up into the chair, then lean my head back and take a deep breath. I acknowledge I finally ended it. I can feel the blood from the deeper wounds dripping onto the floor. I managed to avoid most of the blows so they only grazed me and caused surface wounds, but a few have left deep gashes. Well, what's a few more scars to add to my already extensive collection? Rattling sounds come from the main door, I try to chuckle at the guy's determination to get in here to cuss me out. Even that hurts. My breathing starts to rattle a little bit as pain tears through my right side.

"Reika."

"Who's that?" I can't even lift my head to look at the person who said my name from inside the office.

"Doc. I need to check you over."

"Well, that's the idea, Doc. Pete?"

"Yeah."

"Can you go and tell the noisy fuckers outside that door to keep their fucking voices down please."

"You know they're gonna want to come in."

"Only Marcus can come in." He disappears the way he came. I need to ask him how he did that. Doc comes over and starts asking loads of questions. I know it's rude not to answer him but I can feel exhaustion begging me to slip into the wonderful darkness that edges my vision. My head shoots up as something scratchy and wet runs across my stomach.

"Easy, Reika. I need to clean off the blood so I can see your wounds." Letting him do what he needs to, I drop my head so it rests on the back of the chair. I let my eyes slowly drift close.

"What the fuck, Hellion!"

"Shhh, or your ass leaves, Cheshire."

"Like fuck! You will listen, you little shit. I am so mad at you right now!" Huffing out a breath, a hiss slips past my lips as Doc swipes over a sore spot.

Cracking an eye to see with, Marcus looks like steam is about to come out of his ears. His chest rises and falls quickly and he runs his hands up and down his jeans. He tracks the movements of Doc's hands. His eyes narrow at me as the slosh of the cloth being wrung out in the bucket is the only sound to be heard. Shrugging my shoulders, I close my eyes again and relax further into the chair.

"Look, Marcus," says Pete.

"Shut your fucking mouth, old man! You knew what was going on didn't you?"

Oh, fucking hell no, he didn't! Lifting my head, I glare at Doc so he scrambles out of the way. I stand up on shaky legs as Pete moves forward. Throwing my hand up to stop him, I round the desk toward Cheshire.

"How fucking dare you speak to him like that." My voice is barely above a deadly growl.

"Hellion."

"Don't fucking Hellion me, asshole. Yeah, he knew, but that isn't the thing that's got me wanting to rip your head off at the moment.

"Oh, yeah?" The motherfucker cocks his fucking eyebrow at me.

"One word, Cheshire." I growl, baring my teeth at him.

"What's that?"

"Blondie."

Marcus

Oh, shit!

My mouth opens and closes as my brain scrambles for something to say. Fuck. Shit. How the fuck does she know? Now, I know why Pete said only I had permission to come into the room. How? Fucking how? I haven't seen Blondie in the house since Hellion has been back. The murderous look she is giving me would normally have me fearing for Kane's safety, but honestly, the bastard deserves her wrath.

"Guess you knew?" The betrayal in her tone has me feeling like the worst person alive.

"I was gonna tell you, but then it slipped my mind with everything going on."

"Slipped your fucking mind. You know we fucked, for God's sake, and clearly it was after he stuck his dick in her!"

She starts pacing as Doc throws me daggers. I know, he needs to check her wounds, but she isn't gonna sit still until she gets the answers she needs from me.

"How did you find out?" Looking to Pete to see if he will give me a way out of this, he just mouths *tell the truth* at me. Yeah, great advice, asshole!

"I caught her walking out of his room, buttoning her clothes up." Her eyes narrow to slits. "I put a beating on him for it, and then I left the house and found Liam in the diner."

"You're telling me he fucked her the day of the kitchen incident?" Oh, shit! Her nostrils flare as her movements become jerky. This has Pete standing up straight, watching her. Her eyes darken, then her face smooths out like she's having an internal battle with her demons.

"How did you find out, Hellion?"

"The peroxide bitch told me just before I walked out. All while grinning like the fucking cat that got the cream." She chuckles. "Well technically, she did, since she told me it was more than once and she would be *his* queen."

"The fuck?"

"Your guess is as good as mine, Cheshire."

"Don't let this break you, Hellion. If she hurt you, make the bitch pay. Fuck it, make them both pay." Her eyes bulge at my words. I watch fascinated as her expression changes with whatever is going on in her head.

"You game?"

"You don't even need to ask, Hellion." I grin back at her as Doc coughs to catch our attention.

Thirty minutes later, there is still banging and arguments from the other side of the door, which has had me laughing my ass off. Only five of Hellion's deeper cuts needed stitches, but what has me feeling like shit, and has Hellion saying it's the coolest thing ever, is the scar on her leg that she got from the knife. It now looks like a giant X from a blow tonight. She jokes with Pete that she looks like a treasure map because of all her scars. We can all see how tired she is after today. How the fuck she is still holding a conversation, let alone consciousness, is beyond me. I am going to have to intercept a certain angry asshole who is once again cussing us out through the door when she's ready to leave. Yay, fun. Not.

"Pete, how have they not managed to get in here yet?" I've wanted to ask the question a few times, but Hellion has been my concern. But I ask now as my brothers try again to batter the door down and it doesn't move.

"Ha! I was wondering when one of you was gonna ask." Both our eyebrows hit our hairline as we stare at him.

"Alexander was seriously paranoid, so when he decided on this as his office, he had metal put into the middle of the frame and door to reinforce it."

"No fucking way." Holy shit, that's fucking genius. I can't help the snicker that escapes me.

"Yep, so your brothers are gonna be hurting like a bitch tomorrow based on the force they're throwing into it." We all laugh at this, because they aren't gonna have a fucking clue.

"Okay, now, what do we do about the seriously pissed off

gang leader outside?" Hellion throws out to the room. Even Doc has the look of *oh fuck balls*. We all look between each other waiting for someone to come up with some idea.

"Doc, keep your mouth shut. You two follow my lead. Marcus?"

"Yeah."

"Get rid of your brothers tomorrow, and then bring Blondie to meet me for a little chat." The evil grin on her face has me smiling.

"Yes, boss."

Casually, like nothing has happened, she walks over to the door. They must be damn good painkillers Doc gave her. Either that or she is tougher than the fucking devil. Quickly, but really quietly, she unlocks the door and moves as far back to the right as she can. When the door flies open, I bust out laughing as both Kane and Liam try to stop themselves from face planting the floor. Everyone in the room laughs as we watch them untangle themselves from the mass of limbs they are caught up in. Kane punches Liam as he tries to stand. Hellion laughs even more, making his eyes instantly zero in on her, and the look on his face tells me she's in trouble.

"Pretty Bird?" Her eyes narrow into slits. The look has me praying she's gonna play nice.

"Don't start, Kane. I'm tired and hungry, so get your asses up and let's go." Walking down the corridor with so much sass it's applause worthy, I laugh again at the shocked expressions on everyone's face. Kane scrambles to his feet and sets off after her as Liam turns to me with the with a look saying, spill it. Shaking my head, I walk out with the others, following in her wake.

55

REIKA

Anticipation runs through me as I check and double check everything I need is in the bag. Kane was a pain in the ass last night after we got back, demanding answers for not telling him what was happening. Then throwing a damn tantrum like a child when I told him his reaction was the reason why. Pete tried to explain what he had heard spreading through the underground. Kane's quickly lost his shit and told me that I would not be going anywhere without an escort again. He was seriously lucky I was so fucking tired; I couldn't be bothered to argue with him.

Then he wondered why he got a smack upside the head. The whole reason I did what I did last night was to send a fucking message. Anyone who thinks I can be used in a pissing contest just because of who my father is, has another thing coming. If they come at me, they will leave in a body bag, simple as that. I don't thrive on taking another life, but I am not going to cower like some bitch who needs saving. Over the years, my father's words have been proven time and time again. Do what you have to do to survive! Fight for everything you want! Do not ever cower to anyone!

It took Marcus a while to convince Kane and Liam that they had to do something at HQ today. They only agreed and left when he told them he would stay behind and keep me in check. Checking the time on my phone, I've got about ten minutes before Marcus comes for a talk. Grabbing my bag, I head out.

"Why are you wasting your time with him?" I hear Marcus ask just as the office door opens and he pushes blondie through the door. Without another word he closes the door and locks it from the other side. That's the thing about this office, you need a key to unlock it from either side.

"What the fuck do you want, bitch?" she spits at me. My grin grows at her fire. She has some balls after all, who knew?

"You know what." Walking around the desk to put us closer together, she grins and takes a step forward.

"Ah! Do you want to know all the ways I fucked Kane? That's it, isn't it, Reika?" Anger fills me as I grind my teeth. I can feel my control slipping, the sadistic bitch that lives in my head is screaming at me to end her, but I need to know the truth before I let her out to play.

Slap.

Oh, fucking hell no! The bitch just slapped me and now has a shit eating grin on her face? I lunge forward, and she turns and runs like the pathetic little bitch she is. Grabbing her hair, I spin and launch the cocky bitch into the wall behind the desk. With a battle cry, Blondie shakes off her shock and comes at me.

Crack.

The back hand I just landed has her flying backward into the chair. Her eyes widen. Yeah, that's right, bitch. You don't wanna fuck with me. Ripping the knife out of the sheath, I slam it home as she screams a blood curdling sound. Trying to grab the handle to yank the bastard out, I give her another slap that has her head rolling back. Putting her other hand on the arm I slam another knife through the top of her hand. She screams again, and my body thrums at the sound. I know I look like a crazy bitch. The thing is, I know me and Kane have issues and I don't trust him, but the thought of this bitch or anyone else with their claws on him has my inner bitch planning murder.

"I will have him, Reika!" She bares her teeth at me.

"Is that so?"

"Yeah, they should have killed you. They were meant to kill you!" The roar in my ears kicks up another notch as she smirks at my reaction. I'm frozen in place. My hands start to shake.

"I was the one Liam was fucking in the video. I overheard his plans and I hijacked them. I rang some people to get you out of my fucking way."

Motherfucker! This bitch is the fucking reason for everything.

A scream tears out of me as I throw a punch at this fucker. Her head snaps back and her nose explodes everywhere. My punches are so hard and so fast, her face splits under the power of them. Her screams echo around the room, I think. They sound distorted to my ears. Pulling out another knife, I slam it into her shoulder. My control has snapped. I'm gonna end this bitch where she is. The darkness is all consuming and she will fucking pay for trying to end me.

"Hellion! Hellion, fucking listen to me."

A roar that sounds like a wild animal fills the room. I see shadows moving in my peripheral vision. Hands yank me away as I roar my annoyance at the interruption.

"Hellion!" My vision comes back into focus, and I'm not zeroed in on the bitch attached to the chair.

"What the fuck, Cheshire!" His eyes zero in on me.

"I heard everything. What do you want to do?" The anger in his voice tells me he did hear what she just said. The look he throws over his shoulder at her has a smile coming to my face.

"Do it!" I seethe. This fucking ends today.

Kane

Marcus:
Get your ass back here now Hellion has lost it!!

I'm out of my seat instantly, and I shout over my shoulder to tell Liam to stay put. Without looking back, I run as fast as I can. What the fuck set her off? Within a couple of minutes, I'm out of the building and jumping into my car. The engine roars to life as I slam my foot down hard on the gas and peel out of the lot to the sound of screeching tires. The drive back only takes me five minutes. I jump out of the car and charge toward the house, then head in searching for chaos.

"What the fuck is going on, Marcus?" I find him standing outside the office door.

Without even looking at me, he opens the door and ushers me inside. The room is dark. Hitting the light switch, a wet substance transfers to my hand. What the…? My thought is cut off as my eyes widen seeing Blondie in the desk chair in a bloody mess. Her face is mangled, blood slowly runs down her face; one of her eyes is swollen shut. The door clicks shut and I take a step toward her.

"Touch her and I'll wrap Betty here around your head." The words stop me, my eyes widen as Blondie looks over my shoulders while tears stream down her face. Turning around, my heart jumps at the sight of Pretty Bird. Her voice is layered with so much emotion, it's deepened it from her normal raspy tone. She stands with a leg against the wall. As she pushes off it, a baseball bat swings up and onto her shoulder. My heart stutters as I see the barbed wire wrapped around the end of it.

"What's going on, Pretty Bird?" Unease coats my voice at the look in her eyes. I've seen that look twice before, and both times it ended with fucked-up bodies.

"Ask your bit of ass!" She bares her teeth at me.

"What the fuck?" I don't know what she's on about.

"Thing is, Kane. I don't share."

"Share what? What the fuck is going on here?" Confusion clouds my head.

"You told me not to deny this connection between us, to not fight it and embrace what happens."

"Yeah, I love you, Pretty Bird."

"Stop. Fucking. Lying. To. Me!" She steps closer, the murder in her eyes sends fear spreading through me. "You told me that, then I find out you've been fucking this bitch."

"What?"

"Why are you acting so surprised? You're the one sticking your dick in it." Venom drips from her words.

"I haven't touched anyone since you. It's only fucking you! It will ONLY EVER BE YOU!" I bellow back at her, hoping she will see how fucking stupid this is.

"Stop fucking lying!" I barely manage to duck, as the bat moves across the top of my head. "Marcus, fucking caught her coming out of your room! Do you think I'm stupid?" Her words are filled with so much anger, hurt and betrayal.

Her words register in my brain as the beating Marcus gave me comes to the forefront, his words echo in my head. Realization dawns on me.

"What did you do?" I roar at the conniving little blonde bitch.

"You're meant to be mine. I'm meant to be yours. I'm

meant to be the Queen." The set of her jaw as she stares daggers at Pretty Bird has my anger building.

"I told you. I never fucking wanted you! Then you make all this shit up to destroy what I have with Reika and drive a wedge between me and my brother!" My darkness roars to the surface, begging me to tear this bitch apart.

"It would have happened if they had killed her like they were fucking meant to!" She screams back at me. The roar that leaves me thunders in the room as I grab her chin and the back of her head.

Crack.

My labored breathing fills the room as I look down at the bitch that put my girl in danger. I can't believe it was her.

"You killed her?" At the surprise in her voice, my anger flares again. Launching toward Pretty Bird, she stumbles back, dropping the bat in the process. Gripping her throat, I slam her into the wall.

"Why don't you believe me! You are everything I have ever wanted! Abso-FUCKING-lutly everything!" She needs to realize this.

"Because I never know what is truth or lies!" she screams back at me.

The energy between us explodes, and I slam my lips down on hers. The moan that leaves her has my cock paying attention. Ripping her top from her without breaking our kiss, I drop it on the floor as she tears mine. This is pure chaos; I'm riding carnal desire like a fucking demon possessed. The button on my jeans goes next and my head falls back at the pressure on my cock. She's not controlling this! Wrapping my hand in her hair, I yank her head back. Her eyes widen, then darken as she stares at me, the challenge clear. Adding more pressure to her throat, her breath hitches. I pull her away from the wall, throw her across the room and she hits the desk with an *oomph*. I am on her instantly, applying pressure between her shoulders to forcing her to keep still.

Yanking her jeans down, my dick nearly explodes at the sight of her bare beneath them. The perfect globes of her ass cheeks make me painfully hard. Wiggling my hips, I run my hand up and down from her pussy to her ass crack, spreading her fucking dripping juices. I dip my finger inside occasionally; the sounds she makes at the sudden intrusion are driving me nuts. She is so fucking wet. Dragging her hips back off the desk a bit, I slam home in one hard thrust driving a scream from her. I pound into her pussy with such force the whole desk moves.

"Fuck me, Kane!" Her chant builds as I slide my free hand around her front and run my finger over her clit. The moan she gives has me punishing her, forever questioning how I feel about her. I fuck her so hard, my balls bunch up as the tingle grows. I feel Pretty Bird shaking under me. I don't think so! I slow my thrusts to prolong this; she will come only when I say she can. She cusses me out for slowing down. A twisted grin spreads across my face as I slowly move my hand from her clit across her hip, causing her to shudder again. Wide eyes look at me over her shoulder, her pupils completely blown, as I circle the ring of her ass.

"You ever been fucked here, Pretty Bird?"

"No." The nervousness in her voice has my dick thrumming so hard it's torture.

With a grin, I lift my thumb and suck, her lids are low as she stares at me with a lustful gaze. My thrusts stay shallow and I see she is deciding whether to argue with me again. She's on the verge of exploding.

"Kane!" she growls. As I press into her again, her eyes roll back in her head. I grin. She will learn she is mine and no one will get between us. Pretty Bird opens her eyes to look at me again, and I smirk as I push the end of my thumb into her ass while slamming into her pussy. The sound she makes has me nearly blowing my load.

"You like that, baby?"

"Mmmmmmmm." I pick up the pace, thrusting into her so brutally she can only huff out breaths, but what I want is a scream tearing out of her pretty lips. I continue to slam into her pussy while I breach the tight ring of muscle in her ass, pumping my thumb in time with my cock. Her pussy clamps down so hard on my cock I can't move. Her walls pulse around me, causing me to explode. I roar my release and she screams hers with my fucking name on her lips.

56

REIKA

What the fuck just happened?

I'm pinned to the desk by the fucker behind me as his body shakes from a building laugh. His cock is still buried in my pussy, but the fucker is still hard. I lift my head. Oh, shit!

"Kane?"

"Hmmm."

"Get your cock out of me."

"But I'm comfy, Baby," the little shit whines, like a child.

"Dude, there's a dead fucker in front of me."

Kane pulls out. I stand and pull my jeans up. My top is a no go since the bastard tore it clean off me, a fact I'm sure he's very proud of. Spotting his t-shirt on the floor, I grab it and throw it on over my head.

"Hmm. I like you in my clothes, Pretty Bird." A blush creeps up my cheeks, which has him grinning at me.

"We fucked in a room with a dead body, Kane." I don't know how to feel about this.

"So? The bitch deserved it." The ice in his voice makes my pussy clench, ready for another round. Yes, fucking please, because that was hot as fuck.

"You snapped her neck?" I'm still surprised by this. He did it with such ferocity. I couldn't do anything but watch.

"Yeah, she hurt you." His tone holds so much feeling that my heart stutters.

"Get it through you head, Pretty Bird. I don't want anyone else, it's only you." I, what, ummm.

"I need to know…" Looking up, I see determination in his eyes and the set of his jaw. "Are we all in?" My brow furrows at his words.

"Are we in this together once and for all, Pretty Bird. I am not fucking around. You are mine and I am yours." Holding his breath as he nibbles on his bottom lip, he looks down at me expectantly. My head and heart have a quick screaming match regarding the pros and cons of this.

I take a deep breath and say, "Yes." His lips crash down on mine again as his hand moves to grab hold of his T-shirt.

"Have you stopped fucking yet? I got a boner out here you know!" yells Cheshire. I fall over laughing at the murderous look on Kane's face. Trust Cheshire to pop up in asshole mode.

"You best be lying, Marcus!" I shout back to him. The door clicks, then slowly opens. Kane stiffens. Gripping hold of his forearm to keep him in place, I wait as Cheshire pokes his head round the door.

"You dirty bastards! I'm shocked by your wicked ways, Hellion!" he says in fake shock.

"Eat dick, Cheshire!" Kane smirks at my words as he squints between both of us.

"You took it up the ass. Don't get snippy with me!" Kane doubles over laughing as I throw the nearest thing at the fucker's head, which happens to be the lamp. Cheshire dodges, and it smashes into the wall at the side of the door. The bastard grins at me. I run forward. The little shit cackles and runs flat out down the corridor. Crew members jump out of the way laughing as he charges past them, and I fall a few steps behind. Kane's laughter follows behind me. Don't know why you're laughing, fucker. I'm about to make mincemeat out of your brother!

"Stop running, Cheshire. I won't hurt you too much!" I shout after him as he runs for the front room.

Making it through the door, I slam into Cheshire's back. He stands staring at guests who are looking at us with confusion. My lungs burn. Fucking hell, he's a quick little bastard. I am so out of breath, I double over trying to pull air into my lungs. Kane saunters in without a care in the world and a big ass grin on his face. I smack the fucker in the stomach as a growl leaves me.

Pete, Fox and Paine all stare at me. Kane's T-shirt is hanging to my knees and blood is splattered all over my jeans and hands. Whoops! Pete's face is worried, but what the hell is Paine doing here? I haven't heard anything from him since he dropped me at Pete's. Liam walks in with a nod to Fox. Pete steps forward.

"Now that everyone's here, we need to talk."

Malcolm

After everything I did for those ungrateful little bastards, they choose loyalty to some piece of ass. How the fuck didn't I know that there was a survivor that night? It said in the tabloids that nobody survived. How did they keep her hidden for so long?

The bitch is definitely her father's daughter. The way she laid into me in front of the crew was utterly humiliating. I'll have the last laugh, bitch. Just you wait! Pain rips through my side as I walk up the mountain of stairs to get to my destination. A big fucker blocks my path at the top.

"Turn around, asshole."

"I'm here for the meeting." He radios it in. I wait a few minutes before the crackle of the radio sounds. Listening intently to the voice in the earpiece, he turns the knob on the door without breaking eye contact, like he's afraid of what I might do. He motions me through in the direction of my destination. The luxury of this place has me feeling sick. I'm rich by most people's standards, but this is fucking ridiculous. Especially for the age of the owner. Chatter fills the hall further down where two more security guards stand. Without even looking at me, the double doors swing open. As I step into the room, my anxiety bubbles.

"Is it done?"

"No."

57

REIKA

"What's going on, Pete?"

"Sit down, Little Warrior." Paine looks at me, asking me not to argue. *What?*

"Fox, what's going on?" Kane asks. Fox shakes his head with an unreadable look. I sitting down on the couch. My anxiety builds as Pete walks toward me, then perches himself on the edge of the coffee table.

"I've been working with Fox for a few weeks, Reika, looking into what information we could gather."

"Why?" I haven't got a clue what's going on here.

"Marcus asked Fox to try to find Fancy Pants."

"So?" I'm not intentionally being dense here, but I don't know what is happening. I feel, without having to look, the guys step closer to my back. Pete's eyes widen as he sees it.

"While we were looking, we found some stuff." These riddles are pissing me off now. I am not a goddamn mind reader. I can feel the hold on my temper slipping.

Pete places a file down on the coffee table, sliding it toward me. My hands start to sweat as I look at it. I don't know what it is, but the heartbroken look on Paine's face makes me not want

451

to. However, staying in the dark is not my strong suit. I open to the first page. My heart stops. I gulp at what I see in front of me. It's an in-depth report of the injuries my parents sustained in the attack. The next pages are just your normal things from after people die. Flipping through, I gasp. I hear Pete telling the guys to step back. I launch to my feet with the papers in hand as my eyes read through everything in front of me as fast as I can. Rage boils under the surface. My demons come forward and they are the deadliest they have ever been. Looking around to the only family I have left, I see tears running down his guilt-ridden face.

"I am so sorry, Little Warrior. I didn't know."

My heart pounds in my chest. Chatter breaks out around the room. I watch Paine battle with his emotions as Pete tries to soothe him. He charges out of the room with Pete calling his name.

"Reika." Pete's words are nervous. Pacing seems to be my go to at the moment. My brain goes from denial to heartbreak to rage. I know what I have to do. I can't let this go.

"Pretty Bird?" Bracing my shoulders, I look to each set of eyes in the room. Two of them know what is in the file, but the other three don't.

"Do you trust me?" I ask the guys and look each of them in the eyes for a second.

"Without a doubt, Pretty Bird."

"Then get ready. It's time for war."

58

KANE

It's time for war.

We all watch stunned as Pretty Bird's words echo throughout the room. Her jaw is set and darkness swirls in her eyes letting us all know she's dead serious.

I am still confused though. I'll have to ask her when we are alone what the hell is in that file. When she looked up from the page, stunned and wide eyed, the devastation that creeped across Paine's face made me frown. Whatever it is, it broke him, and he ran. Which is surprising. That fucker went toe to toe with me in the safe house and didn't bat an eyelid. Most people would have run in the opposite direction. But whatever is in that file caused him to charge out the door like his ass is on fire without looking back. My head snaps back to her. Can't she catch a goddamn break? Fuck, that would just be too easy, wouldn't it?

We had such a good time in the office, well, when we fucked. She agreed to be mine properly. Killing Blondie was just a bonus. Honestly, the little bitch deserved it. She was putting a wedge between me and Marcus. Nobody comes between me and my family. Then to go after Pretty Bird like she did; the bitch must have been crazy. She signed her own death warrant that night, and I was just cashing it in.

"Little Reaper, you gonna tell me what you're thinking?" Pete asks with uncertainty.

"I was so close. So, fucking close!" she screams. "If I had known, I would have killed the motherfucker!" she roars, swiping the contents of the coffee table to the floor. The hairs on my arms stand on end as madness shines in her eyes, calling my own. The darkness craving vengeance for it all, demanding payment in blood.

"You will find him!" Pete bellows over her.

My brothers and I look between each other, knowing she is going to explode at this rate. Liam takes a step in her direction to try and calm her down, which has me surprised.

"Back the fuck off, Frosty!" she seethes as she turns her narrowed gaze on Fox.

"The fucker who killed my parents was the one who held me captive! And you only just found out," she seethes as she steps toward him."What use are you? I thought you were meant to be good at this sort of thing, not more useless than the shit I scrape off my shoes," she screams into his face, her rage palpable. Tense silence hangs heavily in the air, like a weighted bullet ready to blow. Fox looks seconds away from pissing his pants, trembling under Reika's wrathful glare.

He was the one? Fuck!

I've never been speechless, but my mouth is sewn shut. Even Marcus hasn't uttered a word. He just stands there, his eyes bulging, his jaw slack. The room is silent enough to hear a pin drop – the calm before the storm. The next moment the spell breaks. A roar fills the room as all hell breaks loose, and Pretty Bird lunges at Fox.

She knocks him on his ass, pummeling his face with all the ferocity of a savage beast, causing a sick feeling in my stomach. Pete just stands and watches while Reika decimates the room. She up-ends the table, smashing it into the TV. Shattered glass and chunks of wood rain down around us. My brothers and I take a step back as Fox crawls out of her path. Blood pisses down his face, a shadow of a bruise showing underneath his left eye and carries on down all the way to his busted jaw.

"Little Reaper?" Pete tries to speak to her.

"Fuck you, Motherfucker!" she roars as she rips the TV off the wall and launches it across the room. Marcus mutters under his breath, "Well, that won't be cheap to fix. I only got that a couple of weeks ago." What's left of it explodes into pieces from the force she threw it with.

"Ah!" All our eyes turn to the voice. Bonzo shakes in his spot, nearly being flattened by the flying object. Pretty Bird glares in his direction, her chest heaving, rising and falling rapidly as she gulps in air. His mouth opens and closes like a fish as he stares back at her, terrified.

"What's up, Bonzo?" Liam asks trying to relax the poor guy. It's fucking comical how chilled he sounds surrounded by such devastation.

"Err. We have a problem." His eyes flick between Liam and Pretty Bird as he takes a small step back out of the room.

"For fuck's sake, man! Just spit it out!" Her words are so full of rage the poor guy whimpers. He looks to me and my brothers for help.

Not a chance, man. I ain't going anywhere near her like this. Do I fucking look like I want to die today?

"The Grimm's have blown up a part of the den."

All our eyes bug out of our heads. My brain runs a hundred miles a minute. What the fuck are they planning? Shit with them is escalating, and quickly! What the fuck is he up too?

A terrifying growl tears through the room. We all look to

Pretty Bird. My blood turns to ice from the devastated look on her face.

"What the fuck is De'Marco playing at?" Marcus asks to no one in particular. That's the fucking question, isn't it?

"What is their end game? They're getting too bold, Kane." Liam turns in my direction as he speaks to me, but my gaze stays on Pretty Bird.

"Was anyone hurt?" The news of the explosion seems to have brought Pretty Bird out of her murderous rage. She looks to Bonzo for his answer.

"Yeah, Reika. A couple of the new cage dancers were there. One of them had brought her daughter in." Pretty Bird's face pales at his words.

"Is she…?" The words are so quiet, I'm not sure if anyone else heard them.

Bonzo gulps, but he doesn't answer. I can tell he is fighting his emotions as they play across his face like an open book. A creak sounds in the room. I turn to Pretty Bird again, and her legs give out from underneath her as her whole body trembles. Rage burns under my skin, Marcus looks seconds away from throwing up, and Liam looks like he is gearing up to burn the Grimm's to the ground. I'm with you on that one, Brother!

"She's… She's in a coma," Bonzo tells the room.

A whoosh of air leaves Pretty Bird. My eyes haven't left her since she dropped to the floor. I walk over and crouch down in front of her, ready to support her if needed. Her gaze lifts to mine, and my heart stills when I see tears brimming in her eyes alongside a look of horror. There's such depth of emotion in her eyes, it really is like I can see into her soul.

"Kill them," Reika mutters so quietly, I don't catch it.

"What?"

Her eyes instantly become devoid of emotion. The tears that were threatening to spill, gone. Her jaw sets to stone, the cold mask of vengeance settling over her face. Slowly climbing to her feet, she looks between me and my brothers.

"Kill them all." Her voice is as cold as the arctic, filled with a command so strong I want to obey. The determination on her face is one of a true queen. One who is there to defend her people, to take control and lead the battle charge when needed.

Marcus sets his shoulders and nods to her in acknowledgement. Liam has a ferocious expression. Even Bonzo looks to her as he realizes what she said is true. They have come after us more in the last few months than they ever have before. We have sent warnings that if push comes to shove, we will wipe them out of existence. Clearly, they're a few brain cells short of stupid. It's time to end this once and for all. "Bonzo, make sure the families are taken care of. Have the crew meet us out back in thirty minutes," I tell him.

"Yes, boss."

He spins on his heel and leaves the room. I look at my queen. She stands with tense shoulders and a look that says she's out for blood. The Grimm's have no clue what is about to head their way.

A smile tugs at my lips as my brain cooks up an idea that, I know in my bones, is the right thing to do. We will deal with the threat from the opposition, then my queen will get what she wants.

Vengeance.

Reika

Pete tries his hardest to speak to me, but I have ignored everyone since my outburst in the front room. I can't bear to look at Kane as guilt racks my body. I was so close to the fucker who killed my parents, and I didn't even know. I helped the fucker hurt Kane! That thought has my stomach churning as I remember giving him the idea to use the SFX patch to make it look like my throat had been cut. No wonder he laughed so much. He wasn't just laughing at them; he was laughing at me for being so naive. But nothing compares to the horror I feel knowing a young girl has been hurt because of the war going on between the two crews. Children are never to be used as collateral. They are not pawns. They should never be touched, their innocence never tainted. This shit has to stop. I know the guys are planning something to retaliate, and I honestly don't blame them. I feel bad for beating on Fox, but the feeling of him letting me down took over and I couldn't control myself. That is the first time I've had an episode where I knew exactly what I was doing.

Standing behind Kane and the guys, I smirk as I watch a couple of the crew members come out with Blondies body wrapped up in a blanket. Bitch deserved everything she got! I still have a hard time figuring out how me and Kane ended up fucking just after he killed her, but if I'm being honest, that shit was hot. Like panty dropping, I want to fuck you here and now, hot. So that's exactly what I did.

Right now, the inner circle stands to the front of the backyard while the crew slowly files in for the meeting. Kane looks over his shoulder at me. His lust-filled gaze has me rubbing my legs together to stop my pussy from throbbing. He smirks at my reaction, which is like a bucket of cold water over my libido. It makes me want to throat punch the fucker. Chatter fills the air as all the crew throw ideas around about why the meeting has been called. But like good little sheep, they wait patiently.

"Silence!" Kane's voice booms over the crowd. The chatter stops instantly because their leader has spoken.

Cheshire throws a look over his shoulder at me that I can't figure out. Then Frosty looks over his shoulder at me with a shit-eating grin. What the fuck are these bastards up to?

"What's the pussy doing here, Boss?" one of the crew members asks. I see the color drain from Bonzo's face out of the corner of my eye.

Kane walks forward with the aura of a happy-go-lucky character, like everything in the world is sunshine and rainbows. The members surrounding the young guy watch like vultures waiting for their prize, but confusion is clear on their faces. I watch in amusement as he drops his arm across the guy's shoulders and gives him a pat on the back. A huge smile on his face.

"What's ya name, kid?"

"Zeke. My name's Zeke, Boss," he answers, his voice wobbles a little, but also holds appreciation for the fearless leader standing next to him.

"What you do here, Zeke?" Laughter is trying its hardest to bubble up out of my throat at the overly indulgent way Kane speaks with hand gestures, making out like he's a teddy bear.

"I'm a new recruit, boss." The guy stands a little straighter at this announcement. The members standing close take a cautionary step back at this confession. Ha ha! Wise choice, fuckers. I fall apart. Raucous laughter spills out of me and a shit-eating grin spreads across my face. I flick my gaze to Cheshire, who slightly shaking his head as he tries to stop his own silent laughter.

"Well, Zeke." The bite in Kane's tone has all the crew members stepping further away from their leader. "What did you just call my girl, there?" His gaze connects with mine, and I laugh even harder at the smirk trying to take over his face.

"Pus.." The poor fucker doesn't even get to finish his words before Kane launches him forward. He lands on his ass in front of Cheshire and Frosty, who look like predators that have been given their first meal in days. Zeke looks up and gulps when he sees his impending doom in their eyes.

I watch mesmerized as Kane turns in a slow circle, his gaze settling on as many members as possible. He commands the whole yard with a simple look. My thirsty, bitch pussy takes notice and starts to throb, excited by the power this one person wields over all these men. This is a power play, I can feel it in my bones. I wish I knew what he was thinking, how that power feels. I would be lying if I said it didn't get my heart racing and my adrenaline spiking. I feel ready to take on the world.

The boys take a step toward the guy on the ground. Cheshire, ever so slowly, rests his foot against Zeke's hand and increases the pressure with a sadistic grin tilting up his lips. Frosty curls down into a crouch. I'm pretty sure the poor bastard has just pissed his pants from that look alone. My eyes dart up as Kane walks toward me, and my mouth starts to water at the dark, demanding look in his eye. The other crew members are shuffling their feet at this turn of events. Whispers start throughout the yard. Kane is now standing at the side of Frosty with his gaze drilling into mine. With a look over his shoulder he whispers 'stop', instantly meeting my gaze again. He stretches out his hand as an invitation to me. I don't question his motives, placing my hand in his. He yanks me forward, tucking me into his side as he turns us around and faces the crew members.

"You all know who this is?" His voice reverberates throughout the yard. A chorus of yes's sound out in the air as they all scuttle closer.

"You all know I lost my mind when Reika was taken." He

leaves no room for disagreement from the crew. I suck in a huge lungful of air. What is he doing?

"We have just found out the person who took Reika is also responsible for her parents murder." His voice is so thickly layered with darkness, I can almost taste it in the air. All eyes swing in my direction, causing me to shuffle my feet. I feel like I am laid bare under a microscope, ready for their inspection. All this attention makes my skin crawl and my darkness rise from its cage.

Kane looks over his shoulder to his brothers. I can't see their faces so I can't see the silent words that pass between them. Kane gives a slight nod of his head and turns his gaze back to me. I hear something being dragged across the ground. I duck down slightly and nudge his arm out of the way, to see the guys pulling Zeke up to his feet. They both look at me like a set of avenging angels. They might look all sweetness and light on the outside, but they're filled with a darkness waiting to break free. I look back at Kane as he steps away from me and closer to the front line of the crew members.

"Reika Martins." He projects his voice to a higher level.

"You are my queen. My one and only. I will follow you to ends of the earth. I promised you we would get answers to what happened in your past." Unease slithers through my stomach, what the fuck is he playing at?

"We haven't got all the answers just yet, however, we do know what happened to your parents." He pulls a knife from the back of his pants. How the fuck did I not know he had that? I look off to the side for Pete. He is nowhere to be seen, which is odd. He must have gone after Paine.

"You asked me and my brother's if we trust you. Our answer is an obvious yes. Then you said to get ready for war." I nod my head in acknowledgement as words seem to be unavailable to me at the moment. My gut clenches as he grips the blade of the knife with his other hand and slices down so it cuts him. My bloodlust rises as I watch his life force slowly drip onto the ground from the blade.

"My army is now your army. My crew is now your crew." He looks out toward the crew waiting for any objections. He is met with nothing but silence. He steps forward, as do Cheshire and Frosty, with Zeke in tow. My stomach drops as both of them raise a hand, grip the blade and slice their hands. Once it's done, they pull Zeke with them as they take up their stance behind their brother. The determination in Kane's face has butterflies flapping in my stomach and bile rising in my throat.

"What are you guys doing?" I hiss at the brothers.

"Reika Martins. I give my control and my crew to you," Kane says, with a stone-like expression that his brothers mirror, like carbon copies.

"You now rule The Damned Crew, my QUEEN!" he bellows the words into the air. The declaration permeates my skin and settles in my soul. I watch in shock and awe as the other men all pass the blade between each other and cut into their palm. As one they lift their bleeding hands and offer them in my direction.

"To the queen!" reverberates around me as all the crew members echo the brothers in acknowledgement. I am frozen in place and unable to say a damn word. I don't know how much time has passed, but every single person in the yard nods their head in my direction. Bonzo has a huge grin on his face. Fox looks as confused as I feel. Kane looks to the sniveling kid in his brothers' arms. Grabbing him around the throat he drags him across the yard; the tips of his shoes scrape along the dirt. Dropping him at my feet Zeke's eyes plead with me, for what I don't know.

"He is an informant for my father," is whispered into my ear as Kane glares down at the fucker, who pisses his pants.

"I-I'm not, Boss," he stutters, looking at me and my dark brooding shadow. Kane lifts his eyebrow at me.

"You have just seen what Kane has done. Witnessed passing of the crew with your own eyes. Heard everyone agree? Yet you ignore me like I am not here?" I chuckle at the fear that flickers to life on his face, the color has drained completely.

"S-s-sorry, R-Reika." I can't get my head to process how stupid this fucker must really be. The murderous waves rolling off Kane have me wanting to climb him like a tree; right here, right now. But this fucker is an informant, and he must pay. I am not naïve enough to think that Malcolm did nothing. I would put everything I own up against the fact he was somehow involved with my parents' murder.

I feel the shift in the air as all eyes drill into me. The crew waits to see what I am going to do, waits for my command. The brothers are giving off serious stabby vibes, which makes me smirk. Kane whispers in my ear, causing a shudder to pass over my body. I wonder if he's into exhibitionism.

"You think because I am some pussy, a piece of ass, that I am not worthy of the respect you would give a man?" I layer my voice with a hint of my annoyance. The guys step further back, leaving me with the sniveling idiot at my feet. I watch in amusement as the guys start muttering to each other, not paying us any attention.

"Yeah, you're only a bit of gash," he spits out at me, then spits at my feet. Silly fucking boy. As I step forward, something cold brushes against my palm. Looking down, I realize Kane has passed me a knife. Sweet! I could so do a little death dance. My murderous inner self thrums at having a weapon in hand. A growl rips through the air and I know he has just pissed off my man. Stalking toward the little weasel, I pick the dirt from under my nails with the tip of the knife.

"Just a bit of gash? Huh." I feign shock. "Not a badass piece of gash? Considering I am now your boss." I watch as the reality of his words slam into him, just like he's been shot by a bullet.

"But, boy…" He tries to scramble away from me, and I know a manic smile carves up my face. Slamming my foot into his chest, I pin him in place and relish the feel of his struggle. I could crush him like a bug. "I may be your boss now, but I have and will always be the God. Damn. Fucking. Reaper." Slamming the blade through his thigh, I smirk as he squeals like a pig. Run, piggy, run. Ha-ha. His fear fills the air as I turn to look at the men that are now staring at me with different degrees of respect.

"I know Malcolm isn't innocent in my parent's downfall, and I will make him pay with his miserable existence. This fucker here…" I flick my gaze back over my shoulder. "Is an informant for that bastard. If you respect Kane, that he has stepped aside and handed the crew to me, then follow me now. Hear my call. Will any of you be my executioner?"

"I will." Bonzo steps forward with a grin.

"I will, boss lady," says another, which sets off a symphony of the "I will" and "Me" throughout the crew. I turn back to the fucker, yank the blade back out of his leg and chuckle as a blood curdling scream fills the air. What a fucking baby. He'd never amount to anything in this world.

"Run, you little fucker. Run as fast as you can."

59

REIKA

The sadistic bitch in me preens as I watch the little shit try to stand on his injured leg. My darkness feeds off his agony. I watch him shift as much of his weight as he can to his good leg, and it wobbles underneath him. I have the urge to kick his legs out and drop him, to see him dragged by his worthless body across the dirt. Ah, that would be fulfilling. But I don't, because of all the bloodthirsty looks zeroing in on him. Like a pack of rabid dogs, the crew stares him down. And like a good alpha, I'll let my pack loose. Darkness thrums under the surface of my skin, egging me on to spill blood.

I was shocked Kane handed over control of the crew to me out of the blue. Oh boy, will we be having words about that later. What if the crew doesn't accept me? Unease and self-doubt creep into my mind and lay their little needles in my head. I watched as they all bled for me, accepting my position as their leader, but I question whether they will be true to their word. Guess we will find out. Kane making the announcement is one thing, but now they must prove they are loyal to the crew and to me. The atmosphere is alive with a current of eagerness, impatience, and bloodlust as they zero in on their prey. The little snitch has made it halfway through the crowd. I'll give him props, he's gotten further than I thought he would.

"You have to test their loyalty, Pretty Bird," whispers into my ear, like static through a radio. Looking over, I find Kane standing at my side with a blank look on his face. I know what he is saying is true, but unease filters through me. Are these men full of shit or do they really care about the crew as a whole? Are they really willing to let a woman lead? I guess there's only one way to find out.

"End him!" My voice echoes throughout the yard, hard and unforgiving as I watch and wait.

The wolves descend on the little shit with ferocity. Maybe my doubts are wrong, and they are trying to prove their worth to me. Screams fill the yard as I watch them start to, literally, pull him apart. I notice a small group off to the back of the violent hoard, watching with sketchy as shit, fear-filled expressions. They mutter between themselves and are not participating. I look at them to memorize the faces of the men I will be watching closely in the future.

Movement catches my eye like a shadow passing on the wind. I looking in that direction, and have to stop myself from laughing. Cheshire is bouncing up and down on the spot like a puppy waiting at the door to go out for a piss. His eyes are begging me to let him join in the fun with the rest of the crew. Frosty is acting, well, frosty. His expression is stoic, giving nothing away. A shudder works its way down my spine. I have just had my first glimpse of the man that has whispers spoken about him in the dark; the one they are terrified will come for them on a command from the leader of the crew. Our gazes clash and I see the anticipation in his eyes. He wants to go and be amongst the chaos. I wonder if it's where he feels the most alive?

I nod to the guys and laugh as Cheshire takes off like a bat out of hell, cat calling as he does. The other twin stalks forward almost like he is gliding across the ground. The crew members part for the brothers leaving a direct path to the weasel curled up on the ground. I can tell, even from this distance, that he is sobbing from the way his whole body heaves. Cheshire grins down. Suddenly he laughs manically and kicks the hell out of him, like a piñata that has fallen to the ground. Thankfully, Frosty takes pity on him, grabbing the back of his neck he lifts him off the ground. The weasel doesn't even open his eyes to look at him. The glint of metal catches the remaining light and shines across the yard. With a quick thrust he embeds the knife in the informant's chest, who now stares at Frosty wide eyed.

The noise level in the yard reaches a new heights as the crew become restless after having their moment taken away from them. They start jostling forward, and one of them stumbles into Frosty. With a ferocious snarl, Cheshire pushes the guy away from his brother, while Frosty growls at a few of the members who are getting braver in their actions.

"Knock it off!" my voice snaps out as I grind my teeth at the stupidity of these fuckers. They are acting like children, throwing a tantrum because they didn't get to break the toy. At my command they all straighten up and turn to me with blank looks on their faces, like they weren't just a second away from all-out war.

"Fucking children, the lot of you." I storm toward them, showing my annoyance at their behavior. I've had enough of this pathetic shit. "If you want to throw a fit over the fact that you didn't get to give the final blow to the little shit, then be my guest and leave." My tone dares anyone to challenge me if they have the balls. I swear I can hear a few sets pop back up inside the stupid fuckers' bodies.

The corner of Frosty's lips twitch, and Cheshire stares at me with his mouth hanging open. They both nod to acknowledge my words, and I watch as the other members step into a line across the yard with the brothers front and center. Kane's hand grazes my lower back as he steps into the line-up with his brothers. All eyes are staring at me, my inner voice is cackling at all these men bowing to my command. The psycho bitch is really loving this!

"Kane has given me the crew." I glare straight at the fucker in question, who smirks at me. "Don't think I'm letting this shit go." He narrows his eyes at me filled with defiance and a little pride shining in his eyes, like he thinks I will give in and let it drop. He hasn't realized yet, but the look just pisses me off more. I glare right back, trying to show him how much trouble he is in. The corner of my lip twitches with a smirk, as he narrows his eyes right back.

"You're in trouble." Cheshire smirks at his brother while chuckling to himself. The corners of my lips lift again as Kane digs an elbow into his side.

"Just because Kane has given me the crew, doesn't mean that they are not in the positions they originally were." Eyes bulge with what the fuck expressions. "Kane is my equal, what he says goes. And these two idiots…"

"Hey!" they both protest.

"Are still second and enforcer. You made an oath to this crew when you joined up and I am not taking away from that." Kane starts to protest. "Fucking hell! Shut it, man!" The death glare he throws my way has me smirking at him, full force.

"Kane is an extension of me, we are the same. So, if he gives you a command nothing has changed. The only thing that has changed is if I give you a command, you follow it. We are both in charge." I meet as many of the members gazes as possible to drill the point home. "Do you get it?"

A collective melody of yes fills the night air. I can feel it in my bones, they will accept this new dynamic. I don't want

Kane giving up his power over the crew. They are going to need him. Call it a gut instinct, but there could be a chance I don't make it out of this war alive. I feel the death glares being thrown my way from the guys; they are practically drilling holes into the side of my head. I don't bother to acknowledge them, which causes a chorus of grumbles from their direction. When Bonzo shocks me out of my inner thoughts and gives me a perfect excuse to avoid them for a little while longer.

"How do, Boss Lady?" His grin is infectious.

"Sup, Bonzo?" I still don't like the fucker after he did what he did with Mel. I really should go and see her grave soon. I am a shitty friend. Since all this crap has taken over my life, I haven't had a chance to go. But honestly, I'm not sure I can bring myself to do it. Right now, I can pretend she is still with me and seeing her grave will bring me out of the lie.

"Well. Um. I wanted to know if there were any hard feelings, Boss?" The nervousness he projects has my inner bitch standing to attention, like a cat that just got a whiff of cat nip. It's so fucking delicious.

"Oh, really?" Sarcasm drips from my voice.

"Well. Um." Looking over his shoulder, Kane has a cocked eyebrow as he stares at us both. I can't tell if there is amusement in his expression or not.

"Look, Bonzo." He stands to attention like a good little solider. "I think you're a fucker for doing what you did." He starts to protest. "But you are a part of the crew and as long as you respect what has been said today..." I stare him down. "I won't need to cut your dick off and feed it to you." His complexion pales at my words. Can't let him think I forgive too easily! Even my inner voice snorts in agreement.

He continues to pale, and I burst out laughing. It's not an empty threat, but I really can't be dealing with his drama today. I have six feet five inches of asshole to have a talk with about how a relationship works, because I am not having major shit like this arranged without me knowing. Cheshire walks over to me and his eyes twinkle with mischief as he smirks at me. Oh, shit! What's he up to? He's like a brother with his happy go lucky attitude, but that look in his eyes scares the shit out of me. You just know the fucker is planning something. I cock my head as I stare back at him, daring him to spill as I know he is dying to.

"Spit it out, Cheshire."

"You gonna punish my brother, Hellion?" His tone is teasing. Fuck my life!

"Who's being punished?" Frosty pipes in as he walks over to us. Kane is talking to a couple of the guys, but the other nosey fuckers' ears all perk up.

"This meeting is over!" My voice booms over all the chatter. I watch silently as they all start to move off and do their own thing; hopefully, going back to the jobs they've been given and not just being lazy shits.

I watch as Cheshire and Frosty head back to some of the crew, shooting the shit with each other. It nearly ends up in an all-out brawl again. My mind wanders to Pete. Where the hell has he got to? I know Paine is feeling guilty, but he shot out of there so fast I didn't even get a chance to talk to him, to tell him not to feel any guilt.

"You wanna talk to me, Baby?" I look up at him. The smirk that greets me makes my annoyance flare. Doesn't he realize I want to strangle him?

"Don't *baby* me, ass wipe." I spit through my teeth.

Spinning on my heels I storm toward the house, away from prying eyes and ears. As I open the door, I throw a look over my shoulder with a challenge in my eyes. I smile slightly when he narrows his eyes and starts heading after me. The cat calls coming from his brothers are seriously messing with my pissed off mood, their childish ways making it hard to cling to my anger. My sole focus is to have this argument in private. My feet automatically start heading toward the office, then I stop short. Luckily Kane doesn't crash into my ass, that would have hurt. I remember what happened in there, so I change course and head toward the gym. I know Kane is following from the thuds that follow mine. He hasn't spoken a word yet and neither have I. Thankfully the gym is empty when we get inside, and I head toward the sparring mats. I can't decide if I want to fuck him or punch him - make him bleed or make him come. It's 50/50 right now.

"What's up, babe?" His tone is cautious which has me wanting to chuckle.

"You decided shit without me?" I try to hide the hurt in my voice, but somehow it slips through. His eyes widen when he hears it.

"I can't risk losing you again, Baby. Me and my brothers had a talk while we were in the office." White noise fills my ears. "This is the best way to keep you safe and help with this war." My darkness flares without warning. I need control, not to be controlled.

"I'm not some fucking damsel, Kane. I don't need babysitters!" Wave after wave of emotion repeatedly slams into me. I can't figure out which one is riding me the hardest, then they all join to make a huge, angry, ball inside my chest that's about to explode. My breathing grows heavy as my palms start to sweat. I feel a tremor snake up my arms. Oh fuck. Oh fuck!

This isn't a good idea. I'm a fucking bomb waiting to go off. My mind is racing as my demons rear their ugly heads, whispering to me that I will fuck this up and kill them all. Everyone's blood will be on my hands. I won't be able to get justice for my parents. I'm not worthy to lead, not worthy to live.

My vision blurs. I can see the concern with a hint of annoyance on his face as his mouth moves, but I can't hear the words. Panic starts to seep into my limbs, static roars in my ears. It's feels like being under water, but nothing can penetrate it. My brain doesn't register anything; it's like my mind has become an empty void. Everything is so messed up. Emotions war within me, but the part of my brain that's still working is trying to figure out how the hell I am having a panic attack. None of my usual triggers have happened. What the fuck flipped the switch?

Everything jolts back into focus as I fight to open my airway enough to allow air into my lungs, but it's halted. The pressure increases as my eyes come back into focus; so does the feeling in the rest of my body. My body responds on its own, as I match the ferocious pace of Kane's kiss. He tightens his hold on my throat a little more. My demons slowly start to trickle away as lust burns through my veins. A growl vibrates against my chest. His hands run back and forth across my stomach, ramping my sex drive up another notch. I wrap my hand around his wrist and drag his hand down the path I am desperate for him to take. Our lips don't break apart as he flicks the button on my jeans and pushes his hand into the front of my underwear. A shockwave of pleasure slams through me as his thumb skims my clit. A hiss leaves my lips, and a smirk spreads across his face that is all male and full of confidence.

"That's right, baby girl. Don't think, just feel. Let your body respond to my touch."

He bites my lower lip before licking the seam of my mouth, demanding entrance with his tongue. I feel the heat rising in my body, the need to take back control. I kiss him back violently, my tongue dueling with his. Our teeth clash as a fever takes over me.

"Oh, Pretty Bird, are you wet for me?

"If you stopped teasing me, you'd find out!" I love the pressure of his hand around my throat. Knowing that if he squeezed too hard, I could lose myself completely. That edge of pain, that chance of losing my breath, sets me alight. I grab hold of his jeans and yank them down so I can palm his cock, to torment him the way he is tormenting to me. He lets out a low groan I feel deep in my pussy.

"Fuck, baby girl, if you keep doing that I won't last. I need to be inside you, now," he growls in my ear before nipping the lobe between his teeth and leaving open mouthed kisses down my neck. I feel his fingers gently glide over my lower lips. I know he feels how wet I am when I hear his sharp intake of breath. I pull his hand out of my underwear and drop to my knees.

"You might want to be inside me, but I need to taste you first." I look into his eyes, and he understands I need this control. He relinquishes it for now, but I know it's only a matter of time until he takes it back.

I pull down his boxers and his hard cock bounces free right in front of my eyes. I can see the wet bead of precum on his tip, tempting me to taste it, so I lick it off. He growls deep in his throat as I swirl my tongue around his tip and over his slit before taking him slowly into my mouth. I feel his fingers dig into my hair and guide me down his length, trying to take back some of my control. I pull back to take a quick breath before taking him deeper and harder than I have before. I feel tears prick my eyes, but I don't stop. I concentrate on breathing through my nose as I start to work up and down his length. I use my one hand to hold on to his muscular thigh while the other gently plays with his balls. He groans loudly and increases the pressure on the back of my head, making me move faster and take him all the way until my nose touches his abs. His hips start to pump his cock into my mouth, as he loses control. I mentally high five myself. I hear him begin to pant as he grows harder still. I rub my thighs together trying to ease some of the tension between my legs, but they are too wet to help me deal with it.

Hands grab my waist roughly and pull me up into the air. Kane throws me over his shoulder and smacks my ass so quickly I squeal. "Time's up, baby girl. I'm gonna fuck you so hard you won't be able to walk for a week and you never forget who owns this pussy."

"Ha! I'd like to see you try, big guy," I growl at him. The only person who owns me, is fucking me. He storms over to the weight bench and places me on my back, ripping off my boots and jeans, then pulls my panties down my legs, torturously slow. Once they are gathered in his hand, he lifts them to his face and inhales. Fuck me, that was the hottest thing I've ever seen. He's a fucking animal. He just smirks and shoves them in his pocket as he kicks off his jeans.

He kisses slowly up my left leg, then starts nipping and licking along my inner thigh. My breath catches in my throat.

"I can't take this anymore. Just fuck me, Kane."

"All in good time, baby. If you're a good girl, I'll make it worth the wait," he chuckles. Throwing my legs over his shoulders, he buries his head in between my legs. I feel his tongue lick me slowly all the way from my slit to my clit.

"Ohhhhhh," I moan, as he sets my nerve endings alight. God, he's driving me crazy and enjoying it way too much. He continues to work my clit with the tip of his tongue in swirling circles as I feel one finger push inside my wet heat. As he begins to pump and find a rhythm, a second one joins in. I feel that tingle start to build low in my abdomen as his pace increases. It feels like lightening is firing all over my body.

"Ahhhhhhhh, Kane... I'm...please," I groan as I feel him bend his fingers toward the sweet spot that will push me over the edge into bliss. He uses the flat of his tongue to roll over my tender nub, as his other hand snakes up to roll my nipple between his thumb and forefinger. It's like there's a direct line from my nipple straight to my clit causing my legs to shake. The tingle grows into a raging inferno, just waiting for release. I can't hold on any longer.

"You won't come till I say so, Baby," he whispers over my sensitive heat, causing my inner walls to clench round his fingers. He pumps a couple more times before he pulls out, leaving me empty and wanting. I feel him drag my wetness round to my puckered hole, circling it gently to mirror the movements of his tongue. As the pressure increases, he pushes through that tight ring at the same time as his tongue spears its way into my dripping pussy causing my orgasm to tear through me and stars to burst across my vision. He doesn't relent as he helps me ride the waves of pleasure that wrack my body. He laps at my juices as if it's the nectar of the gods.

"There is nothing better than hearing you come and tasting your release," he growls.

"Urgh, will you just shut up and fuck me, or should I just walk out of here and find someone who will?"

"Oh, hell no, don't you fucking dare say shit like that! You. Are. Mine," he roars at me. He lines himself up and thrusts into me so hard I feel him bottom out deep inside me as he repeats, "You." Thrust. "Are." Thrust. "MINE!" Thrust.

I feel him possess me, claim me from the inside out. As he thrusts into me, I feel him drive back the darkness that threatened to consume me. Fuck, this man has a hold over me that I never thought possible. That undeniable sensation starts to build again, making all my nerve endings come alive.

"Stop talking and fuck me like you mean it," I growl in his ear. In response, he bites hard on my nipple. I clench hard on his cock, making him groan.

"Hold on, Baby." He grabs my thighs, pushing them against my stomach and slams back into me, deeper than before at a punishing pace.

Gleaming droplets of sweat coat his face and chest. It's such an irresistible sight I push up and lick a trail up to his throat, causing him to moan. I feel the vibrations travel all the way down my body.

"You feel so good, Baby. Get on all fours." I'm flipped instantly before he drives back in, causing my entire body to shake, but it's not enough. He drives into me so hard all I hear is the slapping of flesh every time he bottoms out.

"Kane, I...I...need," I moan. I'm not even sure what I need...but more, just more. I need more.

"I've got you, Baby." Instantly I feel his fingers push inside me, pumping a couple times before finding my clit and starting a punishing pace, circling my most sensitive part as he draws my orgasm out of me. My eyes close of their own accord and lights flash behind my eyes. I lose all control as I detonate around him.

"Argggh," Kane groans as he stutters, losing his rhythm as he swells inside me while my walls spasm around his cock and milk every last drop from him. We're both left panting as the spasms from our high begin to slow. I'm no longer able to hold myself up, and I collapse on the bench pulling him down with me where we're still joined.

"Well, fuck me. I wasn't expecting that," I whisper, feeling like I've lost all control of my body.

60

FANCY PANTS

What a pathetic little shit Malcolm Southbourne is, standing before us trying to explain how he fucked up his task. His very simple fucking task at that; so simple a baby could do it. Trying to defend himself from the wrath he knows he is will suffer through. Personally, I would have gotten rid of the piece of shit long before now, but I wasn't allowed to. The other members all agreed he would be useful in gaining the upper hand in other territories, but the sniveling little fucker has proven he is as useful as chocolate fire guard - soft and floppy, utterly useless, like his dick. I am surprised to hear that Kane and his brothers banished their father without a second thought. The rumors spread far and wide that they jumped to his tune, but evidently, they grew a backbone.

"So, you're telling me, Malcolm, that a little girl got in your way?" Dexter asks, his annoyance easy to spot.

"She's not just some little girl. You are all idiots! She is The Butcher's daughter!"

"We know, Malcolm. We know who she is, but she is only a woman. They aren't built for this life," Cox speaks freely.

"Look at the fucking state of me!" Rage coats his voice, a

smile creeps across my face as I look at him - really I want to laugh at him, he's a fucking mess. "She did this to me! We thought her dad was dangerous. She makes him look like a fucking puppy!" Surprise shows on all their faces as I bark out a laugh. Damn, she is good! All eyes turn to me.

"You have something to say?"

"I know for a fact just how dangerous she is. Her reputation alone from the fight rings is legendary. But I have seen first-hand the tenacity she has when things look bleak."

"Is the girl going to be a problem for us?"

"Immensely. We can't go at her head on. She adapts quickly, and her skills are the best I've ever seen. We need to be smart about it and hit her where it hurts." I'm coming for you and then you will be mine!

Chatter breaks out across the room. All these powerful men telling the others why their way will be the one to stop The Reaper. The one woman who shouldn't be in our world. I lean back and watch as the chaos unfolds; watching, waiting and trying not to piss myself laughing.

"We have to end her before she becomes more of a problem!"

"We need to split her from this fucker's sons!"

"She dies!" My brain jolts back into the room at this.

Standing to my feet, I stare into the eyes of every fucking person in this room. They all shiver at the intensity in my gaze. Their fear is a living thing, coiling round their necks getting ever tighter. They all seem to forget the biggest monster in any room is me. It's a courtesy I allow them, to remain in their positions, because it helps my overall game plan. They all work for me. They live because I decide they are still useful enough to breathe the same air as me. However, as soon as they've served their purpose and are no longer useful, they're dead.

"You forget our plan. She will become my wife like we

agreed in the beginning, or you will lose my backing for everything in the future." My tone dares anyone to argue with me.

"You really think my son is going to allow you to get between them again?" The smug look on Malcolm's face makes my blood boil. He really gets under my fucking skin.

"You really think your boy is a match for me, Malcolm?" Intrigue controls me, as I step out from behind my seat and make my way toward him.

He sets his shoulders and clenches his jaw. I chuckle at the stupidity of this fucker. Honestly, his son being a monster big enough to challenge my own? I don't think so! He is nervous; I can tell by the way his eyes widen just slightly and the increase in his breathing. Slowly I walk a circle around him. I'll give him his dues, he doesn't cower like most do. Canting my head to the side, I watch as sweat gathers on his brow. A sadistic smirk lifts my lips which turns into a full-on all teeth baring smile. My fist connects with his cheek with so much force he is thrown backward. Yells fill the room from the other members of the syndicate while Malcolm groans on the floor. I can hardly contain the chuckle that threatens to escape, the mayhem making my blood sing. Undoing the buttons of my jacket, I slide it off, gently placing it down on the side table. Then I remove my cufflinks as Malcolm watches with terror on his face. They clink as one by one they are placed next to my jacket.

"Do you really think…"

I silence the idiots with a glower over my shoulder. How dare they challenge me! I turn my gaze back to the now sniveling old shit on the floor, crawling backward like a baby to try and get out of my way. I bark out a laugh as my monster becomes restless under my skin, his bloodlust barely contained. The urge to maim and kill has been riding me hard since she was taken. We're in agreement that she belongs to us and us alone.

I stalk my prey with ease as he frantically tries to get away from me, my stride eating up the distance between us. Malcom screams when I stop in front of him. I move my gaze to see what he is screaming about, when I spot his hand under my shoe. A wicked grin instantly spreads across my face. I relish in his agony as I grind my heel down until I hear a crack. He begs like a little bitch for me to stop. So, I apply more pressure until I feel his fingers crush beneath my foot, reaffirming my position over him.

"What the fuck?" Dexter's voice booms. Turning to the others I see a guy who wasn't here before looking pale, and the rest of the idiots moving as far away as possible, as quickly as they can.

Crash.

A chair explodes into pieces against the wall. The others take another step away as Dexter moves through the room like a hurricane, smashing everything in his way. What the fuck set him off?

"That little bitch!" he roars, his hands tangle in his hair making him look slightly unhinged.

"That motherfucker!" He yanks his hair as tears run down his face.

We all look to one another trying to figure out what the fuck is going on. Dexter is normally the calmest of us all. Well, most of the time. His eyes narrow on Malcolm still on the floor as his breathing increases. He sounds like a raging bull getting ready to charge.

"Your fucking son and that bitch killed my baby!" He moves so quickly my brain doesn't have a chance to catch up. Realization dawns on me. Oh!

Broken words fall from Malcolm's lips as he scrambles to

his feet, running from the man who has murder on his face. The other three just stare wide eyed not knowing what is happening. I just want to see what happens - maybe munch some popcorn. Dexter's movements are sloppy, anger clouding his judgment, giving Malcolm the upper hand.

Malcolm.

Agony tears through my body. My nerves feel like they've been struck by lightning. I try to avoid the possessed man who is swinging his fists frantically in my direction, trying to take my head off. What the fuck has been going on at the house? Ducking out of the way of a fist, it skims the top of my head as I run around the desk. Suddenly my airway is cut off. I grab the hand surrounding my throat as I desperately try to pull air into my lungs. My eyes connect with my captor, who grins as he tightens his hold on my neck. My lungs begin to scream as they burn from lack of oxygen. I despise this bastard. Guess this is the result of when power goes to your head.

They don't know, ha, none of them are prepared for Reika. Her father was a mean son of a bitch, but Reika she relishes the pain she inflicts. She's the devil in sheep's clothing. She's a nightmare personified - no one should enjoy feeding off the energy that leaves someone battered to the point of death as much as she does. She scared the shit out of me on the lawn; not that I'd ever admit it to anyone. I know for a fact she was going to kill me. Luckily, she didn't get the chance. My son is a ruthless fucker. Now that they are together, I don't know what this will mean, or how this will impact the syndicate. He has his free will, he's out from under my control. He also has her, and that shit scares me.

"I. Can't. Breathe." I manage to pant the words, hoping this little shit will relax his grip enough to allow some air into my deprived lungs.

"Dexter! What the fuck is going on?" Cox growls.

"They killed her. They killed my baby," he cries in agony as his legs give out from underneath him. I'm not surprised she's dead. Dahlia tried her hardest to get into the power couple plan with my son, but he wasn't having any of it.

The man that brought the news to his boss repeats the information to Dexter. My heart stills knowing my son was the one to end her life by snapping her neck; nicely done though, quick and effective. War is inevitable now; the question is where to stand? They won't let this lie. We have been working too hard to build up our territories, and it has been easier since tragedy befell the king. Now we run the show, and I am not going to let my son or his whore get in the way.

"We need to hit her where it hurts, and make it look like it is Kane's doing," James says. Cal is being quieter than normal. That's what he does, he watches, listens and plans.

The pressure on my throat lifts slightly, and I suck as much oxygen into my lungs as possible. Fuck me, why does it have to hurt so much? My head spins from the sudden influx of oxygen. On unstable legs, I move toward the nearest chair and collapse. My captor moves away and stands in the center of the room with his arms outstretched like a damn deity. What a fucking prick with a God complex.

"Now!" reverberates around the room.

The doors on the far end of the room swing open. I am surprised to hear the clink of metal. Two of the security guards drag a limp body in chains.

"Sorry, Boss. He got outta line," one of them says.

The chilling sound like nails on a chalkboard meets my ears. I watch fascinated as a chair is dragged to the center of the room and the body is deposited on it. One of the guys works to secure the chains to the chair to immobilize whoever this unfortunate soul is. They scurry off quickly as we all watch the guy's head loll on his chest. The others begin to circle around him, like vultures. I stand now transfixed as I watch the youngest of us all start laying into this captive without a second thought. What I find the most surprising is he doesn't make a sound; just the sound of crunching bones can be heard throughout the room. This seems to piss off his torturer even more. He back hands him with so much force the chair tips backwards. My stomach rolls as the guy screams from the impact of his body weight and the chair landing on his wrists.

"Carry on with your conversation. I am just going to play with my new toy for a little bit." Darkness pours off him in waves as the fires of hell dance in his eyes.

"Malcolm?" I'm shocked out of my trance, looking to James.

"Your son killed her."

"I don't know why, but I would put money on it that Reika had something to do with it."

"That's obvious, but what do we do?" Screams fill the room behind me making it difficult to concentrate.

"Dexter?" I say, his red rimmed eyes meet mine with the promise of pain.

"I am sorry for the loss of your daughter. I don't know all the details because my informant hasn't checked in yet, and I'll be fucking gutting him when he does. But I will find out everything I can." I try to appease him with my words. We all must stay united if this is going to work.

"You better, Malcolm, or your head will be on my wall

before the end of the week," Dexter spits in my direction, then slumps into a chair at the side of the room.

"Can you not get your boys in line, Malcolm?" Cal speaks, which surprises me.

"No. They exiled me from the crew." Their eyes bulge at my words. "But I know them better than anyone. I did make them into my image after all. I know how to get what I want." An evil grin spreads across my face as a plan starts to come together in my head. One which will help me achieve my goal and deal with that little bitch, once and for all.

"Do you know why you're here?" The question booms from across the room followed by the sound of flesh hitting flesh, pulling my attention. He demands an answer to his question, but nothing, no reply meets my ears. Just a pained grunt and short sharp pants as the idiot tries to breathe.

"You think this is acceptable?" Another crack follows the psychos' words, but still no reply is given. The silence is driving him to distraction.

"I gave you a home. A fucking family when you had nothing." His voice grows in volume as his rage gets the better of him, but a smirk tips the corner of my lips because the captive still doesn't say a word. Crazed he grips his chin yanking his head up to him, so their eyes meet. Instantly, the rage melts away as a deathly calm mask consumes his face.

"What am I going to do with you?"

61

REIKA

Laughter fills the kitchen as me, Kane and Frosty watch Cheshire prance around grabbing all the stuff he used to make dinner with. He has been on a high since earlier, and I'm surprised at how well me and Frosty seem to be getting on. Listening to the guys shoot the shit with each other brings a smile to my lips and a feeling of contentment settles in my soul. This is a side of them not many get to see; the human side of them, relaxed and having fun with each other. A huge food fight nearly started when Cheshire decided to throw a bag of flour at Frosty. That was fucking hilarious. Then Kane decided to jump in and start slinging shit at them both. My stomach still aches from all the laughing I have done. My mind hasn't wandered to the information I recently learned, and I'm so glad for that. I don't know how much more I can take. A persistent buzzing sounds in the room. None of the guys seem to notice it; clearly, they must be ignoring their phones.

"You gonna answer that, Hellion?"

"Huh." I look between them all with confusion.

"Your phone," Cheshire says as he flicks his eyes to the

counter where my phone is vibrating across the surface. Hitting answer, I put it on loudspeaker.

"Errm. Boss, we got a problem." Rocco's voice sounds nervous.

"Sup, dude."

"The new female fighters are training." His voice holds a hint of fear. I contain the chuckle rising in my throat. Seems I've put the fear of God into him and made him realize women can be lethal too.

"Yeah, and?" I can't deal with any more stupid today.

"One of them is going all out on the others and she's hurt them, Boss. They are saying they don't wanna fight." *Fuck my life. Stupid dumb bitch!*

"I'm on my way."

I cut the call and realize all eyes are on me. Kane steps around the island and slinks his arm over my shoulder, pulling me closer into his side. It's like he can't keep his hands off me. He uses any excuse to touch me. Well that, or he's secretly a teddy bear. A chuckle builds in my throat at Frosty's expression. He has this whole, don't even think about it look. It's different than his normal resting bitch face. Sliding myself off the stool, I pocket my phone, grab my bike keys, and huff out a breath as I turn to leave. So much for a quiet night. Heavy is the head that wears the crown, or some shit like that.

"I'll come with you, Hellion. Then these fuckers can clean up for once." I look back at him and smirk as I'm about to head for the door.

"Hey!" They both protest. I bark out a laugh at the horror on their faces.

"Take Bonzo with you, babe." I plant a kiss on Kane's lips and laugh at the stunned expression on his face.

"Yes, Boss," I mock. I salute him and a low growl rumbles in his chest. Yanking me forward, he slams his lips against mine kissing me violently. I can feel all the emotions from the day through his kiss. He drives his tongue into battle with mine. This feels like a claiming, cementing our new position as joint leaders. Gagging noises fill the room, and my shoulders shake trying to hold in a laugh. Kane's growl becomes almost feral, as I try to pull myself away. The two shit heads behind me continue to gag like the fucking little children they are. Finally, I manage to untangle myself from Kane's death grip. He narrows his eyes at me, and I give him a cheeky wink and jump back as he tries to grab me again. Laughing at the annoyance on his face, I stick out my tongue, joining in with the childishness in the room.

"God, I preferred it when you two had issues," Frosty chimes in.

"Ow!" Cheshire stands at the side of him, grinning, because he just slapped him upside the head.

"Serves you right, fuck face." Kane's voice is thickly laced with annoyance.

"You going with her, Marcus?" Kane asks his brother, like I'm not even standing here.

"Fuck me," I exclaim, throwing my hands up in the air.

"I plan too later." Kane smirks at me his gaze full of lust, sending a shot of heat straight between my legs. The little shit. I rub my thighs together trying to ease the pressure. He catches my movement, and his smirk turns into a full on grin.

"Promises. Promises." I grin at him as I head out with Cheshire hot on my heels. Another round of dry heaving noises fills the kitchen as another 'Ow!' follows the sound of something crashing to the floor.

Me and Cheshire are still laughing as we make it out to the car. Bonzo jogs up from the other side of the garden. The guys do one of those weird fist bump things that guys do as I head toward my bike.

"Where do you think you're going?" Cheshire smirks at me from the driver's side of his Camaro. Putting up one finger to stop his next words, I glare at them both.

"I'm taking my bike."

They look at each other as I swing my leg over. It's been to long since I got to ride this beauty. I seriously can't wait. It took me years to save up for her, and I will not miss out on a chance to ride. Cheshire steps toward me as I pull my helmet on. Before he manages another step, the bike roars to life between my thighs with a deep rumble that sets my pulse racing. Kicking up the stand, I pull down the throttle and speed down the drive. I'm free without any restraints, letting my soul soar as the darkness in me dissipates. Laughing, I watch them in my mirror as they jump into the car and peel out after me. It looks like Bonzo is on the phone. I bet he's getting his ear chewed off thanks to my little show.

Feeling the wind surround me without the shell of a car to protect it, my body thrums to life as my Harley rumbles beneath me. Watching people go about their lives, dashing across the street makes me wish Mel was here. Losing my thoughts to Mel, I throw a promise into the air that I will go see her at the cemetery tomorrow. It's been far too long and that leaves an uncomfortable feeling in my stomach. The warehouse comes into view as headlights flash in my mirror. I know without words they're telling me to move over so they can pull up first. Fucking hell, I feel like I'm being treated like a baby, always needing to have someone with me. I'm the Reaper for fuck's sake. I'm bring fear and pain with just my name. Coming to a stop, I kill the engine and drop the stand. My helmet sits on my tank, and I wait for the guys.

"You sure your bike will be ok here, Boss?" Bonzo inquires. Me and Cheshire look at him with our favorite 'you're stupid' expressions.

Grinning at each other, I yank open the door. Screams and shouts filter down the hallway. It sounds like chaos has erupted in main area we use to train when there isn't a fight going on. "Stay here!" I throw over my shoulders at the guys as I charge toward all the noise. What the fuck is going down to cause this much mayhem? Thankfully, neither of them argues with my order. Me and Kane spoke briefly about 'the ring' being kept out of the crew business. We decided the girls wouldn't fight if they thought it was anything to do with the crew.

I crash through the door. It's utter chaos, absolute fucking chaos. Guys are fighting with each other like rabid animals as some of the female fighters scream at people to stop. Poor Rocco looks like he's about to pass out as he shouts for everyone to stop. Fat lot of good it's doing though, since no one is paying a blind bit of notice to him. Two women are going at each other in the cage. Well, one is trying to block all the hits coming her way, while the other is out for blood. This is madness. I whistle. The noise cuts out instantly, and all eyes turn to me.

"What the fuck is going on here?" My voice is so loud in echoes in the rafters. Sheepishly, they all lower their heads, some even shuffle their feet like naughty kids being told off.

"I asked you a fucking question?" A whole load of um's and wells hit me as I stalk toward my supposed manager, trying to find out what the fuck is happening here. Rocco won't meet my eyes as I glower down at him. Is he serious?

"You mind, bitch? I'm trying to train," a shrill voice says.

Looking around for the owner of the voice, I spot a tiny brown-haired woman in the cage. She's covered in the blood of the blonde who appears to be out cold on the floor. The cocky bitch folds her arms over her chest while tapping her foot. Is she for fucking real? My brow lifts in challenge at the lack of respect as gasps sound throughout the people gathered in the warehouse. Even Rocco steps back. She's got balls, I'll give her that. Either that or she's brain dead!

"Careful there girly! You don't wanna bite off more than you can chew." Sarcasm drips from my tone. Some of the regular's faces pale at the threatening undertone of my voice. I swear I can see the hairs on their arms stand on end.

She scoffs. The mother fucking bitch scoffs at my warning! Is she insane? Rocco, the pussy, runs toward the office like I lit his ass on fire for being so fucking pathetic.

Making my way toward the cage, the others move out of the way, parting like the red sea to let me pass. The bitch still has her arms crossed with a deep scowl on her face as I step toward her. Cockiness rolls off her in waves, and I can't wait to crush her like the filthy roach she is. This has got to be the one Rocco mentioned!

"Stacy?" The broken words fill the arena, causing my heart to shatter instantly. My eyes search for him.

Cheshire is frozen like a statue in the middle of the crowd, heartbreak clear as day across his face. What the fuck went on here? Bonzo glares daggers at the mouthy bitch. Her gaze finally settles on Cheshire, but she brushes him off and turns back to me. A breath hitches. I'm dying to see what's happening as footsteps thunder away from me. Out of the corner of my eye I see Bonzo chasing Cheshire out of the room. I need to know what happened! Anger flares to life under my skin like molten lava. They clearly know each other intimately, if his expression is anything to go by, but this bitch is cold. The dead bitch cocks her eyebrow at me. She's fucking goading me.

"Stacy, don't!" Bray, one of the regulars, calls to her.

"Why? She's just some…"

Crack!

I burst out laughing at the look of horror on her face as she rubs the reddening hand mark on her cheek. Ha! First time I ever bitch slapped a bitch! Whoop! She launches a wild attack at me that I dodge easily with an evil grin on my face as I bounce from foot to foot. I block her movements with ease, pulling a defiant scream from her. I lift an eyebrow and stifle a fake yawn. Fuck, it's like play fighting a toddler. I successfully piss the bitch off even more, and she attempts to up her assault. The other fighters start to cheer as I dodge and avoid everything she is throws at me. As if anyone would expect anything different. Another couple of minutes pass. Her breathing is labored, and her movements are erratic. Sweat runs down her face like a fountain.

My rage hasn't settled at all in the time I have been toying with her. If anything, it's grown into something more palpable. Patiently, I wait as she steps into my space. Sweeping my leg out, I knock her on her ass with a simple rookie move she didn't even see coming. I follow her down as she hits the canvas. With my knee on her throat, I watch with a malicious grin as she claws at my leg trying to get me off.

"One. You clearly hurt my dude, Marcus, and I ain't down with that shit, you pathetic bitch." The guttural growl in my voice stops her poor attempts at trying budge me.

"Two. You've heard of the Reaper, hmmmm?" I taunt her. Color me curious. She tries her best to nod with my knee at her neck, but the slight movement is enough for me to know she does.

Lifting myself up so she is no longer pinned, I extend my hand out to help her up. The arrogant fucker slaps it away and climbs to her feet. The fucking disrespect from this bitch astounds me. Anger is a lovely shade of red on her as it rises all the way up her face. She takes a step toward me, and I can't help the smirk on my face. Yeah, bring it, little one. In a flash, I wrap my hand around her throat cutting off her airway. As my grip begins tightens to crush it, I feel her pulse spike. Pulling her forward so we are nose to nose, her eyes bulge as fear finally flashes across them.

"Three. I am the one who pays you at the end of the night." I chuckle as realization dawns on her face that this is my place. "Disrespect me again, and you will fight me. Mark my words, girlie. I. Will. Crush. You."

Dropping her, I make my way out of the cage to go search for Cheshire and find out what the hell happened between them. If my gut is right, I might be back to knock this bitch into next year soon.

"Who are you?" she croaks, her voice scratchy. Looking over my shoulder, I see her rubbing her neck. You can already see the start of bruising coloring her flesh.

"My name, Stacy, is Reika Martins."

"Yeah, so?" Oh, she gets the stupid award once I find the right trophy for it.

"Everyone else knows me as…" I take a deep breath to draw out my reveal, watching her stiffen with tension. "The Reaper." Her face pales so quickly she practically turns transparent. Without even bothering to look at anyone, I head off in search of my boy. No one hurts my Cheshire and gets away with it.

62

KANE

W hat the fuck is happening? Marcus came charging through the door like a man possessed about ten minutes ago, with a frantic Bonzo chasing after him. Pretty Bird is nowhere to be seen. Panic fills me because she isn't here. I told them not to leave her. I don't like the thought of her being on her own. A door slams upstairs, followed by Bonzo shouting and trying to bang the door down. Liam saunters out of the kitchen looking as confused as I feel about the current turn of events. His eyebrow raises in a silent question. I can only shrug because I haven't got a damn clue. We set off upstairs and the thump of something reaches us as we make it there. Bonzo is braying at the door of Marcus's room like he has the hounds of hell chasing him, and his only chance of survival is on the other side of his door.

"The fuck, Bonzo?" He turns wide eyes to us. Shit, this looks like something serious.

"Sorry, man," he says sheepishly. "You're not gonna believe who we've just seen."

"Who?" I swear if he doesn't give me the goddamn answer I'm going to explode.

The rumble of a bike vibrates the whole house. Just as quick as it's heard, the front door slams open so hard I swear it shakes the foundation. Then footsteps charge in this direction. Pretty Bird stands there with a pissed off expression that has Bonzo gulping.

"Explain, fuckface!" she seethes. You can feel the anger radiating off her in waves.

"Well...erm... I-I-I-I... W-W-We..." he stutters out.

Me and Liam share a look at the way Bonzo stumbles over his words. Looking to my baby, I see the knuckles on her right hand are red and slightly raised. What the fuck? Rushing forward I grab her hand and lift it for closer inspection. She yanks her hand out of mine and glares at me. That's a look that makes grown men run and hide; I'm so confused right now.

"One of you had best explain why the fuck Marcus shot off like he did, and I've just had to smack a bitch?" They've only been gone an hour, if that?

"You had to smack a bitch?" I don't mean for the curiosity to be heard in my voice. Liam snorts out a laugh at her words with wide-eyed respect, that he quickly shuts down when she throws a glare at him.

"Bonzo?" she seethes, through gritted teeth. Those little hairs on the back of my neck stand on end.

"Stacy is here." Liam and I look at each other with matching 'oh shit' expressions. She growls while storming to the door.

"Cheshire, open the fucking door." I feel shitty for my brother, but Pretty Bird won't get any sense out of him now. Not if he's just seen her again after so long. That bitch broke my brother, and I don't think he ever really healed.

The door clicks open as he steps out into the hallway. His emotions locked down, his face a mask of passive indifference. He stands in front of Pretty Bird glaring down at her, but she isn't easily scared off and glares right back at him with her hands on her hips, waiting for answers. Honestly, I've never noticed how comical the size difference is between us all, but seeing my tiny girl looking up at a massive, tattooed man with a 'don't fuck with me' facial expression, I'm dying to laugh.

"Spill it, dickhead." Folding her arms, she starts tapping her foot. "No." His voice is so cold it sends a shiver down my spine.

"No?" Eyes widening slightly, Pretty Bird licks her bottom lip while narrowing her eyes at him.

Me and Liam glance at each other, this isn't going to end well. Marcus doesn't deal well with anything having to do with fucking Stacy. She was the love of his life in high school, and she betrayed him in the worst way possible. When everything came to a head, my brother beat the other guy so badly he ended up in hospital being fed through a tube, for the next year. When Malcolm found out, I took the blame for my brother and dealt with the backlash. I have the scars to prove it, and I'd do it again without a second thought. Marcus was so far lost into a pit of depression, I don't know how far Malcolm would have taken his punishment. Looking back, I'm glad I stepped in.

Marcus didn't talk to anyone for months. He spent most of his time in his room ignoring everyone. He hardly ate. He practically became a wraith and would explode at even the smallest of things. He once stabbed one of the crew for looking at him the wrong way. Well, that was his excuse. Turned out the poor guy had come in for a sandwich and Marcus happened to be in the kitchen at the time. Bonzo takes a step forward, and Liam clicks his fingers to catch his attention, shaking his head in warning. The stare off between Reika and Marcus is still going strong, neither of them wants to back down.

"You heard me. No!" His voice is as sharp as a blade.

Pretty Bird bristles at his brush off. The tap of her foot

becomes more pronounced, and her arms across her chest begin to shake as she desperately tries to hold in her rage. Oh fuck! Me and Liam do the sanest thing, and take a step back until we are a safe distance from these two. Bonzo, the fucking idiot, looks at us confused, his eyes begging us to help. Idiot, move before you get your ass handed to you. Liam must have had the same thought, because he rushes out of our hiding spot and yanks Bonzo by his collar to where we are waiting for the volcano, also known as Reika, to erupt. *Chicken shit!* My inner voice snarls at me, but I stamp the fucker down. I am not getting involved in anything between these two.

There's a reason people are terrified of Marcus. That boy will gut you while he sings one of his favorite show tunes, laughing like an idiot as he does it. We've seen it first-hand more than once. We all have our roles; Marcus is the one that fools people into a false sense of security then tears them to pieces. And Pretty Bird, well I love the bones of that woman, but she is the scariest motherfucker alive. I never feared Malcolm growing up, and that fucker was dangerous. But her, she's ruthless, dangerous, psychotic even. Honestly, it makes my cock hard thinking about the lengths she will go to for what she believes in and the people she loves. She continues to tap her foot, the noise grating on Marcus, because he glowers at her once more before moving away.

"Where the fuck do you think you're going?" she snarls at him.

Reika

The expression Cheshire throws at me pisses me the fuck off. Yeah, granted, I have no right to be pissed about his silence, but that heartbroken look on his face when he saw her gutted me. My eyes flick to the three chicken shits hiding around the corner, peeking out at us like naughty children hiding. I would laugh at that, the big bad crew leader and his second hiding, but this shit needs to be sorted. I need to know what the fuck happened so I can make that bitch pay.

"Go the fuck away! I can't deal with your fucking nagging!" he yells over his shoulder as he storms down the stairs away from me.

"Nagging? Fucking nagging!" How fucking dare he? I roar my defiance into the air, taking off after the fucker. He's just about to step down from the last step, when, without a second thought, I launch myself at his back. We both hit the ground with a thump and roll to the side, my side smashing into a table as we go. I have the upper hand from the roll as Cheshire lies on his back.

"Nagging? Are you fucking serious?" I seethe down at him as I straddle his chest and lock his arms underneath my legs. He bucks underneath me like a wild animal trying to throw me off, while shouting at me. That's it. Scream at me, let it out, let me help you.

"Get the fuck off me, Hellion!" He continues to thrash around, trying to dislodge me, and I stick to him like fucking glue.

"Answer the fucking question! What did that bitch do to you?"

"Nothing!" he roars in my face, causing spit to land on my cheek. His heartbroken expression tells me he is lying; the pain in his eyes crushes my heart. It's so clear this bitch did a number on my boy, and he's as close to me as a blood relative. He is my brother and part of my chosen family.

"Stop fucking lying!" I'm trying my hardest to reign in my rage, but nothing is helping. I don't want to arguing with him like this, but he doesn't get close off and shut me out, not after everything we've been through.

The tightness of his jaw and the stone-cold expression sliding across his face gives me enough warning to prepare myself. He bucks so violently it launches me across the floor in a roll. Shouts erupt. Pulling myself up, I see Kane and Frosty wrestling with him. His chest rises and falls rapidly; his face red as anger rides him hard. Mutters reach my ears. Throwing a look over my shoulder, I spot a few of the younger crew members gossiping like a bunch of girls, fucking teenagers.

"Get the fuck out of here." Their faces pale at being caught, looking at me with wide eyes. Thank God, they don't think twice about fucking right off. I would probably have beat the asses if they hadn't with the mood I'm in.

"The fuck did this bitch do, Cheshire?" I try to show concern in my voice. He's still wrestling with his brothers, like a man possessed. I can't decide if he is trying to avoid the inevitable, or if it really hurts this much to talk about.

Kane and Frosty are barely managing to keep a hold of him as he roars and thrashes like a caged wild animal. Bonzo looks on like he hasn't got a clue what the fuck is happening. I wait as patiently as I can while Cheshire gets his emotions under control. Slowly, I see the fight start to leave his body. His movements become slower, and my heart tightens as his shoulders slump and his head drops froward on his chest. The look that passes between the guys tells me they aren't certain if he is calming down or just playing possum.

"Cheshire?" My voice is uncertain as I step toward him. Seeing him this way is doing something to my soul. His head lifts, our eyes connect, and the hurt and pain in his eyes causes my eyes to burn with unshed tears.

"What did she do? I know you don't want to tell me, but I need to know." He shakes his head in answer, his body slumps forward. Luckily the guys have a tight grip on his arms, keeping him upright.

"She..." his voice breaks, followed by a deafening silence. He doesn't say anything else. Heartbreak is etched on everyone's face seeing the state Cheshire is in. My bloodlust roars to life under my skin. My inner psycho begs me to find the bitch and make her hurt as much as my boy is.

"Someone please tell me. Seeing him like this is, it hurts. It's suffocating my soul." My stomach flutters at my admission, these guys have become so important to me in the short time we have known each other. Kane and I, well that's obvious, but Cheshire is my brother. If someone hurts him, they hurt me. Frosty, well, we are still getting to know each other, but I wouldn't want to see him hurt.

"We were together throughout high school." Huffing out a breath, he stands up straighter and looks me dead in the eye. "She was my everything, Hellion." His eyes shine with unshed tears.

"We were inseparable. She was my one, you know?" He breaks off looking to the side. "But I-I I guess, I wasn't enough." Even his brothers have gutted expressions on their faces.

"Cheshire?"

"It was couple of weeks before the end of senior year. We were getting ready to take the oath. She wasn't happy about it, but she said she understood." Shaking off his brothers, he sits on the floor and starts to draw lines in the carpet with his fingers.

"I was looking for her one night at a party." His hands start to shake, and it makes my heart clench knowing this is it. "She was over an hour late meeting me, so I searched, and found her and Raphael fucking in one of the bedrooms."

Confusion must be written on my face, because he clarifies, "He is De'Marco's cousin."

"You mean the same one who was a friend of yours and now runs the Grimm's?" My heart breaks even more for him.

"Yeah," he croaks out. "I lost my head and stormed off, but the next time I saw him at school, I beat him so bad he wasn't the same for about a year." Frosty's words from our talk earlier rattle around in my head. Kane took that beating for Cheshire to keep him out of their dad's path.

"I found out it had been going on for weeks." A tear rolls down his cheek. The betrayal still raw for him. Even after all this time, his heart still bleeds.

63

REIKA

My mind races as everything pieces together. The look she gave him. Why he ran, and everything else that followed. Before my brain registers anything is happening, I am swinging my leg over my bike. Kane and Frosty race toward me telling me to calm down. The engine roars to life, and I peel out of the yard leaving dust clouds behind me. My darkness is a living, breathing being under my flesh. My rage fuels the bloodlust within it, pouring through my veins like a tsunami. Everything is a blur as I push my bike to its limits, flying to my destination. The warehouse comes into view and the noise from inside can be heard from out here. Must be a big crowd tonight. Quickly shutting off the ignition and dropping the stand, I untie the hoodie from around my waist. I don't even remember grabbing it! I pull it on and leave my hood up as I make my way inside.

The thump of the music fills the air. Along with the roar of the crowd, it's practically pulsating. They're like the hounds of hell crying out for blood. That is exactly what they're going to get tonight too - a show fit for the devil himself. The main hall is packed so tightly with bodies it's hard to push through. Some of the men I push out of the way spin around to give me shit, but think twice about it when they catch my eyes and move out of my way. The guys went all out in doing up the warehouse. Strobe lights fly all over the ceiling in time to the beat of the music. The spectators dance in their seats while watching the blood bath in the cage. Money crosses hands at the betting booth. Lucky for me, that's also where I find Rocco. I pull my hood tighter to cover my face the closer I get to him, then lean to against the wall in his line of sight. It only takes a second for him to spot me in the shadows and head my way.

"Sup, Boss Lady?" he shouts in my ear so I can hear him over the music.

"Is Stacy fighting tonight?" His eyes widen at my question.

"Err. Yeah, she's next up. Why?" The uncertainty in his voice has my lip twitching, and I swear my darkness lets out a happy sigh.

"Who's she fighting?"

"Kerri." His voice still has an uncertain tone to it. This it just made my life a lot easier.

"Give Kerri some money to bow out." A sadistic grin splits my face just as one of the lights hits my face. Rocco shoots away from me at whatever look he sees there.

"Really?" he asks shocked. I bark out a laugh at the horror on his face as I continue to grin at him.

"Yep. Get that bitch Stacy in the cage, and do not let on it is me in there with her." Frantically nodding his head, he heads off to do what I asked. Kicking a leg up to rest a foot on the wall, I lean back and wait.

"Ladies and Gentlemen! We have a new fighter on the permanent card tonight!"

The crowd roars its approval as Stacy jumps into the cage, bouncing from foot to foot as she works through a combination of punches. This sends the crowd into another chorus of cheers and boos. I make my way through the crowd, adjusting my hood as I walk.

"We have more fresh meat tonight! The other fighter is also unknown."

The crowd roars their approval again at Rocco's words. He looks between the two of us. I can't see his face, but I know this is the usual set up. I keep my chin angled slightly down so I can just make out what is going on around me, but no one can see my face under the blaring lights.

"Fight!"

Luckily for Rocco, he manages to get out of the way before she launches into a full-on assault. I dodge every one of her punches, causing a growl to tumble out of her lips and a smirk to spread further across my face. She punches and kicks wildly as I avoid her attacks, allowing my rage to build under the surface, much to the crowd's annoyance as boos and jeers are thrown at the cage.

"Fucking fight me you stupid bitch!" she screams at me.

My smirk grows to a full-on grin as I watch her movements, waiting. Her right shoulder drops just slightly as she throws a right hook. Hooking my left arm around hers, I spin and punch her in the back of the head which has her stumbling into the wire of the cage. Shock registers on her face from the power in my punch. I can't help the chuckle that escapes me.

"Who are you?" she screeches at me.

Beckoning her forward with my finger, a war cry fills the air as she

charges me. Side stepping, I swipe her legs out from underneath her. Looking to the side, Rocco is there with a terrified expression. He knows I never toy with my prey like this, not unless they have done something they shouldn't have done. I allow a few of her punches to land, giving her the false sense of security, then a roundhouse to the ribs has me dropping to my knee.

"Yes! Yes!" she screams to the crowd. Encouraging them to join in with her chant. This fucker watches to much wrestling!

I watch her out of the corner of my eye under my hood. My malicious grin almost splits my face as a laugh bursts out of me. My deep laughter catches the attention of the crowd, who turn silent in an instant. The sound echoes around the high ceiling. Stacy turns to me will a demonic grin of her own. Slowly, I shake my head as I unfurl myself from my position. I turn so I'm facing away from her, and pull the hood back slightly. With the crowd's attention focused on me, they all gasp as realization hits them. Allowing it to drop back on my shoulders, my hair tumbles free. Pulling a tie off my wrist, I pull it up into a high bun on my head. Mutters break out through the crowd. I hear Stacy shuffling her feet.

"The worst thing you could ever do is hurt someone I care about." My voice, filled with malice, rings out around the room.

I hear the squeak of her shoes as the canvas under her feet creaks from the weight of her footfalls. She's trying to stalk toward me without me knowing. My grin grows. I spin just as she sends a jab my way, catching her arm in my grasp just under her wrist. Terror fills her face as she gets her first look at me, and I glare down at the bitch with rage burning in my body to the point I feel like I might spontaneously combust. My grin is all teeth as I tug her arm toward me in a move so quick, she doesn't realize what I've done. Her scream fills the air along with a loud crack as her wrist breaks under the pressure. She drops to the floor clutching her wrist, writhing in agony. My inner bitch thrums in delight, seeking payment for the hurt she put Cheshire through.

"You destroyed him!" My statement is filled with so much

venom, confusion clouds her features. I cant my head to the side, watching her eyes bulge.

"I loved him!" she screams back at me, pulling herself to her feet. Is this bitch serious right now? Love? I bet she doesn't know the meaning of the fucking word.

"How can you say that when you were fucking someone else when he found you?" I bellow taking a step toward her.

"You don't know what went on!" she screams at me. "It has nothing to do with you. You're fucking Kane!"

"How's the wrist, Stacy?" A snort of laughter fills the room. Flicking my eyes to the side I spot Frosty and Bonzo grinning.

"Fuck you!" she screams at me.

"Get the fuck out of my town or I will end you for the pain you have caused him." The command obvious in my tone.

Her eyes widen, then narrow at my words. I turn my back on her and head over to see why these two are here. Honestly, I thought Rocco would have called for Kane to come and remove me from the situation.

"What's going on?" I ask Frosty.

Just as his eyebrows shoot to his hairline, the bitch's foot connects with the side of my head, knocking me on my ass. The crowd that's been too quiet to this point, bellows in excitement at her landing a shot. The noise seems to give her a second wind. She jumps on top of me, landing sloppy punches with her good hand as she tries to protect her other. I grab a fistful of hair and throw her off me. Yeah, bitch move, I know. Climbing to my feet as she rolls across the floor, I rip my hoodie off and throw it over the top of the cage to Frosty who catches it mid-air. Sweet!

"Game on, bitch!" I spit at her.

Liam

505

. . .

My smile widens as I watch Reika's face turn from kinda pissed to downright murderous. Stacy has always been a ballsy bitch though, I'll give her that much. She hasn't realized yet that she has bitten off more than she can chew with Reika. Even though she's only been toying with Stacy so far, Reika has done damage. Stacy is favoring her weaker hand. More than likely Reika broke it. Kane would have come but one of our runners disappeared, and he needed to check it out. *Yeah, and he gets a hard on every time he watches her fight.* My inner voices snarks at me causing a chuckle to bubble in my throat. Bonzo shuffles from foot to foot, his eyes darting all over the place. He's such a fidgety little fucker. I really don't like him, but he's part of the crew, so here he is. Yay. I really need to talk to Reika about that. The dude gives me the hebbie jebbies! Brushing the creepy feeling off, I turn back to the chaos inside the cage. Reika is knocking the shit out of Stacy, who is currently curled up in a ball on the floor screaming bloody murder.

"Erm, Liam?" Rocco stands just off to my right. Slowly folding my arms across my chest, I turn to face him and lift an eyebrow in question. A smile tugs at my lips as he visibly gulps, and his face becomes a tad paler. This is kinda fun. I wonder if this is what Reika feels like most of the time.

"Stacy's had enough, man. You need to stop it." His voice is so meek and mild. Seriously, this guy is her manager? What the actual fuck!

"You're telling me this because…?" I cock my head at him. Annoyance flares under my skin as he starts to shuffle his feet. Wow! What a sniveling little bitch!

"Well. I-I-I-I. U-u-Umm. F-fuck!" he stutters. "Rocco?" I turn so my full attention is on him. "Do I look like your boss?"

"W-w-w-well. No," he stutters through his words again.

"Exactly. Your boss is currently in the cage destroying one of her own fighters. And you want me to do what exactly?" I inquire, letting my annoyance bleed through in the tone of my voice.

"Look, Liam. None of us here are daft enough to try and stop her from killing someone in there." He shudders from the thought of having to do that. What a chicken shit! What the fuck has that got to do with me though? It's not like I'm her boss.

Without answering, I turn my attention back to the cage. The crowd has gone rather quiet, almost eerily quiet. Laughter bursts out of me as I notice Reika is picking a wobbly Stacy up off the floor, and helping her get her bearings, before walking away to wait like a lion about to annihilate its prey. I'll give her respect on this, she is ruthless. I'm pretty sure she fits under the ninja category. When we first met, I thought she was a mouthy bitch who was all bark and no bite. But I'll admit I was wrong. I should never have tried to get rid of her. Guilt still turns my stomach in knots when I think about what I put my brothers through, but after the last few weeks, I know she isn't as bad as our mother. She is good for this family, and I will do everything in my power to prove to her, and them, how sorry I am.

Silence greets me when I pull myself out of my thoughts, no sound of feet moving or even breathing. Looking around everyone is glued to the scene unfolding in front of them, Reika stands over Stacy with a murderous look on her face. The lights are like a halo behind her, giving her the look of an avenging angel. A chuckle bubbles up at that thought. It's rather fitting really, don't you think? As quick as a flash, the atmosphere becomes super charged. You can literally feel the static run along your skin, lifting all those little hairs on your arms as you wait with bated breath to see what is about to happen. I know what she's going to do before anyone else, and I know I can't let her do it, no matter how much I want the bitch to pay for what she did to my brother. Rushing forward, I jump into the cage with a load of curse words following in my wake from the people I sent flying out of my way.

"Reaper!" I bark out, as I catch her wrist in my grasp. Her eyes lift to mine, and the hollowness there sends a shiver coursing through my body. There is no emotion at all in her eyes, only darkness. It's terrifyingly beautiful to see how far into the void she can go.

"He wouldn't want this," I murmur to her, hoping this makes her see sense. Stacy hurt my brother, but I know it will hurt him more if she kills for him. He would be wracked with guilt at her losing a part of her soul because of him.

"She hurt him, Frosty," she snarls through her teeth. "Kane is covered in scars because of this bitch!" she spits the words like venom.

"I love Marcus. You crazy bitch!" The darkness in Reaper's eyes becomes obsidian at Stacy's words. She falls even deeper into the pit of darkness.

"Do you want to die?" I snarl at the stupid bitch. Clearly she still hasn't learned to shut her mouth.

"I…" Stacy's words break off as a demonic growl echoes through the air. It's feral with a promise of pain and violence. Out of the corner of my eye, I spot the other fighters taking steps further away from the cage with terror on their faces. As if the distance will help them if this goes wrong. Reaper's arms shake violently, causing the arm I have a hold of her with to shake along with hers as she tries to rein in the darkness threatening to swallow her whole. I've seen the aftermath of her episodes, but I have never seen her fall into the void. Harsh breaths fill the room as her chest rises and falls rapidly. Her eyelids flutter as she murmurs incoherent words, shaking her head like she's trying to dispel the thoughts in her mind.

"Get the fuck out of her town and do NOT come back!" I spit at the Stacy. My words come without thought as I try to help the stupid bitch. She looks up at death itself as she shakes violently at my side. The look in the eyes of Reaper is enough to get her to listen to my warning. She scrambles to her feet, finally running out of the cage in fear for her life.

"Frosty?" My name sounds hollow and broken as fuck, on her lips. She stares at me like she's looking into a void. Fuck! The internal battle going on inside her to keep her darkness at bay is crystal clear, even for me to see. It's like her demons are moving behind her eyes. As she desperately tries to get it under control, her chest begins to heave. Panic crushes her features as her shakes become so severe, she looks like she's having a seizure. Without another thought, I scoop her up into my arms. Now outside the cage with a human bomb in my arms, I search for somewhere to take her. Not just for her safety, but for everyone else here too.

"Liam! The office," Rocco shouts to me. He hasn't dared approach us; the whites of his eyes are visible from here.

Without another word to anyone else, I take off in that direction. Luckily, the office is at the end of a corridor. Reika jumps out of my arms and lands on the floor in a crouch. Sweat rolls down her arms and back. Fuck! My uncertainty turns to panic seeing how far gone into the dark void she is. I just hope she has the strength to return. How many times is to many for someone to lose themselves in the darkness and return? Is this the last time?

"Frosty?" Her broken words chip a piece of my soul from me, her terror is evident. "Help me?" she pleads, crouching down to her side, I slowly rub circles on her back.

"Shhh. I got you," I coo, trying to calm her down. "What do you need?"

"R-release," she stumbles through her words as she pants, crouched on the floor.

Release? Memories flood me of the jokes me and Marcus have made about Reika losing her shit and Kane having to fuck her brains out to get her to calm down. My brain runs a mile a minute trying to figure out how to help. That's it! Violence. We are very similar people and I need violence to curb my rage. So does she. When Mel died, she pushed my buttons to make me lose it and we fought, she reveled in the pain I caused her, and didn't want me to stop. She pushed me so far it helped expel her own darkness.

"Arrrrrgggggggggh!"

Her soul splitting scream echoes in the hallway, and she is somehow suddenly standing at the other end of it. Rushing forward, I spot a picture in her hand, and a knife is embedded into the door. Her hands shake violently, like she's being electrocuted, as the picture flutters to the floor like a discarded memory. With a roar of defiance filled with pain, she charges into the office and starts tearing the room to pieces. My eyes bulge, but I am rooted to my spot as she attacks it, like a hurricane wiping out everything in its path.

Crack.

She punched a hole through the plaster. Horror fills me as she pulls her hand back out covered in blood, the skin on her knuckles shredded. She doesn't even flinch as it rolls down her hand onto the floor, like a little red stream flowing down a mountainside. Her whole body sways, like it's dancing to its own haunted tune. Another scream and she launches the desk across the room. What the actual fuck?

Bending down I grab hold of the picture and my heart stills. It's a picture of a young Reika, standing with her parents, I'm guessing, as they all look at each other with so much love. Turning the picture over there is another stuck to the other and this one has vomit rushing up my throat. It's from the night she killed Mason in the cage, but there are words written in on the bottom corner. *I'm always watching you. Dad.*

My heart breaks for the girl falling to pieces in front of me. Some sick fuck is not just content with coming after her relentlessly, now they are pretending to be her dead father. Broken sobs fill the room. The last bit of uncertainty I had about this girl crumbling to dust. She is just as dangerous as I knew she would be, but only to those that hurt her family or those closest to her, But underneath that tough exterior, she's broken. Another blood curdling scream fills the air, sounding like a wounded animal. Shooting forward, I duck to miss the fist she launches at my face. Her face is so pale, and her pupils are blown wide, barely any color visible. She's lost in the darkness; there is nothing in the depths of her eyes.

"Reika?" My words are quiet. I don't want to startle her.

She launches forward at me, swinging wildly. I manage to dodge out of the way and restrain her with my arms locking hers at her sides. She thrashes around in my grip, screaming a haunting sound into the room. I spot Rocco and Bonzo standing in the doorway with terrified expressions on their faces. They catch her attention and she starts to struggle to get free of my arms again. I know if she manages it, she will head straight for them, and likely kill them too. I almost lose my grip on her. I manage to lock my fingers to keep her firmly secured. She spins, gnashing her teeth at me.

"Reika!" I roar at her., but she doesn't stop. There is nothing there but the need to hurt something, anything.

"For fuck's sake, Gizmo!" I bellow into her face even closer, then I gnash my teeth back at her in warning.

Her eyelids flutter, as the darkness begins to melt away from her eyes. The screams quiet and the shaking in her body starts to subside.

"Who's doing this to me?" Her words are so low and softly spoken, I strain my ears to make them out. She slumps into my arms like the weight of the world has taken its toll on her.

Shuffling us over to the upended chair, I flip it back on its legs with my foot. I gently place her down and move to my knees in front of her. The darkness hasn't fully left her, but more of the girl I know is back in her eyes. Silence. I don't say a thing as I watch the void dissipate and some of the light return to her eyes.

"Gizmo?" she asks as a slight chuckle escapes her lips. A huge smile breaks out across my face.

"Yeah." I chuckle, and she cocks her head in question. She can't be that dense?

"C'mon girl, you're like a damn gremlin." I chuckle at the 'what the fuck' look on her face. "You look cute and cuddly. But instead of don't feed after midnight, it should say don't piss off or you will bring the seven rings of hell." Laughter bursts out of her mouth, and I chuckle alongside her. Looking around at the devastation in the room, my eyes connect with hers.

"You need a warning label."

64

KANE

My brain is still processing the horrid sight I just witnessed. One of our runners was out on a routine delivery dropping drugs at the usual locations with the usual guys, when I got a phone call saying someone had found him dead and the drugs where gone. They didn't just murder him, they mutilated him. He was barely recognizable as human when I saw what they'd done. Guilt fills me, because at the same time Rocco rang telling me Pretty Bird had gone bat shit crazy at the ring. I had to send Liam to sort her out. It should have been me.

"Kane?" My earpiece crackles as Fox speaks to me from the other car. I'm too tired for this shit.

"Sup, Fox." Even I can tell how tired I am. The member who is driving flicks his gaze to the mirror. I stare daggers at him, and he quickly averts his eyes back to the road.

"Just been notified that some listening bugs were found in the house." I sit to attention at this. "You're not gonna like it, man."

"Tell me."

"A stash was found in Liam's wardrobe."

Motherfucker! I should have known he would be the one behind all this shit, we trusted him. I trusted him. "Fuck!"

The car swerves into oncoming traffic as horns are blasted at us. I feel a little bad for scaring the grunt, but seriously this shit is fucked up. Rage fills me; he's with my baby, my heart. I trusted him to sort out what was going on at the ring. If he has done anything to her, I will fucking kill him. Incessant buzzing fills the car. Realizing it's my phone, I hit accept.

"You finished?" Bonzo's voice fills the car, and my rage ramps up another notch at the disrespect of Liam not ringing me himself.

"Hmmm." Is the only word I manage to get past the huge lump in my throat. My heart constricts in my chest as the gravity of Fox's news crushes me under its weight.

"We will meet you back at the house." The little bastard ends the call. Rage is now at war with suspicion at the lack of knowledge and respect I have just been given.

"Step on it," I spit to the grunt.

"Boss."

Ten minutes later we pull up outside just as Liam's SUV pulls up. Throwing my door open, I am out of the car and storming toward my brother. I freeze in my tracks as Liam climbs out with a shaking Pretty Bird in his arms. My rage at the setup is pushed to the back of my mind for the time being.

"What the fuck?"

"She lost it, Bro. I mean seriously lost it. I managed to pull her out, but she's having another episode."

He doesn't even wait to see if I'm following as he strides past me toward the house. Marcus steps out onto the porch. His eyes widen and practically bulge out of his head at the state of Pretty Bird. Liam doesn't even bother to acknowledge him as he pushes past and heads up the stairs, my legs scrambling to keep up with him. Marcus is hot on my heels. The darkness still shows behind his eyes, but anything to do with her is the priority. Tears stream down her face as she shakes violently on the bed, gripping the comforter like her life depends on it.

"The fuck happened, Bro?" Marcus hisses.

"She nearly killed Stacy." His words are void of emotion as he throws a look over his shoulder. "She was so lost to the darkness, I had to get her out of there."

"Why do you have listening bugs in your room?" The words blurt out of my mouth before I can stop them. His eyes widen at my accusation, then he looks at me with confusion.

"What bugs?" he questions. Marcus's gaze flicks between us in confusion.

"The ones that were found in the bottom of your wardrobe?" I spit. How dare he lie to me?

"I haven't got a fucking clue what you're on about," he seethes. "You might want to concentrate on your girl now. Then deal the bullshit you've been fed, once again, later." A growl rumbles in my chest as I take a step forward. Marcus throws his arm out halting me in my tracks.

"He's right, Kane," his voice is filled with concern.

"She lost her shit. When we got back to the office, she found this fastened to the door by a knife."

He pulls a crumbled item out of his jeans pocket and hands it to me. Marcus moves closer as I open it up. What? My brain can't process the image in front of me. My eyes widen in shock. A young Reika is standing with her parents. They're all staring at each other with so much love. It's obvious they are her parents; she looks so much like her father. But, what shocks me is the fact I recognize the little girl. Memories rush to the surface with one in particular playing in my head. Malcolm dragged us to a business meeting with someone in the middle of nowhere. The place was surrounded by trees and the guy in the picture welcomed us like old friends. He told me and my brothers to explore, but to stay away from the pitch as his daughter was training. Well, we were curious, so naturally we searched for the pitch. We couldn't not do something we'd been told not to do, right? That's when I saw the tiny girl from the picture fighting full grown men, and destroying them like there were nothing more than cardboard cut outs. Marcus's words echo in my head, "I want to learn to do that." That was the only thing said as we watched this amazing creature go round after round with these men, not batting an eyelid. I'm pulled from the memory as a cough fills the room. I stare at my brothers wide eyed.

"We've met her before." Confusion stares at me from their faces.

"Pretty Bird is the one from the pitch at Malcolm's business meeting that day."

We all look at the broken girl laid on the bed. My heart stutters. How did I not know it was her? The defiance and determination in the girl that day is still at the surface of the gorgeous woman she has become.

"Look at the other one?" Liam says.

I cock my head in question, and he just nods at me. Flipping it over I am speechless. The picture is of a demonic looking Pretty Bird, standing in the middle of the cage with an evil grin across her face. Mason's body at her feet. She's covered head to toe in blood and looks like some kind of demon from hell standing over her prey. '*I'm always watching you. Dad,*' is scribbled across the bottom. My gaze shoots to Liam. He nods his head in response to the silent question. This is what's triggered her.

"No. No. No. Noooooo!" she screams. The sound carves through the air of the room.

My eyes dart to Pretty Bird, who is trashing around on the bed with tears rolling down her cheeks. Without a second thought, I'm climbing up onto the bed and pulling her into my arms as she thrashes wildly, trying to fight whatever monsters are in her head. I hear the click of the door, meaning my brothers have stepped out. Sweat rolls off her in rivers down her body. I peel her clothes off to bring her body temperature down. I murmur in her ear and rub circles into her stomach to let her know I'm here, and I am not leaving her.

Reika

Adrenaline thunders through my body as I run for my life. The voices had disappeared, but now they are closer than before. I'm trying to keep my breathing low and my movements silent to escape, but I'm scared.

"She's here somewhere, man," a rumbly voice says, and my body shakes at how close they are now.

Tears rolls down my face. My dad left me and said it would be good training, but this doesn't feel like a normal training session. I have never been here before. I don't know which way home is. I move back as quietly as I can. I freeze as a branch snaps under pressure. My eyes dart to my foot. Oh no!

"You hear that?" Covering my mouth to hide my panicked breathing, I slide my feet backwards to limit the pressure of foot falls on the ground. One. Two. Three. None of my steps make a noise as I move further into the shadow of trees. The moonlight shines through the canopy of leaves every now and then, lighting up the area.

My back hits something and a scream tears from my throat. It is suddenly cut off by a hand over my mouth. I bite, scratch, and kick my captor the best I can. A shudder races up my spine as a slick, wet tongue slides up the side of my cheek.

"Hmmm. Looky what I found, man," the voice says against my ear.

"What you found, Hal?" the other says.

I'm thrown forward away from the guy holding me. My skin splits open on my hands and knees as the forest floor cuts into them. Blood oozes out of my hands, and a whimper leaves my throat. Suddenly, I'm flipped over onto my back. I scream for dear life as one of the men climbs over me and pins me in place. His face is twisted into something that looks like pure evil as he grins down at me. Throwing my head I try to make contact with his nose, but he manages to dodge out of the way at the last second. With a roar, he swings at me. Pain screams through my cheek forcing my head to the side, and my vision starts to darken in the corners. Another pair of feet appear in front of my eyes. The sound of something ripping reaches my ears as I thrash the best I can, trying to break free. Gleeful laughs fill the night as cold air skims over me, making me shiver. Hands runs all over my body. My stomach turns, and bile shoots up my throat. My body shuts down as I feel myself turning numb. I stare into the night sky without moving.

My eyes snap open. I scramble away from the hands rubbing circles on my flesh, falling off the side of the bed and crab crawling away as fast as I can. I am so disorientated. My own screams fill my head from that night. My back slams into something solid, and I tug my knees up to my chin and sob. I feel so cold. My whole body shakes, panic and fear wreaking havoc on my body.

"Baby?" I flinch away from the deep voice, causing a gasp to fill the air. "P…Please don't hurt me?" My voice is low and fractured. Another sob leaves my throat.

My eyes adjust, and I see the furniture in my room. I hug the wall trying to put distance between me and my visitor. Kane sits crossed legged in front of me with a heartbroken expression on his face. He rubs his hands on top of his thighs.

"I'm sorry," I manage to croak out.

"I need you to tell me, Baby. I need to understand." His voice is filled with so much emotion. I shake my head at him, then try to get as close to the wall as possible. If he knows what happened that night, he won't look at me the same way again.

The feeling of phantom hands still flutter across my skin, in all the places their hands were. Fear still rides me hard from the flashback, but my heart stutters at the broken look on Kane's face. I can't cope with the feeling of their hands still on me. I launch forward at Kane, causing him to hit the floor on his back with an oomph. I slam my lips onto his in a desperate kiss. He groans into my mouth as his hands slide up my ass, making me shudder. He breaks the kiss with a smack of his lips, staring at me like he doesn't know the person he sees in front of him. The feeling of rejection flares through me as I stare back at him.

"I love you, Baby Girl, but we can't." His voice sounds so determined, but his lust filled gaze says otherwise. Slamming my lips back down on his, I tug his lip between my teeth and bite on it gently, tugging another groan out of him.

"I can't take the feeling of their hands on me. I need to forget," I plead with him.

"Baby Girl?" His voice breaks as the depth of my words hits home.

"Please, Kane. Replace the bad memories with good ones," I beg, pleading with him. I'd beg for anything to make it stop.

"You need to tell me everything." The command in his tone has a shot of lust going straight to my clit.

"I will, I'll tell you everything. Just give me the best memory ever."

His lips crash brutally into mine, until he takes control of the kiss. He slows the pace from furious to something I have never felt before.

His kisses are soft and gentle as he peppers them across my jaw, following a path only he knows to my mouth. He licks the seam of my mouth with the tip of his tongue asking for entrance, and I open to him like the willing sacrifice I am. His tongue slowly brushes mine with tentative caresses, making me moan as heat ignites in my body. His breaks our connection and looks into my eyes. His almost black eyes are filled with so much emotion, it looks like a storm is brewing inside them; they're like bottomless pools of love, trust and desire. I feel my heart stutter at the intensity in his look. My tummy does a little flip as my heart tries to break out of my chest, sending waves of electricity all over me making my skin pebble.

"I'm going to make love to you, Reika. I'm going to remind you of everything you're worth and how much I fucking love you."

He scoops me up off the floor and lays me down on the bed, so gently it's like he's scared I'll break. He leans over me and takes my lips again, our tongues dance with each other as the intensity of our connection increases, causing me to moan into him. He groans as he pulls back lifting me to remove my top and bra swiftly.

"I'm going to kiss every inch of your gorgeous skin, so all you remember is the feel of my lips on your body and all you think of are my words of love," he murmurs.

Kane kisses me with so much passion, I gasp and open to him. He instantly deepens the kiss and twirls his tongue around mine. He pulls my bottom lip between his teeth and growls softly. He nips it once more before he licks the cartilage of my ear, causing me to shudder. He slowly kisses, licks and nips down my neck to my collar bone before he sinks his teeth into my skin. That slight edge of pain causes my core to go super nova. As I sink my fingers into his hair, he laps at the spot with his flat tongue reminding me just how talented it is and how amazing it feels elsewhere. My core involuntarily clenches as he slowly drives me wild in the most decadent of ways.

"Baby Girl, do you know my heart only beats for you and it will always be yours?" he groans as his fingers quickly undo my pants and pull them down my legs so he has access to my core. He leans up and whispers right into my ear, "Right now all I want to do is sink into your dripping wet pussy, feel your walls hold my cock and milk it till it runs dry."

I almost throw myself off the bed when I feel his fingers glide along my lips as he feels just what his sweet, dirty words and soft touches have done to me. He sinks his fingers deeper between my folds, gathering my juices, and slowly circles my clit in a figure eight. My eyes shutter closed as sensations flow through me like the waves of a building storm. I feel his tongue swirl one nipple making the tight nub even harder before he takes the next one in his mouth. He sucks hard enough to make my back arch off the bed, as he sinks two fingers all the way into my heat.

"That's it, Pretty Bird, I'm going to play you like the best musician in the world. I know how to get the best from you, how to make you feel everything ten times stronger than you ever have. I'm going to leave you trembling and this pussy of mine will only remember the feel of my cock deep inside it. You won't be able to walk properly for a week," he growls. It's such a deep, animalistic sound. I feel the vibrations sink into me only heightening the sensations assaulting my body.

"Kane, I... C-c-c-can't take much more, I'm going to come."

"That's it, Baby Girl. I want you to come all over my fingers. I want you to soak my hand so I can lick it clean before I sink into you with my hard cock."

He curls his fingers so they hit that special spot inside me, making me pant. I feel him sink further down the bed and the tip of his tongue circles my clit. I feel the waves of sensation stop, like they have hit a dam as it builds up until I can't hold it back much longer. I'm dying for sweet release, but he's got my body under a spell. It won't operate without his say so. I'm stuck on the precipice of an orgasm that is going to destroy me.

"Come. Now," he orders, and my body obeys without a second thought. I detonate. The dam bursts and I swear I feel my release flood from me. Kane groans into my ear, whispering something that sends shivers down my spine as my vision darkens.

"Are you back with me, Pretty Bird?" His voice pulls me back from the ecstasy that had taken over and caused me to black out for a minute. I open my eyes and find Kane staring into them, emotions swimming in the depths of his own as his lips gently brush mine. I can feel his hard length slide up from my entrance to my sensitive nub and back down, he's waiting for me.

"I need you to make love to me, Kane." My voice is hoarse from the aftershocks of my orgasm.

He smiles and mouths 'I love you' as he sinks into me connecting us in the most intimate way possible. I feel him begin to move inside me until it's just the tip of him at my entrance, before he thrusts back in; he repeats this pulling almost all the way out, then thrusts back in, sinking deeper than before. He takes his right hand and pulls my left leg over his shoulder, deepening our connection, as his pace finds a steady rhythm. I feel him bottom out inside me reaching places I've never felt anyone before.

Sweat beads across his forehead as he fills me again and again, but the intensity in his eyes never wavers; it's like he's looking into my soul. He's pouring his love into me so deeply

I'll never forget it. I will never doubt how deep his love for me runs. His movements speed up, his legs beginning to shake as he fights his own release.

"Pretty Bird, I love you. I loved you yesterday, I love you today and I'll always love you tomorrow. You are the other half of me. You complete me in a way I never thought possible," he whispers the words in a strained voice, but they have a finality to them. A reverent tone to his voice that makes me realize these aren't just words, this is a promise, a vow to me. To love me, always.

As if his words are magic, my body explodes from within as my orgasm hits me out of nowhere. I can't stop myself from shaking as little electric shocks fire across my whole body. As my walls clamp down on his cock, I feel him swell inside me and the hot jets of his release coat me inside.

His heavy breaths pull me back to the here and now. We share oxygen as we both come down from the most amazing high. He's still semi hard inside me, but refuses to break the connection as he flips me and pulls my back to his chest. My eyes begin to close and just as darkness claims me I hear him speak.

"I love you, Reika."

65

MALCOLM

Raised voices fill the meeting room. The idiots are still arguing over what to do about the problematic bitch. It has gone on for ages. Exhaustion cripples me from not sleeping and hardly eating since those stupid fucking boys exiled me. A putrid stench fills the room from the body still slumped in the chair. Poor bastard! The voices continue to get louder. I shake my head at the stupidity of these idiots.Honestly, they have no idea of the sort of hell they will bring on themselves if they continue on this path. My sons alone are to be feared but the bitch, she is savage.

Their argument continues. What I do find curious, is the smug look on the cocky little bastard's face. I have never liked him since the day I met him when he took over for his father. I knew then he would be up to something; the way he's pushing for command, forcing the other's decisions, he is definitely planning something. Lucky for me, they are all preoccupied with their argument. Artifacts and paintings line the walls in the room. I follow their path, taking my time in studying them one by one, so as not to raise suspicion.

"Where do you think you're going Malcolm?" Cal asks.

"Is it illegal to want to take a piss?" A smirk tips up the corner of my mouth at the repulsed look on his face.

They don't even bother to acknowledge me as I slip out the door into the hallway. I've been here enough times to know there is a bathroom located on the same floor as the office I need to gain access too. Security doesn't stop me as I head down the hallway. This house is built like a damn maze. The whole place is obnoxious, just like the family that owns it. Honestly, I can't understand the thought process of some people. I know the feeling of not having anything growing up and wanting expensive things to remind you where you are now, but this is ridiculous.

Footsteps echo in the hallway, and I slink into an alcove to use a statue as cover. I wait to see which way the person is going, the office I need is just to my right. The sound gets louder as they get closer. The head of security rounds the corner to look at all the doors. Slowing my breathing, I keep as still as possible hoping he doesn't notice me. Thankfully, the sound of his footfalls quiet as he gets further away from my hiding spot. Peeking out, I scan both directions to make sure no one else is here.

After another couple of minutes, I know I am safe and head to the office door. With a twist of the doorknob, I'm surprised to find it unlocked. Trusting bastard! The damn thing squeaks as I gently open it. I glance around to make sure no one has heard the sound. I step in and close the door behind me. The desk is a serious mess with papers thrown all over the place. Dirty cups litter the desk and what looks like traces of cocaine is on the side closest to a pile of files. Dirty bastard! How can someone who seems so well put together work like this? As carefully as I can, I separate the pages stuck together by coffee stains, scanning them for anything interesting. A brown file sticking out from underneath the filing cabinet catches my eye.

Someone clearly tried to force it under the little gap between the base of the cabinet and the floor. Bending down, I slide it out and take a look. The top of the page above the file catches my interest. I pull up the chair and scan the pages. The more I read the more my hearts sinks. That's not possible? She can't be?

"Fuck!" I roar into the office air.

I need to get this information to the boys. They have to know who she is. My mind races at an alarming rate, putting all the pieces of the puzzle together. Everything starts to make sense. Nothing he's done has been for the good of the syndicate. It is all for him. I pace the office, trying to work out the best way to get the information to my boys. If I can save them from the war that's coming, maybe they will forgive me. Fox! I can send him the information. Pulling my phone free and typing out the message as quick as possible, my heart stills at the sound of footsteps echoing from somewhere out in the hallway. Gulping down air, I strain my hearing to figure out where they are. Looking down to the message I notice some of it is jumbled and doesn't make any sense, but knowing Fox, he will be able to decipher it.

Bang!

"Well, well, well. Looks like we caught a little snitch snooping." Ice runs through my veins as the one person I never wanted to see again steps into the room.

66

REIKA

"So, Gizmo, are we going to throw a party or what?" Frosty says over the rim of his coffee mug as we walk through the door.

Kane's eyes turn to me, suspicion is as clear as day in his gaze. Me and Frosty don't ever get on like this, but after everything that happened at the fight ring, I know that we are on the same wavelength. I'll admit the guy ain't all bad.

"Okay, have I been abducted by aliens and taken to a different universe?" Kane throws out into the kitchen. Me and Frosty burst out laughing, grinning at each other. Kane's eyes widen further at us both.

"Kane, call the Ghostbusters!" Cheshire says, sauntering into the kitchen. He looks between us both with a 'what the fuck' expression.

"Bro, I'm not joking. Call them. They are both possessed," he says to Kane, like we aren't here.

I'm still laughing at the brothers' reaction to me and Frosty managing to be in the same room without killing each other. My brain runs wild with a way to torment them both. Sliding onto the stool, opposite Frosty, it's as if he's had the same idea I have. We both grin at each other, mischief is written all over his face. My phone pings on the island, so I throw a look over my shoulder to see what the other two are doing.

Frosty:

We need to prank these two.

Gizmo:

How the hell did you get my number? Stalker!

What you got in mind?

Frosty:

I dunno! You get under Kane's skin.

You tell me?

Gizmo:

He hates pink. But Cheshire is yours!

Frosty:

Fuck! I got it! I'll set it up.

"What are you two planning?"

My scream fills the room and has all three of them covering their ears. *Jesus Christ!* My heart is beating so fast I'm sure it's trying to burst free of my chest. Frosty just grins at me, the little fucker, while my area is cast in shadow from the big bastard standing behind me.

"Nothing, Bro," Frosty says with a sickly sweet voice, taking a sip of his drink to hide his smirk behind the rim.

I can feel Kane's body heat, practically burning me alive from how close he is behind me. Sweat starts to bead on the bottom half of my neck as my brain tries to work out if he read the messages or not.

"Pretty Bird?" His voice is so thickly layered with command, my thirsty bitch of a pussy jumps to life, throbbing between my legs. *Down, you greedy bitch!*

"What, Baby?" My voice is just as sickly sweet as Frosty's. I look over my shoulder to him. He cocks his head and his eyes to glint in a challenge. Cheshire glowers at me over his brother's shoulder. The emotion is too complicated to read on his face, but I see the twitch of his lips. I know secretly he's enjoying this.

"You will tell me, Baby," he whispers in my ear, making a shiver work its way through my body. He leans forward, boxing me in, his chest resting on my back.

Suddenly Frosty jumps and clears the island knocking Kane away from me. They land with a thud on the floor. Frosty has a shit eating grin on his face as Kane throws wild punches at him.

"Gizmo, run!" he shouts at me, laughing his head off as his brother tries his hardest to get free of the death grip he has on him.

Without another thought, I'm running to the door. As Kane cusses from the floor, laughter bubbles up in my chest at how happy I am feeling. This may be stupid, but I feel alive.

"I don't think so, Hellion." Cheshire grins at me as he blocks my way out of the kitchen. His muscles in his arms bulge as he crosses them over his chest.

I bark out a laugh as I continue running at him, his gaze narrows the closer I get. He thinks I'm going to stop. His hands shoot out as he tries to grab me. I drop to the floor on my knees and slide across the floor between his legs, causing him to growl. The carpet stops my momentum as I make it under, then I jump to my feet and I'm off down the corridor. I hear a pissed-off Cheshire giving chase and Kane cussing up a storm from the kitchen as I keep going down the hall.

"Hellion! Get your bony ass back here," he bellows after me.

"Not a chance, Cheshire. What's the matter, can't you keep up?" I throw over my shoulder taunting him. It works as a growl fills the hallway.

Still looking over my shoulder, I'm not paying attention to what's in front of me until my ass lands on the floor.

"Ow!" I shout at the grunt who is rubbing his chest with wide eyes.

"Shit! Sorry, Boss." His voice sounds panicked.

"Fucking hell, man. Kane's gonna bust your ass for that," Cheshire says to the poor guy that looks about a second away from pissing himself. My ass hurts like a bitch. Cheshire extends his hand to me, and I take it. He yanks me up so quick, I barely manage to brace myself so I don't fall face first. I literally end up airborne. He grins at me as I manage to stop my momentum.

"Thanks," I mumble to him as light dances behind his eyes. It makes me happy seeing cheerfulness in his eyes.

"What's up?" I inquire.

"Erm, there's a problem down at the district, Boss." His words come out so fast, I only just manage to make them out. *The fuck is the district?*

Cheshire stiffens at the side of me, and his face shuts down into a cold, emotionless mask; apprehension rolls off him in waves. The grunt's face pales even further than it did when I ran into him. Cheshire spins on his heels, stalking toward the laughter coming from the kitchen. Throwing a look over his shoulder, he clicks his fingers, which has the grunt scrambling to follow him like a dog. I follow closely behind. As the three of us step into the kitchen, I try not to laugh at the sight of Kane and Frosty still fighting like savages on the floor. Their eyes turn to us, then they both nearly fall over each other as they jump to their feet.

"There's a problem at the district," Marcus says.

Both their eyes widen and they're off running toward the stairs. Confusion fills my head. I have never heard of the district before, but whatever it is has all three of them running like someone has just lit a fire under their asses. Determination swells within me. Like fuck am I being left out of this shit! I take off up the stairs after Kane to get answers. I don't even get halfway up when Frosty charges past me, barking orders to some of the members wearing tactical clothing. My eyes bug out of my head as I look around and see crew members filtering in from different directions. Cheshire comes down looking like a man on a mission expression, strapping knives and other weapons to himself.

"What the fuck is going on?" I ask to no one in particular. Loads of eyes swing in my direction, like they have only just realized I am still standing here.

"I don't have time to explain. This needs sorting," Kane says as he walks down the stairs in the same tactical gear as the others. The only difference is he has guns on.

"I'll be ready in five." I head up the stairs.

Just as I brush past him on the stairs, he sticks his arm out to stop me in my tracks. I lift my eyes to his and see darkness swirling behind his eyes. Someone gulps from the bottom of the stairs. I lean against the railing with my left hip and cock my eyebrow.

"You aren't coming, Reika." Reika? Oh, he's gonna use my damn name now?

I push myself off the railing and cock my head to the side, throwing a challenge his way. I allow the irritation to show in my eyes. He just glares right back at me. We are currently in a standoff. Neither one of us is backing down, I can see it in the set of his jaw and the tick of the vein in the side of his neck. Without saying anything, else he continues his descent until he is face to face with the other members waiting for him, his brothers front and center.

Frosty has an apology written all over his face. Cheshire on the other hand has the same don't argue look on his. Some of the crew shuffle their feet, darting quick looks between me and Kane.

"The fuck you mean I'm not coming?" I ask him.

Looking over his shoulder back at me, he just glares and shakes his head, turning his attention back to the men. His refusal to answer pisses me off. I take a step down, the bastard stair squeaks under my foot. Kane turns his attention back to me once more. Some of the crew take a step back at the animosity rolling of him in waves.

"With how hostile you are, I would think there is something there you don't want me to see?" I throw it out there because he has never been secretive with me like he is right now.

"My decision is final!" he bellows at me. Anger flares to life like a living, breathing thing under my flesh. I feel my cheeks start to get warm, so I know they are becoming red.

"Who the fuck do you think you are talking to?" I take another step down the stairs. "You are the one that handed me the crew, and now you're keeping me out of something to do with it?" I spit back at the bastard. His shoulders square and the vein in his neck throbs erratically.

"You are not coming. End of discussion!"

Most crew have slinked further away into the background, some have even left the room. My nostrils flare at the balls of this motherfucker. I don't know what is pissing me off more, what he is saying or the fact that he, the person who has always has my back, is saying it. He stands there glaring at me, like he just wants to get on with his shit.

"I…"

"End of discussion, Reika," he says to me before he storms off. I'm left standing there, gob smacked at what the hell has just gone on. I watch him step out of sight beyond the door with Cheshire following closely on his heels.

"Gizmo?" My chest rises and falls rapidly, I'm clenching my hands into fists then opening them again. I know my nostrils are flaring right now. I'm like a volcano about to erupt at any moment.

"Gizmo?" The stupid as shit nickname reaches my ears again.

"Fuck off, Frosty! Your Master is waiting!"

67

KANE

"If the bastard doesn't hurry up. We are leaving his ass," I shout. I don't have time to be waiting on my fuckwit of a brother.

Just as the crew replies with a round of nods, I spot the fucker jogging across the lawn to where we are all waiting, like a set of idiots, for his ass. The look on his face says he wants to chew me out, which pisses me off because when the fuck did he and Reika get so damn close.

"She okay?" Marcus asks his twin.

"The fuck do you think, man? She's just practically ripped my head off because of you two assholes," he seethes, then climbs into the back of a van, like none of us are here.

Marcus and I stare at each other. My pulse spikes with anxiety, andI notice the slight dip of his Adam's Apple as he gulps at our Liam's words. I know she's pissed off with us, well me, but I don't want her near anything with the person I once called my dad's name on it. The district is what he used as a whore house and strip club for the many business dealings he had with some of the crews from the outer area. I wouldn't be bothered about anything happening to it, but I have to protect the poor women inside; some of them didn't have a choice in being there. Climbing into the van, I wait for Marcus and the others to get into their vehicles so we can head out. Flicking my eyes up to the center mirror, my eyes connect with Liam's as he shoots daggers at me through the glass.

"You know you've got some serious groveling to do when you get back, right?" he spits, then turns away as if my reply isn't important.

I spin around in my seat so I can see him. "What the fuck is your dysfunction, man?"

"My dysfunction? You're having a laugh, aren't you?" he sniggers back at me.

"Seriously, when did you two get so fucking close?" I spit at him, my anger starting to build.

"Dude, do you fucking hear yourself? I realized she isn't as bad as I thought she was," he says, without breaking eye contact with me. "You're the one fucking this up with her. Honestly, we need her here and you became an asshole again."

I know what Liam says is true, but the protective asshole in me is arguing that I was right in my decision. I really am going to have to grovel when we get back. For the next forty-five minutes, I sit in silence in the front of the van. I feel the eyes of my brothers on me occasionally.

"What can I do to make this right?" I ask no one in particular.

"How about a date night?" Marcus throws out, his eyes still glued to the road.

"Date night?" The words sound funny in my throat as I repeat them back over again.

Liam snorts in the back of the van as if this is the funniest shit he has ever heard. I haven't got the patience to argue with him about his snark, but we will definitely be having words later. I have to admit the idea of a date night has a funny feeling showing up in my stomach.

We enter the shitty neighborhood leading up to the district. There aren't many like this around here, but I can see the needles on the ground left by the addicts from the car. My stomach turns as I spot a little boy playing outside of an apartment building. He can't be more five, maybe six, if that. Just as the line of cars pass, his mother comes rushing out to grab him. Her clothes are torn, and she is as thin as a rail. We need to do something with this area after everything is said and done, the residents can't keep living like this.

"Kane, we're here," Marcus says as he throws the van into park and jumps out.

Liam doesn't bother with any more shitty comments as he climbs out and heads to the far side of the road, rifle in hand. Huffing out I breath, I compose myself and push all thoughts of Pretty Bird out of my head. I don't need to tell the crew their orders, they all know what to do. Pulling out my Glock, I head to the front doors of the worst place on earth.

Suspicion and apprehension run through my veins as we work our way through the hallways. There is no one around at all. The whores who are usually running around the place aren't here. It's like a damn wasteland. There are no noises, nothing. If something jumps out at me right now, they're dead.

"I don't like this, man," Marcus mutters behind me.

Mutters break out among the crew that are with us; everyone is feeling the same thing. The hallway comes to an end and opens into the main area which is the point of the strip club. A bar lines the whole wall on the right side and poles are spread out evenly around the place.

"Kane?" Liam asks.

"I don't like this," I reply.

Static fills the room as the radio crackles. "Boss, there's nobody up here," Bonzo says.

"What do you mean, there's nobody there?" What the fuck is going on here?

"There is nobody here. All the rooms are empty," he says.

You know that feeling you get when shit is about to go wrong, but you still have to see it through anyway? We work through the lower areas to confirm it's empty. All the other teams report the same damn thing.

"What the fuck, Dean? You said there was an issue." I snarl at the member in question.

"You got a call saying shit was going down. So, I came and told you all." The sniveling little bastard shakes violently at the expression on my face.

"And what did they say?" My voice cracks out in the hallway.

"Just that there was an issue, Boss," he stutters. A growl tears through the room from Liam, as Marcus moves to the front of everyone taking point.

"And you didn't think that was suspicious?" My anger is reaching boiling point with the stupidity of this clown.

We are all on edge as we trace our steps back the way we came to meet the others back at the vans. As I step outside, a cold blast of air smacks me in the face, forcing a hiss from my lips from the sudden change in temperature. We all move forward slowly, scanning the area.

"Kane?" Liam barks out of nowhere.

Pushing through the others, I make it to his side, and my eyes land on the thing that has stopped everyone in their tracks. My other teams are on their knees with the guns of about twenty or so men pointed at their heads.

"Well look who decided to show up, boys," a smarmy as fuck voice fills the area.

I haven't seen him before, and I definitely don't recognize his voice. His face is hidden in shadows. The only thing I can see is his black shirt and dress pants. I squint into the darkness to try and see his features; frustration clouds my mind because he is hiding himself.

"Do you know what you have done, Kane?" he spits in my direction.

"I don't even know who you are. And honestly, I don't give a flying fuck," I retort, the members behind me snigger at my words.

"I am the head of The Lost Crew, and you, boy, have done the unthinkable," he sneers.

Marcus bursts out laughing, doubling over as tears stream down his face. A couple of the members join in with him. Looking to my right, Liam's lips are twitching.

"What do you find so funny, boy?" the newcomer asks.

"You sound like you belong in Neverland, asshole," Marcus manages to say before he bursts out laughing again.

My lips twitch, trying to lift into a smirk. I should have known Marcus would come out with a smart ass comment.

"How dare you disrespect me!" his voice reverberates.

"Listen, fuckface. I've had enough of your whole, I am in control here, nonsense." I smirk as I step forward. All guns turn to me to take aim. "What are you wanting from all this?" I roll my hand to get my point across that I want him to hurry the fuck up.

Bang!

I duck as the shot rings out. Yells come from the other members who all dropped to the ground. Grunts of pain and roars of defiance fill the air as the crew members that were on their knees fight their captors. My eyes scan the area for anyone that might have been shot. Everyone looks to be accounted for.

"Liam!" Marcus bellows, my eyes dart to his as he frantically searches the area.

"Where's Liam?" he shouts again.

I hear what he is saying, but my mind feels like it's running at a snail's pace trying to catch up with what is going on. Marcus tears through the area looking for our brother. Suddenly manic laughter fills the air. The sounds of fighting stop instantly as the laughter continues to echo. It gives a whole new meaning to the word eerie.

"What the fuck!" someone shouts.

We all watch, horrified, as one of the people with the newcomer pulls Liam out into the open. What is surprising is there isn't any traces of blood on him whatsoever, the guy pulling him along looks vaguely familiar.

"We finish this, Kane, or your brother dies," the leader of The Lost says.

My eyes widen as the fucker holding my brother kicks him in the back of the legs and drops him to his knees. Marcus roars as he tries to get to his twin, some of the crew grab him to keep him in place. The fucker who now has his gun aimed at the back of Liam's head has a shit-eating grin on his face as his stares me down. That's when his face comes to the forefront of my mind. What the fuck? The manic laughter fills the air again.

Bang!

My eyes nearly bug out of my head as the fucker's brains splatter all over the asphalt. A male laugh joins in with the manic laughter, and the owner of the laugh steps out into the light.

"Who the fuck are you?" screams one of The Lost members.

"Ta-dah!"

The newest person to join this shit show is small with a black hood covering their head. Liam slowly unfurls himself from the ground as the person in the hoodie, slowly pulls their hood down.

"Oh, fuck," one of The Lost exclaims.

"What you afraid for man, they are easily dealt with," says another as they start to argue amongst themselves.

"Don't you know who the fuck that is?" says the other one who is violently shaking. I'm pretty sure he pissed his pants.

"That's the fucking Reaper, you idiot."

Pretty Bird stands in the middle of everything laughing her fucking head off, as Liam joins in with her. With her Harley Quinn laugh filling the air and my brother's deep baritone joining in, it sounds like they are making their own song. My mind and body are in a state of shock, not knowing what the hell is going on. I don't know if I want to shout at her or fuck her brains out.

"Sorry, Mister. Was Viper one of yours?" she says in a sickly-sweet voice, with a grin that is all teeth.

"You stupid, skank," the leader says.

"Well, now I'm a little offended." Pretty Bird crosses her arms across her chest and pouts. "I didn't get an invite to the party." Stamping her foot in annoyance, she huffs.

All eyes turn to her as she walks closer to the men in the area, some shake while others take a step away from her. I don't know what they think they are going to accomplish by that, she would still kill them anyway.

"Hellion, what the fuck are you doing here?" Marcus says as he steps toward her.

"Speak to me, asshole, and I will cut your tongue out of your head," she spits out at him between gritted teeth.

"Hell…"

"Don't fucking push it, Marcus!" He shrinks back from her, like a child who knows they're in trouble with the use of their proper name.

The Lost members all watch with twitchy hands as she makes her way toward me. Her whole aura is freaking me the fuck out at the moment. She is covered in weapons, imagine a mix of Lara Croft and Her from Resident Evil. The energy she is gives off in waves has sweat pooling on the back of my neck. Her eyes continue to narrow the closer she gets.

"Listen, you little bitch," the leader spits on the ground near her feet. Her eyes track the line of phlegm that lands on the floor. "This fucker killed my daughter!" he roars.

Pretty Bird cocks her head and pops a hip to the side as she studies his face. Laughter bursts out of her like a tsunami as tears roll down her cheeks. Wildly waving her hand around as she stamps her foot, her laughter continues. The guy's expression turns murderous as he moves again, stepping closer to Pretty Bird. She hasn't noticed the change in the atmosphere as she snorts between laughs.

"I.." She starts, getting cut off as another round of laughter tumbles from her lips.

Bang!

My eyes bug out my head, as the sound rings out. All The Lost members drop to the ground, some screaming like little bitches.

"I will deal with you fuckers in a minute," she says to The Lost, throwing daggers at them, daring them to move. When she realizes they won't be, she turns her attention on me.

"You're in trouble, asshole." Her tone is angry, but the undercurrent of hurt is there. "You said we are in this together, no matter what. Then you don't invite me."

"Can we talk about this later?" I plead with her.

"You two won't get a chance to sort your shit out," the fucker says.

As quick as a flash, Pretty Bird is across the distance separating him from us. A blade glints as she slams it through his right shoulder. He screams as he falls to the ground, clutching his wound with the knife still there. The sadistic grin on her face as she looks down at him is terrifying.

"I'm the reason your daughter is dead," she spits, her voice is colder than the air. "I attached her to a chair with my blades. One of them is in your shoulder." She grins again.

His eyes widen as her words sink in. Next thing I know, all hell breaks loose. The Lost have gained a second wind as the crew come to their leader's aid. Shots ring out, along with screams and grunts of pain – it's chaos. Pretty Bird is further away than she was a minute ago, going toe to toe with two of The Lost. I start to make my way over as one of the idiots charges me with a war cry. *Crack*. His nose bursts open as the lights go out behind his eyes and he drops to the ground unconscious.

"Pretty Bird!" The roar fills the air causing nearby birds to fly out of the trees. The more I try to get closer to her, the further away I seem to be. Scanning the area, I realize the battles going on are pushing them further away. My heartbeat becomes erratic. I stop as more people come from behind crates at the far side of the road. They are all making a beeline for her. The anger explodes through me as I tear through the men blocking the path to my woman. Agonized screams fill the air behind me, but I really don't give a shit. My sight is tunnel visioned on her.

I knock a poor guy flying, then suddenly stop in my tracks. My eyes bug out again at the sight before me. Liam has managed to get to Pretty Bird and they are fighting side by side. I'm awestruck at the way they move together as a unit, managing to avoid bumping into each other as they quickly cut through the people surrounding them. Marcus is off to the other side, fighting like a man out to destroy the world. A chuckle bubbles in my throat as some of the men start toward him, but the one look at his murderous expression has them tucking tail and running away. He looks like a demon bathing in blood as he practically tears men apart. My heart swells at the change in him. This is the enforcer everyone fears. Seeing my family work together to cut down the people coming at us, makes my heart swell even more.

"Wait. Wait, please, I know stuff you don't know." My eyes follow the shrill voice, and a laugh bursts out of me as the leader of The Lost slides across the asphalt trying to get away from Pretty Bird. Making my way over, I laugh because he resembles a piece of meat that has just been assaulted by a meat tenderizer. Sliding my arm across Pretty Bird's back, I pull her into my side. The death glare she givesme has me grinning.

"Ow!" The cranky bitch smacks me in the stomach. I double over, pulling air into my lungs the best I can.

"Argggh! Please don't. I-I can help you." He stumbles over his words as Pretty Bird grinds the heel of her boot into the gash on his leg.

"Speak." Her words are filled with venom, as she grinds her heel in more.

"Your dad killed your mom!" he blurts out. Pretty Bird stumbles back at his admission, confusion etched on her features.

"They died together. I saw it," she screams at him, spit flying everywhere.

"Not yours." His eyes leave her and turn to me. "Yours."

My body turns to ice at his words. What the fuck? My skin tingles in places on my arm. I look down to see Pretty Bird running the tips of her fingers up and down my arm, like she's trying to comfort me. The heartbroken look in her eyes guts me even further; she believes what he is saying.

"You're lying," I roar as I reach down and grab his shirt.

I yank him up from the ground so we are nose to nose. The

terror in his face does nothing to dampen the rage running through my veins like molten lava. Someone coughs behind me, turning us both. I find Liam helping Pretty Bird up off the ground, she's rubbing her right ass cheek. Marcus glares at the bastard in my arms. My hand grasping his shirt trembles. Pretty Bird mutters something to Liam whose eyes widen as he looks at this lying motherfucker.

"I'm not lying." Suddenly he is yanked out of my grasp by Marcus, who looks about a second away from boiling him alive.

"About what?" The words slip through his gritted teeth.

"Your-Your dad killed your mom," the sniveling little shit blurts out again.

"Why?" Pretty Bird asks as she comes to stand next to me. Twining her fingers with mine, I feel my veins start to thaw slightly and I start feeling guilty for hurting her.

"She was going to meet your dad. Malcolm found out she was going to run with you boys, so he had her killed." I'm assaulted with the memory of my mom telling me she will be back soon to take us away from this life.

A roar builds in me, I know his words are true as I replay that memory on repeat in my head. "What the fuck?!"

Reika shouts at the side of me. My vision comes back, and I see the leader of The Lost with a bullet hole through his forehead. Marcus has blood splattered all over his face as the man is limp in his grip.

"Sniper!" one of the other crew members shouts. We all split off in different directions to take cover as shots start.

68

FANCY PANTS

"Is it done?" I spit into the phone at my ear.

"It is, sir." The voice crackles through his end of the phone. "Dexter is dead. He told them about Malcolm killing his wife. I exterminated him before he could say anymore."

I hit the end call button on my phone, then pace back and forth in my office. I knew the fuckwad would fuck it up. He was meant to kill the Southbourne's and bring Reika back to me. Everything I want is within my grasp, but I can't get the final nails in their coffins until she is back by my side. The office door squeaks as it opens.

"You are taking too long to deal with this situation, son." My father's voice has the hairs on the back of my neck standing on end.

"I know, Father." My voice sounds like the broken little boy I once was.

"Do. Not. Fail. Me."

I don't even get a chance to reply to him as he shuts the door, leaving me alone with my thoughts in the silent room. Stamping down my mixed emotions, I remove my cufflinks and place them down on the desk. Slowly rolling the cuffs back so my sleeves are above my elbows, I take a deep inhale to center myself.

"Time to find out how useful Malcolm is going to be," I say out in the open.

69

REIKA

My heart bleeds for the brothers who all stare at each other like their world has just ended. It kinda has as they have just found out their dad was responsible for their mother's . *How could you do that someone you love?* I agree with my inner voice, I can't understand it. My parents would have never done anything like that, they lived and breathed for each other. Emotions mix inside me like they're in a blender. Things with me and Kane are awkward; I'm still pissed at him for leaving me behind. But I love the guy so much. If he was ever taken from me, I would walk through hell and back to find him. Not just him, but his brothers too. We are a team, we will always have each other's backs, and they need me to help them through this.

"Guys." I feel bad breaking the silence, but my teeth are starting to chatter from the cold.

"We need to leave." I try again.

None of them utter a word as they shuffle through the bodies on the ground. The crew that are left fall in to step behind us. A few have superficial wounds from what I can see, but there are a couple who have to be carried back to the vehicles. No one speaks, or even cracks a joke as they can feel how unstable this situation is; honestly, I am glad. One of them on their own would be hard to stop, but all three brothers together is a massive death toll waiting to happen. I watch as they all climb into the vans and the injured are put in too, spinning on my heels I start to head back to where I stashed my bike.

"Where are you going?" Kane voices in a deep rumble.

"I'm not leaving my baby here." His eyes narrow as he takes a step toward me. A smile tugs at my lips. Even in a state of shock he's still a possessive asshole. "Chill, dude. My bike is here and I'm not leaving her behind."

He ponders my words for a second, then he's striding over to me. Looking around him, I see Cheshire and Frosty shaking their heads with slight smiles on their faces. Frosty mouths to me 'make him ride bitch', then smiles wider as he climbs into the front seat of the van. Kane cocks his eyebrow at me in a silent question, and I just shake my head at him, turning and heading off to where my baby is.

Thankfully, everyone was so preoccupied with the shit going down they didn't hear me, because she is a loud, throaty bitch. That is the best damn thing about her, she constantly sounds angry. We round the corner. Kane lets out a whistle as he looks over the beauty. I swing my leg over and wait. His eyes widen when he sees where I am sitting. Cocking his head at me, he just stares. I flick my gaze from him to the bitch seat behind me and his body stiffens even more in surprise. I chuckle at the expression on his face. For five whole minutes the stare off continues between us. Turning her on, the engine rumbles to life underneath me, and I let out a breath of air. I love being on this bike so damn much. The power underneath me is next to none. Well, second best. I'm looking at my other favorite place I love to sit. He takes a step which swallows up the distance between us as he stares down at me. I lift my eyebrow at him. His hands land on my hips in a firm grip that does all sorts of weird things to me.

"Hey!" My protest sounds false, even to my ears, as he slides me into the bitch seat and swings his leg over.

It feels so weird being on the back of my own bike but seeing Kane on it has my hormones doing a happy dance. He looks like it was made for him. I'm so lost in my own thoughts, the brush of hands on mine scares the shit out of me. With a squeak, I realize he is pulling my hands into position. I chuckle at myself for being an idiot, my hands now rest against his abs with my cheek on his back. His body is still tense, anger rolls off him in waves. The t-shirt under my hands pisses me off. I think we both need more of a connection. Sliding my hands down and under I move them back to rest on his abs, skin on skin. At my touch, his body relaxes and the angry energy starts to subside. I hold a little tighter as he tears out of our hiding spot, with a bellow of easy laughter.

The wind is crazy as we head back to the house. Luckily, I am shielded from the impact of the cold air by the mountain of a man in front of me. I know he is getting the brunt of it as he shivers slightly under my touch, but he continues to push her faster. I snuggle closer to his warm body as the lights of the town speed past us; my ass is starting to go numb. I don't know how long we have been travelling for, but I look around and realize we are nowhere near the house. He hasn't said a word since we left the district, but I know he needs the silence. We carry on riding around for another twenty minutes when a house comes into view.

All the vans are outside with some of the crew members still milling about or just chilling around the fire pits. The ones sitting stand to their feet or come over to us. They do the weird manly fist bump thing to Kane and give a nod to me. Frosty is standing on the porch staring at us both, his expression grim.

"Frosty?" My voice is uncertain, the look on his face is not very welcoming at all.

"It's Bonzo." His voice sounds hollow. Kane looks to me, like he is praying for it to be a prank, and my heart stutters for him..

We make our way inside and screams can be heard from the main room. That puts a fire under our asses as we charge down the hall to the room Doc uses for injuries. Kane throws the door open so hard it bangs against the wall, scaring the shit out of Doc in the process. Bonzo is laid out on a trolley screaming like a man possessed, while Cheshire and a few of the other crew members hold him down for Doc to examine him.

"For fuck's sake, man. Stay still," Cheshire shouts down at the Bonzo.

"He's got multiple gunshot wounds," Doc says while trying to avoid the arms around legs being thrown around. "I need to see if he has any exit wounds."

Kane rushes forward to help his brother and crew hold Bonzo. I stand frozen in my spot, watching as blood pours everywhere. It's like something out of a horror show. He's covered in blood and his wails are absolute agony. With Kane helping, they manage to turn him on his side. My eyes bug out of my head at all the little wounds on his back from where the bullets have left his body. Suddenly all hell breaks loose as choked gasps fill the room. They lay Bonzo flat on his back again as he frantically tries to pull air into his lungs. *He was screaming just a second ago!* Doc starts to rush around the room picking up different items, but my eyes are glued to the

Bonzo's lips that are turning blue. The machine he is hooked beeps erratically, then suddenly stops.

Silence fills the room at the long beep of the flatline, telling everyone he is gone. Confusion renders me speechless. How could he go from screaming to nothing? Something crashes to the floor; all eyes turn to Doc who has dropped everything. His expression defeated as his gaze drops to the ground. Some eyes in the room look to Kane while the other's look at me. My body is frozen in my spot as the horror of someone else dying leaves me speechless. All I ever seem to see is death or destruction it's as if it follows me everywhere I go, like I attract it into my life without trying.

"This isn't your fault, Gizmo." The words are a whispered presence from the other brother standing at my side.

"It doesn't feel like that, Frosty." My gaze drops to my feet as I twist my toes into the carpet. "Everywhere I go death seems to follow me." Am I going to be the reason why they die too?

"You're wrong, Baby." The deep baritone of Kane's voice sends a shiver down my spine.

He tilts my chin up, so he can look into my eyes. "You are everything we ever needed to make us whole." I can see in his eyes how much he means those words. It has the opposite effect though, making me feel like an asshole. He is comforting me again when he just found out a shitty truth about his family and his friend just died.

"You don't need to worry about me, Babe. I'm more worried about you guys after everything that has happened tonight," I say to them all, trying to hide how I really feel.

"I think we all knew my dad had something to do with her death, Hellion," Cheshire says as he steps around the trolley to look at me. "Now it has just been confirmed."

The other two nod their heads in agreement with his words.

My heart splits a little further for them, knowing that one parent is responsible for you losing the other has to be a kick in the teeth. My mind works over how everything played out and my gut is telling me it's all too much of a coincidence that they were ambushed like that. How did they know they were going to be there? Who the fuck are The Lost? My brows furrows as my brain tries to piece everything together.

"What's wrong, Pretty Bird?" Kane asks me as he runs his hand up and down my arm.

"Something doesn't feel right." The words blurt out of my mouth.

The guys' eyes widen at the admission, and the crew's heads shoot to look at me. My brain continues to try and make sense of everything as my father's words echo in my head, *'Always trust your gut little reaper. It will never lead you astray.'* My mind jolts to the others as the words play on repeat.

"Has anyone found Paine or Pete yet?" The words fall out of my mouth without me having to think about them.

Just the mention of my cousin's name has the tug in my gut pulling a little harder. The brothers look at me with confusion. "Something isn't right. They knew you would be there. It was an ambush."

Sharp intakes of air fill the rooms with a hiss. I see on everyone's faces that they are thinking about what happened at the district.

"Shit, you're right," Frosty spits between gritted teeth.

"Kane?" My eyes connect with his. "Paine wouldn't drop off the face of the earth like this," I mutter as I twist my fingers together. "Something's wrong."

Kane nods to Frosty, who spins around and strides out of the room calling for a few crew members as he goes.

"Don't panic, Baby. We will find him." His words are a promise which I really hope he can keep.

. . .

Kane

I know Pretty Bird has been worrying about her cousin since he disappeared, and my gut tells me she has every reason to. Thinking back over that shit show, my baby is right. We walked right into a damn ambush. The whore house was empty and the streets outside were deserted. When she says something isn't right with her cousin dropping off the face of the earth, I know she's right. That's why I sent Liam off to go searching for him and Pete. I would normally ask Fox for something like this, but he has a lot of things to do before he steps foot back here. The main one is finding my fuck face of a father. I want to find him even more now after The Lost's leader spilled his guts.

"Fuck it." An idea forms in my mind, we have all been so wired lately we are functioning just for the sake of it. "Everyone get ready, we are heading to The Den."

A round of whoops fill the air from everyone. Even Doc joins in, which is a surprise. We can grieve for our fallen member, but also celebrate his life. A conversation we once had filters into my mind; he told me if he dies, he wants it to be on a mission he for the crew. The crew heads off to get ready, shouting to the others about tonight's plans. Even Marcus has a shit eating grin on his face. Pretty Bird bounces on the balls of her feet at my side of me like the damn Energizer Bunny.

Fifteen minutes later, me and my brothers wait at the bottom of the stairs for Pretty Bird, the others have gone on ahead. Liam is getting restless and muttering about her taking too long because he wants to get laid tonight. Marcus just laughs at his twin's antics. Then their eyes bug out of their heads. I turn to see what has them speechless and my dick grows instantly hard at the sight of my baby in a pair of leather pants and a Rasmus t-shirt. Her hair falls in waves past her chest and there isn't a lick of makeup on her face. She is fucking gorgeous.

"You lucky motherfucking bastard," Liam mutters, instantly followed by an 'ouch.' Looking over my shoulder I notice Marcus laughing, which tells me he has just given him a dig.

She grins at me as she closes the distance between us. My mind instantly starts thinking up excuses to get out of having to go to The Den tonight, so I can peel those pants off her and fuck her until the sun rises.

"Don't even think about it, fuck face." She grins at me as she walks toward the door.

"What?" The words are a little high pitched for me. Both my brothers burst out laughing.

"We haven't partied together," she says as her hips sway in a hypnotic way, drawing my eyes to her ass. "Let's have some fun." She winks.

That woman is going to be the fucking death of me. It was a matter of minutes from us getting into the car, to us pulling up outside The Den. I'm surprised we made it in one piece because Liam drove like a fucking lunatic. Pretty Bird laughed like his driving was the funniest thing ever, while me and Marcus screamed at the psycho to slow the fuck down. We all climb out and I intertwine mine and my girl's fingers. Both of my brothers' grin at me, with a shake of their head. My possessiveness has ramped up to a whole new level, because as soon as she climbed out of the car, I noticed a lot of eyes staring at her.

"Come on, guys." Her excitement fills the air as she breaks our hands and strides toward the doors.

Eyes follow her, causing a growl to rumble in my chest. My

brothers take it upon themselves to deck a few in the line that look for too long. The message hits home as I gnash my teeth to a few more, making them shrink away in fear. The thump of the music vibrates the ground. I get so close to my woman we are practically glued together. Her hips sway in time to the music rubbing against my cock as we walk through the club to the member's area. Most of the crew are already there laughing and shouting at each other. Pretty Bird continues her dance as I flop into a chair and watch hypnotized as her hips sway from side to side.

"Dude, have you seen how much attention you're getting?" one of the members whispers in my ear. I shove him away and keep watching my baby as my dick continues to swell.

Drink in hand, I laugh with my brothers and crew and the tension starts to leave my body. Pretty Bird is in my lap, tormenting the life out of Marcus and Liam, who falls off his chair laughing at her. Contentment fills me as the people I care most about all get on like the have always known each other.

"Hey, Kane."

My eyes look for the owner of the voice. I'm surprised to see a petite blonde in a black dress staring at me with gooey eyes. I cock my head to the side - she seems familiar, but I don't know where I know her from. The heaviness in my lap shifts as Pretty Bird notices the new addition. She flicks her gaze between me and the blonde, flicks her hair over her shoulder and continues to talk to my brothers. The whole area has gone deathly silent. My brothers have an 'oh shit' expression on their faces.

"So, Kane, is she your girlfriend, girlfriend, or are you just talking?" the blonde says in a sickly-sweet tone while twirling a strand of hair.

A few of the crew members slide their chairs further back, as Pretty Bird turns her attention to the woman. Ever so slowly, she turns to me and kisses me with so much possessiveness my inner beast rumbles. Climbing to her feet she turns to the woman, so they are nose to nose.

"Bitch. If I kill you, are you dead, dead or just not breathing?" Her tone has a dangerous undercurrent.

A round of 'oh' fills the area, as the crew hears what my baby just said. Liam chokes on a mouthful of his drink, while Marcus falls off his chair laughing. The blonde tries to look around Pretty Bird, who clicks her fingers in front of her face to bring her attention back to her.

"What the fuck are you looking at him for?" The words have a deeper snarl.

"Well. I. Um…" the blonde stutters her words.

"Answer the question." The sadistic grin on her face as she looks over her shoulder at me has me throwing my drink back.

"Stay the fuck away from my man, bitch." She steps closer to the blonde who falls over one of the crew members legs. "Or your family won't be attending a funeral, since there won't be a body to bury."

The blonde scrambles backward, away from Pretty Bird. Some of the crew stand behind her as she stalks her prey. Managing to get her feet under her, the blonde takes off and knocks some of the other customers out of the way to put distance between them. Pretty Bird bursts out laughing, and the crew members all join in with her. Then she turns to me with a wicked look in her eyes. Climbing to my feet, I grab her wrist and yank her close. She grins as she hits my chest. I slide my hands down her back and grip her ass hard. A slight moan slips between her lips. Lifting her up, she wraps her legs around my waist and starts kissing the side of my neck causing the rumble from earlier to come back. Moving my head slightly, our lips connect in a deeply powerful kiss. Without breaking the connection, I stride toward the door.

"Fuck her brains out, Bro!" one of my brothers shouts.

"Don't break anything!" someone else shouts as the crew all break out into whoops and laughter, shouting abuse behind us.

Our lips are still connected as the cool night air hits us. A shiver runs across her body causing her to grind further down on my cock.

I break our lips with a thwack. "Fuck, babe, you're gonna make me come."

"That's the point, baby," she rumbles back at me.

70

REIKA

Lust roars through me as Kane carries me back to the car. My body is alight with heat and anger at the audacity of the bitch who dared ask if I was his girlfriend. Bitch is lucky I didn't skin her alive for that fucking comment. The click of the car door opening has excitement running through my veins as he places me into the seat. I watch mesmerized as he rounds the hood of the car, my clit throbbing between my legs. The driver's door clicks open, then slams shut as Kane turns the ignition and hits the gas. I jump out of my skin as his hand lands on my thigh. He flicks his gaze to me, and my breath catches in my throat. His hand slides across my thigh toward my clit, causing a moan to slip past my lips. He hasn't even touched me yet.

His thumb presses against the outside of my leather pants. Because of how tight they are, it sends a shockwave straight through my clit. My legs spread wider of their own accord and the grin on his face sends another round of lust firing through my body. He presses his thumb even harder on my clit, rubbing small circles that send bolts of lightning all through my body.

"Put your foot down, dickhead," I snarl at the bastard.

"All in good time, Baby," he purrs at me with a wicked grin.

Fuck this shit! My inner bitch snarls, giving me the perfect idea. Lifting my hips, I flick the button on my pants and slide them down my legs. I hear his gulp as I sit back on my seat, the cold leather against my ass giving me some relief from the burning inferno of my skin. I grin at him as I run my hand across his jeans to his button and undo them in a second. It drives a surprised hiss out of him, making my grin widen as I push my hand into his boxers, firmly taking his cock in my hand. A gasp escapes past his lips as I grin at him, while he narrows his eyes at me. I grin even more as I slide my grip to the base of his cock and back up again, running my tip of my thumb over the head. I feel the bead of pre-cum on the tip and my mouth starts to water.

"You wanna play, Baby?" he growls, making another shiver run through me. A challenge is there. With a wicked grin of my own, I rub the bead of pre-cum around the head and slide my hand down and up, jerking him off as he drives.

The rumble starts in his chest bringing a grin to my face. This huge man become putty in my grasp has a weird sense of satisfaction flashing in my chest. My body freezes as sparks light up my skin. I follow the internal trail to the source and watch mesmerized as Kane rubs firm circles against my clit. My eyes dart to his, and I melt a little further as he grins and gives me a wink. I narrow my eyes in another challenge. He seems all for it. A deep moan passes my lips as my pussy feels full, in a good way. The vicious cycle continues for too long, him pumping his fingers in and out while I jerk him off. The car is full of our joined moans. I feel the tell-tale sparks of an orgasm building as my veins become electrified. He presses his thumb hard against my clit as he continues to torment me in the most delicious way. The atmosphere is super charged, his moans grow deeper telling me he is on his way to coming too. We both speed up our hands, as if it is a race to get the other to come first. Bolts of lust fire off around me again, as his fingers hit the spot I need them to. The grin on his face pisses me off, but my moans tell a different story. Crooking his fingers, he puts more pressure on my bundle of nerves, making me nearly jump off the seat with the power of my orgasm building. Our eyes meet as a superior expression slides across his face, with a grin to match. I react without thinking. Leaning to the side, I swallow his cock in one go. The head pushes past my tonsils. This new angle causes his fingers to hit at a differently, pulling a deep moan out of me that vibrates in my throat. He blows instantly, hot ropes of cum hitting my throat. My head explodes as the mother of all orgasms tears through me. White lights burst behind my eyes. My body shakes violently from the power of it, pulling another moan out of Kane. The orgasmic aftershocks fire off for God knows how long, leaving me in a state of bliss. A screeching sound penetrates my ears as I'm thrown to the side.

"What the fuck?!" I screech, bracing myself for the impact.

Kane grabs the side of my head, so his hand connects with the dash as the car slams to a halt. My brain is still fuzzy from the amazing orgasm I have just had. Lifting myself up so I'm sitting back in my seat. Kane's chest rises and falls rapidly, his eyes glued to my face. The look in his eyes has my pussy growing wetter by the second. A growl rumbles in his chest. Steam covers the windows from our previous actions. I run my tongue across the seam of my lips to give them a little moisture. His eyes track the movement. Suddenly his seat is pushed back as far as it will go and he's pulling me over the center console. My back is flat against his chest, my legs in between his. As he widens them as far as they will go, the deep rumble vibrating my back has my pussy twitching again.

"Naughty birdy," he purrs in my ear, making me shiver. He swipes his tongue up the outer edge of my ear and then nips my lobe causing me to moan again.

"Kane?" The sound is breathless, barely a whisper, begging with him to fill the ache.

"Lean forward and grab me the black box out of the compartment," he commands, and my mind has me complying without a second thought. Pulling out the box, I pass it over my shoulder to him, I try to crane my neck as far as I can to see what he's up too.

"Eyes front, Baby," he snaps out.

Ughh! My pussy is throbbing. My body is on fire, and if he doesn't fuck me soon I'll do it my damn self. Something squelches behind me, and I try to look over my shoulder again.

"I told you. Eyes front." A crack fills the air as my thigh tingles from the slap he just gave me. My lust turns molten lava. Feather light kisses trail down my neck, forcing me to drop my head to the side and back so I'm resting it near his shoulder.

"Do you trust me, Pretty Bird?" he asks as one of his hands makes a line all the way down my stomach to the junction of my thighs.

Slowly he starts to circle my clit again.

"Hmmm," hums out of me in agreement, wanting him to continue what he is doing.

"Lean forward. Hands as close to the windshield as possible," he commands.

I do as he asks lifting myself the best I can, sliding my hands on either side of the steering wheel to get as close to the windshield as possible.

"Show me your ass, Baby." Excitement coils inside me at the thought of him going to town on me with his tongue. He's an absolute God with that thing.

Pushing my ass out as far as I can get it, I wait. My body thrums in anticipation. My pussy gets even wetter at the animalistic growl that fills the car. That sound is a promise of what's to come, and I can't fucking wait for it. A pressure pushes against my ass, causing me to jump forward and hit my head on the windshield. Looking over my shoulder, Kane is looking at me with a huge grin. I know what he's planning, but I trust him to do this. Relaxing myself, the pressure starts again. "That's it, Baby. Relax, it will be worth it. Trust me."

It doesn't hurt as much as I thought it would, but it does feel weird. With a final inhale, a moan tears from me as my ass feels so full my brain starts to go foggy. Pulling me back down into his lap with his hand, I look up to him. He smiles down at me with so much love a lump fills my throat. I have never had anything like this before, and I know I never want to let it go. But…

"You going all gooey on me now, or do you want to fuck me?" I grin as my words hit him, getting the reaction I want.

His eyes darken to the point they look like obsidian stones and the look is pure sex. He lifts me slightly and slams me down on his cock, impaling me in one go. The scream tears out of me before I can stop it. My body shakes as my inner walls tremble. I'm so fucking full. What the actual fuck?!

"I did tell you I would fuck your ass one day, Baby Girl." The triumph in his voice does weird things to me. "We are starting the process."

"What?" The words barely leave my throat.

My eyes widen as a tug on both my breasts makes me look down. I watch stunned as he pulls my nipples sending another shot of pleasure to my clit. He rumbles against my ear, that half a growl then a laugh. Suddenly my ass starts to vibrate. "Butt plugs are the best invention ever, Baby Girl," he whispers in my ear.

The feeling is foreign, but it has little bolts of electricity zapping through my veins. Kane starts to move slowly in and out, he is so slow I decide to take what I want. Adjusting myself into the right position, he follows me up so our bodies haven't broken the connection between my back and his chest. I slam myself down on his cock, forcing a grunt out of him. My lips twitch in triumph as I continue to lift and slam myself home.

"You wanna play, Baby?"

I don't even get a chance to answer as the plug kicks up its vibrating to an earth-shattering level, a guttural moan leaves my lips as Kane pounds into me with brutal force. This is pure madness; the car is rocking and the windows are steamed up. I slam down on his cock as he thrusts up. Our grunts and groans join into a chorus, everything firing on all cylinders waiting for the moment to go super nova. My breath hitches as Kane wraps his hand around my throat, squeezing just enough to make breathing difficult. He continues to pound into me like a wild animal. My brain is fried as the fullness of my pussy and ass drives me wild. Tears leak from the corner of my eyes as breathing becomes too difficult from the pressure. Releasing his grip, I suck in huge gulps of air before his hand comes back into position. We are both chasing our climax as the car continues to rock. The horn even blares every now and then. The burn from the assault on my pussy is fucking glorious. Kane fucks me with such brutality I just hold on, my palm slaps against the windshield to keep me steady and the leverage I need to slam down to meet him thrust for thrust.

"Fuck. Me. Baby." The words fall from my lips like a chant.

White light explodes as my scream fills the car, making my throat raw. Kane isn't happy with that as his pounding picks up to a whole new level. My walls clamp down so hard on his cock, I don't know how he can still move. My clit throbs in time with my walls, stars dancing behind my eyes as darkness creeps in at the sides. An animalistic roar fills my ears as my head is yanked back. Making another orgasm tear through me. The darkness creeps in further as my orgasm releases from my body.

"I knew you could squirt." The pride in his voice lulls me further into the darkness. First time that has ever happened!

Kane

My mind is focused on the absolute carnage of the car. Pretty Bird squirted all over the damn place, I'm covered and my hands are dripping. I lean over to nuzzle into her neck and my hand leaves wet prints on the dash. My dick rises to attention again, and I have to mind slap the fucker down her soft snores fill the car. Fuck me that was intense. Our bodies as still joined as Pretty Bird sleeps on my chest. I really don't want to have to disturb her, but we need to get back to the house. I need to catch one of the crew to clean the car before Liam finds out, or he will lose his shit. That alone has a snort leaving me, breaking the connection between us.

I pull her underwear back into place, adjusting us both so I can wiggle her pants back up into position. Her heads lolls on my shoulder, in the deepest sleep I have ever seen. Finally, after the struggle of pulling her pants back into place while not disturbing her, I open my door and slide myself out. My dick flaps out in the open, but I really don't give a shit. Pretty Bird gets herself comfy in the driver's seat while I pull my boxers and jeans back into place. I lift her into my arms and walk around the car. As stealthy as I can, I open the door and slide her into the passenger seat once again. With a quick kiss to her forehead, I shut the door and round the hood. Just as I'm climbing back in, a twig breaks in the shadows of the trees along the road. I strain my hearing waiting for another sound, but nothing comes. Brushing it off, I climb in and hit the gas to head home.

71

MALCOLM

Agonizing pain roars across my cheek, as the brute punches me again, forcing my head to the side. I'm pretty sure my bone shattered that time.

"Are you going to tell me what I need to know?" The nasally voice of the little fuck really grates on my damn nerves.

"Fuck you!" I spit a clump of blood at his feet. Making him step back with a disgusted look on his face.

Another smack is delivered to my already busted cheek. I'm not sure how long has passed since I was found in the office, but I don't give a shit. The fucker is asking me questions about my sons. I don't give a fuck what happens to the bitch, but he will not harm my sons in any way. I know they hate me, their love for the girl blinding them, but everything I have done is for them.

"Which one of them is the easiest target?" he seethes at me.

I just smile up at the bastard, as I show all my teeth that are left. He won't get a fucking word out of me. Annoyance flickers across his features as he nods to his goon again, who laying into me wildly. I try to keep quiet, but my body is just one massive bruise. I feel fresh parts of my skin break open under the assault forcing grunts of pain to escape my lips. The bastard's eyes widen with joy as he realizes how much pain I'm in. A phone rings somewhere nearby, and the tone hurts my ears.

"What!" the shithead barks into the phone.

Silence, he doesn't say a word as he listens to whatever is being said. I can tell whatever it is pisses him off as he growls throughout the call. The conversation seems to go on forever, making him pace.

"Show me!"

The room grows silent, and the brute stops his attack on my broken body for the moment. My breathing is labored, I'm pretty sure he broke some of my ribs. I try my hardest to do a run through of the injuries I could possibly have. Grunts and groans fill the air. Peeling my eyes open the sight that greets me has laughter bubbling up in my chest. The fucker watches a video on the tv with a murderous expression, clearly it has been filmed with a special lens. I squint to see what's happening, and the laughter that was bubbling up bursts out of my mouth as the bastard grinds his teeth.

"She's mine!" he roars to the screen, spinning around launching a glass at the wall.

My laughter becomes hysterical as I watch the shit show unfold. The grunts and moans on the screen grow in intensity, making his mood even worse. His eyes bulge out of his head as he torments himself further.

"What the fuck do you find so funny?" he spits at me through gritted teeth.

"You really think you are going to come between that? They're fucking like rabbits." Laughter follows my words at the ridiculousness of this whole thing. He had her in his grasp, and she still wouldn't entertain him for anything.

"Your son will die for touching what is mine," he seethes.

I pull myself up a little further in my chains so I can look this bastard in the eye. I know his reaction is going to be painful, but it will be so fucking worth it.

"My son will kill you for watching that." I laugh in his face. "Or maybe she will. Whichever happens is a bonus for me seeing as you get torn to pieces."

Another blow to the head, this time it has the darkness taking hold. I allow it to pull me under with a wicked grin on my lips.

72

KANE

The house is quiet as we pull up. Pretty Bird is still snoring in the passenger seat and if I'm honest, it's the cutest thing I have ever seen. The whole situation bliss swirling in my chest. *Can't we just stay like this a bit?* Unfortunately, fate has a way of smacking me in the face, and one of the grunts comes flying over to the car.

"Boss, there's an issue." His voice is so panicked he shouts the damn words at me, causing Pretty Bird to stir in her seat.

"Shut the fuck up, man," I hiss at him as I flick my gaze to the sleeping beauty at my side.

Luckily, he realizes his mistake and quiets down. Climbing out, I head to her side and slide her out of the door the grunt opens for me. She doesn't even flinch being in my arms, just snuggles closer so her head rests in the crook of my neck. Her feather light breaths tickle my neck as her breathing becomes deeper again.

"I need you to clean Liam's car," I whisper to him.

With a nod in acknowledgement, I head off to the house to put my baby to bed and find out what the fuck is going on. I manage to get into the house and to the room without anyone else causing a hitch. Gently, I place Pretty Bird down on our bed and peel her leather pants off her. Leaving her in just her top and underwear I pull the comforter over her and head off in search of answers. Some of the crew are in the meeting room when I finally track them down fifteen minutes later.

"What the fuck is going on?" I ask the room.

Some of the crew look to the floor while others divert the attention completely, which pisses me off instantly.

"This was on the door when we got back," Liam says as he steps into the center of the room.

He passes me a picture and my eyes bug out of my head at the image that is staring back at me. Pretty Bird is on the ground outside the lake house with Mel's body in her lap. The picture is so close you can see the heartbreak on her face while I try to comfort her.

"How is this shit possible?" My anger becomes palpable; I can taste it in the air.

"We don't know." Liam eyes drop to something on the picture. "Look at the note, Kane."

Following his line of sight, my eyes are greeted with the same writing from the previous picture. *'He will always destroy what is closest to you, Little Reaper. Run as far and fast as you can. Dad.'*

"We can't tell her about this." My words sound hollow to my own ears, but we all know what happened at the ring when she found the previous picture.

"Some bastard is stalking my Pretty Bird and playing games using her dead father. I don't know if it's to break her or to make her unhinged. After the last one she found, they succeeded in their task." My brothers and the crew all nod their agreement. My brain runs at a furious rate trying to work it out if this is someone's idea of a sick game, or if they have ulterior motives.

"She can't be left alone," I say to the room. All eyes lift to me. "She has to be watched around the clock. I don't know what this fucker wants."

Yes, fills the room in reply. I know she is going to lose her shit when she finds out, but that is something I am willing to risk for her to be kept safe.

"You know she will kill us if she finds out," Marcus says.

"What other option do we have?" I say to them both, as quietly as possible. "I have to keep her safe."

"Dismissed," Liam barks out the order to the room. All the members there scramble to follow the command.

"Jason?" I say to one of the inner circle.

"Any news on Paine and Pete yet?" I ask, only hoping a little for some good news for her.

His head lowers as he avoids my gaze. "No, Boss." The words echo like a gong in my head. The pull in my gut happens again at the admission. I think she is right. Everything that is happening is too much of a coincidence.

I wait until all the members depart from the room so my brothers and I can talk freely. There have been too many snakes in the grass for my liking. My brothers must agree with me as no one else speaks as we watch them file out.

"What you think is going on, Bro?" Marcus asks with uncertainty.

"I don't know. But I'm beginning to think Pretty Bird is right," I say to them both.

"She's too observant for her own good, Kane," Liam says to me.

What he says is true, but it has also helped her in more ways than one throughout the years and saved her ass on many occasions. My mind works out everything I need to do before I even realize it. It's like a damn lightbulb goes off in my head.

"She needs me to be the person I was," I say to them both. Their eyes widen at my admission.

"You mean?" Marcus says.

"She needs the soulless." The words echo around the room, like doom itself is here.

"She doesn't need one," Liam says to us. "She needs three."

"Agree?" I say to them.

"Agree," they echo back. We all stare at each other as sadistic grins fill our faces.

Reika

Laughter fills the room, which confuses the fucking life out of me. The people surrounding me all have blurry faces, so I can't tell who's who. One laugh echoes louder than the others, which freezes me in my spot. My heart splits in two as the sound fills my heart dread. I can't seem to stop myself as I follow the sound. Mel is standing at the back of the room with a few people; her face is the only one that isn't blurred.

"Ry!" she screams as she charges toward me, throwing herself at me.

Tears drip from my eyes as I cling to my best friend, my family, for dear life. I don't understand. She isn't here anymore, so why am I able to touch her like she is here right in front of me.

"Shh, Ry. Don't cry," she coos at me.

"M-Mel." The words sound so broken.

"You're dreaming, babe. But it's ok. I am here for you," she says in the 'everything is fine' way she used to do.

My heart stutters at the words. This is a dream. If that's true, I don't ever want to wake up. I wouldn't have to be without her and nothing would be different, just like it was before.

"I know what you're thinking. It wasn't your fault, babe. Everything became too much for me to bear." A smile tugs at the side of her lip even as a couple of tears run down her cheeks.

"I'm sorry I didn't get to you in time." My words are a broken sob. Tears fall like tiny rivers down my cheeks as I admit to one of my closest friends that I failed her. Admitting that to her and to myself opens the flood gates I have been keeping locked all this time. The tears now freely fall down my face as I sob to the one person I would give anything to see again.

"You didn't fail me, Ry." She tries to soothe me with her words, but they don't help.

"I did," is all I manage in response.

"Look at me!" she snaps, tugging at my face so our eyes lock. "You didn't fail me, because you didn't know who had me. I know if you had, the bad bitch I know you are would have burst through those doors and pulled my ass out of there," she says to me with conviction.

"You are not to blame for what you didn't know. But Ry. I need you to be the baddest bitch ever for what is about to come." Sadness fills her eyes at her words.

"What do you mean?" Confusion layers my voice.

"I need you to rain hellfire on all their asses, babe." She grins at me as she steps further away.

"Wait!" The word is pleading; I don't want her to leave me.

"You have everything you need, Ry. Use him, use them. They would scorch the world to ashes for you, babe."

The words echo as the room starts to stutter out and fade to black. I rush forward trying to get to my best friend who is moving further away into the darkness. She smiles at me. The room fades into nothing. It's just a black empty void.

. . .

I shoot up in the bed, my clothes stuck to me with sweat as tears fall down my face. It felt so real. My heart breaks as the room comes into focus and I find myself in our bedroom with a sleeping giant to the side of me. My heart pounds as remnants of the dream still play in my head. With my head in my hands, I sob at the painful feeling of dreaming of Mel. The pain of my failings are always there, and I hate myself for it every day. I haven't had a chance to deal with anything to do with Mel. Then losing Tom because of everything that followed, my pain is still so raw. Climbing out of bed, I throw my clothes on, and tip toe out of the room. Thankfully, I get out without waking Kane. I head down the hallway to the stairs, trying to keep my steps as quiet as I can. I listen for anyone who might still be awake. The house is silent as I descend the stairs and make it to the main hallway. I wrack my brain figuring out where I can go just for a little me time, when it hits me. I have the perfect place. Quickly pulling my boots on, I head toward the door and then stop. If I leave, he will lose his shit. Rushing to the kitchen I yank open the drawer that has a stash of paper and a pen, and frantically scribble a note.

Babe

Don't lose your shit, but I needed to take some time to myself. I will be safe, so don't have to have a heart attack over it. I've got my phone with me so will check in ok!

Love ya .

R xx

I stuff my phone in my pocket. Luckily, I picked up my joggers and not the leather pants. There is a bowl full of keys on the side table. I grab the top set of keys and head out. Hitting unlock on the fob, the lights on Liam's Land Rover flash at me as it beeps. My grin is infectious; this is perfect to get me to the place I need to go. I take time to admire his car. Its black paint works with the black wheels. I open the door to find the interior is exactly the same, black on black. I chuckle to myself as I haul my ass up and into the driver's seat. The size difference between me and the guys slaps me in the face as I have to pull the seat quickly forward to be able to reach anything. Turning the ignition, I throw it into reverse and head onto the road. My dream has seriously messed with me. The first place I need to go is where I have been meaning to for a while, but haven't had a chance.

Twenty long ass minutes later, I watch as the sun starts to shine over the horizon. The red and orange colors blending together has me feeling a little lighter than I did when I first woke up. Finally, the gates to the cemetery come into view. I sit there with the car in park as I stare at the words over the gate. With a deep breath I put my foot back on the gas and brace myself for my emotions as I pass through the gates. Mel's plot is at the back of the grounds. The guys paid for it and Tom helped with the planning of her funeral, because I was so out of it. My mind wanders as I throw the car into park and just sit and stare at her plot. My hands shake on the wheel as I look out to the place my friend is buried. I know she's probably looking down on me right now, screaming at me to stop being a pussy and get out of the car. I chuckle at the thought.

Finally deciding to pull on my big girl panties, I step out. I don't know what I was expecting to find here, but the sense of calm I found wasn't one of them. Her headstone is something she would have been proud of with a picture of her laughing. Tom must have picked it out. Thoughts of the other friend I lost through all this has me feeling sad. We were always so close. Losing Mel hit him just as hard as it hit me. I know he was hurting, but all the cruel words he spat at me at the funeral has my heart growing heavy again. She would have slapped the shit out of him if she heard him speaking to me like that, or me if the tables had been turned and I was the one so angry.

"Hey, sweetie," I mutter to the headstone.

Someone has been here recently because her favorite flowers lay on the ground in a fancy bouquet. The girl went nuts over roses, lilies and orchids. Her obsession with them was so bad, she would buy herself flowers to treat herself, then bitch to whoever she was seeing at the time that they never bought her any and she wanted them.

"Ry?" Hearing my nickname has my heart stuttering. It's your imagination Reika!

"Ry. Is that you?" I close my eyes as an onslaught of emotion tears through me. Have I finally lost myself to the madness?

A hand lands on my shoulder making me scream into the cold morning air. Jumping to my feet, I round on the fucker who just touched me and I freeze. The last person I ever thought I would see again is standing right in front of me.

"Tom?" I sound so unsure of myself.

"Hey, Ry." He sheepishly smiles at me as he wiggles his foot in the dirt.

I don't know what to stay. I am rendered speechless, which never happens to me, but seeing him here after the words he last spoke to me makes this very awkward.

"Sorry, I'll leave you to it," I mutter as I start to take a step around him.

"No!" His words crack out like a whip.

My eyes widen at his tone. I don't want to stand here and look at the person who killed the last piece of my soul with words. Tears gather in my eyes, my arms fold under my chest. I attempt to walk past him and as I pass, his arm shoots out grabbing hold of the back of my top and yanking on it to halt me. It pulls down, causing a sharp intake of air to leave his lips.

"What the fuck happened to you, Ry?" His voice sounds like the friend I once knew, before all the bad shit happened.

"Nothing." My words sound so hollow, my emotions have shut off.

"Bullshit. Your back is covered in scars, Ry."

He must be repulsed by the state of my back. The thought has crossed my mind all the times me and Kane have had sex. How can he look at me the way he does? How does he still find me sexy?

"Ry. What the actual fuck?" He steps closer to me as his face changes from concerned to angry.

"Why does it matter to you? You were cruel to me the last time we spoke." My anger starts to grow at his questions, and the look on his face pisses me off.

I spin, forcing his hand off me. I turn to look at him with venom in my stare. How the fuck can he stand here and pretend like he fucking cares?

"Are you for real right now?" The words spill past my bared teeth.

"Reika, I was hurt and upset about what happened to her," he pleads, which pisses me off even more.

"Where the fuck were you when I went to get her back? Nowhere. I did it on my own. I tried to bring her back, but it was too much for her," I scream at him. "Then you were so cruel to me at the funeral. You blamed me for what happened." His eyes widen as I step closer, my anger riding me hard.

"Ry. I…" he starts.

"You what, Tom? You were hurting?" He nods at my words. "So was I. I tried to do what I could, and it blew up in my face," I scream again, spit flying out of my mouth.

"I didn't just lose one friend that day. I lost you both!"

Finally admitting the truth lifts a huge weight off my shoulders. It feels like I can finally breathe again.

"Ry?" His voice is broken.

"Save it, Tom." My words are pure venom as he stumbles back from me. "I lost you both, then I was kidnapped and tortured by the psycho who killed my parents. So, take your bullshit apology and shove it up your ass."

I leave him standing there, his mouth opening and closing like a fish out of water. I am done with this shit. Dream Mel was right. I did all I could do, and I am not to blame for any of it. Climbing back into the car, my eyes land on Tom who is still standing there with a horrified expression on his face. Normally, I would feel guilty, but I don't. I understand his feelings, but I have to do what is best for me. Turning the car on and putting it into gear, I take off with dust clouds following in my wake. The words from dream Mel repeat in my head yet again, rain hellfire down on their asses! There is one place I need to go. Honestly, I never wanted to step foot there again but it's time to face my demons head on.

The drive to hell on earth isn't as quiet as I hoped it would be. My phone constantly rings and beeps with incoming messages. I'll give the guys their dues, they are persistent in their calls and messages. Because my phone is hooked up to the Bluetooth, I see who keeps calling. It is mostly Kane with the odd occasional Frosty or Cheshire.

73

REIKA

A mother-fucking hour they have bugged the shit out of me. The calls and messages have been relentless. I wouldn't be surprised if they don't have a search party out looking for me right about now.

"What?" Are the first words out of my mouth as I answer the phone.

"What? Are you fucking serious, Gizmo?" Frosty seethes at me down the line, pulling a laugh out of me.

"Bitch, it's not funny. Kane is losing his shit," he says.

"I left a note," I say with a slight chuckle.

"A note! A fucking note!" I hear a roar in the background from the man in question. Fucking hell. I knew he would be pissed but fuck me!

"Put the dramatic bitch on the phone," I say to Frosty.

"Dramatic. Fucking dramatic? Fuck you and your bullshit," he spits at me. "Tell me where you are," he commands.

"I left a note. I'll be fine, Baby." I try to soothe him the best I can.

"Where are you?" he growls back at me.

"Kane. I have some stuff I need to work out, and I can't do

that with any of you looking over my shoulder." Honesty coats my words. I love the guy to bits, but sometimes he can be a royal pain in the ass.

"What stuff?" I hear uncertainty is in his voice. "Do you mean about us?" The silence following his words has me feeling like the biggest bitch in the world.

"No. I have never been more sure about us." I'm hoping my words sink in. "I had a bad dream that made my brain work overtime. Something is coming, and we have to be ready."

"How safe are you going to be, Pretty Bird?" His hysteria has lowered considerably since we started this conversation.

"Baby, I'm going to the safest place on earth. It's like Fort Knox," I say to the man my heart is fluttering for. "I'm going home, Kane."

"Why?" His question is fully loaded.

"I have to face my demons, Babe." My reply is so thick, I could cut the atmosphere in the car with a knife. "I have to be ready for what's to come, and so do you guys."

Silence greets me from the other end of the line. I repeat his name more than once. Did the line go dead? He hasn't said anything to me in reply.

"Kane?" I sound so unsure of myself.

"Sorry, Baby. I get it but come home to me soon. Okay?" My heart flutters at his concern, but my love for him grows even more at his answer.

The line goes dead, and my heart skips to a weird sort of rhythm. My mind feels a lot lighter as I continue my drive back to the worst place in the world. I haven't been near there since I was a child, but I know I might find some answers about my disappearing cousin there. But also, from the stories I have been hearing about my dad, maybe I can find info on the crazy bastards who are relentless in their mission to take me. I hate leaving everything to the guys or Fox. I am more than capable of finding shit out myself. Sometimes I forget who I am and what I am capable of, but that bad feeling in my gut is getting more and more persistent and annoying the shit out of me.

I'm still driving after another hour. People don't know this place really exists. Unless you have been here, you would drive right by. The place is a damn fortress. No one will be able to sneak up on me here, and that thought alone has me relaxing. Kane and the guys would love this place. The thought stops me short. I really should bring them up here when the crazy stops. My inner bitch snorts at me, laughing at the thought of the crazy stopping. Yeah, I don't see it either!

The tree line starts to split wider on the mountain side, it's the perfect hiding spot for something like this. A huge bush type thing stops the land rover and I laugh at the paranoia of my father. To the unsuspecting eye it looks like you have hit some sort of natural block. Rolling down the window and leaning out as far as I can, I hit the hidden thumb print scanner with my thumb. The whole thing pulls opens the rest of the way for me to get to the lodge. I really need to find the damn remote for that thing. During the drive to the door my heart starts beating frantically. I take slow, deep breaths to calm myself and remind myself this isn't another training session. I throw the car into park and climb out. Looking around the place that was my home away from home every weekend and holiday has good and bad memories jumping to the surface of my mind.

The steps creak under my feet as I climb the stairs, making me feel like a little girl again. I stare at the door. The red paintwork is chipped and dull from age. Blowing out a breath of air, the keypad blinks at me like an ominously. Gathering my courage, I put the code in and turn the doorknob. The door swings open, and the first I notice is the smell. It is a dusty, old sort of scent with mildew. All the furniture is the same with the dust covers on it. My father was obsessive when it came to this place. If you so much as left a light switch on by accident in a room with no one in it, he would lose his shit. Laughter builds thinking about all the arguments my parents had over that. All the rooms in this place have good memories. It's the levels below that hold the darker ones. Stopping those thoughts, I head to the back of the lodge where my dad's office is situated.

A sense of déjà vu washes over me. I stand outside the office door and dread fills me. I was never allowed in here as a child. This was for adults only, he used to tell me. My hand trembles as I reach for the doorknob. Blowing out a small breath, I turn it and allow the door to swing open. I wait at the threshold for a couple of minutes. Honestly, I wouldn't put it past the bastard to booby-trap it. My snort fills the air at how nuts my brain is making me. I cautiously step into the room, afraid something is going to jump out at me. I'm a little taken aback at how pristine this place is. A massive mahogany desk fills the center of the room, with the back of the chair to the huge window. Huge floor to ceiling bookcases fill the walls on either side and two leather chairs sit at the perfect angle to face the person behind the desk.

Nothing jumps out at me, thank fuck for that. Walking to the desk, I realize how plush the carpet is under my feet. There is no sound, and my boots practically sink into it. Sitting down on the chair, I see that there are three drawers on either side of the desk. Pulling on the handle of the top left one, I'm surprised it opens on the first try. There's the usual, pens laid out in a perfect line and sticky notes with a notebook. Nothing to rave about so I try the one below. It's all the same through all six drawers - just usual desk crap.

Think Reika! Where would your dad hide his shit? That's a loaded question since I never really, truly knew my dad, it seems. Frustration builds in me at the wasted journey here and I slam my fists down on the top of the desk. Something clicks and my eyes widen as a hidden compartment on the desk pops open. Nah, that was too easy. A lone folded piece of paper sits in the compartment. Pulling it out, my hands shake as I open it and read.

Hello Little Reaper,

If you're reading this little one, things took a turn for the worse and your mother and I didn't make it. I'm so sorry we left you, baby girl. I was hoping it wouldn't come to this, but there were too many snakes hiding in the grass for me to know who I could trust.

I made sure Pete was your guardian and you would be well cared for. Everything that is ours has been left for you. I hope Pete has followed the instructions I left him to tell you everything.

I had some dealings with some very bad people, and they blew up in my face. They will come after you just because of who you are. That's why I trained you the way I did, Little Reaper. It was to prepare you for everything that might come for you. I know you are strong enough to handle it and make the bastards pay for what they did.

Your mother couldn't write you a letter, she is too heartbroken knowing you would be left on your own. She tells me to tell you she loved you with every fiber of her being and she is so proud of you.

You have a cousin called Paine. We didn't tell you about him because we had to keep my brother out of things so you had back up when needed.

I have to go, time is running out. But know this, there is a hidden room in the training room. That will give you some of the information you need. Ask Pete for the rest.

You are capable of anything you put your mind to, and I

love you to the moon and back. You are my everything and my other reason for breathing.

Stay prepared and take what you need.

Dad xx

My tears drip onto the note as I read it over a few more times. My heart breaks for the father I never truly knew. Luckily, Pete told me everything after I shot Kane. I know everything is left to me - the money, the houses, the lot. My heart isn't ruled by superficial things though. I would trade it all in for just one more moment with them. The intruder alarms start blaring around the office and my body freezes. No fucker knows this place is here, the bookcases slide to the side to reveal screens that all have motion sensors on them and videos playing of the surrounding area. A body moves through the shadows at the side of the garage at far side of the property. Running out of the office, I open the weapons door and pull out my guns and make sure I have extra magazines to go with them. The alarms keeping blaring as I make my way to the door which will bring me out behind the intruder. Slowly closing the door behind me, so it doesn't squeak, I keep my body pressed up as close to the building as possible as I move around the lodge. Sticking my head out, I spot the back of the intruder with a gun in their hand staring at something around the corner. As silently as possible, I slide around until I am behind them, then lift my gun to the back of their head.

"Fuck's sake, Gizmo. It's me." The voice is filled with horror.

Keeping my gun aimed, my eyes bug as Frosty turns around to face me with his hands up and his gun dangling on a finger. Terror fills his features seeing the Glock 17 aimed at his forehead.

"The fuck are you doing here, Frosty?" I growl at the bastard.

"I followed the tracker on my car," he says in triumph. "I will say this, Giz, this place is a fucker to find." I can't stop the snort that slips out of my mouth.

"That's the reason my dad liked this place so much." I grin at him as I drop my arm.

We head back inside, both laughing at the situation. Honestly, I think he was half a second away from pissing his pants. A low whistle fills the air as we walk through to the kitchen, I hit the button in the kitchen to knock off the intruder alarm.

"Fucking hell, Giz. Nice digs." The boyish wonder in his voice makes me laugh.

"It's a lodge. Nothing special." It's just a thing to me.

"We never got this close the last time we were here," he says lost in his own world.

"What do you mean when you were last here?" I ask.

"Ah, fuck," he exclaims, and his face pales a little. "Kane's gonna kill me."

I cock my eyebrow in a silent question and try not to chuckle as he shuffles from foot to foot. Clearly uncomfortable with dropping him and the guys in it.

"Spit it out, Frosty, or no coffee for you." I put a hand on my hip as I wiggle the coffee cup in my hand. His eyes nearly bug out of his head at my threat, which makes an unflattering snort leave my lips. Me and Frosty are the same in that respect, we are both fueled by caffeine. I'm pretty sure it takes the place of where my blood is meant to be.

"Malcolm brought us here when we were kids," he says then stops as if that's all the answer I need. I roll my hand for him to continue. "Your dad told us to explore, and we found

591

you training on the pitch. Marcus was so enthralled by you it was funny."

My mind wanders to a time I can think of seeing them, but I can't think of anything too clearly. Anytime I try to think of something from the past it is always the same; the pain is the easiest to remember.

"Kane realized after he saw the picture of you and your family." I cock my head. "The one from the fight ring, Giz."

"Ah." That makes sense. "Why didn't he tell me?" I'm not annoyed that he didn't tell me. I'm annoyed he felt he couldn't tell me.

"You were bad after that shit went down. You lost it, Giz," he says as he pries the steaming cup of coffee out of my hand.

"Question?" I say to him, nearly choking on my mouthful of coffee as he lifts his brows over the rim of his cup. "How paranoid are you to have a tracker on your car?"

"You know how many idiots have tried to steal my baby?" he says.

My coffee falls over the edge of my cup as I snort into it at the seriousness on his face. It's fucking hilarious; the audacity of someone trying to steal his car.

"Laugh all you want, Giz. But that car means more to me than anything," he says with a seriousness I've never seen before.

"Even your brothers?" I can't help throwing the question out there.

"Funny," he replies with a smirk on his face.

The intruder alarm blares again before I answer. I take off running in the direction of the office as the bookcases move again to show me the screens. Bodies move throughout the property in full black clothing and ski masks.

"Who followed you here?" I hiss at Frosty, so much for thinking of this place as my damn sanctuary.

"No one, Giz. I haven't got a fucking clue who they are," he hisses back at me.

As I watch the screen, they move with a stealth only certain people can manage. They are highly fucking trained. Shit! I watch as they take up positions around the grounds. A couple of them are close to the lodge while the others are on the outer perimeter. My eyes dart between all the screens counting in my head how many there are.

"Fuck!" cracks out of me.

I start pacing as my mind tries to come up with a plan, ten of them and two of us. Shit! Frosty hasn't had the type of training these guys have. It's noticeable in how they move.

"Gizmo?" Frosty's expression tells me he doesn't like the odds any more than me. But I have dealt with this sort of shit before, he hasn't. I know Kane would be pissed if anything happened to him.

Without another thought, I run to the weapons room and hit the button to drop the security shutters on the building. Yells fill the air from outside.

"What the fuck?" Frosty glares at me.

"Stay here and stay the fuck out of sight, Liam. I can't have anything happen to you," I say quickly as I put all my knives and guns into their holsters and sheaths. Luckily, my baby is exactly as she was. I check all her pieces to make sure she still works fine, anda huge grin breaks out across my face. I fasten weapons all over. Frosty looks at me with wide eyes when he notices my baby on the counter. One after the other, the click gives me a sense of calm and my body relaxes instantly.

"Fuck off. I'm helping," he spits at me.

I grab the front of his shirt and yank him lose. "They are highly fucking trained, you idiot. They would kill you instantly." I glare at him to get my point across.

Without even looking back, I take off and head to the lower

level of the house. I get to the door and freeze. This place was the worst area ever, I can hear the screams of nine-year-old me as if they are embedded in the walls. The stairs creak going down, but once on the lower level it's sterile and cold, everything in here is some kind of metal. The chains I used to be hung from when going through a torture session are still hanging in my cell, swaying lightly. I recoil as the memories push to the surface.

"Giz. What the fuck?" Frosty turns in a small circle as he takes everything in. When our eyes meet, the look he gives me has a growl building in my throat.

"Don't," I bark at him with my finger in his face.

"Giz. Seriously this shit is fucked up." His voice is filled with so much pity.

"Yeah, well. Welcome to the life of being The Butcher's daughter." I shrug like it's no big deal.

"Look, Liam. I haven't got time for this. Either stay out of the way down here, or if they get in. Head to the roof." My tone dares him to argue.

I slide the wall back at the end of the room and his eyes widen as he sees the tunnel leading away from the house. Stepping in I close it from my side and hit the lock. Thumps hit the metal and I snort a laugh. These tunnels aren't made for escaping, they are to get me around the grounds without being seen. A malicious grin tilts my lips at the carnage I'm about to cause.

Liam

She locked me in! The motherfucking bitch locked me in the damn house! I stare at the massive metal door thing, shocked at her fucking disappearing on her own. If anything happens to that girl my brother will strangle me with my own organs. A shudder runs through me at the thought. Ripping my phone out of my pocket, the screen flashes telling me there is no cell service. Fuck! We're in the middle of nowhere. Rushing back upstairs to her dads office, I find the screens still out. What is on them has my heart practically beating out of my chest. Watching as the bodies move, I see what she means; they all sort of float when they move. They blend perfectly into the shadows. One of the screens shows a guy close to a tree on the far side of the property. He's just standing there looking around as if searching for something when he drops like a sack of shit out of nowhere. My eyes bug out of my head as nothing or no one is near him. There is nothing and he just dropped lifeless. How the fuck is that possible?

It takes about fifteen minutes. I watch with a sick sort of fascination as they all drop like flies. There are two men left closest to the house, the ground opens up and Giz slinks out of it like a panther, then gently lowers the hatch. What the actual fuck? Where the hell did she come from? I notice a zoom button on the keyboard, so I hit the button. It zooms in so close I can see her clearly; she looks like she has bathed in blood. The look on her face terrifies the fucking life out of me. She's enjoying this, she has a sick sort of glee on her face. Both men are unsuspecting of what is standing so close to them. The name Reaper makes perfect sense to me now; she is death itself.

She cuts through the men so swiftly there is a beauty to it. A dance she has mastered over the years, deadly, but flawless. As she looks down on her final prey, my heart races. Without a second thought, I take off in the direction of the weapons room and grab the nearest thing to me without looking at it. I'm up on the second floor in a matter of seconds. At the end of the corridor is a door that is a different color than the others. I pray as I pull it open, hoping it is the one I need. A relieved breath leaves me as the stairs lead up. Taking them two at a time, I come to another door. Quietly this time, I open it and step out onto the roof. There's only a small flat area up here, but it will be enough. Dropping to my belly I crawl across the floor to look out. Giz is still standing over the latest bodies she has ended. Everything screams at me to warn her, but I can't. She hasn't realized how much danger she is in. My heart beats even faster as the new players in the game slink through the night. Thank God they are in the wrong place. I'm just setting up, when a scream of defiance fills the air. My head shoots up at the sound. Horror fills me as five men have her hands behind her back somehow, dragging her backward. Her legs thrash wildly as she tries to do as much damage as possible.

Looking down at the weapon I pulled out, I chuckle at the make of the rifle. The smile spreading across my lips is a promise of death. It's a shame no one will see it. Adjusting myself, I use the scope to choose my first victim. My first shot hits its mark. As the bastard drops, the others search frantically around the area. Aw! They didn't scream. I fire at the next two, one after the other the bullets hit their mark. They drop, leaving two. There's a commotion between them. They must decide their direction as they start to drag her along the ground, but Giz isn't planning on going anywhere. She drops to the ground, and I fire. I chuckle silently to myself as their heads explode. I managed to get two for the price of one on that shot. Looking through the scope again, Gizmo has managed to get rid of her bindings. She's glaring in my direction with her hands on her hips. She slinks back into another hatch on the ground and disappears out of sight. That is so fucking cool! I really need to ask her if I can keep this. I head back down into the lodge. Let's see how grumpy she's gonna be?

"Are you fucking serious right now?" Spinning to face the pissed of gremlin, I grin at her. "What happened to staying put, Frosty?"

"Errm. Did you not see the assholes trying to kidnap your ass?" I cock my eyebrow at her, which only works in pissing her off even more.

"I had it handled." Anger layers her voice. I can't decide if it's because she needed help, or the fact that I did it without her permission.

"Giz, can I keep this?" I ask trying to lighten the mood. I lift the rifle up and grin like an idiot. "This blew two of their heads off in one go." Her eyes widen a touch at the excitement in my voice.

"Fine." She rolls her eyes at me. "It was a good shot, I'll give you that." She smirks as she heads off toward one of the rooms. Holy shit! Did she just compliment me?

"Did you plan on the whole bathed in blood look?" I can't help wanting to annoy the shit out of her. "Cause I gotta tell you, it really works for you." I grin at her.

She looks over her shoulder and lifts her brow. A smirk tugs at her lip, and that's all the answer I need. This is the reason why her and my brother are meant to be together - their crazy plays well together. He may be one scary son-of-a-bitch when he wants to be, but if it was a choice of taking him on or her, I'd pick him every fucking time.

74

KANE

I have tried calling Liam so many times my fucking thumb aches from hitting the screen. All I get is a dead tone. Nothing. I need to know everything is okay with her. My heart relaxed when we realized she had taken his Land Rover, because he is so paranoid he has trackers on everything he owns. So, we knew where she was, but that isn't what has me worried out of my fucking mind. Not long after she left, reports started coming in that the Grimm's were attacking multiple areas of ours. All hell has broken loose. Some of the locals have been spotted leaving, while the few retired crew members have all called in and said they want to help. It's a fucking war zone out there!

"Bro!" Marcus shouts.

"What?"

My mind feels too full. There is so much shit going on it doesn't want to function properly. If I could split myself, it still wouldn't be enough.

"I got a lead on where some of the Grimm's are hiding," Marcus says, walking into the office.

I practically fall out of my chair at his voice in the room.

The snarky bastard laughs because he scared the crap out of me. Thank fuck I managed to catch myself on the edge of the desk before the chair went fully over, because if it had I wouldn't have lived it down.

"How reliable is this source?" I feel like a dick questioning him, but shit is happening way too fast for my liking.

I know the question has pissed him off as he cocks an eyebrow at me and grinds his teeth. He has been so out of whack recently, I can't blame him, but I can't have him running off on a shit source and getting himself injured, or worse. What happened with Bonzo still sits at the front of mind; it would break me if anything happened to my brothers or Pretty Bird.

"It's reliable, Kane," he seethes at me, his chest rising and falling rapidly.

"Bro, look I believe you," I say as gently as possible. "I'm just on edge with how fucked up everything is."

I know it's worked as his body starts to lose some of the tension coiled inside him like a snake waiting to strike. The thing with my younger brother is when he loses his shit. He doesn't just get mad, he gets volatile. Everything within a fifty-foot radius dies, there is no reasoning with him. He becomes single minded in his quest of destruction.

"We going to check it out?" His voice is so uncertain now, I really wish I could kick my own ass. With a nod, I stand and head out of the office. We best start making plans on what we are going to do.

Time seems to move like a whirlwind. We are on our way to the location Marcus was given. The convoy isn't as big as I would have liked; unease stirs in my gut. A phone ringing pulls me out of my inner thoughts.

"Hey, Bro. You alive?" My head snaps up as Marcus asks the question.

"Yeah, luckily." Liam's voice echoes through the car, my heart beats a little faster.

"Where are you?" I ask. Marcus smirks at me.

"Ah. I was wondering how close you would be to the phone." The tinkling laugh that fills the car over the hands free has my body coming alive.

"What does Liam mean, Pretty Bird?" I try to keep the fear out of my voice, but it doesn't work.

A smile tugs at my lips, as we listen to Liam getting chewed out by her. His reasonings fall on deaf ears as she chastises him like a child. Marcus looks at me with a 'what the fuck' expression. Seeing it has laughter bubbling out of me at how well they are both getting on. It's refreshing but weird as fuck.

"Drop me in it again, asshole, and I will confiscate your new rifle," Pretty Bird shouts to my brother, who practically whimpers like a kicked puppy. Marcus slams on the brakes as the other cars swerve to avoid us, my eyes narrow on him at the stupid move he just pulled.

"The fuck, bro? I don't plan on dying anytime soon," I throw at him.

"Hellion, what do you mean his new rifle?" I stop the next set of words when I realize what the fuck he has just said. I cock my brow at him as he just shrugs at me.

We both listen intently as they give us a play by play of what happened. My emotions go from anger to murderous, then horror. Finally, the only thing I am feeling is pride. This woman that walked into my life like a giant mouthy thorn is what I never knew I needed. Her darkness plays well with mine, but she also can step up when needed and deal with shit on her own. Liam is gloating about grabbing a rifle and killing five of them that tried to steal my woman. A growl rumbles in my chest at the thought, and all three of them burst out laughing.

"Who were they?" I ask.

"Haven't got a clue, Babe, but they were specially trained." I listen to her words. "If the tunnels weren't there, it could have gone badly."

I respect her honesty, but her confession that it's a fluke, that it went right, has my darkness roaring to life and thirsting for blood. My silence sends another round of tinkling laughter from her.

"So, what you guys up to?" she asks ever so sweetly. I shake my head at the change of subject before I can answer.

"We got a lead on some Grimm's hiding out," Marcus blurts out. "So, we are gonna check it out. The town has become a war zone."

"What you mean?" they both say at the same time.

"Locals are leaving. The Grimm's are getting braver each hour," I say before Marcus.

"Ah, can't really blame them, Bro," Liam says.

"Why have they suddenly gotten this brave?" Pretty Bird muses. It wasn't really a question, her tone tells me she just said her thoughts out loud.

"Good question, Pretty Bird. That's what we are hoping to find out," I answer her.

"Be safe, Kane. Something feels off about this." Her concern has weird feelings settling in me.

"When are you two back?" I change the topic back to them.

"We got something I want to check out before we get back, Babe." Annoyance builds that she isn't coming back now.

"What's that?" Marcus asks.

"We are going looking for Pete and Paine." I knew it had something to do with them. My emotions go haywire, but I know why she has to.

My eyes catch a reflection in the side mirror. Looking to investigate further, I notice it's one of the grunts from the car behind. As he gets close to the window, he raises his hand to knock, then nearly falls on his ass when he sees me looking at him. I narrow my eyes at him in warning not to disturb us. He takes off back to the car, so clearly my look was enough. Remembering our task, I know the guys are getting restless.

"Stay together and watch each other's back," I say in my commanding tone which gets a snort from the pair of them. "Check in regularly."

"Aye, aye, Captain," she sasses me, which has my brothers laughing.

I end the call without another word. Marcus's eyebrows hit his hairline at the lack of goodbye, but I would get side-tracked if I said anything else. Just listening to her made me want to command them both back, but I know that would have a mistake. Marcus knows this as well as I do, but he doesn't like it. He reluctantly resumes our journey, grumbling under his breath. My mind wanders to her, and I slap it down. She has her shit to do. You have yours. Stop being a pussy whipped bitch!

For thirty minutes the car is silent. Marcus and I haven't said a word to each other, both of us are lost in our own thoughts. Honestly, the closer we have get to our destination, the more my unease grows. Marcus pulls over and climbs out. I wait and watch to see if anything sticks out, which it doesn't. A homeless looking dude walks over to him, and they start talking. Marcus throws a look over his shoulder and I know that's my cue. Climbing out, I head over to them.

"Sup, man," the guy says to me.

With a nod, I listen. The conversation isn't what I thought it would be, him being a source, but something just feels off. Watching him intently, that feeling in my gut screams to life even more, he's too fidgety for my liking and he isn't keeping eye contact.

"Tell me the truth, man," I say with a deep rumble as horror fills his face.

"What? What?" His eyes dart everywhere but at me.

Marcus side eyes me, in a way that says, 'what the fuck am I missing?' My warning bells continue to go off in my head and I don't want to waste another second here. Spinning on my heels, I head back to the car and climb in. Raised voices can be heard, Marcus is furious at the informant. The little shit takes of like a bat outta hell in the opposite direction. Marcus charges back to the car and jumps in, turns the ignition and slams his foot down on the gas. Something has him rattled as he drives like a madman.

"Dude, what the fuck?" I shout at the crazy bastard who is likely to get us killed.

He carries on his mumbling without answering and pushes his foot flat to the damn floor. My heart practically drops out of my ass and is laid somewhere on the road behind us. Marcus sniggers at the horror on my face. It pisses me off, but the fucker still doesn't tell me why he's driving like an absolute psycho. The car behind flashes his lights at us repeatedly, but he just ignores them.

"Marcus, what the fuck?!" I try again.

Nothing not a damn thing from him. Unease swirls around me and the look in his eyes, something is seriously wrong. He is so close to losing it and I don't know why. Honestly, I brace myself for the possibility that we'll crash, so when the car slams to a screeching halt my head hits the dash, full force, and the pain is eyewatering. I feel something drip onto my face, using the center mirror I growl at the cut on my forehead that is dripping blood down my face.

"You fucking idiot!" I bellow.

Turning my eyes to him, I come up short as his breathing is increased and his eyes dart around. Looking out of the window, I see we are home, but what has my gut screaming again is the fact there isn't a soul around. Without thinking, I jump out and make my way toward the houses. The guys shout at me to stop, but it's as if my body has been taken over and it's moving on its own. The firepits are still lit, and a couple of seats have been turned over, but that is all. The front door opens at my touch with an ominous creak that has all the blood rushing to my head. The quiet is so eerie, there is no movement in the hallway.

"Marcus, what the fuck is going on?" I ask to the presence behind me, he must have run after me.

"I don't know. But, Kane, the rat kept saying I'm sorry before he bolted." The nervous tone he has, makes my darkness unfurl itself from the pits of my soul.

The atmosphere is charged with a weird sort of feeling. Neither of us know what we are gonna come across, and we need to be prepared for it. Marcus checks the living room as I check the kitchen, both of us come up empty. Heading further into the house, the pounding in my ears grows so much it starts to cause a headache. All the rooms off the corridor are empty; it didn't take long for us to check. The weird tug in my gut has me feeling all sorts of emotions.

"I'm gonna check upstairs" Marcus says, before heading in that direction.

My feet continue to move on their own deeper into the depths of the house. My gut roars with apprehension as I stop outside the gym doors. Taking a deep breath to prepare for whatever I find, I push through the doors. Vomit hits the back of my throat at the horror show in the room. I have no words to describe what the fuck I am seeing. Only thing that comes to mind is they look how Jesus did, nailed to the cross. Fifteen men are nailed to the walls. But what has me wanting to throw up all over the floor is that their bodies have been mutilated.

"Kane, they…" Marcus's words break off.

Turning away from the scene I look to my baby brother,

who has horror all over his face, as he looks at all the bodies. I don't have any words; I am still shocked myself.

"This is my fault," he blurts, which pulls me out of my trance.

"No, it's not," I argue.

"Kane, if we hadn't left, they wouldn't be dead!" he roars at me, guilt clearly ruling him as his voice breaks.

Striding forward, I grip his shoulders. He lowers his gaze to the floor. "Look at me!" He doesn't lift his head or acknowledge anything, which guts me like a knife to the stomach.

"Marcus, you are not to blame." I try again.

"Boss?" My eyes dart to the doors, seeing the other guys there has me feeling lost.

Their faces are different; some are angry while others look on terrified at the show. What piques my interest is one of the grunts staring at something by the side of the door. Striding over, I stop short at the words written in blood.

This is our town. Leave and you will survive.

75

FANCY PANTS

E verything seems to be going right for once, it's nearly time for the whole thing to come to an epic conclusion.

"You fucking idiot." Turning, my father storms into my room. His eyes are bloodshot, and he has a demented look on his face.

"Why. What have I done wrong now?" I blurt in a flippant tone. My eyes widen as I realize my mistake. Oh shit!

"She fucking killed them all!" he roars, spit flying everywhere.

I stare, stunned by my father's words. This has really shaken him. He paces across the office like a pissed off lion; I can't understand a word he is saying. After the initial shock of his announcement, it is replaced by amusement. She's stronger than we thought. For ten full minutes, all he does is pace and mutter to himself. Honestly, I'm surprised at how shaken he is by this. He knows who her father was, and what that fucker was capable of. Why is this such a surprise?

"What's so surprising about it?" I ask with a shrug. He spins to face me, nostrils flaring and a bright red face.

"She shouldn't have been able to beat them!" he roars.

"Why?" Confusion clouds my mind, but my question clearly pisses him off further.

He roars his anger into the air and swipes the contents of my desk onto the floor. I'm used to my father destroying my stuff, but the bottle of whiskey he has just smashed all over my floor annoys the fucking life out of me. It's my favorite brand.

"You are such a fucking idiot," he seethes.

"Huh." A snort passes my lips. "The only one I can see here acting like an idiot is you."

His eyes narrow on me like a fucking homing beacon, he charges toward me, but I step out of the way in time. This angers him even more, and I laugh out loud again. How can one little girl make men like my father lose their shit like this?

"They were highly trained mercenaries." His words stop me in my tracks.

I stare wide eyed at him; he nods in answer to my silent question.

"Exactly."

76

REIKA

"**D**ude, turn that shit off," I say to the six foot five idiot driving the car. "It's making my ears bleed," I protest further.

"You just don't appreciate good music, Gizmo," he retorts, with a snort of laughter.

The fucker is lucky he's driving, or I would slap some sense into him. But I don't feel much like dying today. If that happened, I think Kane would bring me back from the dead just to scream at me, and then possibly kill me again. I'm still surprised he was ok with us searching for Paine and Pete, but I know they have other stuff they need to deal with. My thoughts instantly go back to the constant unease in my gut. There's more going on here, there must be. It's too much of a coincidence that everything has turned to shit so quickly.

My mind goes over everything repeatedly, trying to figure it out and hoping to remember something I missed before. I am lost inside my own head for the entire journey as Frosty drives to our destination. The only useful thing I found inside my dad's office was a mention of Deacon Anders. There was a picture of my dad, Deacon, and a little boy who looks like a younger Paine. They all had huge smiles on their faces. They looked happy, like they didn't have a care in the world.

"Gizmo?" Frosty's voice fills the car. My head snaps in his direction. His eyes hold a cautious look as he turns to look out of the windshield.

The house in front of us looks like it has been abandoned for years. Weeds nearly cover the entire property. I'm shocked to think that someone could be living in this environment. The house has a basic style and sits on what looks to be a shithole of a street. There are pieces of bricks, rubbish and other junk littered everywhere. A dog barks off in the distance as I just stare. Honestly, I'm not sure I'm ready for what I might find.

"You sure you wanna do this?" The unease in Frosty's voice has my own nerves fluttering to life.

I just sit and stare at him without saying anything. I don't want to be here. But I can't leave my cousin out in the world and not know what the hell is happened to him. Paine's phone goes to voicemail and Pete's doesn't even connect. It's been too long since I have heard anything from either of them. We both climb out of the car and walk toward the door. My heart rate picks up as apprehension creeps into my body. Unease rolls off Frosty in waves, and the way his eyes are constantly scanning the area has me seriously on edge.

The paint on the door is chipped and cracked in places, with mold patches everywhere. It has definitely seen better days. The boards creak under Frosty's weight. My palms are slick with sweat as I lift my fist to knock. I wait after knocking for a few moments to see if anyone is home. There doesn't seem to be any life in the house, no movements or anything. Annoyance starts to build in me at the wasted journey. With a huff, I turn on my heel, climb down the steps and head for the car with my shadow in tow. Luckily, he doesn't say a word. As I climb into the car, a shiver runs down my spine as though someone is watching. I make a scan of the area, but don't find anything. Frosty watches as I get myself comfortable. His features tell me he is concerned over something, but I don't know what.

"Spit it out, man," I demand.

"You sure this is a good idea?" he asks, with a hint of hesitation.

I give a shrug in reply. I'm not sure of anything anymore, and I don't like feeling so out of control.

"Giz?" Frosty says. "Gizmo."

I'm lost in my thoughts trying to figure out where to go from here. I know without a doubt something is wrong, but I need to find Paine.

"Reika!" Liam screams in my ear.

"The fuck, man!" I bellow.

He nods in the direction of the creepy house; I lift my eyes. Shock renders me speechless as an elderly woman stands in the doorway, staring at me. Slowly, her hand lifts from her cane and beckons me with a finger. I turn to look at Frosty; his eyebrows have become a part of his hair.

"Hello?" I say to the lady as I climb out of the car.

She just watches as I slowly make my way over. I don't even know why I'm creeped out, but something has my palms sweating and sweat gathering on the back of my neck. Her gaze narrows the closer I get, but her eyes are alive with something as she tracks every step I take.

"My God, you look like your father, Reika," says the elderly woman. I stumble back at her use of my name.

"How do you know me?" The question is harsher than I meant it to be. A wheezy chuckle fills the air as the lady stares in amusement. Cautiously, I take the first step up onto the porch. A smile tips the corner of her lips.

"It's good to be cautious, dear," she chuckles again, "but I mean you no harm."

Get it together, Reika! It's just an old lady who may have some answers. I'm still freaked a little by the knowing look in her eye as she watches everything I do. A door bangs closed behind me. I look and see Frosty as he steps out of the car, his eyes narrowed on her.

"Well, are we just going to stand here and have a staring contest, or are you wanting to talk?" Her question catches me off guard as I open and close my mouth in response.

With a tut, she turns slowly and wobbles into the house. I'm surprised how fast she moves considering how unstable she looks on her feet. I'm standing at the threshold looking into a house that gives me weird vibes. She looks over her shoulder and lifts a brow at me. I walk into the hallway, and I'm instantly met with the smell of old, dank furniture and years' worth of dust. A sneeze has me nearly jumping out of my skin. I spin and find Frosty standing behind me, rubbing his nose as another round of sneezes has tears leaking from his eyes.

"Sorry for the dust and clutter. My old bones aren't what they used to be," she says.

I lift a brow at Frosty and he just shrugs and grunts as he battles to stop another sneeze that's fighting to come out. I chuckle as he starts again. Clinking draws my attention further into the house. As I watch, the lady fills a cup with sugar, coffee and milk.

"Sugar?" she asks.

"Are you a serial killer, lady?" Frosty manages to squeeze out in-between sneezes. "Cause I'm kinda getting Ted Bundy vibes here." My laugh doesn't come out nicely, but more like a shocked, what the fuck snort. The old lady chuckles as she takes a seat at the kitchen table.

"I'm not a serial killer, young man," she says, then chuckles and shakes her head at him. "I just know things." My interest is piqued.

"How do you know my name?" I ask her again. She lifts her hand to the seat opposite her at the table. Not wanting to be rude, I take a seat and we just look at one another as she slides the cup across to me. I busy myself loading it up with sugar and milk.

"I know your name, my dear, because I have pictures of you from when you were a young girl." My heart drops into my stomach.

"What?" My voice is harsh.

"Can you pass me that purple album from over there, please, boy?" she asks Frosty as she motions to the item on the side.

He jumps up and grabs it, passing it across the table. The fact he didn't want to get close has me chuckling again. Our eyes meet and he looks at me as if the lady is a kook, making another snort of laughter bursting from my mouth.

"What a handsome man you have in your life, Reika." Coffee splutters out of my mouth and nose.

"What?" I croak as I try to clear my airway.

"You look good together," she says as she looks between me and Frosty. Laughter bubbles out of me. The horrified look on his face says it all, and it's the funniest fucking thing I've ever seen.

"She's my sister-in-law, lady," he blurts, causing another round of laughter from me.

The confused look she gives us both has tears running down my cheeks. It's cute in a weird sort of way how she assumed we were a couple, but what has me laughing again is how Kane would have reacted if he was here. She lifts a brow at me in question.

"I'm with his older brother," I say while she flicks through the pictures in the album.

Ten minutes of silence pass as she continues her search.

Some of the tension starts to leave my body. I know Frosty is still uncomfortable; he stands just off to the side with a pissed expression.

"Is he a looker like him?" she asks.

I snort again and smile. She smiles back and it makes me feel a little soft and gooey inside. I don't know why I am so bothered with what she thinks of me, but the longer I spend here, even without answers, the more comfortable I feel.

"These are pictures of Thornton and Deacon when they were younger." She slides the pictures over to me.

My gasp is short as I look at a picture of my father, who must be around nine years old, with another boy of the same age. They both have popsicles in their hands and mud smeared across their faces. They each have an arm wrapped around the other. They look so innocent and carefree.

"Here are some more."

She continues to pass picture after picture. There are photos from when my father was a small toddler up to the age of around twelve. All in different situations, playing out on a bike or at a park. The boy from the first picture isn't very far in any of them. If he isn't directly in front of the camera, he is somewhere in the background. Tears gather in my eyes at the snapshots of my father's life.

"He was a very troubled young child when he came." I look to her and she's staring off into the distance. "He wouldn't have much to do with anyone, until Deacon came a few days after he arrived.

"What?" I don't know what she means.

"These are the pictures from when your dad and uncle lived here." Her answer makes no sense. "Your real grandparents came and took Thornton back when he was twelve, but from the age of one, he was with me."

"You mean my dad was in foster care?" I ask quietly.

"Yes, my dear." A tear drips from the corner of her eye as she looks at me. "After he left, he managed to find Deacon and stay in touch, but I didn't see him again until he was a grown man bringing me pictures of you." The sadness in her eyes has me feeling like the world's shittiest person.

"I'm sorry, I don't know your name," I say in a hollow voice.

"Cynthia, my dear. Cynthia James." She smiles at me.

"I wonder why my dad never mentioned you?" I murmur to myself.

"Because, my dear, your father was involved in a very bad world thanks to his parents, and he said he didn't want that spilling into my life." The sad look on her face as she looks at one of the pictures on the table guts me.

"Do you know my father is dead," I blurt without thinking.

"I do. I did try to find you after it happened, Reika." My body freezes. "But I couldn't find you." Tears track a clear path down her face now. "I'm sorry."

"Why did you look for me? My dad left it in his will that Pete was to look after me," I inquire.

"Because I didn't want you to have the life he did. When I saw him again as a man, he wasn't the little boy I remembered." She takes in a deep breath. "He was cold and calculating. It just wasn't what I wanted for him."

"He did some bad things, Cynthia, but I know he had his reasons behind it," I say, trying to relieve some of her guilt.

"Actions always have consequences, my dear, and I fear they may want the payment from you," she says.

Her words render me speechless as I stare wide eyed at her. I spot Frosty out of the corner of my eye, and his face matches mine. Her words are so accurate it's chilling. Payment is coming due, but the question I need the answer to is from who?

"Your concern is right. A lot of things are happening, and I don't know why," I say to the woman who looks heartbroken, "but Cynthia, I'm looking for Paine." Her eyes widen.

"He's okay?" she croaks.

"That's why we are here. He went missing a few weeks back and hasn't been seen since," Frosty says, joining into the conversation instead of observing.

"What happened?" Her tone has a lot more life to it now.

"We found out we were cousins after something bad that happened to me, and he was wracked with guilt," I say. Just speaking that out loud has my emotions all over the place.

"I don't know where he is, Reika," she says in a sharp tone, "but you need to find him."

The afternoon passed quickly after I told her I would find him. We spent the rest of our time sharing stories about my father.

"Gizmo, we have to get back or check in with Kane." Frosty says breaking up the conversation.

Rounding the table, I hug the woman who has helped me learn more about my father and promise to come visit her again as soon as I can. She looks a lot happier now than she did when she first opened the door. I feel happier too after talking to her, but the feeling of impending doom is still there. I am leaving for now with answers about who my father was, but nothing to help me navigate the shit show that is my life.

77

MALCOLM

Time has blurred into together for me as I sit and wait in the belly of the beast. I always thought I was the scariest person in any room, my ruthlessness unrivalled. How wrong, was I? My body is broken beyond repair and my mind fractured into tiny pieces. Emotions I have never felt before torment me in these darkest of times, and when the shadows come calling to take payment for my insolence. Screams fill the air around me from the other captives in their cells. Groans or screams are often let free, but the screams of one captive happen for the longest and seem to go on forever. I don't know who they are or why they are here, but they seem to be the favorite for dishing out punishment.

"Boss man says we will have full control soon." I peel open my good eye, as two men walk by my cell.

"Everything is falling into place, and it's moving quicker then he thought," says the other in excitement.

"I can't wait until the damned fuckers are dead on the ground, and I can walk in their blood," says another.

"Best give him his delivery man," they say as they walk off laughing.

The scream I hear every day, echoes through the air as they laugh. Guilt has me dropping my head in defeat. Why did I ever let it get like this?

78

KANE

My anxiety has reached a stupid level as I sit here and listen to Marcus talk shit about the instructions Liam left him for date night. What the fuck are these two idiots up to? After Liam rang and said he and Pretty Bird would be coming back tonight, my body filled with excitement at seeing her, but also nervousness as Liam asked Marcus if he has everything planned. Even Pretty Bird was stumped while the twins gossiped like a set of girls. Her reaction put me at ease, but the laughter that followed something Liam said scared the shit out of me. Liam also filled us in on the situation they had found themselves in.

"Marcus, what the fuck are you up to?" My annoyance is clear as the psychotic fucker bounces around the kitchen singing.

"You and Hellion are gonna go on a date night," he squeals.

"Dude, what the fuck is wrong with you?" My tone rises a little closer to horror.

"Love is in the air, everywhere I look around," the nutcase sings, shaking his ass like a stripper.

He continues to ignore me and shake his ass. I'm horrified

at the stupidity he is showing for whatever they have planned, and the whole dancing shit show is collecting a damn audience outside the kitchen. Crew members laugh at him while waiving dollar bills in the air.

"Honey, I'm home!" echoes through the hallways. My heartrate picks up.

"Thought you wanted to scare the shit out of him, Giz?" Liam's voice questions, which makes me smirk.

"Well, thanks for that asshat. Now he knows were back!" she exclaims, making a laugh burst from me as she shoots the shit with my brother.

"Dude!" he shouts back. "You just shouted 'Honey, I'm home' down the hallway."

"So, what, dickhead? I didn't say which hallway," she argues back.

I honestly thought Pretty Bird and Marcus were dangerous together. But I'm pretty sure that her and either of my brothers is dangerous for my sanity.

"Pretty Bird, get your ass in here and stop leading my brother astray!" I shout out.

"Yeah, Giz, stop being a bad influence," Liam shouts out loud, then laughs his head off. Marcus joins in, echoing his laugh instantly.

"Fuck the both of you!" she shouts back, then laughs as a roar of pain follows.

Her laughter grows as she charges through the kitchen like a damn maniac. The roar follows behind. I choke on my water as Liam comes into the kitchen with what's left of some food on his face.

"Dude, get your woman under control," he shouts at me. "She just hit me with a fucking burger." I burst out in full blown belly laugh. Tears stream down my face, as I watch a bit of sauce run down his cheek. The next thing I know I'm flat on my back laughing even more.

"Yeah, and I wasted it on you, fuckface!" she exclaims with her hands on her hips looking like a pissed off hobbit, which draws another round of laughter from me.

With a huff, she steps over me, and I catch her ankle, so she drops to the floor wailing and kicking her legs.

"Get the fuck off me, you idiot," she scolds, but her eyes give her away. She is dying to laugh.

I pull her toward me by her legs. Laughter falls from her as she squeals and throws punches that are light when they land. I grin down at her, and her eyes widen as she notices our position changed to have her pinned underneath me.

"Hey there, Pretty Bird," I purr, that makes her shiver beneath me.

The grin she gives me has my cock growing and a lust firing off through me. Coughs ring out around us, but it's not enough to make us break focus. The little witch gives me a devilish wink as she wriggles underneath me, causing my already painful cock to throb even harder.

"Take it to the damn bedroom," Liam shouts at us, making Pretty Bird snigger.

"Bro, they gotta get ready for date night," Marcus throws back.

Fuck! What is with them and this damn date night? The little minx grins at me as she slides herself from underneath me and stands with a hand extended to me.

"What do you say, Kane?" she purrs. "Wanna get ready for date night?"

I climb to my feet and twine my fingers with hers as I yank her forward. The squeal that leaves her throat has me grinning as I connect our lips so brutally, she sucks in a breath, allowing me access. Our tongues dance in the most seductive way; it's forceful and all consuming. Tiny bolts of static tingle under the surface of my skin. Pretty Bird breaks the kiss with so much force, I am left sucking in air to fill my lungs. We both stare wide eyed at each other. I will never get enough of the feeling when our bodies connect. She lifts a brow in a question, and I grin back at her as I drag her out of the kitchen toward the stairs.

We don't even make it fully through the bedroom door before our lips are on one another again, in a battle for dominance. Our teeth clash with so much ferocity, I could blow my load any second. A sharp sting registers in my brain, making me break the connection. Pretty Bird grins at me as I run the tip of my tongue across my bottom lip and the same sting happens again. Narrowing my eyes at her, her grin grows as I realize she bit my lip. That realization has another shot of lust headed straight to my dick, while her eyes twinkle with mischief. Stalking her forward, I see the change as her eyes darken with lust.

She backs up keeping her eyes on me. She sucks in a gasp as my hand clasps around her throat applying the slightest bit of pressure, keeping her back against the wall. My lips land on hers continuing our delicious battle for control. The moans that leave her have me wanting to tear off her clothes and fuck her raw against the wall. That thought has a grin tipping my lips as I watch her suck in air. My eyes stay locked with hers as I gently run the tips of my fingers from her shoulder across her collarbone. Keeping to the path, I continue down toward her stomach. Her breathing has become rapid, but in a shallow sort of way. Her lust filled gaze has me mesmerized.

"Take off your pants," I command, causing another shiver to dance through her body.

My eyes stay glued to her hands as the little minx strokes and pulls her nipples on the way to do what I asked. Her moans continue to grow as she flicks the button on her jeans and agonizingly slowly pushes them over her hips. Once she passes the restrictions of that perfect little ass of mine, they drop to the floor, leaving her bottom half bare to me. I lift my eyes to meet hers, and the defiance that shines back has saliva pooling in my mouth. I cock my eyebrow in a warning, and she purrs in the back of her throat as she steps out of the jeans and flicks them to the side. Applying more pressure to her throat, she moans again. I step so close we look joined. I tap her right ankle making her lift a brow in question.

"Open up, Baby. I want to see what's mine," I purr next to her ear, as I run my tongue up the side.

I feel her weight shift as she opens for me. I growl in approval as she gives in to my commands. Keeping my hand on her throat, I drop to my knees in front of her and run my tongue through her lips. The taste already has me wanting to bow to her every command. She tastes like my favorite flavor of candy; saliva pools in my mouth even more. The moan that escapes her lips has my cock growing painful. I adjust my position on my knees to relieve some of the strain. Grabbing hold of her legs I lift one over my shoulder, causing another guttural moan to leave her. I do the same to the other leg, so she is supported by me along with her shoulders against the wall, my hand on her throat keeping her in place.

Pulling her forward, I shift myself to get a foot underneath me, then stand to my full height. Her fluid fills my mouth, forcing a moan so deep she shudders, pushing herself down on my face in demand. I've barely even started yet as she trembles above me, her legs clamped around my head. My control snaps and I dive in, licking and biting her clit. She thrashes around from my onslaught. I play her body to the tune I want to hear. While she moans and commands me to eat her like I mean it, I push her into the wall harder by her throat and keep her suspended above me. I push my index finger into her pussy and the greedy thing tries its hardest to clamp down. My tongue is working her clit like a tornado as I add another finger, pumping them in and out as fast as I can.

The moans turn to a choppy 'Oh my God' as I feel her start to tremble above me. Her fluid drips like a water fountain in a constant stream. I suck and lick to make sure I collect every single drop. Her hand yanks my hair painfully as she yells out that she's close. Slowing my fingers and tongue, I allow the orgasm building to die down. I tease and play causing her to threaten to gut me in my sleep if I don't let her come. I chuckle at her ferocity, which makes her clit vibrate in my mouth and a moan fall from her lips.

Feeling her fall under my command has me in a state of ecstasy. The little trembles in her body have subsided, and a murderous chorus of cursing has another chuckle building in my throat. I start to pump my fingers again, adding a third, when I look up to meet her eyes. I watch in awe as her murderous intent flickers out, turning into a state of bliss. Her hand lands on the back of my head, forcing my head back between her legs. I alternate between fucking her brutally with my fingers and toying with her clit as I hum against her sensitive nerves. Her legs tremble against my back and a chant of don't stop is bellowed into the air. I up my pace to a frantic level as the sound of her lust fills the room. A scream tears from her throat as I bite down on her clit just enough to send her over the edge. Her breathing is choppy and all over the place as I work her over to help with the aftershocks of the orgasm that just tore through her. My dick throbs painfully in my pants as her shudders slow.

"Guys, you ready or what?" Marcus shouts through the bedroom door. I growl in annoyance and Pretty Bird to chuckles.

Our eyes connect as I look up to her from between her legs. She runs her tongue across her bottom lip, pulling another growl from me. No matter how much they protest about us being on a schedule, I think me and Pretty Bird are on the same wavelength as I start to pump my fingers inside her again.

"Guys?" Marcus shouts again.

"Fuck off, we're busy!" we both growl without breaking eye contact.

"Oh," is the only thing he says, before silence.

I continue to work her over with my fingers, watching her eyes become stormy.

"You know they will keep bitching?" she says on a chuckle.

"Yeah, I know," I mumble. She continues to grin down at me.

"What you thinking, Big Man?" she questions.

I flick the button open on my jeans and wriggle out of them. Pretty Bird is still on my shoulders, making me harder just thinking about it. I grin in answer as her eyes widen hearing the thump of my jeans hitting the floor.

"Fuck me like you want to, Baby," she purrs.

The slow movements of my fingers pick up the pace as I thrust them deeper. Her breathing hitches as I kiss across her stomach and tits, pulling a nipple and biting down gently. She throws her head back and moans in response, jiggling my shoulders slightly. I drop her legs to my elbows as I keep my hands on her back to steady her. I allow her body to slide down my stomach, pulling my fingers out of her pussy. Her eyes bug out as she realizes her legs are above her head.

"Kane?" she groans.

I slam into her with a brutal thrust. She screams and shatters around me as another orgasm tears through her. Her pussy clamps down on my cock so hard, it's like she's trying to join us together permanently. She stretches forward and slams her lips down on mine as I thrust into her with a brutality I haven't before. This is a fucking whirlwind. Her nails scrape across my shoulders, a sting tracks the line she marked, making a growl slip between my lips as she swallows it on a moan.

The pictures rattle on the wall, the sound of flesh hitting flesh echoes throughout the room. Sweat runs down the back of my neck as I fuck my woman harder. Her screams fill the air along with my grunts. The tingle in my balls starts as my mind becomes fuzzy, the feeling continuing to radiate through my body. Pretty Bird screams again, and hot jets of my cum explode like an eruption, making my legs turn to jelly. I barely manage to keep us both upright as my legs buckle beneath me. Not wanting her to get hurt, I drop to the floor as our kiss becomes sensual. Not in our usual brutal way, this isn't a fight for dominance between us.

79

REIKA

My heart races like a freight train as my head is pressed to Kane's forehead, both of us trying to catch our breath. My body is still alive from multiple orgasms, and I feel like I'm floating.

"For fuck's sake!" Liam shouts through the door this time. "You two ready yet?"

"Give me ten," I shout back.

Pulling myself up to separate our bodies, I stand and make my way toward the bathroom. My head spins and I stumble on my way there.

"What the fuck, Pretty Bird?" Kane says, panicked.

I shake my head to try and clear my brain. "Chill out, man, I haven't eaten today," I say.

"You had food when you came in," he says.

I lift a brow at him. Yeah, I did have food when I came in, but I hit his idiot brother in the face with it. My stomach growls in protest of the lack of food, and another wave of dizziness hits me. I manage to catch myself before I face plant, as frantic hands run across my back.

"What the fuck, babe?" Kane growls.

"I hit Frosty with the burger, dude, so I didn't get to eat," I answer.

"Get ready and I'll grab you some food," he says.

I plonk my ass down on the edge of the bed as he tears through the room in a state of panic, throwing clothes on. I can't help but snort laughter at his actions.

Kane

I can't believe she hasn't eaten. My anger toward myself is unrivaled, but knowing she wasted food hitting my brother pisses me off as I charge down the stairs to the kitchen. I pass a few of the crew members on the way down that burst out laughing. I haven't got time for their shit! I continue my journey and it's the same thing, everyone I pass starts laughing. I slide across the kitchen floor as I fight to try and keep myself upright. Both my brothers jump back as my legs come out from underneath me.

"You, asshole, make Reika some food," I seethe at Liam.

His eyebrows hit his hairline as a snort of laughter slips through his lips. Marcus just stares at me wide-eyed. They turn to each other, and burst out laughing. Has the entire crew gone nuts? Pulling my ass off the floor, I glare at the two laughing hyenas.

"What?" I ask.

"I wasn't sure you'd like the color," Marcus throws back at me in a girly voice.

"Yeah, Bro, it really brings out the color in your eyes," Liam says, then doubles over laughing. What the fuck? I look down and what stares back at me fills me with horror.

"No," I shout as I charge out of the kitchen to the mirror in the hallway.

I can't believe my fucking eyes, my reflection has me horrified. I hear cackling behind me again, turn and see them with tears streaming down their faces.

"What the fuck have you done?" I spit through my teeth.

I'm in a pair of bright pink fucking sweatpants and a pink T-shirt with some weird pink unicorn thing on it. Disgust and horror war within me. I take in my reflection as my brothers continue to howl. The motherfuckers! This is why the crew laughed when you passed. White hot rage sparks within me at the balls on these two, at the audacity to fuck with my clothes. What the fuck? We aren't in high school. I'm just staring at myself, as they continue to fall apart behind me.

I charge back up to the bedroom, where Pretty Bird is laying on the bed. Looking like she hasn't moved an inch from the time I left. I rip open the wardrobe doors and horror fills me. All my black and grey clothes are now different shades of pink. There is even some fluffy shit hanging on one of the rails.

"What's up, Baby?" she asks.

I snort in response as my brain quick fires all the multiple ways I can kill my brothers and make it look like an accident.

"Where are my fucking clothes!" I roar back out into the hallway, which has more laughter reaching up the stairs.

I've never wanted to murder them so much in my life. They often piss me off like brothers do, but this is taking it above and fucking beyond any of the stupid pranks they have ever played on me. I remember once Marcus put some weird see-through stuff on the toilet so when I went for a piss it went everywhere but in the toilet. I can't figure out how or why they would fucking do this. This isn't the time to be playing stupid fucking games with each other.

"It really suits you, Baby," Pretty Bird says, then laughter fills the bedroom.

I turn to look at her, as she howls with laughter holding her stomach. Tears roll down her cheeks. Her laugh is then echoed by two others. Looking over my shoulder, I find Liam and Marcus standing in the doorway. Every time one of them looks in my direction and the laughter intensifies.

"Start fucking talking," I say to all three of them.

The little shitbags all turn wide eyes on me like they had nothing to do with it. But I can smell the bullshit a mile away. My eyes narrow on each of them when a memory flashes in my mind.

"You two?" I point between Pretty Bird and Liam.

Pretty Bird starts laughing so hard she falls off the damn bed, and Liam trips over nothing as he ends up flat on his face on the bedroom floor. Marcus starts laughing at the two other fucking idiots, and I'm just standing here looking like a unicorn threw up on me.

"He needs glitter to go with the Pinky Pie top!" Pretty Bird screeches as she jumps to her feet, running to the bathroom.

"Oh, hell no!" I bellow as I chase the psychotic little hobbit.

Unlucky for me she has two idiots who seem to like the idea of her grabbing fucking glitter. Marcus dive bombs me clean off my motherfucking feet. I land on the bed, throwing punches trying to knock the bastard off me, which the he just laughs at. Liam jumps on the bed and pins my arms down above my head. My roar fills the room as my brothers fight to keep me in place. If I get out of this, both of these bastards are on bathroom duty for months. That thought has a smile tipping my lips.

"Hellion, Kane's gonna give us bathroom duty," Marcus shouts.

"Why?" she shouts back, as rattles come from the room. Followed by drawers opening and slamming shut.

"Because," Liam shouts.

The high-pitched squeal that fills the air has my ears ringing. Pretty Bird saunters back into the bedroom with a look of triumph on her face. She holds up a little box thing in her hand with a huge fucking grin.

"Pretty Bird," I chastise, "don't even think about it." As soon as the words leave my mouth, I realize my mistake.

She lands on top of me, pulling her legs into position as I thrash underneath her. She's like a damn monkey that seems to superglue themselves to you and won't let go. Their laughter fills the air. As my assault becomes more violent, something swipes across my eye. Pretty Bird smiles so wide the fight is knocked out of me for a second. Liam starts puckering his lips at me and laughing, while Marcus keeps a tight hold on my legs. Every time Pretty Bird looks like she's gonna fall, he grabs hold of her.

"Why are you doing this to me?" I ask between pants.

"You need to get that stick out of your ass, Bro," Marcus says.

I'm so fucking confused at what they mean, when they all burst out laughing again.

"Errm. Boss?" All our eyes turn to the doorway to of the grunts.

"One fucking word and you're out," I seethe at him. It's bad enough some of the crew saw me on my way to the kitchen.

What the hell is happening here? Throwing my head up, I manage to catch Liam under his chin slightly. As he falls, I thrash my legs so much Marcus is knocked off the bed. Pretty Bird just stares down at me with an 'oh shit' look and I smirk as I grab hold of her hips and lift her off me. Once I'm standing back on my feet, I look back to the new addition to the room.

"What's happening?" I ask, my breathing is still labored.

"The Grimm's are attacking The Den," he stutters out.

A growl tears through me instantly. What the fuck are they playing at?

"Set a fucking meeting up with De'Marco, now!" I command. He jumps out of his skin and runs off to do as I ask.

"Kane, you and Hellion have a date tonight," Marcus says.

I look at Pretty Bird who looks a little deflated at the comment. I watch her as she squares her shoulders and sets her jaw.

"You two go," Marcus says. "Liam can hold stuff down here, and I'll meet with De'Marco." My heart stops at that. With Stacy being back, there is a chance he could run into her. I look to Liam who gives me a nod; that's all I need.

"You sure man?" I question.

He looks at Pretty Bird, who seems too quiet for the conversation. Her face is stoic as she waits to see what will happen.

"Yeah, Bro." He smiles at her. "Go out and treat your woman," he says, which has a smile spreading widely across her face.

"Oh, and you are going to Rossi's," Liam says.

A huge growl fills the room as all eyes turn to Pretty Bird who is holding her stomach laughing.

"You know I'm hungry, Baby," she says sheepishly.

"De'Marco says he will meet you in twenty, Boss," says the grunt.

I rush to the side of the bed, as I tear the god-awful pink shirt off. Luckily my clothes from earlier are there.

"They're in my side," Pretty Bird says through a grin.

I head over and nearly rip the door from the wardrobe. Low and behold, a bag is at the front with all my clothes in it. I throw a look over my shoulder. She smirks sweetly at me as I shake my head. Pulling out jeans and a T-shirt, I put them on in record time. Marcus and Liam are nowhere to be seen.

"You ever been to Rossi's?" I ask. Pretty Bird shakes her head in response.

80

REIKA

I've never been to a restaurant like this. Well, honestly, I can't remember the last time I was in a restaurant. I'm trying my hardest to act like there is nothing wrong, but Kane hasn't realized he didn't wash his face before we left. The waiter gave a confused look at the make up on his face, which had me choking on my glass of water. But in true Kane fashion, he just death glared the poor guy until he left. I thought it would be awkward for us, but it isn't. After talking about the stupid prank and why we did it, he agreed it is funny now, but wasn't at the time. He did make me promise to never put him in pink stuff ever again. Our food comes just as my stomach protests again and another wave of dizziness hits me.

"You really need to take better care of yourself, Babe," he says to me like he's talking to a naughty schoolgirl.

"Yeah, I know," I mutter, because he is right, "but with everything going on, it's just been a lot."

He nods his head in agreement. We have hardly spent any quality time together since the incident with Blondie, and it feels weird to be doing it now. Marcus meeting with De'Marco while we sit here like a regular couple is just strange. I have never wanted the sunshine and rainbows sort of shit, but this is nice. Hearing him laugh as I told him how creeped out Frosty was by Cynthia, then telling him everything she told me about my dad makes it all the more real that we are really doing this - trying to be a normal couple in our fucked-up world.

"Is it strange for you?" he says over a forkful of Bolognese. "Being here?"

"Yeah and no," I reply which has him cocking his head to the side, the hair on the top of his head flops into his eyes and my pussy comes alive.

"What do you mean?" His voice is layered in uncertainty.

"Yeah, because not that long ago I was fighting in the ring to make ends meet," I say. His eyes become downcast at my words. "And no, because it just feels right being here."

"Yeah, I know what you mean, Babe," he says. "It's been a lot."

I have to agree with him, our conversation breaks off as we both dig into our food, much to the delight of my stomach which I'm pretty sure was on the verge of eating itself. I've heard about this place from Mel. She used to gush over the food here when she came on dates.

"I saw Tom at the graveyard," I say. Kane cocks his eyebrow.

"He saw the scars on my back and started running his mouth." I try to make my tone void of emotions, but my anger slips through.

"Are you wanting to try and get in touch with him?" His question catches me off guard and I choke on my pizza. Yeah, I know. Classy.

"No," I blurt out. His eyes widen at the ferocity in my tone.

He nods and continues eating his food. The meal passes quickly as we laugh, joke and talk about the most random things. He fills me in on more shit the guys did to him when they were younger, and I decide to pull up my big girl panties and tell him about my life. I have to give him his dues, he doesn't react like I expected him too. He did growl occasionally, but the table is still standing. He listens so intently as I tell him about all the bad shit that happened with training, about the pity in Frosty's face as he saw the torture room at the lodge, and everything in between. He nearly choked when I told him about all the shit that went down with Stacy and how it made me feel. The heartbreak Cheshire had on his face and how it gutted me for him. That's why even though it feels like there are fire ants crawling underneath my skin, I tell Kane the fears I have about us.

"I always thought I was easily forgotten," I mumble as it feels like a knife is twisting in my gut. "Dad was never one to really show me how much he cared, but then I found that letter at the lodge.

"I never knew he could be like that, and it kills me to know I will never get the chance to learn who he really was on the inside." A small tear drips form the side of my eye.

"I know, Baby," he coos. "Your dad went about things the wrong way. But he loved you," Kane says.

I know he's right, but it's still hard to picture him being the loving doting father everyone else thought he was.

Tonight has been a whirlwind and I am dying to unbutton my jeans. My stomach feels like it's ready to burst. We both get lost in our own heads for a little while. I wouldn't be surprised if he isn't thinking about the shit show of a father he has.

"Fuck," he says as he jumps to his feet.

"What's up?" I jump up ready for action, my muscles coiled, ready to strike. He turns the phone to me so I can see and my heart sinks.

· · ·

Liam:

Someone tried to kidnap Marcus after the meeting!

I'm just about to ask who would be stupid enough to do that. I've seen the darkness that lays in wait behind his eyes. They either have a death wish or they're stupid. The phone beeps again.

Liam:

Get back here now we have an issue!

My brain starts to run a thousand miles a minute trying to figure what the hell could have Frosty so panicked, and fear for Marcus has me grabbing hold of all my shit. Kane throws some bills down on the table. Neither of us say a word as apprehension builds in my stomach. Kane mutters the whole way back about who would try and kidnap Marcus, and what happened with De'Marco. While my brain takes me down the rabbit hole. Thank God Kane is driving like a NASCAR driver, we get back in record time. Crew members are everywhere. The yard is full of them, but what has the unease growing in me is how they all look to the floor as I make my way to the house. Blood curdling screams fill the hallway as I head off in search of Liam. Doc nearly barrels me over as he rushes down the hallway.

"Shit, I'm sorry, Reika," he stutters with a fearful expression.

"Doc, what's going on?" I ask. He looks at me terrified, and stutters through a load of words that make no sense.

"Giz?" I turn around and find a pale Frosty watching me from the living room. "Let Doc work, okay?"

"Why?" My voice is hesitant.

"Pretty Bird?" Kane says as he strolls through the front door, his eyes widen seeing Doc in the hallway.

I look between all of them. Frosty is looking like he's a second away from running. I'm pretty sure Doc is close to pissing himself.

"Someone tell me what the fuck is going on!" I roar, my anger has taken over instantly, without any warning.

Marcus walks through the door to the basement, wiping blood from his hands. He has a sadistic grin on his face, his eyes filled with darkness. My own rears its head at not getting any answers. Frosty pales as I narrow my gaze at him. Doc whimpers at my side.

"It's Paine." My heart stops, as I turn to look at Doc.

I don't think as I take off in the direction of the room I know Doc uses to treat the crew. A few of them are waiting outside the door, but as soon as their eyes land on me they run in the opposite direction. My hand trembles as I grab the door handle and turn it. Beeps fill the shadowed room as I step in, my brain is silent. I slowly make my way toward the bed.

As I look down to the body lying there, my chest constricts like something is crushing it. Air won't fill my lungs. My breathing comes in choked gasps. My cousin lays on the bed in a mutilated mess. He has cuts and gashes all over his face and neck. The covers are pulled up tight to his neck, so that's all I'm able to see, but that's enough. Dark spots creep into my vision and my legs give way. The beeps fill my head as I see Paine on the bed, his chest rising and falling only slightly.

"Pretty Bird?" Kane's voice feels like a sweet caress against my mind.

"Kane, be careful you don't know how unstable she is going to be." someone else mutters.

I feel the darkness pulling me under again. I want to hide from the reality that awaits me when I open my eyes.

"Baby?" His words feel like they are reaching into my soul, trying to pull me out.

The light hurts and has my head screaming as my eyes flutter open. Kane, Cheshire and Frosty are all leaning over my body with scared expressions.

"What happened?" I croak out. They all look to each other, and gulp. Kane helps me up into a sitting position, and I realize I'm on the floor in the treatment room. Pulling me closer to his chest, he cocoons me in his arms.

"You fainted when you saw Paine," Cheshire mumbles quickly.

My mind reels at the feeling of helplessness as I remember my cousin laying not five feet away from me, looking like he's a second away from dying on me. I manage to wriggle out of Kane's arms and crawl on my hands and knees toward the bed. The room spins again as I pull myself up.

"Here," Frosty says passing me a chair.

With a slight smile I take it and sit down next to the bed. Doc watches my every move with a jittery one of his own.

"I'm okay, Doc." I try to reassure him.

The lights are on, so I get to see the full effect of the damage to his face. A gasp leaves me at the mottled color of his skin. As gentle as I can, I sweep the hair off his forehead and stroke the bit of healthy skin I can find.

"How bad is he?" I ask.

"He's been starved and is dehydrated," Doc says, then gulps, "but he has superficial wounds all over."

"Superficial?" I ask, confused.

"Yeah, he has lacerations everywhere, but there are some

deeper wounds as well." A growl rips out of my throat without warning, and poor Doc jumps back.

"I knew something was wrong." Guilt slams in to me. I couldn't find him.

"Baby, we were looking for him," Kane tries to reassure me, stepping closer.

"Yeah, but look at what the fuck has happened now!" I shout, hatred for myself poisoning every word.

They all start to give words of reassurance, but all it does is piss me off even more. Paine looks to be in worse condition than I was when he got me out.

"How did he get back?" The question stops them in their tracks.

"He was left on the doorstep, Giz," Frosty mumbles.

"What?" My voice is barely a whisper.

"One of the guys found him on the doorstep," Frosty mumbles again.

My mind agonizes over the fact that I was out having date night with Kane, while my cousin went through torture and was dropped on the doorstep of my home.

"Leave us." I say. The words croak out around the huge lump in my throat that blocks my airway.

The door clicks as they quietly leave the room, leaving me alone with the constant beep of the heart rate machine. That beep is the only way I know that he is alive. All the emotions I have bottled up for so long come out like a tsunami. I can't stop the silent tears as quiet sobs wrack my body.

81

KANE

Five days. Five fucking days have passed since Pretty Bird told us to leave the treatment room. She hasn't left his side unless she needs to go to the bathroom. She has eaten in the room and slept in the chair. We have all taken turns to spend time with her in the room and get her anything she needs. Doc has tried more the once to get her to sleep in our bed, but she shut that down instantly. Paine has woken up a few times since being here, but he hasn't been able to tell us much. He has slept a lot, which Doc says is a good thing. His body needs to recuperate. Liam is keeping an eye on everything with the crew, and Marcus is playing with his new toy down in the basement. Unfortunately for one of the idiots that tried to kidnap Marcus, he is learning why my brother is the most feared enforcer. I'm surprised to hear voices as I get to the treatment room door.

"I'm sorry for scaring you." The words are broken and quiet.

"It's okay, cuz. You're here now," Pretty Bird tries to soothe him.

Not wanting to disturb them, I head to the kitchen to find a boat load of caffeine.

"Kane?" I look to the hallway to find Doc shuffling his feet.

"He okay, Doc?" Uneasiness grows in my gut.

"Yeah. He will be ok." He continues to shuffle his feet.

"What's up?"

He huffs out a breath as he walks over to the island with his hands in his pockets, not meeting my eyes. He pulls something out and slides it across the island to me. I'm surprised to find a USB there.

"This was in his pocket, when he was brought in," he says in a whisper.

"What is it?"

"I don't know," he mutters.

I look at the small black thing with a feeling of doom and I don't know why. Who would put something on the body of a guy who has been so badly beaten?

"What's that?" Pretty Bird mumbles as she rubs the sleep from her eyes.

Her hair is all over the place and she's in the same clothes she was wearing when we got back from our date night. Her eyes look hollow and all her energy is missing, her snark isn't there. Screams echo around the house again from the basement, pulling a small chuckle from her.

"Take it he's having fun?" she sniggers.

"Marcus has tortured the guy for hours trying to get as much info as he can," I say.

Pretty Bird walks straight over to me and settles herself against my side, giving me all kinds of warm fuzzies as she seeks out comfort. Sliding myself off the seat, I put her in my place, grab her cup and make coffee.

"Anyone gonna tell me what that is?" She points to the stick of doom.

"It was in Paine's pocket," Doc blurts. I glare at the idiot as Pretty Bird sucks in air.

"What's on it?" she asks, with a yawn.

"We don't know," Doc blurts again, as I slam the coffee cup down on the counter.

The cup cracks along the bottom as Doc jumps out of my line of fire. I can't believe he opened his fucking mouth about the USB stick. Pretty Bird has enough to deal with at the moment. She doesn't need to be worrying about that. I can see how tired she is, the exhaustion radiates off her.

"We need to know." Her words sound tired, but I know she won't take no for an answer.

"You sure?" Annoyance flairs on her face.

She doesn't even reply as she stands up with coffee in one hand and swipes the USB off the island with the other. She heads out of the kitchen shouting for Marcus and Liam as she goes. They both pop up from wherever they have been, looking at me in a silent question. I just shrug as I follow Pretty Bird. She heads toward the office.

My heart rate goes mental as she sits in my throne behind the desk and takes a deep breath. As she puts the USB in place, we all suck in a breath. My brothers and I all shuffle closer to the screen, Pretty Bird's hand trembles as her finger hovers over the pad. The atmosphere is supercharged as we all wait with bated breath to see what the hell is on this damn thing. The click of the pad, echoes around the room. Pretty Birds gasps as a video loads up. The first thing we see is Paine, bloodied, tied to a chair.

"I didn't want it to come to this, Reika," a weird sounding voice says through the speakers, "but you left me no choice." Pretty Bird growls in response.

I watch with wide eyes as I am slapped in the face with the one thing that stole my everything. A person walks across the screen in a well fitted suit, a mask covering their face.

"Kane?" Marcus and Liam hiss quietly.

Horror fills me, as the memories of the video I watched of Pretty Bird dying flash through my mind.

"Fancy Pants," Pretty Bird hisses with so much venom, we all snap our gazes to her.

Her chest rises and falls rapidly as the growl building within grows to a terrifying volume. My mind closes off just slightly as the words from the video echo.

"He helped you and he got hurt for it. Doesn't that make you feel like a monster, Reika?

"How does it make you feel that one of your friend's killed herself from what I did to her? She screamed for you. Begging for you to help her."

Anguished sobs fill the air, but I am still lost in what is unfolding in front of me.

"Screaming as we took what we wanted from her over and over!" Vomit flies up the back of my throat as gagging noises fill the room.

"She was so much fun to use as we saw fit. Every time I was buried inside her, she fought like a wild animal."

Manic laughter fills the room.

"She broke when she realized you weren't coming to save her. That the infamous Reaper was no help to her, and she was left to rot. I wonder will you fight as much as she did?"

"Kane," someone shouts.

"Now is the time to play, Reika. Come find me, I know you want to."

Laughter echoes through the room as the person talking steps in front of the camera in a full-face shot, then the camera stutters out and a video that has me horrified, fills the screen. The grunts and moans falling from the speakers has me and Pretty Bird staring at each other in shock.

"Guys?" Marcus asks.

The video stops as the masked face comes back in front of

the camera, the heavy breathing sending a shiver down my spine.

"I am always watching you, Reika. You are mine."

The camera zooms out so the person can be seen and there is open space around them in the shot. Suddenly the background fills with different pictures of Pretty Bird that have me feeling violated on her behalf. Some are of her in the shower in the house or asleep next to me. Some are pics taken when we have been having sex, like the video that has just been played from near the car. The laughter starts again as the masked person slowly lifts the mask up and over their face.

"I'm gonna fucking kill him!" My roar fills the room as I grab the laptop off the desk and throw it against the wall.

"Motherfucker!" both my brothers roar.

My body takes over as I tear through the office, destroying anything in my path. Pictures get ripped off the walls as my darkness roars to life. I should have fucking known it would be him. The crunch of something draws my attention as I find my hand embedded in the wall of the office. I pull it back out; my hand is a bloodied mess.

"Kane!" Liam screams at me.

I spin to him as my nostril flare with my rage. My eyes widen as I find Marcus trying to pull his hair out as he roars. I freeze as I notice Pretty Bird just stares off into space, not really seeing anything. Liam is muttering to her how sorry he is, trying to pull her out of her own mind.

"Who is it?" her voice is lifeless as she asks.

"De'Marco," Liam spits through his teeth, prompting another roar from Marcus.

Pretty Bird lifts her head as if she is looking directly at my brother, but there is nothing behind her eyes, just an endless void.

"Who?" she asks again.

"The leader of the Grimm's," my brother answers.

82

REIKA

My mind is worse than hell, as that name echoes through my head. The masked figure taunts me about Mel, over and over, until everything becomes blurs together and I can't tell what is real anymore. De'Marco did this to Mel? He did this to Paine? My darkness is out and begging to pave the way with his blood. He defiled my friend and broke her spirit. Why? The questions rattle around inside my head as my body becomes a twitching live wire. Roars fill the room from Marcus as he tries to tear his hair from his head, but I can't bring myself to care about the brother who is in self-destruct mode right now. De'Marco took pleasure in taunting me, in telling me to find him.

My mind snaps back, becoming as clear as day. I stand up from my seat behind the desk. I make my way across the office to a chorus of shouts asking what I am doing. My body feels like it's on autopilot as I walk through the hallways. Murderous intentions filter into my head, giving me all the best ideas on how to kill the motherfucker painfully. A smirk tilts my lips as I think of all the ways that it is possible. The door creaks and the cold air hits me full force. I gasp in shock at the sudden change in temperature. A wheezing sort of rattle filters up to my ears. My steps echo on the stairs as a shiver sweeps across me. The door to the basement room is slightly ajar, the rattle happens again as something coughs on the other side of the door.

"Is someone there?" the voice croaks.

I step into the room and find a man hanging from the ceiling in chains, his body broken. His face is so badly swollen shut there aren't any features making him recognizable.

"Hellion?" Cheshire says from behind me. The guy trembles in fear at the sound of his voice.

I smirk as I look over my shoulder to my shadow. I see the darkness he tries so hard to hide, front and center. It's as if our demons are speaking to one another. Marcus sweeps past me into the room and unfurls something on a metal table. As the item is opened, the guy shakes violently with each resounding clink. My inner darkness drinks it all in.

"Where is he?" I ask the mystery man.

"Wh-Who?" he stutters back.

His scream tears through the air as Cheshire lands a vicious blow to his ribs.

"Where is he?" My tone is so cold, it feels like the temperature in the room drops.

"I don't know who you mean," he stutters again.

I lift a brow to Cheshire who is waiting on me, the sadistic grin that spreads across his face is all predator. Screams reverberate around the room as Cheshire sets in on the man. Beating him until his screams turn into hollow groans. But my friend doesn't stop there. The assault continues to increase in pace as he asks where we can find his master, every insufficient response intensifying the attack. My rage builds with each shitty answer he gives. I launch forward, knocking Cheshire out of the way, and I wrap my hand around the guy's throat.

"Where is he?" I scream in his face, my spit flying everywhere.

"I don't…" he stutters.

I spin to the table of horrors and grin as I spot all the instruments lined up neatly. From scalpel's, to knuckle dusters to big ass knives,my inner psycho is squealing. I pull on a duster and face the guy again.

"Where is he?"

Whack!

"Where the fuck is he!"

Whack!

My rage turns molten as he keeps his mouth shut. I drop the knuckle duster back on the trolley and pull up my next object.

"What are you doing?" the guy whispers out in a broken voice.

"Where is De'Marco!" I scream, as I yank his head back he lets out a blood curdling scream.

"With the syndicate!" he screams.

My hand lashes out, as my darkness roars in delight. The thump has my face splitting into a malicious smile as I look over to Cheshire who grins right back. I swipe the new ornament off the floor and head back up the stairs. Just as I'm about to step through the door I hear raised voices.

"It was De'Marco," Fox's voice shouts.

"We know," Liam roars.

I walk over to the kitchen, placing the new feature onto the kitchen island. All three of them jump away from the head sitting in a pool of blood on the counter.

"Reika?" Fox whispers with a horrified expression.

I tilt my head to the side and watch him as his eyes flick between me and the head. A smile fights to break through my stoic look. Marcus cackles at the horrified looks in the room. A chuckle builds in the back of my throat.

"What have you two done?" Kane asks.

"We got rid of the problem, Bro," Marcus says, which has the bubbling laugh bursting out of me.

"So, Fox, what have you found out," I inquire as his complexion pales further.

"Little Warrior?" My heart stutters at the tired voice as Paine wobbles into my line of sight. His eyes bug out as he sees the head on the island.

"What are you doing up?" I say as I rush over to my cousin.

"Any reason why Dean's head is bodyless?" He cocks his head at me and smirks.

"Ah, so you know who he is?" Kane asks.

"You knew you were a part of the Grimm's?" Fox asks my cousin with a suspicious look.

He looks down at me guiltily and I see the torment in his eyes. Stepping closer to him, I try not to hurt him too much as I wrap my arms around him and give him the hug I have been waiting for.

"When I found out she was my cousin," he starts, "I knew it would be better for her here than with that psycho."

"Do you know who she is?" Fox asks. We all frown at Fox with a what the fuck are you on about expression.

"Just as I thought," he mumbles rubbing his chin.

"Reika there is a reason why De'Marco is so dead set about you being his," Fox says. I lift a brow urging him to continue.

"You are the true leader of the Grimm's," he says with a serious face.

Me and the guys all burst out laughing at his ridiculous statement, tears stream down my face at the idiot who has been fed false information.

"Laugh all you want fuckers, but Reika is the leader of the syndicate." My heart stops.

"What?" I croak as the guys all turn to me, wide eyed.

"Your dad ruled the Grimm's, but was also the King of the biggest underground organization on this side of the state." I just stare.

"All the families have one who sits in a seat and a King or Queen is chosen to lead."

"And Reika?" I lift my eyes to meet Fox's.

"De'Marco killed your parents." His face is wracked with guilt as he looks anywhere but at me.

My mind once again becomes numb as everything I have pieced together slots into place, like puzzle pieces and they fit perfectly. I know what I have to do, and the time is now to show these bastards once and for all.

"Send the head to the syndicate," I say as I turn on my heels and leave the room.

Kane

I'm at a loss for words about everything that has happened over the course of our time together but seeing Pretty Bird become devoid of emotion has a new anger building within me. I knew she wasn't in the right frame of mind to listen to anything else Fox had to say, I sat with him and my brothers as he told us everything he found out about De'Marco and the syndicate. He also gave me the disturbing news that he found Pete dead. He is just waiting on the confirmation before we tell Pretty Bird. I don't know how well she will take another loss. Luckily, Paine is back on his feet and regaining strength, which seems to pull her out of the darkness when needed. I can't say the same about Marcus, he is lost in the darkness all the time now, and that terrifies me and Liam. Pretty Bird has come down a few times and told us we need to get ready to make them pay. She doesn't want to leave it too long before dealing with De'Marco.

"Everyone ready?" I ask the room. Looking at my watch I know she will be down any minute to discuss the plan of attack.

"Yes, Boss," the inner circle says. Liam and Marcus grunt their approval.

"Everyone here?" Pretty Bird asks, walking straight through the room to the seat I am standing behind.

I pull it out for her, and she gives me a wicked smile as she takes her seat at the head of the table. Everyone has been filled in on what went down. They are all chomping at the bit to end this shit once and for all.

"Fox, is the shipment still going ahead?" She turns to him.

"Yes, Reika. They will be there in three hours."

The grin that splits her face has some of the crew gulping out of fear. I chuckle, because they are the same ones who kicked up a stink about a woman having a say.

"Let's get this done."

83

KANE

Wance all watch from our hiding places around the
warehouse, looking at the little displays Pretty Bird
gave us. Apparently, she took them from her dad's lodge, which
is cool since we can see what is going on in the warehouse. We
watch as they all flit about without a care in the world, not
knowing what is waiting for them. My woman looks demonic
as she stands beside me in a long black leather coat, jeans and
her boots. Fucking gorgeous.

"It's time," she says, stepping out of the shadows and
heading to the doorway.

We all follow the one leading us into the belly of the beast.
Liam has his mask in place, his face not giving anything away.
Marcus bounces on the balls of his feet with a shit eating grin,
excitement rolling off him in waves. We all creep silently down
the hallway. The voices in the main area get louder as we make
our way. Pretty Bird doesn't duck down like some of the others.
No, she throws the door to the main room open with huge grin.

"Tag, you're it! I found you, De'Marco," she shouts, then
proceeds further into the room.

Clapping fills the room, as the man in question steps

forward in front of Pretty Bird. A growl grows in my throat at the way he looks her over, like a lion looking at its dinner.

"Well, well. What do we have here?" He says with a click of his fingers.

Men pour out of the back of the wagons in the room, surrounding us. I step forward as a gun points at my temple blocking my path to Pretty Bird. I should have fucking known the bastard would have pulled something like this. But what he doesn't know, is my woman has set them all up. We willingly walked into an ambush so they would think they had the upper hand. The atmosphere is supercharged, as the Grimm's face off with us.

My brothers and I become restless as Pretty Bird gets separated further from the group as they march her toward De'Marco. My anger simmers under the surface, waiting to explode, as I watch that motherfucker circle my woman like a damn vulture with a glint in his eye. Every now and then his gaze flicks to mine and the fucker grins, trying to taunt me into doing something. I manage to hold myself steady until, the fucker runs his fingers across her cheek while grinning at me like he just won the damn lotto. Marcus catches my eye; with a subtle shake of this head, I know he is telling me to keep calm. Everything has been planned we need to stick to it, or this is will to end in disaster.

"What's the matter, Southbourne?" De'Marco sneers across the warehouse "I'll give you your dues, you have excellent taste in women. She is lovely." The growl from Pretty Bird should have been enough to warn him. But no, he licks his tongue up the side of her face and my brain explodes.

"Keep your fucking hands off her!" I roar, it echoes all the way up to the rafters.

Liam and Marcus grapple with me, trying to stop me from charging across this place and ripping his face off. I really want to rip his fucking head off! The bastard grins because he's managed to get a reaction out of me, which pisses me off to astronomical levels. I feel like the human torch from that movie, but I can get hurt by the flames. My body feels like it's being melted off. I'm still struggling in my brothers' hold, causing De'Marco to smile at me with a smug look. My growl echoes around the room. Pretty Bird catches my attention over his shoulder. She blows me a kiss and throws a wink at me. This has my body temperature dropping slightly. Liam turns a knowing smile on me having seen what Pretty Bird had done. My body relaxes further with the reassurance on Liam's face. Marcus feels the fight go out of me and gives us both a confused look.

"So, Reika, have you agreed to be mine yet?" he asks in a sickly-sweet tone as he circles her once again. My whole body vibrates. What I'm going to do to the bastard when I get my hands on him.

I don't see or hear a reply come out of her mouth, but whatever look Pretty Bird has on her face pisses him off. His body stiffens and his features turn stormy. His hand snaps out and grabs hold of her by the back of her neck. My body instantly coils as he yanks her forward so they are so close they look like they are joined together. He leers down at her in triumph, looking down the front of the top.

"Arrrrrggggggggh!" Tears through the area as De'Marco drops to the floor like a bitch, holding his junk. "You fucking bitch!" he screams as tears stream down his face. Sniggers fill the air from the Damned Crew and the Grimm's turn to their boss with shocked faces. But what has me chuckling, is the tinkle of laughter that grows more manic by the second as my baby glares down at the supposed King on his knees.

"Aww, did that hurt, De'Marco?" she says ever so sweetly.

"I fucking told you to be careful, boy." The words fill the room along with the clomp of footsteps on the concrete floor.

"Sorry, Father," De'Marco mutters as he pulls himself back up to his feet, glaring at Pretty Bird.

My brothers and I all stare at each other in surprise. "Father?" I mouth to my brothers, and they both lift their shoulders in reply. He's a street kid with no family? That's what he said for all the years we knew him. The clomp grows louder as the new person walks across the warehouse. My eyes bug out of my head at the man in an expertly fitted suit. Strangely he has a mask covering his face. It's identical to the one De'Marco had on in the video. I am even more confused as all the Grimm's practically bow to the guy, who is making a beeline for Pretty Bird. She doesn't give anything away as she squares her shoulders and lifts her chin in defiance. A snort fills the air from the mystery man, like he expected that reaction, and my anger starts to build again. This new person isn't someone we know, and now knowing he is De'Marco's father has changed the whole situation we prepared for.

A growl fills the room. "I knew you were going to be trouble, girl. So, I made sure to take out an insurance policy," he seethes as he grips Pretty Bird's face harder.

"Kane. Don't you dare move," Liam hisses at me under his breath.

"Oh, yeah?" she spits back at the newbie the best she can. Even the grip he has on her doesn't stop the venom dripping from her words.

"Yeah." he says, as he slides the mask up slowly to reveal his face.

"You motherfucker!" me and my brothers roar in unison. The click of safety being clicked off stop us short.

Pretty Bird stands frozen to her spot. I can't see her face, but her anger is apparent to everyone in the warehouse as her shoulders rise and fall rapidly. I still can't believe who is standing in front of her, like it's the most normal thing ever. My attention snaps to the sound of something being dragged across the floor, the clinks remind me of chains. So, when I see some of the Grimm's dragging a body across the floor, chains clinking together behind it, I'm not surprised. I don't have a clue who the hostage is.

"Daddy?" says the voice of a broken child who has seen a ghost for the first time. Pretty Bird looks at the guy with horror on her face, her lower lip trembles.

"Daddy?" she whispers again in shock and the emotion has an imaginary knife gutting me.

Pete has a gleeful expression on his face as Pretty Bird watches the Grimm's dragging her father across the floor and dumping him at her feet.

"I told you. I took out an insurance policy, girl," he says to her.

"Why?" Her voice breaks as she kneels to her father, feeling the betrayal of the man she has seen as her family since his death.

"He had everything I ever wanted," Pete says in such a calm way, it sends a tremor down my spine. "He ruled the syndicate, he ruled the Grimm's and had the perfect fucking family," he hisses between gritted teeth. De'Marco growls his agreement beside his father.

"How?" Her words are hollow. I can't tell if it's from shock or if everything hasn't quite sunk in yet.

"Someone pulled you out of the fire when they shouldn't have," he replies flippantly. "So, I went back in for your father."

"I saw him die," she screams at him. "It's not possible."

"When I got inside, he still had a slight heartbeat. So, as

you say when you surprise someone…" He grins. "Ta-Dah." He jumps and throws his arms out in a flamboyant gesture.

Pretty Bird turns back to her father, who looks like he's a second away from death. Bruises and gashes litter what I can see of him, and the signs of old injuries are clear even from my distance. She's whispering something to him.

Bang!

"Noooooo!" Her scream tears my soul straight out of my body.

Reika

"Daddy!" My screams fill the air.

"Please, Daddy," I scream as I try to apply pressure to his chest. "Please, don't leave me," I beg to whoever will hear my pleas. His breathing stutters as he coughs, and bloods flies out of his mouth. "Daddy, no!" I beg him again. His eyes meet mine, and his blood continues to fill between my fingers as I try to save him.

"Please, Daddy, you can't leave me." My soul shatters. "Not again, Daddy, please."

I watch my father fight to breathe, tears streaming down my face. My eyes widen at the amount of blood managing to escape through my fingers. His breathing has become rattled and choked. Blood flies from his mouth as he coughs again. My heart beats frantically as I try to remember my training to deal with wounds.

"L-Little," the words are strangled and broken, "Reaper."

"Daddy?" I lean down further to try and hear what he is saying.

"S-Show. T-Them. Why. They. Should…" He breaks off into another coughing fit, pushing more blood through my fingers.

"Should what?" I ask.

"Fear you." As the last words fall from his broken and cracked lips, his breathing stutters to a stop. His body becomes still.

"Noooooo!" I scream as I rock my father's body back and forth, praying to all the gods I can think of to bring him back. I need him!

Show them why they should fear you. His words echo in my head, as I sit on the concrete floor holding him in my arms. His words aren't broken as they repeat over and over in my head. My darkness awakens with a battle cry inside my mind as my whole body fires off like a rocket. The continued roar in my head has my vision tinting red, as my body becomes numb. A bloodthirsty void is all I feel inside myself that is crying out for revenge. Slowly, I slide my father onto the ground as I pull myself up to my feet. Silence greets me, my only friend in that moment.

"Aww, what's the matter, Little Reaper?" The person I considered family sneers at me.

Lifting my head so our eyes meet, his complexion instantly pales at the look on my face. He stumbles backward as I cock my head at the little shit standing next to him and grin. I know the look on my face must be terrifying because he trips over backward trying to get away from me.

"One. Two. I will kill you. Three. Four. You can't run no more."

War cries fill the air as Pete turns on his heel and runs as fast as he can. My vision is laser focused on him as I stalk him through the warehouse. I avoid the flying bodies as I pass the Grimm's and The Damned fighting like this is the final battle in the war. Manic laughter builds in my throat as Pete tries desperately to open the doors leading out of here. Not a chance, fuckface! I knew the locks were a good idea. My grin is vicious as I watch him scramble, trying to find a way out. I watch as he falls over bodies that lay dead on the floor and all my mind is thinking of is all the ways I am going to kill this bastard that ruined my life.

"Reika, can we discuss this?" he begs as he runs for his life.

I cock my head and continue to stalk him; my silence is answer enough for him as he searches around. An agonizing roar fills the air. Looking over my shoulder I see Kane and De'Marco in a brawl. No weapons in sight as they fight hand to hand. Unluckily for the father son duo, he isn't faring well next to my man. The grin I turn on Pete would have been terrifying if the space wasn't empty. What the fuck? Something clinks and then the sound of weird footfalls echo around the room, I look up and I smile at what I see. Perfect!

I skip my way through the crews fighting each other, throwing a few punches on my way laughing like a damn maniac. I reach the stairs to the catwalk. As I work my way up, I have a great viewpoint to see what is going on below. Some of the Grimm's are trying their hardest to break free through the doors, while others are getting dropped instantly by either a bullet or other weapon. Laughter bursts out of me as Marcus dances between different groups chopping people's heads off with a machete in one hand and a gun in the other. A shadow catches the corner of my eye on the level above and I take off in a sprint. Pete, the little shit, is trying to use the different levels to get away. I look up and find a skylight. Fuck! My arms pump furiously as I push my legs as fast as they will go, jumping over the obstacles in my way.

I make it onto the level I have just seen him. Trying to slow my breathing, I stretch my hearing as far as it will go, but with all the noise down below it's hard. I duck just in time as a whoosh passes over the top of my head. Pete stands in front of me, a murderous look on his face, with a huge metal pole in his hand. He swings it round in a circle like I do with betty, something clinks to the floor. My eyes dart down to see the pole I just knocked over. The smile that tugs at my lips says, 'Game on, bitch!' I drop to my knees and grab the pole as Pete's slams down on the center of my back. A scream tears from my lips as pain radiates through my body.

"Reika!" Kane's roar fills the air.

Black spots dance in front of my eyes. I shake my head to clear the fog. With a roar, I launch to my feet and tackle the bastard to the floor. He screams like a girl. After all the emotions of everything, I snap. I land blow after blow while screaming down at the one person I thought loved me, other than my parents. His bones crunch under my fists, making my inner darkness preen like a bird fluffing its feathers. His screams fill the air as I shatter his cheekbone and I grin, all teeth, at him.

"Arrrrrgggggggggh!" Pain radiates through my scalp as I am dragged backwards.

I'm pulled up onto my feet. Spinning, I'm shocked to find Malcolm standing with strands of my hair in his hand. I grab his wrist and twist; a loud crunch sounds as he roars. I grin at him. I lash out with my leg and hit Malcolm in the chest; his arms fly all out as he goes over the side of the catwalk. I turn, Pete is back up, bouncing on the balls of his feet. My pole has fallen somewhere, but he is still equipped with his.

"This is mine!" he yells as he charges toward me.

I manage to duck under the side of his arm, switching our positions. I dodge each swing of the pole, barely. He manages to slam it into my right side and I feel bones break under the impact. I back up to keep out of striking distance. Air flutters across my back, and the clink of metal catches my attention. Just to the side of me, chains swing from the next level above. I take off running, the pain radiating through my body brings tears to my eyes. Pete's footfalls are right behind me as I push my body to its limit. I make it to the next level and grab a length of the chain. I yank on it, but I am met with resistance.

"Time to die, Reika."

He swings for me again. I wrap the chain around the pole yanking it out of his hands. His eyes widen at his lack of weapon, as I grin. He throws caution to the wind and he charges. I throw an uppercut that stuns him enough to have him stumbling back. With a grin, I wrap the length of chain around his neck and headbutt him. He stumbles back and falls over the rail. I feel like I'm floating, as air whooshes around me. I continue to fall as Pete screams, then his wails cut off as his neck snaps. My mind reels as I realize the bastard pulled me over. My hands flap around as I try to find something to catch onto and my screams fill the air. I manage to catch a length of chain, as my hands slide down the burn in my palms is real.

Kane

Terror fills me as Pretty Bird screams when she falls from the catwalk. I roar and throw my fist into the bastard De'Marco's face, knocking him out cold.

"Liam!" I bellow as I charge toward the stairs.

He kills his opponent and charges after me without asking anything. I nod my head to what has my heart beating out of my chest and he looks terrified as she tries to stop her decent. We make it up onto the catwalk and my hand shoots out, grabbing hold of her wrist. I feel it crunch under my grip. As she screams, bile hits the back of my throat. Groans catch my attention. As I start to hoist Pretty Bird up, her hands start to slip through mine.

"Dad?" Liam hisses, his attention on something over the edge.

I reach over and grab the back of Pretty Bird's top, and with a roar, I manage to pull her up to the rails. She grabs hold of a bar and pants, my heart crumbling at the wheezing in her chest as she tries to breathe deeply.

"You crazy bitch!" my sperm donor screams, making Pretty Bird choke out half a laugh with a hiss.

"He attacked me when me and Pete were fighting," she explains. If that motherfucker wasn't swinging from the rafters by his neck, I would rip the bastard's heart out.

"Can I kill him?" Marcus shouts up to us.

I'm surprised to find De'Marco awake on his knees in front of my brother. The murderous look on his face, tells me all I need to know.

"Do it." I barely get the words out before his head hits the floor in one swoop and my crazy ass brother whoops into the air like a kid at Christmas.

I anchor Pretty Bird to the rail with my arms. I watch Malcolm try to get himself off the top of the wagon, his eyes widen as he sees Pete's body hanging from the rafters. My rage grows further with indecision, one part of me thinks fuck him. But the logical part knows he is the leech of this family. I look to Liam and he switches positions with me. I head to the side and hop over the rail, becoming air born for a few seconds. My landing rattles the wagon as Malcolm turns wide eyes on me.

"Son, help me," he pleads, palms in the air. "De'Marco and Pete tortured me."

As if that would make me think any more of the waste of

space. He thinks he can do shit and get away with all of it.

"Kane, please," he begs, snot running down his face.

Everything about my mother flashes before my eyes. The times we laughed when I was younger or when my brothers and I would do something stupid, and she would help us hide it from him. She was the light of my life back then and she is gone, because of him. I cannot allow him to destroy anything more.

"Kane!" Liam screams.

I look over my shoulder and stumble seeing a limp Pretty Bird in my brother's arms. His face is almost see-through from where I am standing. Pulling out my gun, I take aim.

"You wouldn't, son?" The uncertainty has me grinning.

"Kane, for fuck's sake!" Liam screams again.

Bang!

The light dulls in my father's eyes. I would have loved to see it drain from him, but heavy footfalls tell me Liam is on the move. Looking at the aftermath, I see a lot of the crew have survived. Marcus and Liam are charging toward the only door that has been left open. I jump down off the wagon and race after them. I make it to the car just as Marcus was about to set off.

"Get in!" he roars at me.

I scramble into the back with a passed out Pretty Bird. My stomach is in knots as I watch for her breathing. It's shallow which causes me to panic even more. Thankfully, Marcus hits the gas, and we squeal out of our spot with dust clouds behind us. The drive home only takes us minutes with the way Marcus has driven us back. As soon as we stop, I haul my ass out, pulling Pretty Bird with me. With her in my arms, I charge through the door.

"Doc!" I bellow into the hallway, Marcus and Liam are just coming through the door.

"What the hell happened?" Doc says as he walks out of the kitchen.

"She passed out," Liam answers.

The lump in my throat is restricting my ability to talk, as he ushers us into the treatment room. Placing Pretty Bird down on the bed, Doc instantly gets to work. He's pulling different stuff out of his cupboards; Pretty Bird's hand is in my grasp.

"Kane, I need you to move," Doc spits at me.

"No." The growl tears from me. I am not leaving her. He shakes his head and turns his eyes to my brothers.

"Kane," Liam says. "Let Doc do his job," Marcus says after.

My heart is hammering in my chest as I leave her behind on the bed. When beeps fill the room, my head snaps around to see Doc hooking her up to a heart rate machine. He gives me a tense smile as the door closes, blocking her from view.

Hours have passed as we wait for Doc to tell us what the fuck is going on. Marcus has threatened to kill so many people I have lost count. The crew members left at the warehouse all file into the house. We have been waiting for them to fill us in on the body clean up. What surprises me, is the number of Grimm's that have come forward and said they want to be under Pretty Bird's command, she should take her place. The door squeaks and a tired looking Doc walks toward us.

"Doc?" My heart is in my throat.

"Reika and the baby are fine."

THE END.
(Or is it?)

665

EPILOGUE

Reika.

"Can you fucking idiots behave yourselves for a second." Seriously what the fuck is wrong with them?

"Sorry," echoes from the idiots standing around the bed.

"You okay, baby?" Kane asks me.

"What do you think, fuckface," I seethe at him. "I am the size of a whale and have to decide which idiot is going to be in charge of the businesses." He drops his head sheepishly.

"Hey!" A round of protests come from said idiots.

I glare at Liam, Marcus and Paine. They cackle like a set of naughty kids. Fuck my life. Kane has been unbearable after finding out I was pregnant. It was a shock to me as I never really thought of myself as having kids. But after seeing the baby on the ultrasound, my heart melted, and a fierce protectiveness came over me.

"So, Giz, how's my niece or nephew cooking?" Liam asks

with a grin. I growl in response as another round of laughter fills the air.

"Look, idiots," I shout. "We need to sort out who is running what since the crew has grown massively."

"Yes, Boss," they all sass me. They are lucky I can't beat their asses right now.

"Marcus."

"Yeah, Hellion?" he says, waiting with bated breath as he bounces on the balls of his feet.

"Strip club?" I smirk at him as his eyes widen with a strange sort of joy.

"Fuck, yes!" he shouts, jumping around like a psycho.

"Liam."

"Yeah, Giz?" He's leaning so far forward I'm surprised he hasn't fallen face first.

"Fight ring."

"Fuck, yes." He jumps up laughing. I feel bad as Paine looks deflated. Me and Kane both smirk at each other.

"Ow!" I exclaim as a weird pain washes over me.

"Paine," I pant out.

"Yeah, Little Warrior." He looks so concerned for me.

"The Den." I smile as his eyes light up.

Another pain tears through my stomach and I roar in pain. The guys look at each other with panic stricken faces, and turn to look at me as the pain happens again.

"Doc!" Kane shouts.

Doc comes charging through the door and as soon as he sees me, he chuckles.

"Out," he shouts to the hovering bodies. "Get out now." He shoos them away.

Reluctantly they all leave. Kane and I share a look as he walks to the door, and Doc and his helper close it.

Kane

My eyes sting as I force them open for the hundredth time in the last ten minutes. I know things are okay from the abuse being screamed through the door at me, occasionally. This has the three asshats sitting next to me laughing like a set of hyenas. I'm getting worried though. I haven't heard anything in a while. Then a tiny cry splits the air, and my heart drops into my stomach. Liam hugs me first, then Marcus. Paine is last as he slaps me on the back as the door to the room opens. I fight with them to get through first. Pretty Bird is on the bed smiling at me with exhaustion on her face as clear as day. Her hair is stuck to her head and sweat lines her face. I rush over to drop a kiss onto her forehead. She murmurs something as the other three crowd around the bed, smiling down at the love of my life. The helper turns and walks to me, a bundle of white in her arms. She smiles as she passes the baby to Pretty Bird, who looks like an expert already. My heart is in my throat as I look to her and that cry fills the air again. Pretty Bird lifts the bundle up and my arms tremble as I hold the tiny thing in my arms. The blanket falls away and my heart stops as everything zeros in on the stormy eyes staring back at me.

"Daddy, meet Rikki," Pretty Bird says, "your daughter."

Reika

"Cheshire, will you put her back in the crib." Honestly, the little shit bag just grins as he rocks Rikki in his arms. Why do they all feel the need to disturb her when she's fast asleep? I haven't slept properly for the last six weeks. Haven't they realized there is a chance they could die?

"Hellion, come on," he pleads in a childish voice, as he gently lays her back in her crib. "You can see how cute she is. I just want to squish her all the time," says the six foot five, heavily tattooed enforcer that I watched make a grown man shit himself the other day at Headquarters, because he stole his last lollipop.

"Boy, I am telling you now. If you don't get your ass out of here. The grunts will be pulling your intestines out of the waste disposal for the next few weeks." His face turns ashen in an instant, as he falls over my feeding chair at the side of her crib. Trying his hardest to put distance between us. I chuckle darkly as he throws his hands up in surrender. A small cry echoes around the room as Rikki wakes up. Marcus runs out of the room as fast as he can.

"Kane," My voice bellows throughout the house, he comes running into the room. "Deal with Rikki!" I snap as I stride out of the room looking for the little shit.

"What's Marcus done?" he calls after me, causing me to snarl and scare the shit out of one of the grunts who was heading in my direction. I chuckle as he takes one look at me and turns around to go in the opposite direction.

"Not so fast shithead." I call to him, and he freezes in place. I can see his hands tremble. "Where is he?"

"B-Boss. I- I," he stutters through his words. My nose crinkles up in disgust as I see the wet line forming a trail down his pant leg.

"Go get cleaned up you little bitch," I say as I head in the direction he tried to disappear. "If you piss your pants again, boy. I think you might need to make a change to your life choices."

My head snaps left and right as I check every room, heading closer to the front of the house. A commotion catches my attention from the kitchen as someone says something about Marcus having a death wish. A round of laughter echoes around the house, and I hear Rikki start crying louder from my position at the top of the stairs. My blood boils at disrespect these idiots are showing. They know the rules when she goes down for a nap, they shut the fuck up, because that is the only time I can get some sleep.

As quietly as possible, I stalk my way through the house. A couple of the older members spot me and casually head out of the front door, shaking their heads as they go. Yeah, you know it boys. I take a quick look around the entrance of the kitchen. Smiling to myself, I spot Cheshire and Frosty laughing at something someone has said.

Rikki's cries are louder this time, and they all freeze, and lift their heads up to look at the ceiling.

"We're safe aren't we?" Frosty mutters to his brother.

"Yeah man, Hellion will be trying to settle her." he whispers, as he rubs the back of his neck.

"You sure, Bro. Because Giz scared the shit out of me before the baby, but now? I ain't dying because you couldn't follow the rules."

"Yeah. how do you all want to die?" I inquire as I step out of my

hiding spot into the kitchen. "I'm taking requests." All eyes snap to me, and they all look terrified.

"Hellion. Come on now, you love me." I stalk him across the kitchen. Frosty dives out of the way, leaving his brother on his own to face me.

"Do I now?" I ask in a calm tone, he goes almost see through as the crew members all gasp, like a set of girls.

"Arrrrrggggggggghhhhhhhh." A member rolls through the

entrance of kitchen, all our heads snap in his direction as he smashes into the island unconscious.

"Oh, Reaper. Where are you, you little bitch?"A growl rumbles in my throat as I ignore Cheshire. I storm my way through the house, making out of the front door in record time.

The sight before me has me stopping short and someone slams into my back.

"Who is it, Baby?" I look over my shoulder to find Kane pressed up to my back, with both his brothers flanking him. All three of them have a murderous expression. I step further out so we aren't all standing on top of one another as I get my bearings. I face forward, a huge smile on my face.

"Boys, meet Ryan."

ACKNOWLEDGMENTS

Thank you all, who have made it this far to the end of Reika and Kane's story. I do hope you loved them as much as I do, it feels so strange now. Knowing my debut series is complete as this story has spent a lot of time in my head over the months. Keeping me awake on a night with their arguments in my head and all the stupid stuff they would do. Long nights and a lot of coffee later, we have the damned crew wrapped up. I have met some amazing people on my journey since I bit the bullet and decided to follow my dream. I can't thank you all enough, it means a lot. The knowledge I have gained from each of you has been epic and really helped me when I felt I was trying to tread water with weights on my ankles.

To my readers your support is invaluable and I am so thankful you have read the crazy from my brain and I hope it gave you a lot of laughs on the way. Being a new indie author is scary and is nerve wracking for the soul. But I am so glad I did it, the excitement you guys have over a story that you enjoy is amazing.

Thank you all for the love and it's now time to start the next lot of crazy. Hopefully you want to continue to learn about the dark areas of my mind. If you do well buckle up honey it's about to get wild.

Turn over for the blurb to my next release.

Black Frost Academy: A Dark Bully Romance.

I don't belong here, I know it the second I step into Black Frost academy for the first time. The opulent setting screams of money and is shrouded in secrets but this isn't my world.

Bound by a promise made to my aunt that I'm determined to keep, I lockdown my fear and embrace the fresh start I've been given.

All I have to do is keep my head down and stay out of trouble, which isn't easy for someone like me.

But then I meet them – the Gods.

And finding myself the recipient of ice-cold distain. Inexplicably lands me in the crosshairs of two rivals.

With the school divided, I'm caught up in a dangerous game of cat and mouse.

Where bullies are pitted against each other, andinfatuation takes a deadly turn.

With neither side willing to concede, enemiesand allies alike wait with baited breath for the winner to claim their prize.

The girl that doesn't belong here.

Me.

If you have any trigger this book is NOT for you!! If you still want to know what they are join my reader group to find the list

** This is a why choose romance where the FMC will have multiple partners and doesn't have to choose. There will be HEA at the end as this is a standalone.**

ABOUT THE AUTHOR

Tatum is a mum of two girls, while also being a writer, Netflix and coffee addict. She loves to write dark stories with both why choose and MF romances that will take you on one hell of an emotional rollercoaster. Characters that will have you blowing so hot and cold you won't know how to feel at any given time and who love to shatter your heart. Does she laugh while she puts the shards back together? Maybe just a little bit.

Visit her online:
www.tatumrayneauthor.com

or join the Trouble Makers or newsletter on website to stay up to date.
You can find the reader group here: https://www.facebook.com/ groups/tatumraynesreadergroup/?ref=share_group_link

ALSO BY TATUM RAYNE

BROAD CREEK PREP

(Dark, Academy, MF Romance)

Broken Prince

BLACK FROST ACADEMY DUET

(Dark, Bully, College-age Academy, Why choose Romance)

Black Frost Academy

Return to Black Frost Academy

THE DAMNED CREW

(Dark, Mafia MF Romance)

Ruthless Monsters

OTHER AUTHORS AT HUDSON INDIE INK

Paranormal Romance/Urban Fantasy

Stephanie Hudson

Xen Randell

C. L. Monaghan

Sorcha Dawn

Harper Phoenix

Sci-fi/Fantasy

Devin Hanson

Crime/Action

Blake Hudson

Jack Walker

Contemporary Romance

Gemma Weir

Nikki Ashton

Anna Bloom

Tatum Rayne

Milton Keynes UK
Ingram Content Group UK Ltd.
UKHW010937280823
427620UK00001B/7

9 781916 562042